Sean Slater is the pseudonym for Vancouver Police Officer Sean Sommerville. Sommerville works in Canada's poorest slum, the Downtown East Side – an area rife with poverty, mental illness, drug use, prostitution, and gang warfare. He has investigated everything from frauds and extortions to homicides. Sommerville has written numerous columns and editorials for the city newspaper. His work has been nominated for the Rupert Hughes Prose Award, and he was the grand-prize winner of the Sunday Serial Thriller contest. His debut novel, *The Survivor*, was published to rave reviews. *Snakes & Ladders* is his second novel.

Praise for *The Survivor*

'A satisfyingly authentic debut from a man who really does know about the bleak side of the human psyche . . . written with an unexpected gentle irony, and featuring a lead character that the author clearly likes, it's a neat, stylish thriller from a writer to watch'

Daily Mail

'The USP of this energetic debut thriller is that it's written about a Vancouver cop by a Vancouver cop . . . In fact Sean Slater writes the sort of pacy superior pulp you'd expect from an author who'd never eaten a doughnut on a dull stakeout'

Daily Telegraph

'Fast-paced, gripping and impossible to put down, Sean Slater's debut novel is an explosive, action-injected tale told by a great new talent. A fantastic read'

CHRIS CARTER, author of *The Night Stalker*

'*The Survivor* grabbed me by the throat from page one and held on until the very end. Slater's debut is a rocket-paced evocative thriller. Gritty, dark and graphic, *The Survivor* is at times hard to read but always harder to put down. A terrific read'

DANIEL KALLA, bestselling author of *Pandemic*, *Blood Lies* and *Of Flesh and Blood*

Also by Sean Slater

The Survivor

SEAN SLATER

SNAKES & LADDERS

SIMON &
SCHUSTER

London · New York · Sydney · Toronto · New Delhi

A CBS COMPANY

First published in Great Britain by Simon & Schuster UK Ltd, 2012
A CBS Company

1 3 5 7 9 10 8 6 4 2

Simon & Schuster UK Ltd
1st Floor
222 Gray's Inn Road
London WC1X 8HB

www.simonandschuster.co.uk

Simon & Schuster Australia, Sydney

Simon & Schuster India, New Delhi

A CIP catalogue record for this book is available from the British Library

ISBN 978-0-85720-040-2

Typeset by Hewer Text UK Ltd, Edinburgh
Printed and bound in Great Britain by CPI Group (UK) Ltd, Croydon, CR0 4YY

Acknowledgements

In *The Survivor*, I thanked everyone in the world who has ever supported me in my writing career. In *Snakes & Ladders*, I am being more specific. This book would not be what it is without the help of my usual advisers:

- Joe Cummings, my plot & character mercenary
- Kirk Longstaffe, my idea bouncer and information safeguard
- And my dear wife Lani, who not only acts as my first reader and editor, but who endlessly takes care of our home so I can actually have a few hours here and there to write these novels.

Professionally, I have to thank everyone at Simon & Schuster UK, especially:

- Libby Yevtushenko for being such a wonderful editor
- Clare Hey for her tiresome diligence in ironing out the wrinkles
- Suzanne Baboneau for giving me the opportunity to break into the writing world

- And everyone else there who has worked so hard with regards to typesetting, proofing, cover art, publicity and so on.

I would also like to thank everyone at the Darley Anderson Agency for their constant work behind the scenes:

- Rosanna Bellingham
- Madeleine Buston
- Mary Darby
- And, of course, Clare Wallace.

It is always an unexpected delight to receive an email from any one of you.

Last, and certainly not least, I have to thank my fantastic agent, Camilla, who acts as an editor, agent, negotiator, adviser, friend and counsellor – heck, this woman wears so many hats, she needs a walk-in closet at the office. Life in the writing world would not be as exciting or enjoyable without her. She has been a godsend, pure and simple.

For anyone I might have missed, apologies all round.

Sean

This book is dedicated to three amazing men:

To Gramps, for always being there for me.

To Dad, for finally finding your way and coming through
at the end.

And to Larry 'Big Poppa' Oakley, who has always been a
rock of support for everyone in the family.

Snake Eyes:

Definition:

1) The lowest possible roll of the dice (two ones) in a game of Craps, or
2) *Extremely* bad luck

Day One

One

The black mask was made entirely from leather. Rectangular slits were cut out over the eyes and mouth areas, and running down the back, interlacing through the eyelets, were a pair of long, thin straps.

The Adder tightened these straps, firming the mask to the back of his head as he stared at the young woman before him. Her name was Mandilla Gill. *Mandy*. And he knew her well.

She was pretty and young – nineteen to be exact – and bound to the chair not by any physical restraints but by the medications he had given her. More important than all of that, she was about to be freed from the cold darkness of this world. It was time for her salvation.

The Beautiful Escape.

'Please,' she said. Her voice was soft, distant, barely a whisper.

'Everything is all right,' he told her. 'Do not be afraid.'

The girl looked like she wanted to respond, but said nothing back.

The Adder scanned the room. It was dark and cold, and the walls reeked of old, set-in dampness. All across the floor was litter – old newspapers, dirty clothes, garbage of all kinds. The Adder walked across the trash to the other side of the room and stared at the camera he had placed just outside the window.

The angle was perfect. And it had to be.

Satisfied, he turned around and knelt before the girl. Already her breathing had slowed to a critical level and her eyes were taking on a lost, distant look. Even in the pale dimness of this room, the Adder could see that.

There wasn't much time left.

'Please,' she said, and this time her voice was far away from him. So very, very far.

'Do not be afraid,' he said again. 'I'm freeing you.'

The Adder smiled at her. He held her head in both hands. Stared deep into her eyes. And made sure that she saw he was there for her.

'Fly away, Little Bird,' he told her. 'Fly away.'

And Mandy Gill did.

She was *soaring*.

Two

Snake Eyes.

Mandy Gill's life crapped out on a cold and grey winter day. The dice of life were loaded against her. They always had been, ever since the day she'd been born. She died isolated, in a sad and lonely place. And the worst part about her death was that it could have been prevented.

If anyone had cared.

The thought of this filtered through Jacob Striker's mind as the homicide detective pulled his cruiser up to the old hotel. The place was a shithole. Old boards covered the broken windows; gang graffiti painted the walls, and crabgrass mixed with dirt made for a front lawn. This was the Lucky Lodge Rooming House, and anyone who lived here wasn't so lucky.

Mandy Gill was the perfect example of this. Her last trip out of here would be under the stiff white plastic of a coroner's body bag – an undignified end to an unfair life.

Game over. You lose.

Striker's fingers clenched into fists as he climbed out of the unmarked patrol car. He hated this place. Always had. This entire area, too. It was Strathcona, a one-way ticket to nowhere for the mentally ill and drug-addicted. Too many checked in, so few checked out.

Such was life at the Lucky Lodge Rooming House.

Over the years, during his stints in Patrol and Homicide, Striker had been here too many times to count. Overdoses. Suicides. Forcible Confinements and Murders. All bad, no good. But being here today was especially terrible.

For personal reasons.

Striker killed the thought and walked down the cracked-cement walkway, which was covered in rotting leaves and half hidden in the four o'clock dimness. The cold January air was crisp with the hint of coming snow, and blowing in angry gusts. It ruffled his hair and stung his skin.

Striker reached the door, shouldered it open and went inside.

The foyer was dark, and the walls held the smell of old dampness. Striker avoided touching them. Everything was quiet and calm. The nearest hall light was burned out, and the only other light that existed was down at the far end of the corridor.

It flickered strangely.

Striker walked down the hall and took a closer look. What he saw was not surprising for this area – the light wasn't coming from a bulb, but from the flame of a candle, flickering in the draught. He reached out, pawed the wall, and hit the light switch.

Nothing.

The building had no power.

In his coat pocket was a flashlight. Striker fished it out and turned it on, then made his way up to the third floor on steps that sounded weak and hollow. At the top, he turned left and surveyed the hall. Through the yellow gloom, he spotted a man in a blue uniform.

Patrol cop.

Striker shone the beam on him. The cop was young. Asian. Looked no more than twenty years old and fresh out of the academy. Definitely out of his element. He had his own flashlight out and was shining it nervously around the hall. When he spotted Striker, he let out a heavy breath.

'Hey,' he got out.

Striker stepped up to the doorway. 'You got a name?'

'Yeah, Wong. I'm on Charlie shift. Team Two-Ten.'

Striker looked at the man's badge number and saw that it was 2864 – over a thousand numbers higher than his own badge number. It made him feel old. He nodded at the young constable. 'I'm Detective Striker from Homicide. Where is she?'

'Just . . . just over here.' The kid shone his flashlight into the nearest room. Unit 303.

'Have you touched—'

'Nothing. I didn't touch a thing. Not a single thing.'

Striker was pleased to hear that; the kid had been taught well.

He turned his attention to the room before him. Everything was still, and darkness hung about the air in different shades. In the centre of the room, lying back in an easy chair, was the body of Mandy Gill.

The rest of the room was empty.

Striker frowned and looked at Constable Wong. 'Where's your partner?'

'Partner? I . . . I don't have one. I'm one-man.'

'You mean you're at a Sudden Death *alone*?'

The kid shrugged. 'I had to be. There was no one else to go. Thought someone else would clear by the time I got here. But so far, you're the only one.'

'You got balls, kid. Next time wait.'

Constable Wong never took his eyes from the body. 'She looks . . . fresh.'

Striker nodded sadly. The kid was right; the death looked somewhat recent.

'She's listed in the directory only as Gill,' the young cop

offered. 'But I haven't had a chance to confirm anything yet. I could run out to the car for the laptop, if you want.'

'There's no need to,' he said. 'You're right about her identity. Her name was Mandy Gill and she was nineteen years old.'

'Oh, you already researched her?' the cop asked.

Striker shook his head sadly. 'I *knew* her.'

Three

The body of Mandy Gill had been discovered by accident. The original call to the Lucky Lodge had come in as a Suspicious Person complaint from an anonymous caller. A shadowy figure had been seen lurking in the bushes behind the dilapidated building, somewhere close to Union Street.

That in itself was nothing out of the ordinary – SusPers were a dime a dozen, especially in the Strathcona area – but lately, over the past nine months, the City had been having problems with an arsonist. Because of this, the area from Union Street to Pender had become a top priority. So a unit had been dispatched immediately.

Newbie cop Wong drew the short stick. Working a one-man car, he had attended the scene and stumbled across the sudden death.

Mandy Gill.

Striker stepped into the small apartment, being mindful of where he placed his feet. The air was just as cold inside the building as it was outside, and he found that disheartening.

He looked around. The suite was minute, built into two separate rooms: one washroom and one common room, which was complete with a kitchenette, sitting area, and one shabby, single-mattress cot, which was tucked away in the far corner.

All in all, it was a sad statement of this girl's life.

Dirty dishes filled the sink. A carton of milk was left on the stove. And old newspapers and junk mail littered the counters and floor.

After a long moment, Striker stepped into the centre of the room and stopped avoiding what needed to be done. He shone his flashlight on the dead girl before him and really *looked* at her.

It pained his heart to do so.

Mandy Gill was sitting back in an old easy chair that was made from threadbare fabric. She was positioned to look out of the only window the room had – a cracked pane that faced west. In her hand was an empty vial of pills, and in the corners of her mouth was the white crust of pill paste. Her chest was completely still.

Even in the unforgiving glare of the flashlight's white beam, it was apparent that all the colour had drained away from her dark brown skin, turning it more of an ash-grey colour.

Striker leaned closer and studied her face. The underlying musculature was slack, and her eyes were wide open and milky, staring through the window at a world that was as cold to her now in death as it had been in life. An empty expression marred her face, and it struck Striker like a physical blow.

Mandy Gill looked sad, even in death.

Striker killed the thought. He turned and located Constable Wong, who was standing quietly in the doorway.

'When did you arrive on scene?' he asked.

'Huh?'

'How long you been here?'

'Uh . . . twenty minutes, maybe more.'

Striker nodded. 'Did you clear the place?'

Wong jabbed a thumb over his shoulder. 'All the other apartments are unoccupied. In fact, she's not even supposed to be in here. This place was condemned over a month ago. Everyone was supposed to have moved out by now. Who knows why she's even here.'

'She's in here because she had nowhere else to go. You got the manager's number?'

'In the car.'

Striker forced a smile. 'Well, we can't read it from here.'

Wong clued in and left the room. When Striker heard the young constable's police boots clomping down the steps, he focused his attention back on the dead girl before him. He tried to think of her as 'the body' or 'the deceased'.

As anything but Mandy.

It was impossible. His conscience would not allow it. Memories hit him, and all of them sad. He had hoped she would escape this place. This area. This rotten city altogether. But like so many others before her, she hadn't left. And in the end, she'd found her own way out.

The only way she knew.

'I'm sorry,' he said softly. 'I should have done more.'

He reached out and gently touched her face.

And he frowned.

She was still slightly warm.

A thought occurred to him. He stood back up from Mandy Gill's body, walked into the kitchenette, and approached the stove. On it sat a carton of milk. He touched it.

It was still cool.

Not a lot of time had passed since the woman's death – too much for any hope of resuscitation, but not a lot in terms of a crime scene. And every Sudden Death had to be considered a crime until ruled otherwise. He took out his pen and notebook, and wrote down: *Time?* When he looked back up again, his eyes found the throw-rug on the floor and lingered there.

The rug was an old thing, probably something Mandy had

snagged from the Salvation Army or the First United Church. Green threadbare fabric, just like the recliner, with dirty yellow flower designs.

But the colour and pattern were not what stole Striker's attention – it was the strands of the carpet. The indentations in the weave. And the more he looked at it, the more he realized that the chair had been moved from its normal resting spot. Now it was angled westward. Facing out of the window.

It was odd.

Had Mandy wanted to watch the setting sun during her death? The timing would seem to suggest so. And if not, what had she been looking at?

Striker approached the window. Outside, the dusk was slipping slowly by. In the coming twilight, streaks of blood-orange sun blistered the charcoal sky, making the world look warmer than it actually was.

Three storeys down, the next neighbouring lot was vacant.

Striker scanned the area. The lot was filled with construction debris from the demolished house. He was about to focus his attention back on the room and begin sorting through Mandy's articles when something outside the window caught his eye – a glint of something metallic in the sun's fading rays. On the ledge, just outside the window, was a small object with a circular glass front.

A camera.

It was facing inside the room.

Striker grabbed on to the window and tried to lift it, but time and rot had caused the frame to swell. As a result, the window was wedged tight. Impossible to open.

Whoever had placed the camera on the ledge had done so from the outside.

Striker considered this. He leaned forward for a closer look, then heard a soft, raspy sound behind him. He spun around, not knowing what to expect.

After a short moment, he relaxed. It was just air escaping the body – a normal occurrence during the beginning of decomposition. Relieved, he turned back to focus on the window once more. What he saw shocked him.

The camera was gone.

Four

The Lucky Lodge was small for a rooming house. Each floor had only three units per side, and each unit was an SRO – Single Room Occupancy. Because of this, there were only six rooms on the third floor, and only three of them faced west – one on either side of Mandy Gill's unit.

The window ledge where the camera had been set lay closer to the south neighbour than the north, so Striker headed for unit 305. He kept his pistol drawn and made his way towards the hall.

Without the ambience of Constable Wong's flashlight, the darkness of the complex seemed thicker than before. Deeper. And as if to make the situation even harder for him, the blazing orange light of dusk faded completely as the sun slipped in behind the blackish western cloud banks.

Striker stood behind the cover of the door frame and angled his flashlight. It was a mini Maglite. It didn't hold a candle to the full-sized ones patrol members used, but it was all he had. He rotated the lens to turn the narrow beam brighter and shone it down the hall.

Everything was still. All the doors were closed.

'Vancouver Police!' he yelled. 'Make yourself known!'

No reply came back, only silence.

For a moment, Striker considered waiting for Constable

Wong. Rookie or not, two cops always gave better odds – and that was on the assumption that there would be only *one* threat awaiting him in the other room.

But thoughts of a suspect escaping ate away at him. He readied his pistol and slowly moved down the hall. When he reached the door to unit 305, he stopped. Listened.

Nothing but silence.

He reached out and grabbed the doorknob. The steel was cold to the touch. When he turned it, the knob refused to move. It was locked from the inside.

'Vancouver Police!' Striker said again. 'I know you're in there. I need to talk to you about the tenant in the next suite. Open the door.'

Again there was only silence. And then . . . .

A *sound*.

It took Striker less than a second to identify it – the soft, scraping noise of a window being raised.

He took a quick step back, then jumped forward and kicked the heel of his foot between the doorknob and frame. Entry took only two kicks. The steel lock remained intact, but the rotting wood of the frame let loose a loud *snaaaap!* and broke inwards. The door flew back, slammed into the wall, and Striker aimed his gun and flashlight all around the room, hitting each of the four corners.

No one was there.

He quickly surveyed the room. The layout was a mirror image of Mandy Gill's unit. Kitchenette, cot, washroom and main sitting area, all in one. The kitchen was vacant. The underside of the cot was visible with no one beneath it. And the bathroom had no one inside.

The window was wide open.

'Fuck,' Striker growled.

He hurried across the room to the window and looked down at the vacant lot below. With the sun all but gone, the shadows were wider and deeper. Everything was grey and black now. Impossible to distinguish.

There were many places to hide.

Striker assessed it all – from the huge commercial garbage bins of the back lane, to the underground parking lot on Gore Avenue, to the heavy row of bushes that flanked the communal area of the Prior Street Park.

Everywhere he looked there were escape routes.

He spotted Constable Wong returning from his patrol car.

'Cover the southwest corner!' Striker ordered. 'Someone just took off from this room! Call for more units and a dog. I'll take northwest!'

The young constable froze, though for only an instant, before nodding and racing south. When he disappeared behind the curve of the next building, Striker turned back and ran for the doorway. He was barely halfway across the kitchenette when his shoes caught on something. He stopped running, looked down. In the dimness of the room, the objects he had stepped on were not easy to define, so he shone his flashlight on them.

Not plastic, but wire. Trays of some kind.

Refrigerator trays.

The thought had barely crossed his mind when the fridge door came flying open. It hit Striker with enough force to send him reeling backwards. He landed hard on the floor, and rolled. He raised the gun, shoved his back tight against the far wall, and readied himself for an attack.

But none came.

He looked across the room. Racing for the window was a figure – average height. Lean build. Dark clothes.

'Stop! Police!' Striker ordered.

But the suspect ignored him.

Striker scrambled to his feet and dived towards the window – but the man was fast. He was already three-quarters of the way out by the time Striker reached him. He grabbed on to the suspect's hand and yank him back. But it was too late. The suspect slipped out of reach, and Striker was left standing there, clutching one of the man's black leather gloves.

The man plummeted three storeys down. No scream, just silence. He hit the crabgrass, rolled down the small slope of hill, then got back to his feet.

Striker tried to flood the man with light from his flashlight, but from three storeys up the beam was too weak. All he saw was black clothing. A dark hoodie. And beneath that, what appeared to be a black leather mask. The suspect leaned down and picked up his camera. Then, for a brief moment, he looked back up at the window.

'Don't move!' Striker ordered.

But the man ignored him again; he turned and raced into the shadows of the south lane. And then he was gone.

Five

Five minutes later, Striker looked up and down Union Street for the red and blue glow of the Canine Unit's lights. When he didn't see them, he got on his phone and called the Central Dispatcher, Sue Rhaemer.

'Where the hell's the dog?' he demanded.

Rhaemer paused for barely a moment, and Striker knew she was checking the GPS. 'He's just a few blocks out.'

'Well, tell him to get his ass here *now*.'

Striker had barely ended the conversation when the dogman's emergency lights tinted the air and a white Chevy Tahoe came racing around the bend of Gore Avenue. The man behind the wheel was Harry Hooch, one of the department's best dogmen.

The Tahoe came to a sliding stop on the icy road surface and stopped right in front of the Lucky Lodge. Hooch climbed out. He was shorter than most cops, maybe five foot seven, and he was rail-thin, weighing less than a hundred and sixty pounds. But what Harry Hooch lacked in height and weight he made up for with his steel determination. He yanked open the rear door and Sable jumped out. The Shepherd's colouring was completely black. Even in the grey light of the coming night, her coat glistened.

'Where's the scent?' Hooch asked.

Striker pointed to the area where the suspect had fled. 'Landed there. On the slope beneath the window.'

'Anyone else?'

'None. The area's clean.'

Hooch said nothing. He got the Shepherd to sniff the glove, then led the dog across the lot and got to work.

Striker watched eagerly as the Shepherd scoured back and forth in search of the trail. When the dog finally picked up the scent, she beelined down the south lane of Union.

Hooch went with her, and so did Striker. The dogman didn't want the extra protection, and the scowl on his face showed that; like most dogmen, Hooch liked to play the game solo. But Striker wasn't about to leave him without proper cover. Especially when they had no idea what they were dealing with here.

He ran with the man.

The dog continued the trail southeast, eventually turning down Malkin Avenue. As they ran, Striker mapped out the area in his head, and cursed.

'What?' Hooch asked.

'He's heading for the train yards.'

Hooch made no reply, but the tightness of his face showed his own frustration. The train yards were always a bitch during tracks. Too many obstacles: the fenced-off areas, the moving freightliners. And, of course, the endless streams of the homeless people who camped out behind the industrial area, or grouped together down by the bottle depot and recycling plant.

All in all, it all made for a difficult track.

When they reached the dead-end stop of Glen Drive, Sable stopped running. The dog dropped her tail low and began running back and forth all along the gated area that led into the train yards. Hooch gave the dog more leash and marched impatiently with her.

Striker took the moment to scan the area and catch his breath.

The cold air stung his lungs and it was dirty, stinking of diesel gas fumes and smoke from the industrial plants. Not twenty yards away stood a tall chain-link fence that separated the federal land of the national railway with that of the City. Behind it were pockets of homeless people. Small fire-lit camps dotted the rail yard.

'Tracks gonna get messed up in there,' Striker noted.

Hooch shook his head. 'Track doesn't lead there anyway.'

'Then where's it go?'

'Right fucking *here*.'

Striker looked all around the immediate area. There was nothing here except a dead-end street, a gravelly roundabout, and a row of old vacant warehouses.

'It's a dead fucking end,' Hooch griped.

Striker watched where the dog was pin-balling back and forth on a small strip of gravel, less than twenty feet long. Using his flashlight, he lit up the area and focused on the road's surface. It was a mess of concrete and rock and dirt, and there were no discernible tyre tracks.

Hooch's posture slumped, and he began reeling in the dog. 'He had wheels parked here, Shipwreck. No doubt about it.'

Striker nodded in agreement.

'Or a ride waiting for him.'

He looked all around the area for witnesses, or better yet, video surveillance. But aside from the video cameras that CP Rail owned – all of which faced inwards towards the train tracks – there were none to be seen.

Hooch reeled in his beast. 'It's done, man. He got away.'

Striker shook his head. He offered the dogman a weak grin and held up the black leather glove.

'Not completely,' he said.

Six

By the time Striker made it back to the Lucky Lodge, Felicia was on scene. She was speaking with Constable Wong – although from Striker's vantage point, it looked more like an interrogation than a discussion.

A smile broke his lips; Felicia was always so intense. It was one of the things he loved about her.

Under the pale light of the street lamp, her breath looked like steam. Striker hoped she wasn't grilling the kid too hard. Wong was only a rookie. Had just a few months of road time under his belt and was now stuck in the middle of a strange Sudden Death call that made no sense.

Welcome to the Force, kid.

Felicia spotted Striker and her expression turned even more serious. She stopped talking mid-sentence, left the young constable hanging, and came marching up the sidewalk towards him.

'Any luck?' she asked.

Striker nodded. 'Lots. All *bad*.' He relayed the entire call to her from the second he'd heard the dispatch over the air until the moment when the dogman had lost the track out by the train yards. When he was finished speaking, Felicia made a sour face.

'Train yards, huh?'

'Yeah. He had wheels, too. I'm sure of it.'

She thought this over. 'Long way off to park his wheels.'

'For sure. And yet the safest place, too. Who's gonna notice anything going on down there at Glen and Malkin? It's the industrial area. Dead-end streets. No video of any kind. Only people down there are the homeless, and they don't want to get involved. When you think about it, it's actually a perfect place to hide some wheels.'

'Which leaves us with jack.'

'Not entirely.' Striker held up the glove once more. 'Got this from the suspect. Ripped it right off his hand during the struggle.'

'We'll have to hit the lab.' She grabbed the keys from his pocket, hurried back to the trunk of the police car, and returned with a brown paper bag. She wrote the time, location and incident number on the outside of the bag in thick black felt, then held it open for Striker to drop the glove inside. When he did, she put the bag back in the trunk and handed him the keys.

It wasn't until she had marked the time of transfer in her notebook – continuity was *always* a bitch in court – that she took a long look at Striker and assessed him. The skin around her brow tightened and her eyes turned soft.

'Your forehead,' she said, and reached out to touch it.

He leaned back. 'Leave it.'

'It's been bleeding, Jacob.'

'I know that. And it stopped.'

'What happened? You get hit? He hit you? You need someone to look at that.'

'I'll live, Feleesh, really.'

She gave him another one of her long, drawn-out motherly looks, and Striker ignored it. Before she could say more, he turned back towards the Lucky Lodge.

In the five o'clock darkness, the building looked even more

dilapidated. He took out his flashlight and set the cone to the halfway setting for equal amounts of intensity and expanse. Then he began scouring the crabgrass, taking slow careful steps – the last thing they needed right now was to step on and destroy any trace evidence.

Felicia came up beside him to assist in the search.

'He ran this way,' Striker explained. 'Landed right over there beside the power box. Look for footprints and any electrical stuff, too. Wires, a lens, whatever. Maybe he left something behind.'

They moved closer to the area where the suspect had landed.

'It's so cold, the ground is like rock,' he said. 'When he landed, he must've landed hard.'

Felicia kept looking. 'He get hurt?' she asked without looking up.

'Dunno. He could've – though you'd never know it from the way he raced out of here.'

'I'll call the hospitals.'

'That's not a bad idea.' Striker pointed to the east. 'Maybe he sprained something. Broke a bone, if we're lucky.'

Felicia thought this over. 'If he was high, he could've fractured a bone and not even known it – but he will later when the juice wears off.' She got on the phone and called Central Dispatch. She got them to flag all the hospitals for patients coming in with injuries that could possibly be related to a high fall.

While she did this, Striker continued searching the outer perimeter for evidence. He did a grid search, line by line. It was an arduous process, but the best way to go. In cases like these, it was one hundred per cent necessary.

No evidence could be overlooked.

Not three minutes later, he found a footprint. It was not overly far from where the suspect had landed – just east of the utility box – in a patch of earth that had been recently covered with fresher ground from the construction work in the next-door lot.

Striker squatted close to the footprint. It was a right-foot imprint. Standard size, maybe a ten or eleven. But that was not what got his attention. What stole his focus was the sole pattern in the mud. It was a checkered tread, and the grooves were deep. The imprint itself was level for the most part, but wore away almost completely near the toe.

Striker looked around the area, and found a left-shoe imprint that matched in size and tread. He noted that the toe of this shoe was not as worn as the right.

When Felicia finished her phone conversation, she joined him once again. He showed her his find.

'What does that wear on the toe tell you?' he asked.

'The wearer had an awkward gait. Maybe from some type of previous injury. Or a leg length discrepancy.'

Striker agreed.

They marked the area off for Ident to do a casing of the shoe prints. Then they continued the search.

Nearly a half-hour later they had cleared the lane, the vacant lot to the west, and were now performing a final search of where the suspect had landed. Striker paused for a moment to look up at the window. Unit 305. From down here, it looked awfully high up.

Felicia nudged him. 'He had a mask on, right?'

'Yeah. Black leather thing. Narrow eye slits. Kinda like the one you wore on our first date.'

'Yes, well, I like to surprise my men.' Felicia looked up to the same window. 'No power at all, huh?'

'All the power's been cut off, and it looks like it's been that way for a long time. We'll check with the City for an exact date.'

Felicia thought this over. 'This guy . . . could he have been a squatter?'

'Maybe. Or even some toad with a warrant. Who knows? Anything's possible at this point. But it doesn't explain why he'd have a camera set up outside her window.'

Felicia nodded, but said nothing.

Striker swept the flashlight through the blades of crisp grass. He was just about to leave the area when he spotted a glint of silver, coming from beneath the edge of a utility box. An object was there. He crouched down, gloved up with latex, and picked it up.

'Interesting,' he said.

'What is that?' Felicia asked.

Striker wasn't sure yet. The object looked like a broken-off piece of equipment – a tiny plastic box with a sensor attached to it. There were no part numbers on it. No model number. No serial.

He shrugged. 'Might be junk for all I know. We'll get the tech boys to look at it later.' He slid the object into a small paper bag he had folded up in his pocket, wrote the details on the bag, then took a final look around the scene.

He made his way back towards the front entrance of the Lucky Lodge with Felicia by his side. Patrol were now on scene and they had cordoned off the area with yellow police tape. Some of the cops were doing a secondary canvass.

It was much appreciated. But unfortunately it didn't diminish the amount of work still required, and Striker started a list in his head. They still had to reassess the primary crime scene, investigate the secondary, get Ident down here to photograph and mark everything, and, lastly, they had to hit the DNA lab to have the glove bagged and tagged for testing – and all had to be done before this night was through.

As if on the same wavelength, Felicia said: 'This week is killing me. It's only Wednesday and it feels like Friday.'

'Well, get used to it,' he replied. 'Our long day just got a whole lot longer.'

She said nothing for a moment as she looked up at the blackened windows of the old building where Mandy Gill had died. When she looked back at Striker, her dark eyes were concerned and focused. 'This is creeping me out,' she said. 'Seriously. What kind of sicko films a suicide like that?'

Striker gave her a hard look and spoke determinedly.

'The kind we're going to catch,' he said.

Seven

The Adder – for that was how he thought of himself – opened up the hidden hatch in the floor and stepped down on the first rung of the ladder. The wood was old, and it squeaked beneath his weight as it always did. Hinted at giving way. If that ever happened, the results would be dire. The drop below was nearly twenty feet in total, and on to concrete.

But the rung held, and the Adder continued down the old ladder into the murky darkness below. His mind was not on the possibility of a fall, but on other things. More pertinent things. Tonight had been a first.

Caught . . .

He had almost been caught.

It was unthinkable.

Shaking, as much from the astonishment as from the excitement, he found his special little corner of his room – the Place of Solace – and dropped to his knees. His mind was reeling. Going a million miles a second. Thoughts too fast to string together. The sounds were back again:

The laughter.

The powerful thunder.

The screams.

And finally, the silence . . . That god-awful, overwhelming *silence.*

The Adder could not catch his breath. Could not breathe. He lay down on the cold hard concrete, ignoring the pain in his back and hip – a result of the fall – and reached up blindly for his iPod. When he found the device, he grabbed it with his shaking hands. Fumbled to make the headset cover his ears. And inserted the headphone jack. Once done, he thumbed the Play button and his ears filled with static charge – the wonderful, soothing, blessed, healing sound of white noise.

It was the only thing that helped.

Eight

The doorway to Mandy Gill's room had a wide yellow slash of police tape across it, set up by rookie cop Wong. Striker was glad to see it. Locking down a scene was always best practice. He gave the young constable a nod. 'Tape off unit 305 as well. No one in or out but Ident. Keep a log. And you're gonna need a second unit up here, too.'

'Delta Thirteen's already en route, Detective.'

'Good job.'

Striker turned away from the constable and went inside Mandy Gill's unit. The first thing he noticed upon re-entry was the empty pill bottle still clutched in the girl's hand. It was a small plastic vial. Blue cap, white label, with some black and white lettering. Standard stuff.

Cross-contamination was always a worry at scenes like this, so Striker removed his latex gloves, stuffed them in his back pocket, and re-gloved with fresh ones. Then he knelt in front of the body.

He gently prised Mandy's thumb and index finger back – they went easily; full rigor had not yet begun – and removed the bottle from her possession. He turned it around and read the label.

Lexapro.

'Jesus,' he muttered.

He looked up and spotted Felicia in the entranceway. She was setting up a Sunlite, one of the portable lighting systems the department used. It was actually designed for film sets, but worked perfectly for odd situations like this. Once turned on, the entire room was illuminated.

To Striker it was a depressing sight. The room looked better in the dimness of the flashlights. With the bright glare of the Sunlite making every inch of dirty floor and grimy countertop visible, the true filth which Mandy Gill had been living in became apparent – garbage on the floors, water damage and mould in the corners, a dead rat on the kitchen counter.

He turned his mind away from the depravity and got Felicia's attention. Held up the empty pill bottle. 'She's on anti-depressants,' he said. They both read the label:

Pharmasave.
Prescription number: 1079880 – MVC.
Quantity: 50 tablets.
Dispensary date: Jan 28th.

Striker did a double take on the date.

'The twenty-eighth,' he said.

'That was just yesterday,' Felicia noted. 'Tuesday.'

Striker thought this over. Fifty pills dispensed just twenty-four hours ago, and now there were none. It was more than enough for anyone to overdose. He wrote down all this information in his notebook, then placed the bottle directly beside the chair leg for Noodles, the Ident tech, who was already on his way. Then he stood up and looked around the room some more.

He felt at a loss, and he wondered if his guilt was clouding his vision. Despite the oddity of the camera being set up outside the window and the subsequent altercation with the suspect – evidence which was all circumstantial, by court standards – there was no *physical* evidence of foul play. At least none he could detect on the body, or anywhere in the primary crime scene.

Suicide was still not out of the question.

Especially not when considering this was Mandy Gill. Striker knew her well. He had for several years, ever since he'd met her at one of his daughter's Sports Day rallies. Mandy had been sixteen years old then, just a few years older than his daughter, Courtney. She had been living in the Dunbar area, not overly far from his own place. She had been a sweet young girl, polite and gentle, but she had already been suffering from depression problems, even back then.

There were reasons for it. Biochemical issues aside, the poor kid's mother had died from cancer the previous winter, and her father had been a cold, distant man who had eventually found his way back to jail on aggravated assault charges. With no siblings for support, Mandy had been alone in this world.

Just like she had been found tonight.

The thought pained Striker. 'I should have done more,' he said softly.

He stood there and thought of all this, and didn't move until Felicia called out to him: 'Look at this.' She was in the kitchen, scouring through the cupboards.

Striker crossed the room, the garbage that covered the floor crunching beneath his shoes. Once beside Felicia, he saw the tray of plastic bottles in her hand. There must have been over forty of them.

'Jesus, that's a lot,' he noted.

'It's all Effexor,' she said.

'*Effexor?* Let me see that.' He took one of the bottles and read the label. On it was the same pharmacy name and prescription number as the Lexapro. The combination of the drugs told him what she'd suffered from.

'She was bipolar depressive,' he said.

Felicia looked up. 'How do you know?'

He gave her a hard look. 'Personal experience – they put Amanda on the same stuff, after her first suicide attempt.'

Felicia looked back at him, her face taking on a concerned look. She said, 'Oh,' and then became quiet. For a moment, the silence of the room was uncomfortable, and Striker's thoughts filtered back to his wife and all her depression problems.

It was a memory that would never fade.

He prayed that Courtney was different from her mother – God knows she had the same stubbornness and unpredictable, fiery disposition that Amanda had always displayed – and it often worried him that she would develop the same depression problems, too. That she had suffered a serious spinal injury this last year and was now going through occupational therapy didn't help matters much. Lately, she'd been distant and moody. Brooding, really. Typical for a sixteen-year-old girl, he told himself. Or as Felicia always put it, bang on for a Scorpio.

He moved over to the window and gave her a call. She answered on the fifth ring.

'Hey, Pumpkin,' he said.

'Oh, hey, Dad. Let me use my psychic powers here – you're gonna be late again.'

'Funny girl. But I think I already am.'

'You definitely are. I was giving you an out.'

He laughed softly. She knew him too well. Knew the job.

'It's a bad call, bad day,' he explained. For a moment he considered telling her it was Mandy, but then he reconsidered. This might not have been a close friend of hers, but it was someone she knew. He'd tell her in person. It was better that way.

'Dad?' she asked.

'How'd it go with therapy today?'

'I didn't go.'

Striker said nothing for a moment, then continued, 'Look, Courtney, we've been over this before. You *need* to go to therapy. It's not an option. Without it, you won't regain full function. Even Annalisa—'

'I don't like Annalisa. She's a bitch.'

Striker took in a deep breath. He caught Felicia staring at him, eavesdropping openly on their conversation like she always did, and he turned away. 'Look, don't call her that. I don't like it. It's not respectful. And besides, the woman's only trying to help you.'

Courtney let out a bemused laugh. 'Help? You call that help? It doesn't help *anything*. And what would you know anyway? You're not the one going through this!'

'I'm not, am I? You'd be surprised to know—'

'I have to go, Dad, the bath is running.'

'Courtney—'

The line went dead.

Striker felt his fingers tighten on the phone as he stood there listening to the silence. Finally, he dropped his hand and stuffed the iPhone back into his inner jacket pocket. He gave himself a few seconds to get grounded. It had been like this with Courtney a lot lately – the angst, the anger and defiance, the never-ending rollercoaster ride of ups and downs.

Amanda all over again.

He turned around and met Felicia's stare. 'If you want to be a part of the conversation next time, just come over.'

Felicia didn't bite. 'She mad at you again?' she asked.

'She thinks I'm the Antichrist.'

'Well, *all* women think that.'

She laughed softly at her own joke; Striker did not. He examined the room and saw nothing but the sad signs of mental illness: counters covered with old dirty dishes; spoiled food on the tables; heaps of unwashed clothes in every corner; and stacks of newspapers piled up randomly all around the room. The entire place looked like it had been flooded and then drained, with everything left lying where it landed.

He crossed the room to the kitchen area and looked at the piles of papers on the countertop. They were bills for an old cell phone. And for credit cards. Letters from creditors. Job application forms coupled with received rejection forms.

Everything in the room signalled the downward spiral of depression, and no one had caught it. Striker was in the process of making a list of what he was seeing when a short, portly cop with white bushy eyebrows appeared in the doorway. His stomach hung way down low and he waddled more than walked. He took a few steps into the room and spotted Striker.

'Shipwreck.'

Striker looked over at the man. 'Hey, Noodles.'

Noodles. Real name: Jim Banner. Striker had requested him personally. Noodles was the Vancouver Police Department's best Ident technician. Hell, he was the best tech Striker had ever worked with. The Noodles nickname had come from a near-death experience Jim had suffered when choking on creamy linguine at the Noodle Shack up in Burnaby. It was a nickname Banner had always hated, but one that would forever stick.

That was the police way.

'You friggin' detectives,' Noodles growled. 'You're ruining my social life.'

In the sombre setting of the room, it was all Striker could do to force a grin. 'You need friends to have a social life, Noodles.'

'I was sitting there with Jack Daniel's when you called.' He dropped his tool box and gear just inside the door. 'Why the hell didn't you just call Marty? He's already on duty.'

'This one is important to me, Noodles. I wanted the best here.'

The Ident tech raised an eyebrow and made a *whatever* face, but clearly liked the compliment. 'The best, my ass,' he said. 'You can blow as much sunshine up my ass as you want, Shipwreck, but it don't change nothing – you owe me one for this.'

'Pick your poison.'

'Jack Daniel's. Gentleman's blend.'

'Done. Now get to work. Time is important.'

Noodles said nothing; he just did his own visual assessment of the scene, then opened his camera box. Striker relayed the whole experience to him, in exact detail, then guided him around the room, from the body of Mandy Gill to the kitchenette and, last of all, to the window area where the camera had been set up on the ledge.

'When I saw the guy, he had gloves on, but maybe he took them off at some time before I got here. I'm hoping for some prints around the lower pane,' he explained. 'Especially on the outside of the window, right here, where the lens was located.' He pointed to the exact area to be precise. 'Check all the pill bottles as well. I've already handled the one by the chair – gloves on – and Felicia touched the ones on the counter. Gloves, too. When you're done with this, I need the entire fridge in unit 305 dusted. Prick was hiding in there.'

'In the suite?'

'In the *fridge.*'

Noodles raised an eyebrow in surprise, then promised to have it done before going home tonight. For a brief moment, he focused on the body of Mandy Gill and his round, old face took on an expressionless look. After a moment, he shook his head and spoke.

'She was young.'

'She was a good kid,' Striker said. 'It's not right.'

The words felt heavy and the mood darkening, so Striker gave Felicia a nod to leave and they said goodbye to Noodles. Now that Ident had arrived and the scene was secure, he wanted to get out of there ASAP. For many reasons. Noodles worked faster when alone; the glove had to be properly bagged and tagged for DNA; and, without a doubt, Car 10, the Road Boss, would be pulling up on scene any minute. Striker wanted to be clear of this place – clear of this entire area – when the man arrived.

He and Laroche didn't exactly see eye to eye.

Nine

Striker settled into the driver's seat, and Felicia into the passenger's. He'd barely driven a half-block down Union Street before he hit the brakes, stopped hard, and stared out of the window at the building on the other side of the vacant lot.

It was an old house, a three-storey, directly west of the Lucky Lodge. Out front was a billboard notice from the City, explaining that construction would soon be underway. The place was going to be rebuilt into a quadplex.

Typical for the area. More money that way.

Most of the windows were boarded up, and on the ground beneath some of the planks Striker could see piles of broken glass. A big red Realty Inc. sign hung off a post out front, swaying in the growing night-time wind. Striker stared at it for a long moment.

'What?' Felicia asked. 'You got something?'

'I'm not sure,' he said and got out of the car.

Immediately, harsh winds blew his hair about and he buttoned up his trench coat. He slammed the driver's side door, rounded the car and started into the vacant lot that separated the two buildings.

Felicia got out too and followed him.

When Striker reached the centre of the vacant lot, he stopped. He looked across the way – at Mandy Gill's window, then at the empty three-storey behind him. At the very top was an attic. Its windows were covered with broken shutters. Everything inside appeared dark and still.

He pointed at it.

'The attic. It's directly across the way from Mandy's room. And it's one floor up – a perfect spot for a vantage point.'

Felicia came up beside him for a better look, so close he could smell the vanilla scent of her perfume. The wind whipped her long hair across her face and she used her hand to hold it down.

'The attic looks right into her window,' she agreed. 'Wanna check it out?'

Striker nodded. He crossed the vacant lot, weaving around the construction debris and potholes, until he stepped on to the next yard. Directly in front of him was the house. East side, ground floor.

He took out his flashlight and shone it on the building. The walls were made of wood and stucco that was broken off and chipped in large patches. Old rickety planks covered up most of the windows, and the one in front of Striker was no different. He gloved up with a pair of leather Windstoppers – they were thick enough to stop the glass from slicing him – and yanked hard on the lowest plank. It creaked and groaned, but remained firmly in place.

'The wood is strong,' Felicia remarked.

'Long nails.'

Striker left the boards in place and made his way around the house with Felicia following. By the time they'd seen all four sides – and that included a heavily planked front door, complete with iron bars – he was satisfied the place was secure.

Felicia shivered from the cold. 'We done our tour here?'

'You can wait in the car, if you want.'

'Wow. Touchy, touchy.' She looked up at the top two floors.

'All the other windows are too high. Someone would have needed a ladder to get up there.'

Striker didn't disagree. The other windows were definitely out of reach. To complicate matters, the house was built on a slope. The next floor was over ten feet above the outside ground. The attic was another two floors above – far too high for someone to reach – but something about the attic called out to him. Then he figured out what was bothering him.

'The boards have been removed from the attic window . . . and that doesn't make sense. No Break and Enter toad is gonna climb all the way up there to force his way inside, not when he can just crowbar one of these bottom windows open. The only reason for breaking off those attic boards is if he did it from the inside – to get a better view.'

Felicia saw his point. 'Of the Lucky Lodge.'

Striker turned his concentration to the ground-floor windows in front of him. After a more careful look, he noticed something odd with one of them. Compared to the other windows around the house – all of which were also boarded up – the planks on this one were different. They were stronger wood. Cleaner. Newer. And when he shone his flashlight on the boards, the shiny silver of new nail heads gleamed back.

He pointed this out to Felicia. 'The other boards on the other windows are old, but this one's been boarded up recently. And look at the angle of these two – they've been driven in poorly. By the looks of it, the guy was left-handed.'

Felicia looked at the nails and agreed. Then she squatted down low and shone her flashlight through the frozen blades of grass. 'Look here. There's small bits of glass. Just tiny stuff. Cubes, really. But it's there. It's almost like someone broke the window, then boarded it back up and cleaned the mess.'

Striker called up Dispatch, gave her the address, and asked if there were any recent break-ins reported to the house. When the answer came back no, he hung up and fixed Felicia with a stare. 'When's the last time you ever heard of a B and E guy repairing a place before he left?'

'Never.'

'Exactly.'

He reached out again with both his hands, grabbed hold of the upper plank, and reefed back on it with all his might. The connection was strong, and it took several attempts before the nails loosened, but in the end the planks gave way and tore out of the frame. Striker threw the planks into the construction site, and looked in through the window.

Behind him, Felicia made an uncomfortable sound. 'We don't have permission here, you know.'

He turned around. 'What?'

'Technically, we're breaking and entering this place. Maybe we should get hold of the property rep.'

Striker let out a small laugh, one that pissed off Felicia – he could see it in her eyes. 'I'm not waiting around here for three hours so some idiot can let us in the front door – and that's *if* he even comes down here, and *if* he consents to us searching the place. Right now we're going in under exigent circumstances.'

Felicia raised an eyebrow. 'Exigent circumstances?'

'I'll work it out later.'

Before she could argue the point further, Striker used the last remaining broken plank to rake away the small teeth of sharp glass from the window frame. Then he shone his flashlight through the window.

Inside was the living room. Thick drapes hung across all the other windows, keeping the place entombed in darkness. Clear plastic hung over the couch and love seat, and boxes filled with other unknown belongings were stacked in the far corner. No lights of any kind were on. Not even the stove or microwave clocks in the adjoining kitchen.

'Looks like the power's been cut here, too,' he said.

Felicia said nothing back. She stepped forward, right up to the window, then searched the darkness of the room and frowned.

'Let's call for a dog,' she suggested.

'And let some mangy mutt destroy any evidence left behind? Forget it, I'll risk this one on my own.'

'But Jacob—'

'I'm going in, Feleesh. Just cover me, okay?'

Striker took off his coat. He draped it across the window frame to cover any leftover slivers of glass that might cut him. Then he drew his SIG Sauer, ducked low, and stepped in through the window frame.

The first thing he noticed inside the living room was the scent of dampness; it lived in the walls and unused furniture. The smell reminded him of an old folks' home. He shone his flash-light around all four corners of the room, spotted nothing of interest, then stepped forward and peered into the kitchen. It was the same. Dark. Bare. Still.

The place looked deserted.

'Hold up,' he heard from Felicia. 'I'm coming with you.'

He smiled at that. He knew she would come, in the end. She was stubborn, like always, but forever faithful. It was her best quality.

When she reached his side, he motioned for her to cover their backs. She did. Once in position, Striker led them on. They slowly made their way to the west side of the house, then started up the staircase. They cleared each floor as they went, room by room, passing two bedrooms and a bathroom, then an office, master bedroom and ensuite on the top floor.

Felicia looked around the area, cursed, shook her head. 'This is the east side of the house,' she said. 'I don't see any window.'

Striker pointed up. He walked back into the hallway. Hanging down from the ceiling was a long nylon cord with a handle at the end. He grabbed it, then fixed Felicia with a hard look.

'Be ready,' he said.

'Go,' she replied.

He gave the cord a hard yank. A loud groan filled the air, and a fall-down staircase descended from the ceiling, bringing with it a cloud of dust and particles of sawdust. Once the staircase was resting on the main floor, Striker gave Felicia the nod, and he started up the stairs. The angle was steep, and the wood was old and rickety, but he continued up. Ten steps later, he was standing in the entrance of the attic.

It was dark and dusty, cold and quiet.

He shone his flashlight at every corner. Saw no one there. But on the east side of the attic, he spotted the window with the broken shutter. The sight of it excited him, and he started that way, then stopped. He slowed himself down, took a moment to assess the area. He shone his flashlight across the wall and saw nothing of interest. Then he aimed the beam at the floor. What he saw there made him pause. By the base of the window, in the dust, were two sets of markings. They were faint and faded and indistinct, but they were definitely there.

Felicia joined him in the attic entranceway and took note of the tracks in the dust. 'What do you think they're from?' she asked.

Striker dropped into a squat position and studied the markings. Two one-inch trails, perfectly parallel.

'Suitcase maybe. A stand. A generator. I'm not sure.'

He stood up, stepped to the side of the markings, and approached the window. As he neared it, he looked down and across the way. Directly below was the beginning of the vacant lot. Directly across the way was the Lucky Lodge.

'You got your monocular on you?' he asked.

Felicia nodded. 'Always.' She fished it out of her pocket, a token from her surveillance days.

Striker had always planned on getting one himself. He took the monocular from Felicia and used it to look across the way. The scope zeroed in on Mandy Gill's room – a perfect unobstructed view. He could see her kitchenette, the doorway to the hall, the doorway to the bathroom and then Mandy herself, dead in the chair.

Noodles was still on scene gathering evidence.

For surveillance of unit 303, there was no better position.

Striker handed the monocular back to Felicia and turned on his flashlight. He swept the beam around the window, but saw no prints of possible value. Lastly, he illuminated the broken glass and shutter, again looking for fingerprints. He found none, but what he did find was equally telling. He reached out through the window frame and picked up a shard of broken glass. Stuck to it was a small strip of black material.

Felicia made an excited sound. 'Is it leather?' she asked.

Striker nodded. He dropped the evidence, shard and all, into a paper bag, marked it, and carefully pocketed it. Then he turned around and found Felicia's eyes.

'Tape everything off?' she asked.

'Yeah,' he replied. 'There's no doubt about it. He was here.'

Ten

Ten minutes later, Noodles had made his way over to the attic and was now taking pictures and bagging samples. He stood up awkwardly in the low-ceilinged attic, and rubbed his lower back, all the while complaining about it.

'You guys'll have me here till the early morning light,' he griped.

'You're breaking my heart,' Striker said.

'Like you have one.'

Striker let the banter go, and mentally went over what they had. The entire building was taped off now, with patrol cops stationed as guards at the front and back of the residence.

Striker left the scene under the command of Sergeant Mike Rothschild – an experienced old-schooler who had been one of Striker's first NCOs many years ago.

Striker and Felicia returned to the car. After Striker hopped in the driver's side, Felicia slammed the passenger-side door closed and bit her lip. 'Foul play is looking more and more reasonable,' she said.

Striker shifted in his seat. The leather was cold and it felt stiff against his back. He started the car and got the engine going. Turned on the heater. Switched the setting to defrost.

'Yes and no,' he finally said. 'Sure, it looks bad. No doubt about that. But what do we really have here to suggest this is anything other than a suicide? And by that I mean *non-circum-stantial* evidence.'

'Non-circumstantial?'

'The physical evidence all points to a suicide.'

'That someone *filmed.*'

Striker nodded. 'I'm not arguing that; hell, I'm the one who found the guy. It's creepy, no doubt. But what really is that? We got a guy in the next suite filming Mandy with a set-up video camera. Why? For all we know, he had a thing for her and was videotaping her before her death. For all we know, he was there trying to get the camera back before we found it.'

'Or maybe he was filming us, for that matter,' Felicia said.

That notion bothered Striker. It was a possibility he hadn't thought of. But a legitimate reality. 'You could be right about that,' he said. 'One of these YouTube idiots. Or maybe another media-seller.'

'Sounds weak when you say it.'

'And it might well be,' he said. 'All I'm saying is that we don't know *why* this happened. Hell, we don't even have possession of the camera.'

'What about the leather strip we found on the broken window?'

Striker nodded. 'I have no doubt Ident will match it to the glove I tore off the suspect – the material is the same colour and texture. But even then, so what? What does it actually prove?'

'It proves we got a sicko on our hands.'

Striker grinned darkly. 'The world is full of sickos, Feleesh. Again, what does it prove? That someone who filmed Mandy was in the next-door apartment. He was also in the house across the way. Could've been a squatter, for all we know.'

'I doubt that.'

'I doubt it, too. But that's what we got right now. We need

more.' He turned silent as he thought things over, and he revved the engine a few times to warm it up faster. After a long moment, something occurred to him and he turned to face Felicia once more. 'If Mandy was forced to eat those pills, then they were already ground up into powder when she took them – I saw the paste in her mouth.'

'Saliva over time can do that,' Felicia said wryly.

Striker gave her one of his *I'm not a moron* looks. 'There was pill dust around her lips as well, and she also had bits of it on the corners of her mouth. The pills were crushed, Feleesh; she didn't chew them. So either she hated taking medicine in pill form and always ingested them as powder – or someone made her take them. It's one or the other.'

Felicia crossed her arms to keep warm. 'If there was a struggle, you'd think she'd have fought back.'

'There are no defensive wounds.'

'Could she have been bound?'

Striker bit his lip as he thought that over. 'I looked for that, and I didn't see any ligature marks. But if something happened to her first – if she were held down, or bound, or drugged – then that would explain it. My bet would be drugs.' He flipped through the pages of his notebook, then wrote down a few theories. 'You can damn well *zombify* a person with a lot of over-the-counter meds – sleeping pills, Valium, anything they can crush up and slip into someone's drink.'

'GHB,' Felicia noted.

Gamma Hydroxybutyric Acid was the most common date-rape drug on the market.

'That shit renders victims damn near immobile,' she added.

'And it can kill in larger doses,' Striker said. 'That might end up being another avenue we need to pursue. For all we know, this could end up being a case of a date rape gone wrong.' He wrote this down in his notebook. 'Tox tests will help.'

Striker was about to say more when his cell phone buzzed. He reached into his jacket pocket and pulled out his iPhone. Across the screen were two words: *Larisa Logan*. He saw the name, then shook his head and swore under his breath. He hit the Ignore button and stuffed the cell back into his pocket.

Felicia took note. 'Who was that?'

Striker gave her a glance like he didn't want to get into it. When Felicia didn't look away and just kept staring, waiting for an answer, he relented.

'Larisa Logan,' he explained. 'Works for the Victim Services Unit. Third time she's called me in two days.'

Felicia shook her head. 'Well, here's a novel idea – why don't you actually answer the phone? Or at least call the woman back?'

Striker said nothing for a moment. He used the sleeve of his coat to wipe away some of the remaining moisture on the driver's side window. Then he fiddled with the defrost controls.

'Jacob?' Felicia persisted.

He sighed and met her stare. 'Look, Larisa's the counsellor who put me through the department-ordered sessions after Amanda's death, okay? That's her fifth call this week.'

'Then why don't you just call her back?'

'Because I know what she wants.'

'Which is?'

'To do her yearly follow-up sessions, I'm sure – the woman is relentless.'

'So then do them.'

Striker said nothing, he just exhaled. The sessions with Larisa were difficult; they brought back too many painful memories. And there was enough on his plate right now with work and home life. Already, he couldn't sleep at night. And on top of all this, there was his relationship with Felicia: off again, on again, somewhere in between – he never knew which way they were headed.

Off again right now, and he wasn't happy with it. Whenever he asked her what the problem was she said: 'There's just too many issues to deal with.'

It was her standard response.

Lately, everywhere he turned there were problems. Even the good things felt hard. And he was tired of it. He didn't need any more stress put on his shoulders. And dredging up the memories of Amanda's depression and suicide would only make matters worse.

He was avoiding all that. Purposefully.

Felicia suddenly made an *Ohhh* sound and seemed to catch on. 'My God, Jacob, I'm sorry – I never even realized.'

He looked at her, confused. 'Realized what?'

'*This*. I mean, here we are at a suicide, and the woman has almost the same name as your wife. Mandy. Kinda like Amanda. I'm sorry, I should have known. I never even thought—'

'You're reaching here, Feleesh. And for the record, Amanda died a long time ago.'

'What does that matter? My God, if I'd realized—'

'A long time ago, Feleesh.'

She gave him an uncertain look, like she wasn't sure which way to take the conversation. In the end, she kept quiet. The passenger window was still fogged up, so she took a moment to power the window down and up. When it remained fogged, she wiped away the condensation with her hand. Afterwards, she turned in her seat and met his stare once more. She spoke softly.

'Maybe you should see Larisa one more time.'

Striker groaned. 'Oh Jesus, not you, too. Leave it be, Feleesh.'

'I'm just saying—'

'You're always *just saying* something. Serious. Just let it go for once, will ya? Let this one ride.'

Felicia's eyes narrowed at the comment, and for a moment she looked ready for a fight. She tucked her long dark hair back over her ear and her mouth opened like she was ready to say more.

Striker looked away from her. He was in no mood for small talk or bullshit. And in even less of a mood for arguing.

DNA tests needed to be done.

Eleven

Before Striker could put the car into gear, the bright glare of head-lights caught his eye. When he looked over into the centre of the street, he saw two men with video cameras and one woman with long blonde hair holding a microphone in front of a white media van.

The evening news.

'Jesus, they're here already?' he griped.

Felicia sighed. 'They must've seen the police lights and the dog track.'

'Just say nothing and get in the car.'

Striker powered down the driver's side window. The blonde woman took notice and hurried over, almost slipping in her high heels.

'Detective Striker. Detective Striker!' she called.

'No comment,' he said politely.

He tried to show no emotion. But it was hard. There was no doubt in his mind that he and Felicia would now be on the local news tonight, and that irritated him.

Felicia shook her head as she looked at the news crew. 'Must be a slow night,' she noted.

'For *them*,' Striker replied. 'For us, it's about to get busy.'

He put the car into Drive and pulled out on to the road. The lab was waiting.

*   *   *

For the first few minutes of the drive, silence filled the car. Felicia was reading through Mandy Gill's long and troubled history, and Striker had taken a handful of aspirin to get rid of the headache that was growing behind his eyes. When they reached the corner of Clark and Broadway, Felicia looked up, confused.

'Why are we going this way?' she asked. 'The lab is south.'

Striker said nothing as he navigated around a parked bus and continued west.

'Jacob?' she persisted.

He glanced over at her. 'Using the police lab will take months,' he explained. 'Weeks, in fact, even if we could put a rush order on it. No, we're going private on this one.'

'Private? You know how much that costs.'

'Don't worry, I got it covered.'

'*You* got it covered? Like, personally?' When he didn't answer right away, her eyes narrowed. 'What are you up to now? How are we going to pay for this?'

'Contingency fund.'

She gave him one of her probing looks, and Striker felt her hot black eyes bore into him. He ignored the feeling and pretended to be oblivious – like he always did when trying to avoid a discussion with Felicia.

They continued on to their destination, swerving in and out of the seven o'clock lingering rush-hour grind. When they reached the fifteen hundred block of West Broadway Avenue, Striker pulled over to the north side of the road and stopped in a No Parking Zone. He threw a Vancouver Police placard on the dashboard.

Above the Chapters book store, GeneTrace Laboratories occupied the top two floors of the Bosner Tower, a ten-storey, glass-and-steel monstrosity that took up the entire southwest corner of the Granville–Broadway intersection.

The windows were all tinted black, and the moon and car lights reflected off the glass panes in a display that looked eerily festive.

Striker had been here before.

Many times.

Obtaining DNA results was an arduous and painful process if you went through the proper channels. The police lab was a nightmare – great technicians with no support. Wait times could be as long as two years, sometimes even three, if the crime was only a property-related offence.

With the private labs, a complete test with 16-loci quality could be attained in as little as seven days. Less, if the customer was willing to buck up. Private was always the best way to go. And as far as Striker was concerned, GeneTrace was the cream of the crop; they had state-of-the-art facilities and the latest, ground-breaking technology. All of which the customer paid for – and paid dearly.

'What contingency fund?' Felicia asked.

Striker just gave her one of his trademark smiles and opened the car door.

'Don't ask questions you won't like the answer to.'

He grabbed the paper bag with the glove in it from the trunk, turned around, and marched across the street to the Bosner Tower.

Being just after seven, they had plenty of time. GeneTrace Laboratories was open until ten, though Striker often made arrangements for after-hours drops. The owners of GeneTrace were good businessmen.

And cops got preferential treatment.

Inside, the waiting area looked more like a trendy cappuccino shop than a science laboratory. Black leather Casa Nova sofas, white marble floors, and stone-and-glass coffee tables were the norm. Standing tall in the centre of the foyer was a hand-etched sculpture of a pair of chromosomes, made from transparent glass. Behind that was a thick granite countertop, on which stood several black leather folders, which looked more like fancy menus at a five-star restaurant than catalogues for DNA testing.

Felicia walked ahead and picked one up.

'Wow,' she said. 'They do everything here from paternity tests to mitochondrial DNA.' Her eyes turned to the price list and her brow lifted. 'For this kind of dough, they should at least offer us a martini while we wait.'

Striker grinned. 'Martini? Hell, they should offer us lines.'

He'd barely finished speaking when the front-desk clerk returned. He walked, almost stork-like, in huge awkward strides with his head bobbing forward with each step; Striker half expected the man to preen himself. His face was thin, and it looked disarmingly young behind the glasses he wore. When he spoke, his voice was high. Fluttery.

'Good evening. Welcome to GeneTrace. How can I help you?'

Striker approached the counter and badged the young man – an action which seemed to leave no impression on the young clerk – then dropped the brown paper bag with the glove in it and the brown paper bag with the glass shard in it on the granite countertop and met the man's stare.

'Vancouver Police,' he said. 'We need DNA on this glove. And anything you can do with this glass shard – there's a leather strip on it we think is from the glove. We'll need it matched.'

'That's not a problem.'

'We need it done *fast*.'

'That is also not a problem.' He spoke with an air of arrogance.

Without another word, the clerk pulled a form and a pen from beneath the counter and handed it to them. When Striker accepted the form and began filling out the necessary details – type of test required; suspected location of DNA on the item procured; and all the necessary contact numbers – the clerk cleared his throat.

'And do you have a suspect comparison sample?' he asked.

Striker shook his head. 'We want the results run through the DNA Databank. See if there's any Known Offender hits.' He met the man's stare. 'And we want the results in less than forty-eight hours.'

The clerk frowned. 'I said fast was not a problem, not light speed.'

'This is important.'

'I'm sure it is,' the man said, and that arrogance was back. 'Unfortunately, the lab is *extremely* backed up right now – we've been tasked with assisting the Pickton investigation. So even with a rush, it's going to take some time.'

'Like I said, we need them fast.'

The clerk's face took on a distant, detached look, as if this was a line of questioning he was all too used to. When he spoke again, his speech sounded prepared and overused. 'This is DNA we're talking about, Detectives, not fingerprints. The culture has to be grown.'

Striker put on his best smile. 'So it's not like *CSI*?'

The clerk's face tightened for a moment, then lost the frown. A grin spread his lips and he let out a small laugh.

'Expect four days,' he said. 'Three at the minimum. But leave the sample with me and I'll see what I can work out with the lab people. Forty-eight hours seems quite unlikely at this point in time, but you never know.'

Striker cast Felicia a glance. After she nodded, Striker turned back to face the clerk. 'Thanks. We really appreciate your assistance with this.' He shook the clerk's hand, then handed him a business card and wrote his personal cell number on it. 'Call me the moment you know. Night or day.'

'Of course.'

The clerk rubbed his nose and read through the DNA form, making sure all the boxes were properly filled out and checked. When he reached the bottom of the page, he looked up and met Striker's stare.

'And what authorization number should I use?' he asked.

Striker didn't hesitate. 'Eleven thirteen.'

He saw Felicia flinch at the mention of the badge number, but he paid her no heed. Seconds later, when the clerk excused himself to print up the proper labels for the sample and grab one of the Time Continuity forms the police required, Felicia rushed up to the counter and elbowed Striker.

'What the hell is wrong with you? That's *Laroche's* number.'

Striker shrugged. 'Has to be. With a bill this big, only an inspector can sign off on it.'

'But he *didn't* sign off on it – we haven't even spoken to him yet.'

Striker raised an eyebrow. 'Really? I must've been mistaken then, because I could've sworn you told me he'd given us authorization.'

Her reply was cold. 'No. I didn't.'

'Hmm. Must've misheard you then.'

'Jacob—'

'We really need to communicate better in the future.' When her cold look remained fixed on him, he added, 'Just be happy he took the badge number. Otherwise we would've had to use Plan B.'

'Plan B?'

'You would've had to sleep with him.' When she didn't laugh and her glare remained the same, Striker splayed his hands in surrender. 'Come on, Feleesh. It'll be fine. Trust me.'

She lowered her voice. 'I've heard that one before, Jacob. You're going to get us suspended.'

He stopped leaning on the counter and turned to face her. 'That won't happen. And besides, you know how it works around here – you honestly think Laroche is going to authorize private funding when all we got right now is circumstantial evidence? Lots of luck.'

'That's exactly my point.'

'Well, whatever happens, *I'll* wear it. As far as I'm concerned, I thought he had approved this. Whoops. My mistake.'

'Let's just get the hell out of here,' she said.

'We can't go just yet. He needs me to sign the continuity form,' Striker said.

Felicia just gave him one of her sharp looks before turning away. She shook her head, brushed her long dark hair over her shoulder, and focused on the gigantic painting on the far wall – a recreation of Michelangelo's *The Creation of Adam*, except in this painting, Adam wasn't touching God, he was touching a spiralling strand of DNA.

Striker watched Felicia from behind, feeling the cold shoulder she was giving him. It was all right; she had reason to. He completely understood that. What he was doing could get them into major shit. Yet again. And sooner or later, a suspension was bound to happen. Lately, he'd been cutting more corners than a Vancouver taxi driver. But he couldn't help it.

That was the only way things ever got done around here.

He was just about to force some conversation with Felicia – try to smooth things out a little – when his cell went off. He whipped it out, read the screen and saw Mike Rothschild's name. He picked up.

'Sergeant,' Striker said.

'Hey, Snow White, how's life in the forest?'

'We're real busy here, Mike.'

Rothschild laughed at his irritation. 'I got some news for you.'

'*Good* news?'

'Yeah. The camera cunts showed up.'

Striker felt his jaw tighten. 'The media? Again?'

'You said it. What ya want me to tell them?'

'Who the hell leaked?'

'Find me a magic mirror and I'll tell you.'

Striker thought over their options. Dealing with the media was always a hassle. They distorted facts to make articles more sensational, and they had no respect for a person's privacy. Whether the victim was alive or dead, young or old, passed away or horribly mutilated and murdered – it was irrelevant to the media. All that mattered was how many viewers were watching. Or how many papers sold. Everything was numbers and headlines.

'Tell them it's a suicide at this point, but the investigation is ongoing.'

'Done.'

'That's all and no more, Mike – I want to keep a tight lid on this one. Real tight.'

'So I shouldn't tell them we suspect Taliban involvement.'

Striker smiled grimly at the comment. 'At least then I'd have a suspect.'

He hung up the cell and pinched the bridge of his nose. There was pressure there, building up behind his eyes. The aspirin did jack shit; the headache was growing.

He should have expected it. So far everything was going

sideways. Mandy was dead. A suspect had escaped. Felicia was pissed at him again. And now the media had shown up, asking questions on a case where he still had no real proof of anything. What was this – a strange suicide? A date-rape overdose? A snuff film?

Or something even more dark?

The thought left him sick. A ball of stress was knotting up his insides, getting tighter and tighter with every turn. This call was a bomb, he knew, and the fuse had already been lit.

Sooner or later, it was going to blow up on them.

Twelve

How much time had passed, the Adder had no idea. Whenever the sounds returned – the laughter, the thunderous cracks, the screams and then the silence – he always scrambled for his white-noise device. Only when it was turned on full, with the headphones jammed right into his ears, was there ever peace. And time had little meaning.

Regardless, time *had* passed. And his mind had finally calmed to a much more logical level where he could think again. Rationalize. Assess.

He got the glove.

This was disconcerting. Not because it made him easier for the police to identify or catch, but because it had never happened before. This was an unprecedented error.

The first time he'd ever come up Snake Eyes.

From now on he would have to be smarter than that. From now on he would wear a layer of latex beneath the leather gloves. As a necessary precaution. Because the damage was already done.

There was a link now.

With that notion came the other thoughts – the ones that left a tingling sensation running amok throughout his insides. Had he touched anything when the glove had been torn off? And if so, what? Had he left fingerprints back at the scene?

He felt his facial muscles tighten with the thought, and he

could not relax them. This cop was smarter than most. He had connected the fridge trays with his hiding spot. And he had remained calm and logical and tactical. When the big detective had zeroed in on the fridge, the Adder had had no choice but to react.

No choice.

The anxiety swelled up again, too much to contain. And the Adder leaned back and let out a sorrowful sound. He crawled across the cold cement floor to the far wall with the cabinet. He took hold of the edges, then paused for a moment to look up at the hatch in the ceiling.

It was locked and in place.

Safe.

The Adder slid the cabinet out of the way. It was heavy and scuffed on the floor as he did it but, like always, he got it to move.

Located in the wall was a small hollow. There lay his silver container – his own personal holy grail. A case which he cleaned and polished several times a day, so much that it glowed like a mercury halo. Inside it were his DVDs and Blu-ray discs.

Inside it was his salvation.

He took hold of the case, removing it so gently, so carefully. He set it down on the soft burgundy towel he kept on the ground, then opened the case. He stared in wonder. Two rows of DVDs and Blu-ray discs. His files. His wonderful, beautiful movies. Thirty-six to be exact.

There should have been thirty-seven.

Mandy Gill's movie was still missing. And it was going to be a problem.

The sight of the empty DVD space brought the darkness back, but before the thought could settle in his mind, the bell went off. The noise so sharp – not only in its sound but in what it signified – that he stiffened like he'd been whipped across the back with a belt.

The Doctor was calling.

And that was never good.

The Adder felt a shiver run through his body, and he quickly regained his senses. He closed the silver box and gently placed it back in the hollow. Then he took hold of the cabinet and slowly, carefully, slid it back into place, hiding the hole in the wall.

He scrambled up the ladder and undid the latch.

When he stepped inside the study, the contrast between the rooms was alarming. His was cold; the Doctor's so very hot. His was dark and gloomy; the Doctor's so bright and glaring. And his room offered a safe, protected feeling, one that may have been false and imagined, but one that was there nonetheless. Here, in the Doctor's office, there was always a sense of danger. Of threat. Of despair.

And it was very, very real.

The Doctor was already there, sitting in a high-backed leather chair. The darkness made the world out there appear hidden, indistinct.

It matched the mood.

'I am not happy,' the Doctor finally said.

The Adder looked down. 'I know.'

'You have been very foolish.'

'It wasn't my fault. The police . . . they were just suddenly *there*.'

'Did they see your face?'

'They know nothing.'

'Did they see your *face*?'

'No.'

'They had better not. We've got a lot of work to do, you and I, and I can't have you getting into trouble like this.'

The room was silent for a long moment – a time that could have been minutes or seconds to the Adder, for time rarely flowed normally. Then the Doctor spoke again. Simple words. Brief and direct.

'You know the rules.'

The Adder's head snapped up. 'But it wasn't my fault!'

'Fault?' The Doctor laughed. 'What does that matter? Fault? Was it *William's* fault?'

The Adder said nothing, and he began to shake all over.

'No,' he said softly. 'No,' he said again.

And he did as he was told. He followed the rules. He succumbed.

He went to the well.

Thirteen

'We need to do more research on Mandy,' Striker said.

It was one of his own personal rules. *Know the victim.* This was crucial. And to a point, he already did. He had known Mandy years back when she had attended the same school events as Courtney, and he had dealt with her a few times just last year when he had filled in for Bernard Hamilton.

Hamilton worked in the mental health car – which was essentially a mobile unit, composed of one officer and one social worker, who partnered up to help the mentally ill people of the Downtown East Side.

All the past connections helped, but they weren't enough. Striker wanted to know everything about the girl.

Especially her recent history.

Felicia buckled up her seat belt as Striker pulled out on the main road and headed for the downtown core. 'I'll go through the CAD calls,' she said. 'See what else was going on in that area when Mandy's call came in.'

Striker nodded in agreement.

CAD was the Computer Assisted Dispatch system that was used whenever 911 calls and general requests from the public were made. It was documented every time a patrol member took a call. Maybe they could find some connections there.

God knows, it was as good a place as any to start.

They headed for headquarters. While en route, Felicia grum-
bled about the day never ending. Striker took a quick look at
her. Her eyes appeared heavy and were underlined. Seeing that,
he took a detour through the Starbucks drive-thru on Terminal
for some much-needed caffeine. He grabbed himself a tall
Americano, black, and a protein bar.

'What do you want?' he asked.

'Eggnog latte. With a slice of raspberry loaf with lemon-
cream-cheese icing.'

'Why don't you get something decadent for a change?'

'I'm low on carbs and sugar and caffeine, Jacob, now is *not*
the time. And after that little stunt you pulled at the lab, this
treat is all on you.'

He smiled. 'I wouldn't have it any other way.'

When the coffees and food came, Striker paid for them and
handed the cardboard tray to Felicia. Then he headed for 312
Main Street. Headquarters.

Destination: Homicide.

It was less than a mile away.

A half-hour later, Striker sat back in his office chair and rubbed
his eyes. They were dry and grainy. How could they not be? The
computer screen assigned to his desk was an outdated piece of
junk. The monitor was on the fritz – the colours all seemed a
tint or two off – and it was not even a widescreen.

He glanced over at Felicia. She had a better chair, one made
from leather and high-backed, and also a brand-new widescreen
monitor. A twenty-four incher. And newer technology. LED.
Striker looked at it.

'How the hell d'you ever get that anyway?' he asked. 'I've had
a requisition order in for six months.'

'Connections,' was all she said, and went back to her reading.

Striker said nothing. He just stretched his hands high above him and felt his back crack. He stared at the window. Outside, everything was black and deep and cold.

He was glad to be inside the office.

His thoughts turned to Courtney, and he made a call home and hit the Speakerphone button so he could talk while he worked. The phone rang six times before the answering machine picked up. As usual Courtney had changed the voice message again, like she did every week:

'If you like it then you better . . . leave a message,' she sang.

The words were familiar, but Striker couldn't place them. Some song on the radio, he guessed. It usually was.

'It's Dad,' he said. 'Pick up.'

When Courtney didn't answer, he repeated himself, then finally gave up. He hit the End button and disconnected the call.

Felicia swivelled around in her chair. ' "Single Ladies",' she said.

'Huh?'

'The song on the machine. It's "The Single Ladies". By Beyoncé.'

Striker just nodded. 'Sure.'

She stared him down. 'You have no clue, do you?'

'Sure I do. Beyoncé – lead singer from Guns N' Roses.'

Felicia laughed out loud, and Striker smiled weakly back at her.

'My eyes are turning to sand,' he said.

She tore off a piece of her raspberry loaf and stuffed it in his mouth. 'You at least getting anything?'

'Besides a headache? No, not really.' He swallowed the loaf and glanced back at the computer screen where he had opened four different pages from PRIME.

PRIME was the Police Records Information Management

Environment – a huge, widespread database that contained everything from basic police reports to hidden intelligence files. It was but one of a dozen different databases the cops used.

All of which were essential.

Striker spoke again. 'There's a ton of stuff here on Mandy. File after file, and most of it is Mental Health Act. She was a very sick person. Listed EDP everywhere.'

EDP – Emotionally Disturbed Person.

'And then there's a dozen more street checks,' he continued. 'She was run by Patrol tons of times, just for acting strange. Then there's the rest of the standard calls – a lot of Disturbances and Suspicious Circumstance incidents, most of which were because she was off her meds again. Acting all loopy. She's also done a dozen different voluntary transports to the psych ward at St Paul's. So she was at least cognitively aware that she was having problems.'

Felicia glanced at the list of files and frowned. 'Hey, you authored some of these reports.'

Striker nodded. He told her about the times he had replaced Bernard Hamilton in the mental health car, and also about how he knew the girl from before. From when Mandy had attended the same school as Courtney.

'Wow. So she went from Dunbar to Ditchville,' Felicia said. 'The poor kid. Did she have any family?'

Striker threw his pen on the blotter. 'Her mother died of cancer a few years back. As for her father, he's in jail.'

'Jail? What for?'

Striker didn't want to get into it, but he explained anyway: 'After Mandy's mother died, when she was still living in Dunbar, she was going to the same school as Courtney. St Patrick's High. They knew each other.'

'How?' Felicia asked.

Striker gave her a cross look. 'From hanging out and smoking outside the school fence – I could have killed Courtney when I caught her.'

Felicia grinned at that.

'Anyhow,' Striker continued, 'that was when Mandy's depression really deepened. I must have picked her up a half-dozen times when she'd run off. And every time, I took her back to her father and told her she had to keep taking her meds. It was a never-ending cycle.'

Felicia shook her head. 'So?'

'So, what I didn't know at the time was that Mandy's father was abusing her. Sexually. Which was one of the reasons for her growing depression, why she kept taking off all the time.' He shook his head as he relived the moments. 'Every time I picked her up, I was taking her right back to the monster. I'll never forgive myself for that.'

'She never told you?'

'No, but I should have seen it. There had to be some signs. There had to be *something*. I was so preoccupied with Amanda's depression problems at the time, I never saw it . . .'

'It was a bad time for you, Jacob.'

'Bad for her, too.' He pushed the keyboard away and rubbed his eyes. 'Either way, Mandy's father was caught, but by that point in time the damage had been done. Mandy was put under government care for a bit, but you know how it is. She bounced around a lot, and to be honest, I lost track. If it weren't for the problems we were having with Amanda, I would have taken the kid in . . . Ah fuck, I *should* have taken her in!'

Felicia reached out and touched his arm. 'You can't save the world, Jacob.'

'She was one girl.' He looked back at all the reports and felt sick to his stomach. 'Anyway, she had no siblings. And only one cousin, a guy named James John Gill. You'd know him better as Jimmy J.'

'Jimmy J? – You mean *Gonzo*?'

'The one and only.'

Felicia thought it over. 'Didn't he die over six months ago? In that meth lab explosion on Blenheim?'

Striker nodded. 'Damn near obliterated himself.' He thought it over for a while, then added, 'They never did recover all the money.'

'Because it was blown to shreds.'

'Was it?' he asked. That was probably the case, but there were no absolutes in this world. Definitely not in the business of policing. He took a moment to write this down in his notebook, then picked up his half-full coffee cup and rolled it back and forth in his hands. He was just about to return to reading the computer screen when Felicia made a *hmm* sound.

'What you got?' he asked.

'Maybe something, maybe nothing. Listen. There was a driving complaint. Brand-new SUV, a Beamer—'

'Probably an X5.'

'Sure, whatever.' Felicia was terrible with makes and models. 'Anyway, the complaint came in just five minutes after you went over the air requesting a canine unit. This guy was really flying. Doing nearly a hundred, according to the complainant. And he blew right through a stop sign. Almost caused an accident. Never even stopped.'

Striker thought this over. 'Where?'

'Vernon Drive and East Hastings Street.'

'That's not far from Mandy's place,' Striker noted. 'Just a few blocks east and north.'

Felicia nodded. 'It's *real* close. Vehicle was racing north, then made a hard left turn on Franklin. That's when the complainant lost sight.'

'Any details?'

She read on. 'The vehicle was dark, maybe black, with shiny chrome mags.'

'That's standard dress, right from the factory. Any plate?'

Felicia just shook her head. 'Not even a partial.'

Striker thought this over and dumped out his cold coffee. He sat up in the chair and smiled.

'No plate *yet*,' he said. He stood up and grabbed his notebook.

'Where are you going?' Felicia asked.

'Put on your coat,' he said. 'We're going to Vernon and Hastings. I've been there before. That intersection has a Chevron on the southeast corner.' Striker's smile widened. 'They got *video*.'

Fourteen

The Chevron gas station located on the corner of East Hastings Street and Vernon Drive was a magnet for trouble. Had been ever since Striker joined the VPD. And the details showed that: the front door was always locked after ten; the front window was made out of safety glass; and the bathroom used a black light source for illumination, not white, because it made it harder for junkies to shoot up in there when they snuck inside. All in all, Striker had been to the Vernon Drive Chevron more than a hundred times, kicking out the junk monkeys and drunks, and chasing down shoplifters and armed robbers.

Because of this, he knew the staff well.

'Hey, Wanda,' he said as he entered the store.

The large woman with the wild hair looked up from behind the register and beamed. 'Detective Striker!' she said in an overly loud voice. 'Now just where have you been, my big beautiful man?'

'Cloud eight,' he replied. 'Still trying to work my way to Nirvana.'

Wanda laughed in big heavy gusts, then hurried around the counter. She was a big woman. Her hips were so wide they barely fitted through the desk opening, her knees were knocked, and her breasts were so large and heavy they came close to popping the buttons of her uniform. She gave Striker a bear hug that lasted embarrassingly long, then let go almost unwillingly.

Felicia stood there watching the show with a half-smile on her face. She gave Striker an odd look, and he just shook his head. He'd known Wanda Whittington for over ten years now, and the woman would never change. At five foot five and nearing two hundred and forty pounds, no one would ever be accused of calling the woman dainty. But her build was never what he noticed; it was her heart. Wanda was a good person.

Striker introduced the two women, then got right down to business.

'We need help,' he said to Wanda. 'A big SUV came rampaging through here, sometime between four-twenty and four-forty earlier today.'

Felicia nodded. 'The driving complaint was called in at exactly four twenty-eight.'

'Do you remember it?' Striker asked. 'This guy was apparently driving balls to the wall.'

Wanda Whittington thought it over, her big brown eyes taking on a faraway look behind her chubby, freckled cheeks. She scratched at her hair, then let out a frustrated sound and shrugged.

'It was just so damn busy today,' she said. 'I'm sorry.'

'Don't be,' Striker said. 'Either you saw it or you didn't. Was anyone else on shift with you at that time?'

She absently rubbed the knuckles of her left hand. 'Well, Davie was *supposed* to be working with me today, but he never showed – he's probably drunk again. You know how he is. Called in three times last week saying he was sick, but everyone knows he's on the sauce. And on the cheap stuff, too. Likes the red can.'

Striker just nodded. He'd known Davie for almost as long as

he'd known Wanda. A nice, harmless guy. But he had a problem, no doubt. Like half the population down here.

He looked past Wanda, past the black-light washrooms, at the manager's office. The door was painted blue and had a brand-new peephole installed. It was closed and more than likely locked.

'You still got video back there?' Striker asked.

Wanda nodded. She returned to the register, locked the till, then grabbed the office key they kept hidden behind the money-drop box. She rounded the counter and passed Striker by.

'Follow me, my beautiful man.'

She walked up to the blue door, unlocked it, and disappeared inside. Striker started to follow her. When Felicia didn't join him, he stopped and turned to face her. 'You coming?'

She didn't respond at first, she just kept looking out of the window. To the north. 'The caller said the Beamer turned left on Franklin,' she recalled. 'Vernon and Franklin . . . isn't that the corner where we attended that suicide last year – the one in front of the plastics warehouse?'

Striker nodded, seeing her point. 'They got video, too.'

'I'll head down there and see what I can dredge up. In the meantime, you finish here. Pick me up down there when you're done.' She leaned close, smiled, and whispered, 'Want to borrow my rape whistle in case things go bad?'

'You mean in case things go *well*.' He smiled back at her, then shook his head. 'If I can handle you, I can handle anyone, especially Wanda. I'll pick you up in twenty.'

Felicia just rolled her eyes, gave his face a pat and left the store. With her gone, Striker locked the front door for Wanda – to prevent anyone from coming inside and stealing products – then entered the back room.

To reach the office, he had to cut through a small narrow

stock room. Walls of motor oil, and candy bars filling the shelves. Everything smelled of lemons from the car deodorizers.

Tucked away in the far back corner of the store was a small nook, used to house the security system. Wanda was already standing over it, leaning forward over the desk. With her there, there was little room left for anyone else – much less a man of Striker's six-foot-one, two-hundred-and-twenty-pound size. He did his best to lean over her shoulder and watch the security surveillance feed.

The video system was new, and that made Striker smile. The old one had been a software program called Omni-Eye. Striker had used it before. The program was slow, buggy, and crashed halfway through most of the applications – especially when burning video evidence for court. It was also not uncommon to burn the video, then leave with a blank DVD.

'You guys switched to digital,' he noted.

Wanda just shrugged. She used the mouse to navigate back through the video timeline.

Unlike most gas station security systems, the video for the Chevron at Hastings and Vernon was excellent. The new owner was a former military officer and, as such, took security very seriously. Striker had never met the man, but he sure appreciated all the benefits. He looked down at the timeline and said, 'You're getting close, Wanda. Slow the feed down.'

She did.

The machine read 1625 hours, and the angle of the exterior camera caught the northwest corner of the lot. This was the Vernon Drive entranceway. The camera had been placed there to catch the never-ending stream of Gas-n-Go fraudsters, which was becoming a pandemic nowadays. With any luck, the driver of the SUV would be driving tight to the kerb, and thereby visible. Any further out than that, and they'd be shit outta luck.

Striker watched the feed at normal speed.

'I shoulda been a cop,' Wanda said. 'Or at least married one.'

'You say that every time I see you.'

'Because you never take the hint.'

Striker grinned. He was about to say something back, when he spotted a black SUV on the feed. The caller was right – the driver had been driving like an idiot. The vehicle raced down Vernon Drive, punched straight through the stop sign, and bulleted across East Hastings Street. It happened in less than two seconds. Given the time of day and the thickness of the rush-hour traffic, it was a wonder that no one was hurt. The vehicle was going so fast, Striker had to back up the video twice and slow down the speed to have any hope of making out the details. With the video in slow mode, the make and model of the SUV became apparent.

It was a Beamer, no doubt. And he had been right about the model.

An X5.

As for the driver, it was impossible to tell. The distance was too far and the angle bad. The speed of the vehicle also made the quality poor – not blurry, but definitely indistinct.

Striker doubted if the tech guys could even sharpen it.

'It's not very good, is it?' Wanda asked, frowning.

'It's better than what I had coming down here.'

Wanda smiled at that.

The front door alarm buzzed – more customers trying to enter the gas station – so Striker told Wanda to go unlock the front door. She could leave the video with him. He knew how to work the system.

He spent the next ten minutes trying to magnify and sharpen the image. It wasn't easy. But when he was done, he was fairly certain that the first letter in the licence plate was a J.

The rest of the letters and numbers were impossible to make out.

He snagged a disc from the shelf, slid it into the tray, and burned a copy of the feed for the Forensic Video Unit. They could do wonders with digital files nowadays, but Striker had little hope in what they could find. The problem wasn't just the clarity – it was the angle.

J was likely as good as it would get.

He saved the file on the hard drive, started a new video time-line for the store, then left the office and closed the door behind him. He'd barely gotten three steps into the store before he ran right into Felicia, who was rushing in through the front doors.

'You get anything?' she asked.

He gave her a flat look. 'It's a Beamer. Dark, possibly black. An X5, just like we thought. The first letter in the plate looks like a J. But that's as good as it gets.' He looked at her hopefully. 'Any video on your end?'

'No,' she said, then smiled. 'But I did one better – I found us a *witness*.'

Fifteen

They drove two blocks down to the warehouse where Felicia had already gotten the business owner, John Gibson, to start writing up a proper witness statement. GPT Industries – Gibson Plastics & Tubing – was a square cement warehouse that sat on the corner of Vernon Drive and Franklin Street.

Striker knew this area well. They were dead smack in the heart of the Franklin industrial area. He had done a hundred stings here over the years, all related to sex and drugs because it was the hottest spot for all different flavours of the sex-trade industry. When someone on Franklin Street said they blew their tranny, they weren't talking about the transmission of their Oldsmobile.

The warehouse was old, looked ready to crumble, and sat less than a hundred metres from the train tracks and overpass. Striker pulled their cruiser up front and parked in the gated lot. With Felicia by his side, he walked under the broken yellow neon sign that now read only *GPT Indust* and climbed the cement stairs.

Inside the warehouse, the air was no warmer than the freezing chill outside. All the workers had long gone home for the day, and because of that the place looked deserted. The air stank of diesel oil and some type of plastic glue. Together, the two scents produced a strange, caustic smell.

They entered the main office.

John Gibson was sitting behind an old monstrosity of a desk that looked to be made of metal. He was an older man, probably mid-sixties, with a short, wiry build and thinning grey hair. His hands were dirty and calloused, but they looked strong enough to tear phone books in half.

In front of him on the desk sat his statement, already written. Even from where Striker stood, the writing looked like chicken scratches on the page. It was full of spelling errors. Striker said nothing; it was typical for this area. And for all the bad grammar and spelling errors, he appreciated getting the statement. It was one more than they already had.

Gibson looked up with a pissed-off expression on his face. 'Back already, huh?'

Felicia smiled. 'Yes, we finished up with our other witnesses. This is Detective Striker.'

'Nice to meet you,' Striker said.

When John Gibson just grunted and gave a half nod, Striker grabbed the statement paper and read it over. The statement was brief, not even half a page long. Most of it was no more than a nonsensical rant. Clarification on many points was necessary. He skimmed down to the part about the driver and the licence plate.

What he saw made him smile.

The details on the driver were vague at best – the person was unidentified with no description – but whoever the driver was, he was definitely alone. And, more importantly, the last two numbers in the plate were listed.

Seven and nine.

Striker looked up at the old man. 'Seven and nine? You're sure about that, Mr Gibson?'

'Damn right, I am. One hundred per cent. I remember it perfectly cuz that's my kid's birthday – seventy-nine.'

'And you saw just one person inside the vehicle?'

'Yeah, just the one – the cocksucker.'

'Male or female?' Striker asked.

'Couldn't tell either way.' The man's fingers clenched into fists. 'Goddam prick was driving too fast again. Almost knocked the load right off my forklift.' He jabbed a finger towards the front road. 'He's always driving too fast. He's a fuckin' *nimrod*. And I'll tell ya this: he ever stops out front – even *once* – I'm gonna get him outta that truck and kick his fast-driving ass all over Franklin Street. Goddam cocksucker's gonna kill someone one day, he keeps that up!'

Felicia stepped forward. 'You said, *again*? Have you seen this vehicle before?'

'Sure. Lotsa times. He's always coming this way. Always driving like a fuckin' nutcase.'

'How often?' Striker asked. 'Any particular days?'

The older man thought about it for a long moment, then shook his head. 'I can't make no rhyme or reason outta it. Just seen him down here lots. Always driving too damn fast.'

Striker looked at Felicia and saw that she understood the significance, too. They had a pattern of driving behaviour here, and a regular route travelled. It was good news and bad – good because it would be easier to track this person down; bad because it made it less likely the man was connected to Mandy Gill's suicide. For all they knew, the driver was just another John, coming down here to get his rocks off, then hauling ass to get out of the area.

Striker wrote down the last two numbers of the licence plate, which now gave them three out of a possible six letters and numbers. *J* for the first three letters; *79* for the last two out of three numbers. It made Striker smile.

They now had enough for a motor vehicle search.

He handed the written statement to Felicia and asked her to do the Q and A with Gibson. When she took it and sat down in one of the office chairs, Striker left the room and hung out in the warehouse, where he could be alone.

He got on his cell and called up Brian Greene, a contact of his at the Insurance Corporation of British Columbia. Striker knew the man well from a previous motor vehicle accident in which Brian's sixteen-year-old son had gotten critically injured. Striker had located Brian, picked him up, and driven him Code 3 to Burnaby General Hospital to see his son before the emergency surgery. Driving lights and siren with citizens in the car was a departmental no-no, regardless of the son's injuries, and it could've gotten Striker into hot water. But that became a moment that Brian Greene would never forget. Ever since then the man had been a reliable and useful contact.

The call was answered on the third ring.

'Brian Greene,' the man said.

'Brian, it's Jacob Striker.'

'Detective! Long time no talk.'

'I'm surprised you're still there. It's late.'

'Yeah, well, we had another after-hours meeting. The tenth one this month, I think. Everything's always a crisis around here, right? I was just about to leave.'

'Well, lucky me for catching you.'

'That depends on what you need. How's life with the Vancouver Police Department?'

'I'm just one lotto ticket away from retirement.' Brian Greene laughed, and Striker continued: 'How is Jonathan doing?'

'He's *walking*. He's walking and he's doing well. Finishing his degree at UBC. Philosophy. Which means he's never leaving home, I guess.'

'You got a professional student on your hands.'

Brian laughed. 'Yeah, I think he's gonna live at home till he's thirty!'

Striker smiled at that. It was good to hear the boy was doing well. Back then, at the accident scene, he didn't think Jonathan Greene was going to make it. And the memory of that moment stirred up some hard emotions.

Striker changed the subject. 'I'm calling because I'm in need here, Brian. Can you do a search for me – completely off the record?'

'Any time. You just give me the plate number.'

The words were music to Striker's ears. Normally, the Insurance Corporation of British Columbia was sticky when it came to the private information of their clients, and unless the circumstance was labelled *Life or Death*, any help from the corporation required a warrant.

No exceptions ever.

Having a contact like Brian Greene made all the difference in the world.

'Juliet for the first letter,' Striker said. 'Next two letters unknown. First number is unknown. Last two are seven and nine.'

'In that order?'

'I think so.'

Striker heard the clicking sounds of Brian's keyboard, then a moment of silence before the man responded with a whistle.

'That's never good,' Striker said.

'Ten *thousand* hits, man. Got any other details to narrow it down a bit?'

'You bet. It's a Beamer. An X5.'

A few more clicks.

Brian said, 'Okay. One hundred and thirteen hits.'

Striker thought it over. 'Try Beamers that are less than three years old.'

A few more clicks, then: 'Good one. You're down to twenty.'

'Black in colour.'

Brian punched the detail into his keyboard, then let out a laugh. 'Okay, now we have five.'

'Put the location of the registered owner as Vancouver only.'

'Now you got three.'

Striker smiled. 'Give them to me.'

Brian did.

Striker wrote the plate numbers down in his notebook, then asked for the details of each one – the name of the registered owner, the address listed, and so forth. When Brian Greene gave him the details of the third and last plate, one detail in particular caught Striker's attention and a smile broke the corners of his mouth.

'Interesting,' he said.

Sixteen

At first the water of the well stung his skin like a cold fire. But soon the sting went away and was replaced by a swelling numbness that started in his fingers and toes. It then inched its way slowly throughout the rest of his body like long probing tendrils.

The Adder swam in place, desperately trying to keep his lips above the water. It was a difficult task. The Doctor had laid planks across the top of the well and, as a result, there was less than a few inches of space between the top of the splashing water and wet hard planks above.

The darkness made everything worse. All the Adder could see was a mass of blackness; it was everywhere he looked. And when he reached out for the sides of the well in an effort to hold himself above the water, the only thing his fingers touched was slime-coated stone.

Cold and hard and slippery.

Many times already, he had fatigued. Taken in a quick deep breath. And let his body sink beneath the top of the water into the depths below. Never once had his naked feet touched the bottom. No matter how far down he dropped – so low he feared he would never reach the top again – he never touched the bottom.

In some ways that was good. After all, what was down there? An end? Or would currents suck him away to other underground chasms? And was there something down there? Something *alive*?

That thought terrified him. More than once, something had brushed his leg – a fast and fleeting sensation. But one he was certain of.

Something was in the well with him; he just didn't know what. After that first touch, the Adder had struggled to stay near the top, swimming so hard the flesh of his lips tore as they raked against the rough wooden surface of the planks above.

A whimper escaped him, for he knew he was failing now. His body was too numb. His limbs too tired. They were giving out on him. And despite the fear he felt, despite the anxiety of what lay below, a part of him rejoiced in the suffering.

For this was how William must have felt.

The Doctor was right about that; this was what he deserved. A fated and fitting punishment. For he had failed. And all because of the cop. The big homicide detective who had slipped out of the shadow like a snake through water – a demon from out of the darkness – and tried to suck him down with him.

The memory was still fresh, and it made the Adder's heart race.

The next time things would end differently.

Seventeen

Felicia and Striker sat in their unmarked car, which today was an old Ford Taurus. John Gibson had finished the question-and-answer session with Felicia, and she was now in the process of folding and tucking the statement into a file folder. She slid the whole thing into her briefcase in the back seat, then turned to look at Striker.

Her pretty face looked tired. Her dark Spanish eyes were underscored with sleep lines, and the way she hunched forward made her body look deflated.

Striker couldn't blame her for being exhausted. The last two days had been hell. Before tonight's incident, over Monday and Tuesday, they'd each put in over thirty hours. And even this morning, they'd started their shift at four a.m. in order to investigate a lead on a different case. The expectation had been to leave early this afternoon, at maybe at two or three, and go home for a good night's rest.

Mandy Gill's death had changed all that.

Felicia stifled a yawn and covered her mouth. 'My God,' she said. 'What time is it, ten?'

'Close enough; it's just before nine. You gonna make it there, Bella?'

She gave him a look of daggers. 'You know I hate it when you call me that.'

'*Mamacita?*' When she didn't see the humour in it, he changed the subject. 'You learn anything else from the statement with Gibson?'

She nodded. 'Sure. He's angry and he's an idiot.'

Striker smiled at that. Felicia got this way whenever she was tired and irritable. He changed the subject again. 'We got three possible hits on the Beamer,' he started. 'The first one is Juliet-Juliet-Mike, One-Seven-Nine.'

Felicia punched the numbers into the computer, into the Vehicle Query, and searched the plate through the police and motor vehicle databases. 'Beamer,' she said. 'An X5. Comes back to a woman named Elin Forslund.'

'What's her record?'

Felicia looked through the PRIME information, then shook her head. 'Clean as they come, including her driving record. No criminal history whatsoever. Works as an consultant at a video game company. Dream-Makers. As for the vehicle information, it says here the plate is invalid. Insurance expired yesterday. She's got only a temporary operator's permit now.' She looked at Striker. 'You see one of those in the video?'

'No, but they're not always the easiest to spot.'

She nodded. 'Fine. We'll keep this one a limited possibility. What's the next plate?'

'Juliet-Mike-Delta, Seven-Seven-Nine.'

She ran that plate. Got some hits back. 'Okay. Registered owner and listed driver's licence come back to one Clayford Ozymandias Kennedy.'

'Holy shit – *The Third?*' Striker asked.

Felicia smiled. 'No kidding. Nice parents – what, were they trying to get him beat up at school, or something?' She read on. 'Okay, he's fifty years old. Works as an investment broker, by the looks of things. Works for ING Direct. One speeding ticket. No criminal history whatsoever.'

Striker nodded. 'Where's he live?'

'Downtown core.'

That was the direction the vehicle had been heading in. 'Contact number?'

'Cell only.'

Striker took it and made the call. Two minutes later, he had his answer. Clayford Kennedy was currently in Kelowna at an investor conference. He'd been there all day long, with his vehicle, and he had proof of this. Striker hung up.

'Scratch him off the list for now,' he said. 'We'll have to confirm the details later.'

Felicia made a note of the name, then looked up. 'And the last plate?' she asked.

Striker smiled. 'This one intrigues me. Juliet-Alpha-Papa, Nine-Seven-Nine.'

Felicia typed in the information, then sent the request. When the responses came back, she read them out slowly: 'Okay, we got some hits here. Primary driver licence on file belongs to a man named Erich Ostermann. Forty-eight years old. Lives out west towards the university grounds. Point Grey, I think.'

Striker read the screen, too. 'Look at the address.'

She did. 'Belmont Drive. So what? Like I said, that's way out by the university grounds.'

'No, not his home address. Look where he works.'

She skimmed through the list of addresses on the main screen. 'There's a few of them,' she said. 'This guy works in many places: 512 Granville Street . . . 2601 Lougheed Highway . . . 330 Heatley Avenue—' She hesitated. 'Why does that address sound familiar?'

'Because we've been there before. It's the address of the Mental Health Center.'

'Strathcona,' she said and looked east. 'That's just down the road from here.'

Striker nodded. 'Looks like Mr Ostermann is *Doctor* Ostermann.'

Felicia read through the file and clarified, 'He's a psychiatrist.'

Striker looked at the list of places where Dr Erich Ostermann worked. One stuck out to him. 'Riverglen Mental Health Facility,' he said sternly. 'Mandy Gill was a patient there for a brief period of time. She also spent time at the Strathcona Center.'

He put the car into Drive and pulled out on to the road. They headed for Heatley Avenue.

Eighteen

When Striker and Felicia arrived on scene, they found that the Strathcona Mental Health Center was closed for the night, and the emergency number listed on the front door was actually the number for Car 87 – the officer-and-counsellor paired unit of the Vancouver Police Department's Mental Health Team.

It was a dead end for now.

Striker looked at his watch, saw that it was now nine twenty, and shrugged. 'We could always go see Dr Ostermann at his home. You up for a trip out west?'

Felicia nodded, but her posture spoke otherwise.

Striker bribed her. 'I'll buy you another eggnog latte on the way – as rich and creamy as you like it.'

'A double-shot,' she added. 'I'm gonna need it.'

Striker smiled at her; she was a trooper. They got back into the car, and Striker headed west.

The Ostermann house was located just to the east of the Endowment Lands, on one of the most expensive – and widely unknown – jewels of the city, Belmont Avenue. Striker had been to the area once on a million-dollar fraud call. That was ten years ago. He doubted that the road had changed any. Just multimillion-dollar homes for multimillion-dollar families.

As they turned off Burrard Street and drove along the forever-busy grind of West 4th Avenue, Felicia brought up as many

PRIME pages as she could, and read through the known police history of Dr Erich Ostermann.

'He's listed in the database a ton,' she said. 'But always under the entity of *doctor*. He's related to a gazillion mental health files – everywhere from Riverglen, way out in Coquitlam, to the Strathcona Medical Health Center in the Downtown East Side.'

Striker zigzagged around an Audi sedan turning left on Arbutus and gunned it to get through the yellow light. He turned his eyes from the traffic to Felicia. 'Go over his driving record again.'

Felicia brought up his driver licence history and said, 'Wow. This guy's a road criminal. Got over twenty tickets for everything from speeding to running stop signs. It's a wonder they haven't suspended his licence yet.'

'I guess being a psychiatrist has its privileges.' Striker thought this over. 'So Erich Ostermann is the good doctor in the medical clinic, but a road warrior when he's in his vehicle. Kind of a Jekyll and Hyde guy. Interesting detail. Says something about his character, I'm sure.'

Felicia was less impressed. 'It also says something else, unfortunately – that him blowing that stop sign was probably just the regular driving pattern for him. He does it all the time and probably wasn't evading anything.'

'Maybe. And yet, there *is* a connection between Mandy Gill and Riverglen. It's a lead still worth investigating.' He glanced at Felicia, then floored it to the twenty-two hundred block of West 4th Avenue. He drove into the oncoming lane of traffic and parked the cruiser in an open stall, facing the wrong way.

Felicia put a hand over her heart. 'Jesus, Jacob, are you trying to kill us?'

'If I wanted to be suicidal, I'd just propose to you.'

She gave him the ice look, and he just smiled back. He then pointed to the Pharmasave drug store next to them. 'Important stop.'

'Why? What are we doing here?'

Striker just smiled at her.

'What can I say?' he said. 'I need my meds checked.'

The Pharmasave drug store, located on the corner of 4th Avenue and Vine Street, was one of the few pharmacies in the area that was open twenty-four hours a day, seven days a week, all year round. More importantly, it was one of the few places where Mandy Gill had ordered her medication from – even though it was a twenty-minute bus ride from her Strathcona apartment.

The electronic doors parted as Striker approached them, and the warm store air was a sharp contrast to the howling cold outside. Inside the store, the soft coma-inducing sound of muzak filled the air and shoppers lined up wearily at the front till. Striker searched the store for the pharmacy and found it in the far rear corner.

He and Felicia made their way down.

Behind the counter stood the pharmacist. He was an East Indian man with large glasses, tall – damn near six foot six – with overly long arms and hands that appeared disproportionately small. Striker watched him stomp back and forth behind the counter, then stop to give his assistant shit about something. She was a small Japanese woman, and she looked tired.

'I'm sorry,' she explained to him. 'I've been up the last three nights with my boy. He's been sick.'

'Don't bring your family problems to work.'

'I didn't mean to, it's just that, well, I thought you said to—'

'I know what I said,' the pharmacist snapped. 'God gave you ears, woman. Next time use them.'

The diminutive woman nodded obediently and said nothing, but her face remained fixed with a rock-like expression.

'Minimum-wage help,' the pharmacist muttered, then carried on with his work.

Striker took an immediate dislike to the man. He approached the counter and pulled out his wallet. When the pharmacist finally deigned to look over, Striker flashed the badge and motioned for the man to come closer.

'Detective Striker,' he said. 'Vancouver Police Department.'

The pharmacist said nothing back; he merely pointed at his name tag, which was labelled: *Pharmacist*. 'It's been a very busy night. What do you need of me?'

Felicia laughed softly. 'What do we need of you? Wow, formal.'

Striker took over the conversation. 'We have a bit of a problem,' he explained. 'A woman who buys her medicine from you is having some very serious mental health issues – I'd like to see the referrals you keep on record.'

'Everything is electronic nowadays.'

Striker blinked. 'I think you're mistaken. Her *history* is all electronically stored, but I'm talking about the referral pads themselves. The paper slips, specifically.'

'I don't know,' the man replied. He took off his glasses and began cleaning the lenses. 'We're very busy tonight.'

'It's important.'

'Do you have a warrant?'

Felicia stepped up to the counter. 'According to BC Medical, you're supposed to keep all referrals on site for three years before purging. Are you not doing this? Because if not, this is very serious. It constitutes a breach of MSP protocol.'

'A breach?' the pharmacist replied. A sour look took over his face and he put his glasses back on. 'I think that's hardly justified.'

Striker took advantage of the moment. He pulled out his notebook and showed the man the information he'd written down from the pill bottles at Mandy Gill's residence:

Pharmasave.
Prescription number: 1079880 – MVC.
Quantity: 50 tablets.
Dispensary date: Jan 28th.

'I want to see the referral slip written for these pills.'

The pharmacist looked at the page for a long moment, like it was an unwelcome bill or the results of a herpes test. He did not move away from the counter.

'Might I inquire as to why?' he finally asked.

Striker gave Felicia a quick look, then continued: 'As I explained, it's related to one of this doctor's patients. A woman we are currently investigating for some very violent offences. Stalking, home invasion, forcible kidnapping – I really can't say more. But I will add this: time is crucial here.'

'Do you have a warrant for this information?' he asked again.

'There's no time for that,' Felicia said.

'Then I can't help you.'

Striker said nothing for a moment. He put on his best surprised look, then nodded slowly, acceptingly. 'That's fine with me,' he said. 'It's completely within your right to refuse, sir. Just give me your identification and I'll write up the form.'

'Form? What form?'

'The *Refusal* form.'

'Why would you need my name on that?'

Felicia cut in. 'It's a matter of civil liability.'

'Li-liability?'

'Of course,' Striker said. 'Without a warrant, you have every legal right to deny us the information. But you do have to give me your name and details so I can keep a record of it – that's the *law*.'

'But . . . . but why?'

'What is your name, sir?'

'Parm-Parminder. Parminder Sanghera. But why—'

Striker pointed his pen at the man. 'Because if something bad happens to the doctor, the Vancouver Police Department certainly isn't going to wear it – especially not in civil court.'

'*Civil* court?'

Striker made an annoyed sound, then spoke in his best condescending manner as he explained the situation. 'Legal and civil court are two entirely different matters – you should know this if you plan on denying possibly lifesaving information to the police.'

The tall pharmacist suddenly seemed smaller. He took a step backwards. 'I really . . . really don't want to be a part of this.'

Striker ignored the request; he wrote into his notebook:

I, Parminder Sanghera, have been informed of the possible threat to the life of Dr Erich Ostermann, and deny Detective Jacob Striker of the Homicide Unit of the Vancouver Police Department the medical information requested (prescription history of Mandilla 'Mandy' Gill), with full understanding of the possible consequences (loss of life) involved.

Striker showed this to the pharmacist. 'Now just sign and date it.'

The pharmacist looked at the wording and his face paled. He wiped away the sweat from his brow and stepped back. 'Well . . . well, hold on a moment. What exactly is it you wish to know?'

'We don't *wish* to know anything,' Felicia said. 'We *need* to know.'

'Yes, yes, yes,' he replied. 'I can see that now. Yes. But what exactly is it you need to know?'

Striker held up his notebook. 'Where this referral came from.'

The pharmacist looked at the numbers and letters, then relented. 'It's already right there in your notebook, Detective. MVC is the clinic abbreviation. The referral came from Mapleview. Mapleview Clinic.'

Striker took in the words, then shook his head. He had hoped for Riverglen, but nothing was ever that easy.

'What doctor?' he asked.

'Dr Richter,' he said.

'Richter?' Striker said. The name was one he had never heard of. He had been guessing Ostermann.

'That billing number is for Dr Richter,' the pharmacist continued. 'But Dr Ostermann is the one in charge of that whole clinic.'

'Dr Richter,' Striker said again. He wrote it down, then put his notebook away and took a long hard look at the man before him. 'You did the right thing here today.'

'Maybe even saved a man's life,' Felicia added.

The pharmacist, looking grey, just nodded. He asked if he was free to go, Striker said they were done, and the man left the counter area altogether, disappearing into the back. Once he was gone, Striker gave Felicia a nod and a smile, and they left the store.

It was getting late, but they were determined to see Dr Erich Ostermann before the night was through.

Belmont Avenue was less than ten minutes away.

Nineteen

They were barely back inside the car when Felicia bundled up her coat and cranked the heater to full. With the hot air blasting against his skin, Striker almost didn't feel the vibration of his cell phone. He whipped it out and read the name on the screen: Noodles. AKA Jim Banner from Ident. He picked up immediately and stuck the speaker to his ear.

'Give me some magic, Noodles.'

The man laughed. 'Hey, if I was a magician, I would've pulled your head outta your ass years ago. But you're lucky enough anyway. I did manage to find us some prints out there.'

Striker felt a jolt of electricity. 'Where?'

'On the fridge. Inside surface. On the door.'

'Any hits?'

The Ident tech let out a frustrated sound. 'Can't run it. The print is only a partial.'

Striker cursed and deflated back against the seat. He looked over at Felicia, who was looking at him hopefully, then gave a head shake, signalling *no*. 'How good of a partial?' he asked.

'Not very – but it is something for us to work with. You get me a suspect or comparison sample, and I'll see what I can do to match it up. Won't hold up worth a shit in court, but it might give you a lead to work on.'

'Keep searching,' Striker said.

And Noodles just sighed. 'Friggin' chain gang,' he said, and hung up.

A partial, Striker thought. Shit. Nothing ever came easy on an investigation. He put his cell away and pulled back on to West 4th Avenue once more. They headed for Point Grey.

Where the Ostermanns lived.

Twenty

The Ostermann House sat high above the main roads, on Belmont Avenue, looking over the violent pounding surf of the Burrard Inlet. The lot, nestled just east of the hundred-hectare wilderness of the Endowment Lands, was massive by city standards, and outlined by rows and rows of maples and Japanese plum trees.

Striker drove by the front of the house and spotted the black BMW X5 on the driveway's roundabout, behind the gated entranceway. He came to a complete stop and assessed the place.

It was impressive. Everything was obviously top-notch, with no dollar spared. The whole lot was lined by tall grey stone walls with white stone pillars at each corner. Old-fashioned lanterns, in the form of iron sconces, lined the cobblestone driveway and walkways. And dotting the rest of the yard were stone sculptures and Japanese rock gardens. Standing direct centre of it all was a marble fountain. The water was turned off.

'You need to be born with a silver spoon in your mouth to live here,' Striker noted. 'This is *wealth*.'

Felicia didn't respond, she just kept reading through the files. Finally, she made an *ugh* sound and slapped the laptop.

'That doesn't sound good,' Striker said.

'It *isn't* good,' she replied. 'I've been researching this Erich Ostermann guy the entire way here. And aside from driving like an idiot, the man is a five-star human being.'

Striker put the car into Park. 'Lay it out for me.'

So she did.

'According to all the files I see here, Erich Ostermann is a psychiatrist well-respected in his profession. He's won numerous awards for Clinical Leadership and Outstanding Community Support. But his real claim to fame is that he's the doctor who started EvenHealth.'

'EvenHealth . . . I've heard of that.'

'You should have. It's everywhere. Essentially, it's a platform for equal access for marginalized people who are suffering from mental health disorders.'

'So it's treatment for the poor.'

'Exactly. And Dr Ostermann is the Grand Poobah of the whole thing. EvenHealth is his brainchild.' She read on. 'So he works privately in his own practice as well as for the government-subsidized Riverglen Mental Health Facility out in Coquitlam.'

'Busy man.'

'There's more,' she said. 'Ostermann further donates time to the Strathcona Mental Health Team – which is where we were earlier, down on Heatley Avenue – and works in the more impoverished areas of the city, mainly the projects on Raymur Street and Hermon Drive.' She looked over at him. 'All in all, it's the résumé of a reputable and amazing man.'

'Who works with a lot of mentally ill people,' Striker added. 'Some of whom are very violent.'

Felicia met his stare. 'You think the guy you fought with might be one of his patients?'

'He might be a lot of things.'

Felicia said nothing back; she just flipped through the electronic pages, then let out a bemused laugh. 'Christ, Ostermann even donates to the PMBA.'

That made Striker pause. 'You're kidding?'

'I wish I was, but no.'

He grimaced. The PMBA was the Police Mutual Benevolent Association. Money from the PMBA went to helping out cops who were down on their luck, and towards special police projects that would have been otherwise fiscally impossible. Inspector Laroche was heavily involved with the PMBA, too. Striker wondered if he and Ostermann had ever crossed paths.

Felicia closed the laptop. 'All in all, this lead is feeling more and more abysmal.'

Striker reached over and re-opened the laptop. 'A résumé means nothing. Colonel Russell Williams was commander of our country's largest air force. He was a highly decorated officer and a good husband for nineteen years – but that didn't stop him from killing innocent women while wearing their bras and panties.'

'Maybe.'

'Maybe nothing. That's the way it is. And at this point, no one is accusing Dr Ostermann of anything – he's just a Person of Interest. But I will tell you this: *how* he answers our questions will tell us as much as what he tells us. Will he be honest, or will he lie? That's always the question.'

Striker put the car back into Drive and drove up to the gates. He hit the intercom, and they waited for the response.

'Hello?' a woman finally asked.

Striker shoved his badge up to the camera lens that was built right into the stone wall and spoke loudly.

'Vancouver Police,' he said. 'We need to speak with Dr Erich Ostermann.'

Striker and Felicia were allowed into the house by the doctor's wife. Striker gave her the once-over, taking his time as he did so. Lexa Ostermann was a beautiful woman. Thick straight hair the colour of honey fell down past her shoulders, framing a face of creamy skin and deep brown eyes. When she offered him a smile, Striker felt her magnetism pull him in. It was impossible not to feel it. Even in her mid-forties, Lexa Ostermann was elegant and breathtaking – no doubt the perfect trophy wife for her husband's professional parties.

She met Striker's stare. 'Right this way, Detective.'

She led them from the entrance hallway to a small library. The room was dark – wooden walls, wooden floor, and wooden shelves. Soft golden track lighting lined the ceiling. In the far corner of the room, next to the bay window, sat a gas fireplace. Lexa Ostermann flicked the button on the wall, and flames shot up behind the glass.

'Please,' she said. 'Be comfortable. The doctor will be with you shortly.'

Striker detected a slight accent. 'Czech?' he asked.

She smiled at the comment. 'Let's just say European. It sounds more modern.' She reached out and touched his shoulder. 'I must say, though, I am impressed, Detective. You have a good ear.'

'I have a good many things.'

She smirked. 'I'm sure you do.' When Striker said nothing back, she touched his shoulder again and continued talking. 'I came over here when I was very young. I'm surprised you heard my accent at all – most people don't.'

'I'm not most people.'

She laughed again. 'I can see that.'

'Will your husband be here soon?' Felicia cut in.

'My husband . . .' Lexa Ostermann nodded slowly and the smile fell from her lips. 'Of course.' She turned around and walked out of the library. At the doorway, she stopped, fidgeted with her hands and turned back to face them. She looked directly at Striker and the confident look in her eyes seemed to fade. She suddenly seemed smaller and weaker. *Concerned.*

'Is . . . is everything all right, Detective?' she asked.

Striker nodded. 'We just need to speak with your husband regarding one of his patients.'

Lexa Ostermann's face tightened and her big brown eyes got wider. 'Dr Ostermann is very protective of his patients,' she said softly. 'Please, be careful how you word things with him. He gets upset rather easily.'

'We'll be nothing but professional,' Striker promised.

'Thank you, Detective.'

'Of course. It was nice to meet you, Mrs Ostermann.'

'The feeling is mutual.'

She offered Striker another wide smile – one that appeared forced rather than breathtaking – and then disappeared down the hall. When she was gone, Felicia sat back in one of the reading chairs.

'You can put your tongue back in your mouth; she's gone.'

Striker blinked, then looked at her. 'I have no idea what you're talking about.'

'Sure you don't. *I have a good many things . . . I'm not most people . . .* God, you win the award for corny.' She picked up one of the magazines from a nearby table and flipped through it.

Striker looked back down the hall to where Lexa had walked only seconds ago. A bad feeling pooled in his guts. She seemed nervous, and she looked almost afraid. It concerned him. After a moment of thought, he turned to face Felicia.

'Did you find that odd?'

'Your excessive flirting? No.'

'I mean Lexa,' he said. 'She looked . . . nervous, or something. And did you hear how she referred to him? *The doctor* will be with you shortly. Not *my husband* or *Erich* – the doctor.'

Felicia put down the magazine and nodded. 'Actually, that was odd. I noticed it, too.'

Striker let the thought sit in his mind for a while as he moved around the small library and assessed the place. Directly ahead of him, to the north, was a large bay window with a seating area and the gas fireplace Lexa had turned on. Everything beyond the window was black – impossible to see with the contrast of the dark outside and the light inside – but Striker knew this area. Out there was the back yard, followed by the cliffs and the inlet beyond.

He continued looking around the library. On the fireplace mantel were four separate photographs. One, he presumed, for each member of the family. Not together in one, he noted, but each on their own.

A family together, but apart.

The first photograph was of Lexa Ostermann. She was smiling back over her shoulder. Seductive, beautiful, confident. Just like she'd been in the foyer. Striker stared at the picture long and hard. The woman was magnetic, and he felt an unexplainable concern for her.

Felicia took note of him staring at the picture. 'Maybe she has a wallet-size one she can give you for your alone time,' she said.

Striker ignored the comment. He pulled his eyes away from Lexa's photograph and studied the next ones. The second photograph was of a young man. Could've been seventeen, could've been twenty – it was hard to tell. He was lean and wiry, with pale skin and eyes so green they looked like coloured contacts. His jet-black hair was thick and wild.

Felicia came up behind him and stared at the photograph.

'He looks very serious,' Striker noted.

'He looks like a model from an Axe deodorant commercial,' Felicia said.

'Now who's being corny?' He looked at the next photo.

It was of a young woman. Beautiful, much like Lexa. Same face, same creamy skin, same eyes. Just the hair was different. Her hair was almost as black as the young man's, and long and thick and straight. Her eyes were dark. Darker than her mother's – even blacker than Felicia's. The faint grin on her lips looked forced, crooked somehow, and didn't show at the corners of her eyes.

'She's beautiful,' Felicia said. 'Both these kids could be models.'

'She looks lost,' was all Striker said.

He moved up to the last photo.

It was of an older man. Late forties or early fifties, but in good shape. Reddish-brown hair that was kept short, yet still managed to curl on him. It matched his goatee. His eyes were an unnatural green – matching that of the boy's – and were hidden behind a pair of round tortoiseshell spectacles. Overall, the man looked quite astute, orderly.

'The good doctor,' Felicia said.

Striker agreed. He walked back across the hardwood floor. To his left, the walls were lined with wooden shelves containing leather-bound books on psychiatry. Titles with syndromes – Conduct Disorder, Antisocial Personality Disorder, Post-traumatic Stress Disorder, and more.

Striker grinned. 'Looks like the study guide for getting promoted at the Vancouver Police Department.'

Felicia laughed softly.

On the right side of the room, on more rows of wooden shelves, sat sections of non-fiction books, ones unrelated to the profession of psychiatry. Striker saw that they were set in rows by category: True Crime, Homicides, Police Procedurals. A lot of books on police investigation and procedure.

He was leafing through one he recognized from his earlier training days – *Integrated Practical Homicide* – when a voice spoke to him from behind.

'Good evening, Detectives.'

Striker turned around and saw a scholarly looking man – the man from the picture on the mantelpiece. Dr Erich Ostermann. In person, he was far fitter than his picture suggested, and he had a certain presence in the room.

'I am Dr Ostermann,' he offered. His eyes focused on the book in Striker's hands. 'Brushing up on your skills, I see.'

Striker smiled. 'Surprised to see a book of this kind in your library – it's one we actually use for training purposes.'

Dr Ostermann waved a hand dismissively. 'Oh, that's just Dalia. That entire shelf is hers.'

'Dalia?' Felicia asked.

'My daughter. She can be excessively morbid at times, though I will admit to leafing through the pages once myself. Grim to be sure, though a bit compelling. I can understand her fascination, but I do try to steer her away from it.' He smiled at them both. 'We all have to deal with death eventually, but right now there is life. We should live it.'

'I won't argue with that,' Striker said. He reached out and took hold of the doctor's hand. Shook it firmly. The action made the man flinch and, after the handshake, he stepped back awkwardly.

Striker took note of this. 'Are you all right?'

'This? Oh, I pulled my back a little, is all.'

Striker forced a grin and pushed the issue. 'Tough session at the clinic, I guess?'

'Something like that.'

'Something like that,' Striker repeated.

Dr Ostermann merely nodded. 'Lexa tells me this visit has something to do with one of my patients?'

'Yes,' Striker said. 'A woman named Mandy Gill.' He watched the doctor's face for a reaction.

'Mandilla Gill?'

Striker nodded. 'She was your patient.'

'Oh yes, for some time now. A constant work-in-progress, I'm afraid.' He sighed and appeared tired all of a sudden. 'What has she done this time?'

'She's killed herself.'

The doctor's face paled and he froze for a moment. 'My God, I didn't know. No one told me . . . *When?*'

'This afternoon,' Felicia said.

Dr Ostermann rubbed a hand through his goatee, his face turning red. 'She was depressed again . . . I should've sectioned her . . . I *should* have!'

Striker spoke up. 'Mandy was very troubled for a long time,' he said. He explained the most basic details of what they knew to Dr Ostermann – leaving out the camera and the physical altercation he'd had with the suspect – then got down to the business of the BMW X5 being in the area. 'Were you anywhere near there today, Dr Ostermann?'

The doctor took a moment to think. 'Well, no, not near Ms Gill's place – she lives down on Union Street. But I was in the Downtown East Side today. I had to drop by the clinic for some rather important files.'

'Which clinic, if you don't mind me asking?'

'Strathcona. On Heatley.' Dr Ostermann adjusted his glasses, then looked over at Striker with a concerned look on his face. 'May I ask why this is important?'

Striker nodded but did not answer the question. 'What were you driving today?'

The doctor shrugged. 'My own personal vehicle.'

'Which is?'

'A BMW. An X5. It's black.'

'And were you alone?'

'Yes, completely. Detective, have I done something wrong here?'

Striker looked up from his notebook and met the man's stare. 'We're just verifying things, sir. We have to. And these are all pretty standard questions.'

Dr Ostermann said nothing. He moved to the corner of the room where there was a liquor cart and poured himself a glass of amber-coloured booze. He brought it to his lips, drained the glass, then refilled it.

'I must say,' he began. 'I've had the unfortunate experience of having my patients commit suicide on previous occasions, you know. Yet no officer has ever asked me questions like this, so forgive me if they don't *sound* standard.'

'That's fair enough,' Striker replied. 'But this time there are unique details we need to rule out. Your vehicle was seen in the area at roughly the same time as her death. You were also her doctor. Time and connection, that's why we're here – to gain some history on Mandy Gill, because right now we have nothing.'

Dr Ostermann made a sad face. 'That's because there's not much to know, I'm afraid. Mandy didn't have any family. Her mother's name was Janelle. She passed away years ago, not that it mattered. All ties had been severed between them years before. When Janelle and the father broke up, she just packed up her things and moved out east. Left everyone behind.'

'Mother of the Year,' Felicia said.

The doctor only nodded. 'It was quite sad. After her father's incarceration all Mandy had left was one cousin, and he perished in an explosion – a fact I'm sure you're already well aware of.'

Striker nodded but said nothing to that fact. 'What about friends?' he asked. 'Did she have anyone close to her?'

The doctor said nothing for a long moment. He took off his glasses and rubbed his eyes. 'Mandy was close to only one other person that I know of – another patient of mine, in fact. It was a relationship I never approved of from the start, and I did everything in my power to put a stop to it.'

Striker and Felicia shared a quick glance.

'Who?' Striker asked.

The doctor bit his lip as he mulled it over. 'I'm sorry, but I can't say anything at this point in time – patient confidentiality and all.'

Striker stepped forward. 'I'm not going to lie to you, Doctor. There are some things about the death that are concerning to us – things I cannot discuss. But I really would like to speak with this other patient of yours who knew Mandy. It's absolutely crucial.'

Dr Ostermann sipped his drink. Swallowed. Let out a fluttery breath.

'I understand that, Detective. I do. But this particular patient of mine is very . . . *fragile* right now. And this will most definitely come as a shock to him. There's no telling how he'll react.' He frowned. 'Not well, I presume. Let me talk to him first. I'll inform him of what has occurred. Then I'll explain to him that you will be in contact.'

'I would appreciate that, Doctor. As I've said, this is very important, and time is critical.'

Dr Ostermann looked up at the clock. It was now just after ten. He extended his hand. 'Very well. I will call you first thing in the morning then.'

'As early as possible,' Striker replied. He thanked Dr Ostermann for his time and gave the man his card. Then looked at Felicia, and they took their leave. At the door of the library, Striker stopped. He turned back and met the doctor's stare one last time.

'One more thing,' he said. 'Do you ever work at Mapleview?'

Dr Ostermann shook his head. 'No. I work at Riverglen now. I also do some outreach programmes. Actually, I do quite a few of them with many different Mental Health Teams. Strathcona, for one. Am I not in your police database?'

Striker ignored the question. 'Must be a difficult job at times.'

'The career of a psychiatrist is never easy, Detective. There always seems to be another tragedy waiting around the corner.' Dr Ostermann gave them both a quick look and forced out a waxy smile. 'My profession is much like yours, I fear. In some ways, our paths are quite similar. We'll talk tomorrow, either here or at Riverglen.'

Felicia said goodnight, but Striker only nodded.

'Don't worry,' he said. 'We'll find you.'

Twenty-One

They were leaving.

Striker reached for the front door of the Ostermann house when it suddenly opened on him and a cold powerful wind blew inside, filling the foyer with an immediate chill. Stepping through the front door were the two people Striker had seen in the photographs on the mantelpiece, back in the library.

The first one through the doorway was the young man. Maybe seventeen. He moved with the awkward laziness of every teenage boy Striker had ever known – a kid whose body was growing too fast for his mind and coordination to keep up with. His wild, jet-black hair looked blown all over the place – or maybe that was the way it naturally stood – and his deep green eyes focused on Striker with a look of ambivalence.

'Ah, the children are home,' Dr Ostermann said. He gestured to the young man. 'This is my son, Gabriel.'

'Nice to meet you, Gabriel,' Striker said.

Felicia said hello, too.

Gabriel said nothing at first; his eyes just moved from Striker to Felicia, then stayed there for a long moment. He smiled.

'Yes,' he said. 'Hello.'

'And this, of course, is Dalia,' Dr Ostermann continued.

Striker turned his eyes from the young man to the young

woman. In some ways, they looked similar. In others, completely different.

'It's good to meet you,' Striker said to the young woman.

She just looked back at him, saying nothing. Finally, she nodded slowly, as if only now making the connection that he was standing in front of her.

Striker found the moment odd. When he gave Felicia a quick glance, the expression on her face told him that she felt the strangeness, too. He looked once more at Gabriel, then at Dalia, and felt an underlying tension in the foyer as they looked back at him.

But they didn't really *look* back at him; they looked at nothing. The boy's green eyes were piercing and focused; the girl's were black and hollow and distant, and they looked right *through* him. Analysed him.

He didn't like it.

'We really should go,' Felicia finally said.

Before Striker could respond, the girl spoke up. 'Why are they here?' she said to her father.

'It's nothing,' he said.

The girl's eyes never shifted. 'It's obviously something, or they wouldn't be here.'

The doctor's face turned red with embarrassment. 'It's none of your business, child. It's regarding the clinic.'

Gabriel's eyes suddenly lit up. 'Are they here about Billy—'

'*ENOUGH!*' the doctor roared.

The girl and boy didn't so much as flinch; they just stood there and said nothing. As if hearing the commotion, Lexa quickly appeared at the top of the stairs.

'Children, children,' she said softly.

She came down the stairs into the foyer and ushered the two youths away from their father – away from Striker and Felicia.

As she did so, she stole a quick glance at Striker and said, 'I'm sorry, there is just . . . a lot of stress, right now.' Her beautiful face was hard, and her eyes almost watery.

Striker put on his best warm smile. 'You're talking to a father who has a teenage daughter – I know.'

Lexa said nothing more. She guided Gabriel and Dalia away from their father towards the kitchen area. Striker watched them move down the hall, fleeing more than walking, with Lexa looking back over her shoulder a few times as they went. There was a strange expression on her face, one Striker couldn't define.

He didn't like it.

When he turned his eyes back to Dr Ostermann, the man looked like a victim of high blood pressure. His face was red and the veins in his neck looked close to the surface of the skin. He fumbled off his glasses, wiped his brow with his sleeve, then looked back and forth from Striker to Felicia and back again.

'I apologize for that,' he said. 'I didn't mean to be so . . . so . . . *vocal.* But I cannot – I *will not* – have my patients' privacy breached. It's unethical and it simply cannot be allowed.'

Striker said nothing.

Felicia said, 'We understand.'

The doctor nodded, as if thankful. 'I will call you first thing in the morning – *after* the appropriate contact has been made.'

Striker took the hint and said goodbye, as did Felicia. The moment they stepped outside, the front door closed behind them. They returned to their car and drove up to the gate. When it opened, they pulled out on to the road and drove down the snaking route of Belmont Avenue. It wasn't until they were almost a mile away that Striker felt the pressure lessen.

Felicia was the first to speak. 'Nice family.'

'Sure. If you're one of the Mansons.'

They drove towards 41st Avenue. That was where the office

of Car 87 was located, the Mental Health Team car. It was also the location where the staff personnel files were kept.

Which was a necessary step.

If Dr Ostermann did work with the Strathcona Mental Health Team, it meant he was also linked to Car 87. And to work with Car 87, everyone required a portfolio of their personal history, which included everything from emergency contact numbers to a criminal records check. Dr Ostermann would have his file there, and Striker wanted to see it. There was more to Dr Erich Ostermann than the man was showing them.

Striker could feel it.

Felicia looked at the way they were headed. 'Aren't Car 87 headquarters south of here?'

Striker nodded. 'We got one quick pit-stop to make first.'

When he took a left on 12th Avenue, Felicia understood. They were going to Vancouver General Hospital.

That was where the morgue was located.

Twenty-Two

The Adder sat on the grey concrete of the floor in the dimness of the room, and felt the cool dampness of the walls invading his core. No matter what he did, he was never warm. Not here in this room. Not anywhere. He was always cold.

Cold like the water in the well.

He stared at nothing for a long time, and listened to the sounds that came from above. The Doctor was up there. In the study. And dangerously close to the edge again.

The Adder tried not to think about it.

He stood up from the floor and walked to the far wall, where the cabinet stood. Behind it were his beloved DVDs and the back-up hard drive. More than anything, he wanted to watch his movies. To relive that wondrous moment. That instantaneous miracle.

The Beautiful Escape.

But he could not turn his thoughts from the detective. The man was a force like no other. And the man was in pain. The Adder could see that just by looking at him. Bad things had happened in the man's life. He had researched it, researched this man. More than anything, the Adder wanted to release him from the chains of this world. To set him forever free.

And to watch the bliss in his eyes when it happened.

He didn't understand it himself. The greater the challenge,

the more beautiful the release. It was odd. And the mere thought of such a moment was so powerful that it sucked him away. And time passed. When he finally awoke from the reverie, his face was bleeding and he realized he had been scratching it again.

It was unimportant.

He moved over to the cabinet and turned on the computer. Pale blue light – as cold as the blood in his veins – artificially tinted the room. The Adder signed on to the computer.

Logon: William
Password: Flyaway

He hit Enter and the Windows screen flashed up. There was no screen saver. No saved image on the desktop. Just an icy white screen, because that was how he felt. All icy white.

He double-checked his internet options to be sure that privacy was set to maximum. Then he logged on to the relay computer he kept off-site. It was a necessary tactic. If the cops ever did manage to trace his IP Address – which was almost impossible considering he used proxy servers *and* ran his requests through other unprotected Wi-Fi users – poor eighty-nine-year-old Martha McCallum would find the cops kicking in her front door in the middle of the night and searching her crawlspace.

And even that did not matter. The computer was set to delete All History every night using the KillDisk program.

As a last wall of defence, the Adder always used his Anonymous-Sender account because the host company purged their servers every twelve hours. Even if the cops did get a warrant – which was highly unlikely – the information would be gone by the time they executed it.

Everything was one hundred per cent *safe*.

And yet still, it was not enough for the Adder. Overconfidence had been the downfall of many before him. So he spoofed his IP Address regularly. And he changed the way he did things every single time so that there would be no pattern. With all the steps the Adder had taken, he was confident he had created a non-entity on the net and an email host with no traceable account.

It made him smile every time he logged on.

With everything set in place, he was ready. He took one last look at the hatch above the ladder, making sure it was secured and locked in place – for an action such as this would *enrage* the Doctor – and then he began typing his email.

Addressed To: *Homicide Detective Jacob Striker*
Subject: *Snakes & Ladders*

Twenty-Three

The Vancouver morgue is located on the north side of Vancouver General Hospital, behind the police and ambulance parking area. No signs show the way. There's just a pair of grey doors leading to a cargo elevator. That's it.

Striker had been there too many times to count. Long-forgotten memories bombarded him, one after another, whenever he came here – the murder victims, the car accident casualties, and of course the never-ending string of suicides.

Like his wife's. He would never forget the day he came here to identify Amanda. The walls had seemed warped and the lights far too bright and the body cleaners smelled like Lemon Pledge. That was a memory that refused to leave him. He doubted it ever would.

They took the elevator down two levels into the morgue and Striker moved over to let Felicia stand by the doors. Her claustrophobia was always two seconds from exploding, and she almost jumped from the booth when the doors were half open.

Striker followed. Once in the hall, the stale smell of old paint and dampness hit him. The building was old. The morgue, equally so. He walked down the long dim corridor, turned right, and stopped at a drab grey door. This was the main entrance to the morgue.

Where he had identified Amanda.

The moment hit him hard. So many memories. All bad. This was a sad and despondent place, one he never wanted to see again. And yet here they were, like always.

He opened the door and stepped inside.

On the nearest examination table lay the body of Mandilla Gill. Nineteen years young. A plastic white sheet covered her body and neck, but her face was exposed, which was abnormal. Clearly, the Medical Examiner, Kirstin Dunsmuir, was prepping the body for examination.

Striker looked around; didn't see the woman anywhere.

'You see Dunsmuir?' he asked Felicia.

'The Death Goddess?' Felicia shook her head. 'No. And I'm thankful for it. Small miracles, you know.'

Striker didn't disagree. Were it not for the heaviness of the moment, he might have smiled at that. Felicia didn't like Kirstin Dunsmuir, which was unsurprising. Most people didn't like Kirstin Dunsmuir. And he was included in that group. The woman was colder than the stiffs she worked on, and equally fun at parties.

He killed the thought. He gloved up with fresh latex and moved towards the body on the steel table. In the harsh brightness of the examination lights, Mandy Gill's skin looked almost ashen. Her face was slightly deflated from the draining of fluids, but the muscles around her eyes were still somehow tight. Striker had hoped the woman would look more peaceful in death, but she did not.

He pulled back the sheet and studied the body below. The prep work had already begun.

Felicia saw this, too. 'Dunsmuir's probably tagging the undergarments right now. Maybe we should wait for her before touching anything – you know how she is with this stuff.'

Striker didn't really much care. 'I'm not touching anything just yet. I'm just looking at a few areas.'

'For what?'

'Signs.'

He reached up, grabbed hold of the examination light, and tilted the face of it downwards, so that the brightness of the light shone directly on the body. Lividity – the pooling of the blood – was showing like a faint purplish line now, running all along the lower fifth of Mandy Gill's body. Her facial muscles were stiffening, mainly the eyelids and cheeks.

Rigor was setting in.

Striker looked past all of this and focused on the skin. He swept his eyes around the most common injection areas first – the shoulders, the arms and wrists. When he saw nothing out of the ordinary, he started back at the toes, then slowly, patiently, worked his way up the body, looking for anything that stood out as irregular.

When he reached the neck, he found it. A small mark, almost imperceptible, even with the bright glare of the examination light – definitely impossible to detect back in the dimness of the victim's room.

'Right here,' Striker said to Felicia. 'Left side, just lateral to the base of the neck. Over the first rib area.' He pointed out the area of skin to Felicia, and she shook her head.

'I don't see it.'

Striker took out his pen and pointed to a small precise area where the skin had a slight mark on it.

'See that?' he said. 'The tissue is slightly swollen here. Just barely, but when compared to the right side, you can see there's a difference.'

'Why?'

'Because, I believe, she was injected here.'

Felicia made a face. Looked again. 'You're sure?'

'Positive. And the swelling indicates Mandy was alive when it happened – otherwise there'd be no immune response. If you look close enough, there's a small mark right *here.*'

He pointed and Felicia shook her head. 'Since when do injections leave a mark like that?' she asked.

Striker gave her a dark look. 'They don't – unless someone's resisting and the needle tears the skin.' He was about to say more when a cold voice filled the room.

'What the hell do you think you're doing?'

Striker looked up to see a very unhappy Kirstin Dunsmuir. One look at the medical examiner and Striker could see that she'd had more work done to her face. Cosmetic surgery. The woman was addicted. She crossed her arms over her breast implants and sneered at them through her collagen-filled lips.

'Why are you touching my subject?'

Striker just pointed to the area he was looking at. 'I think she was injected here, can you take a look for me?'

Dunsmuir said nothing for a moment, her icy blue contacts staring Striker down. She strode across the floor with her blue autopsy gown flapping behind her like a cape. Once beside the table, she gave him a long hard look before seeming to relax a little. She put on her glasses, examined the skin, then nodded slowly.

'Yes, it would appear she's been injected.'

She stood back and put on a forced smile, one that showed every one of her capped teeth. 'Excellent detail,' she said to Striker, 'and if I ever again catch you touching one of my subjects before the autopsy is done, I'll have you banned from the lab.'

Striker felt his jaw tighten. His first instinct was to tell the woman off – he had every right to be in here. Mandy Gill was his victim first; her subject second. He could have argued that point and won.

But what was the point in that? He knew Kirstin Dunsmuir well. The Death Goddess had earned her reputation for a reason. And fighting with her would only complicate the investigation.

'I'm sorry,' he offered. 'I wasn't trying to overstep my bounds here. It's just that . . . I *knew* this woman. She was a good person. She didn't deserve this.'

The medical examiner didn't blink. 'If you knew her, you should remove yourself from the case.'

Striker let the comment go. 'Look, I didn't mean to step on your toes or break your lab policies. I'm just worried that this is more than a simple suicide.'

Kirstin Dunsmuir made no immediate reply. But Striker's words seemed to placate her. Her posture relaxed. 'I'm just starting my assessment now,' she said.

'Good. Can we get some toxicology on this one?' Striker asked.

'I always do tox tests – when it's warranted.'

Striker nodded. 'What are we looking at for timeline here?'

'For the tox tests? I'll expedite them. But we're still looking at a while. Twenty-four hours, for sure.'

'It's appreciated,' Striker said. The smell of the body cleaners was getting to him. So were the memories. He handed Dunsmuir one of his business cards with his personal cell number on it. 'Call me the moment you know.'

Dunsmuir took it and said she would. Then Striker gave Felicia the nod to leave, and they did. Once back in the hall, Felicia looked over at him. Nodded approvingly. 'I thought you were going to tear her head off in there.'

Striker shrugged. 'More flies from honey,' he said softly.

He walked down the hallway, the hard sound of his heels echoing against the walls. With every step, the lighting seemed to grow darker and the long corridor narrower as they closed in on the cargo elevator.

Striker couldn't wait to get outside. He needed some space, some fresh air. A moment to think. But more than anything, he just needed to get out of the morgue and away from Kirstin Dunsmuir.

He was suffocating on the darkness.

Twenty-Four

Striker got the car going immediately. Got himself focused. Again, they headed for the headquarters of Car 87, with one purpose – to see if the clinic had a personnel file on Dr Erich Ostermann.

At this point, anything on the man would be helpful.

It was going on for eleven o'clock now, which didn't matter as far as the headquarters were concerned because they were open twenty-four hours a day. Whether it was a nurse, a counsellor, or one of the officers involved, someone would be there.

They drove on. The traffic was surprisingly bad, given the time of night. And it thickened the further they went.

When they got stuck at a red, Striker pulled out his cell phone. He tried calling Courtney to tell her not to wait up for him, but then got directed immediately to the answering machine.

She was already on the line.

That usually meant at least a half-hour wait, so he left her a brief message, then hung up the phone. Felicia hung up her own phone as well. When she let out a long sigh, Striker didn't like the sound of it. 'What now?' he asked.

'I just tried their office. A few of the nurses are there, but Car 87's gone home for the night. We can't get to any of their files till morning.'

Striker cursed and thought this over.

'Screw it. We'll drop by the office anyway. See if anyone else there can help us. Maybe one of the nurses has access to the files.'

The light changed from red to green and Striker hit the gas. Not ten minutes later, they pulled up in front of the building, just in time to see a familiar figure emerging.

Constable Bernard Hamilton was sneaking out of the front door.

Striker knew it was Bernard. He was the only cop around that owned an entire wardrobe of pastel-coloured dress shirts, complete with matching ties. He was a strange-looking man. He was thinning badly on top, and in an effort to divert attention away from his baldness, had grown the rest of his hair into a long ponytail, which he then braided down his back.

Striker didn't like the man. Never had. As far as he was concerned, Bernard Hamilton was a lot like Inspector Laroche – a by-the-book guy, but only when it served his purpose. Bernard Hamilton cared more about stats and commendations than honest-to-God police work, and his only goal in life was to see his face on the Officer of the Year plaque.

Whether he deserved it or not.

Striker had done the man some favours in the past, covering him when he needed a day off for personal reasons – which was, of course, *not* by the book. Bernard Hamilton owed him one for that, and for many other things over the years. It was time to collect.

Striker rolled down the window. Cold air blustered inside the car. Striker ignored the chill and waved the man down. 'Bernard! Hey, *Bernard!*'

Hamilton looked up, unwelcome recognition filling his face. 'Striker,' he said. 'What are you doing here?'

'Planning my retirement. You got any room in there?' When Hamilton didn't so much as break a grin, Striker got right down to business. 'We're here about the Mandy Gill suicide down on Union Street.'

Bernard shuffled his feet and blew into his hands. 'Yeah, I figured as much. I heard the call.'

'What do you know of her?'

Bernard Hamilton shrugged as he came closer. 'Not much more than's already in her file. No family or friends. On social assistance. Suffered from depression. And she self-medicated, like everyone else down there. You know how it is.' He pulled out a pack of smokes and lit one up.

'What kind of self-medication?'

'What kind ya think? Crack, mostly. Some heroin too, though. She could be a little speedball queen.'

Striker made a note of this for the toxicology tests, then texted the information to Kirstin Dunsmuir. While he made the text, Felicia interjected.

'What about this doctor Mandy was seeing – Dr Erich Ostermann?'

Bernard blew out a trail of smoke. 'Ostermann? Don't know him personally. But he's a good man, from what I hear. Created EvenHealth, you know – he's won awards for that. Got some publicity from it. Good stuff. Front page stuff. TV, too. BCTV news, I think.'

Striker didn't much care about the accolades. He put his phone away and asked, 'What do you know of the man's work?'

Bernard bundled up the top of his coat, hiding a pastel blue shirt and matching tie, and turned away from the wind. 'Fuck, it's cold out here. Can we do this later?'

'Just answer the questions,' Striker said.

Bernard took another quick puff and cursed. 'Ostermann

does a lot of work with high-risk offenders. The criminally insane. The mentally ill. Stuff like that. Works mainly out at Riverglen.'

'Can I see his file?'

Bernard said nothing for a moment, he just stared back blankly.

'You mean his *personnel* file?'

'What other one is there?'

Bernard shook his head. 'Sorry, man, they did away with all that after one of the patients stole a folder. One of the docs complained about it and the board ruled it a breach of privacy. The office got rid of all the staff's private data six or seven months ago. Shredded everything.'

Striker gave Bernard a queer look. '*All* of it?'

Bernard asked, 'Why are you so interested in Dr Ostermann anyway?'

'Because he's not being entirely forthcoming with us. I think he's protecting one of his patients. Billy something. I need you to look into it. And while you're at it, keep an eye open for a Dr Richter. His name was seen on Mandy Gill's referral pad.'

Bernard bit his lip. 'I dunno. We're pretty busy right now.'

'I'm not asking.'

Bernard let out a heavy breath. 'What the fuck is that supposed to mean?'

'You owe me one,' Striker reminded him.

Bernard threw his cigarette on the ground and crushed it with his foot. 'Fine, then, fine. Tomorrow, maybe.'

Striker nodded his understanding. This was Bernard Hamilton's passive-aggressive way of trying to get out of doing the job. Striker pretended not to notice.

'No maybe,' he said. 'I'll call you tomorrow.'

'Uh sure.'

'Track you down if I have to.'

'I'll look into it,' Hamilton said, the irritation in his voice now audible.

Striker smiled. 'You're a saint, Bernard.'

Felicia always giggled at that joke, and Bernard just scowled.

'Whatever, Striker. I'm freezing my balls off here, and I'm not getting paid for it.' Bernard Hamilton turned about, his pony-tail snapping across his upper shoulders, and stormed down the road towards his car.

Striker watched the man climb into a new-model Audi located on the east side of the road. The lights turned on, the motor revved, and Bernard Hamilton took off down the road. He was just barely out of sight when Striker's cell vibrated against his side. He plucked it up and saw that he had voicemail. He scrolled back through the received calls and frowned when he saw the name:

Larisa Logan.

The counsellor from Victim Services.

He let out a groan.

Felicia looked over and smiled. 'Just call her back and tell her you don't want to talk about Amanda right now.'

Striker met her stare. 'You don't know Larisa – she's a pit bull. The woman's jaw locks and she never lets go.'

'Then tell her now is not a good time.'

'She'll say that means it's *exactly* the right time.'

Felicia grinned. 'She's persistent, I'll give her that.'

'Stubborn as hell is more like it – similar to others I know.' Before Felicia could respond, Striker hit the Voicemail button and then punched in his password. There was only one message waiting, and when he hit Play the sound of Larisa's voice was completely unlike anything he remembered of her from the past – high in pitch, unsteady, and speaking too fast:

'Jacob, it's me, it's Larisa . . . Look, I just saw you on the news and . . . . I need to speak to you. About what happened. About Mandy Gill. She didn't kill herself, Jacob. She was murdered. And I can prove it.'

Twenty-Five

The phone message shocked Striker and he called Larisa's cell number. It went unanswered. He dialled and waited for her to pick up three more times but to no avail. Finally, he got hold of the police department's Info Channel and asked them to look up Larisa Logan's home number. He called that, too. Again, there was no response.

'This is bullshit,' he said.

Felicia agreed. 'Let's just go there already.'

'Already one step ahead of you,' he replied and hit the gas.

Larisa Logan lived in Burnaby, just a few blocks outside the boundary of the City of Vancouver. From Striker and Felicia's location – the twenty-seven hundred block of Granville Street – the drive normally took twenty minutes.

Striker made it there in ten.

The listed address came back to a small rancher-style house, located on the north side of Parker Street. In the dark of winter, the place looked abandoned and secluded. A barren cherry tree covered most of the front yard, its long bony branches reaching up into the night sky like arthritic fingers. Inside the house, all the lights were turned on. But there was no movement inside.

Striker parked the car and jumped out. Felicia followed suit.

'I don't see any movement,' she noted.

'Me, either.'

As he spoke, Striker absently touched the butt of his pistol, tugged on it to make sure it was snug in its holster. Then made his way up the sidewalk.

The front stairs were slippery with frost, and he took them slowly, one hand on the railing, one hand free and ready for a quick draw. When he reached the front door, he saw that it was already ajar. Just an inch, but definitely open.

He showed this to Felicia.

'Be ready.'

She drew her pistol and took a position of cover on the right side of the door frame, out of the direct line of fire; seeing this, Striker took the left. When they were both lined up, he gave her the nod and then knocked hard on the door.

'Larisa!' he called. 'Larisa, it's Jacob Striker. With the Vancouver Police Department!'

No answer.

'Larisa, I got your message!' he called again.

But still, nothing.

He pushed the door all the way open, and it moved silently, exposing the hallway, living room and kitchen beyond.

'Larisa!' he called. 'It's Jacob Striker! Felicia Santos is with me. We're coming inside!'

He and Felicia moved inside the foyer, then shut and locked the door behind them – they didn't want anyone sneaking up behind them. Once done, Striker gestured for Felicia to cover the right side of the room. When she nodded her understanding, he took the left. Together, they cleared the entire floor, room by room, starting with the den and office and finishing with the bedroom and ensuite in the back of the house.

They found no one.

'She's not here,' Felicia finally said. 'Shit. Where did she call you from?'

'Her cell.'

'Was she home at the time?'

'She didn't say. It was a message.'

He spoke the words without paying attention; his main focus was on the area around them. Something about the room bothered him. Something about *all* the rooms bothered him. Tugged away at the back of his mind like an invisible string.

He holstered his gun and moved slowly from the bedroom, down the long carpeted hallway, into the living room and den area. He stood at the entrance to the kitchen and looked back and forth between the rooms.

Felicia followed him.

'What is it?' she asked. 'What's wrong?'

He said nothing and just looked around. On the kitchen counter and table were piles of dirty plates and leftover food. By the stove, a pile of spaghetti had been dropped on the floor and never cleaned up. In the far corner of the room were piles of newspapers and bags of empty cans.

'The place is a pigsty,' he noted.

'Some people are messy.'

'This is beyond messy. And the door was left open. With the heat blasting. I know Larisa – she would never live this way.'

'How would you know? Have you ever been to her place before?'

'No. But I have been to her office. And in her car. Everything is always neat and tidy. Clean. *Orderly.* This . . . this isn't her.' He walked outside and checked the address. It was correct. They were at the right house. 'Maybe she moved,' he added. 'Maybe someone else lives here now.'

'Let me get the computer,' Felicia said. 'I'll check out her history, see what I can drum up.'

He nodded, and she returned to the car.

While she was gone, Striker made his way back down to the bedroom. On the bureau was a family photograph. The picture was of Larisa with two other women, so this was definitely her house.

It struck him as odd.

He moved closer and focused in on the photograph. It looked like Larisa and her family – presumably her mother and sister. They were smiling, happy, looked like they had been laughing about something.

A hidden joke between them all.

Striker continued looking around. Piled beside the photograph was a stack of newspaper clippings. And on the wall were more of the same. Stories. Articles. Clipped out and stuck to the walls. Some were from tabloids and magazines; others from more reputable sources.

He read through them all. Across the front of one story – where a man had thrown himself out of a window on the sixth floor of the Regency Hotel – someone had used a big thick felt pen to write: *LIES! LIES! LIES!*

The collage of articles made bad thoughts filter through Striker's head, and he hoped he was wrong in what he was thinking. Then he heard Felicia re-enter the house through the front door. He went to meet her.

When he reached the living room, he found her standing at the kitchen table with the laptop open. She was reading through a list of entries on the PRIME database.

'What you got?' he asked.

She gave him a queer look. 'How well do you know this woman, Jacob?'

'Well enough.'

'Do you? When was the last time you talked to her?'

'I dunno. A while ago,' he admitted. 'Probably just over a year – why, Feleesh? What are you getting at?'

'I'm getting at *this*.' She turned the computer around so he could see the screen. The first thing that caught his eye were three letters, marked in big red font:

MHA.

'Mental Health Act?' he said. 'What the hell?'

Felicia nodded. 'Turns out this Larisa you know has had a lot of problems since she left the Victim Services Unit.'

'Problems?' Striker looked up from the laptop. 'What do you mean?'

Felicia took the laptop back and clicked through the electronic reports. 'According to PRIME, Larisa Logan has been listed as a Disturbed Person numerous times.'

Striker raised an eyebrow. *Disturbed Person* was a politically correct label for bat-shit crazy.

'Must be a mistake.'

Felicia continued reading through the reports. 'I wish it was, Jacob. But I don't think so. It looks like Larisa actually left her position with Victim Services twelve months ago and took some kind of personal leave. Could be stress-related. I'm not sure. It doesn't really say.'

Striker closed his eyes and thought back. 'Twelve months . . . . That was right about the time I had my last session with her. Or maybe thirteen months – it was before Christmas. And then she took stress leave?'

Felicia grinned. 'Yeah. Must've been your boyish charms.'

He didn't respond. He just began reading through the reports.

While he did this, Felicia took a moment to look around the room. After a few minutes, she returned with a large piece of paper in her hands. On it was a list of strange scribblings. It was confusing and nonsensical. Written gibberish. But some names were there.

Striker saw two names that he recognized:

Mandy.

Billy.

He pointed to them. 'That could be Mandilla Gill. And that could be this Billy guy . . . Ostermann's patient.'

Felicia didn't look so assured. 'There's over thirty names here, Jacob. It could be a lot of things with all these scribblings. But yeah, sure, the names do match.'

Striker read through all the scribbles until he spotted one name he did not recognize. Unlike the other names, this one had been underlined several times:

Sarah.

He wrote the name down in his notebook.

Felicia held up a pile of more newspaper clippings – tabloid stuff about everything from medication frauds and passport scams to the existence of aliens and demons. 'Jesus Christ, Jacob, look at this stuff. Aliens? Demons? The woman's gone right off the deep end.'

Striker said nothing and finished the report he was reading. When he was done, he skimmed through the list of call incidents. There were many: *Disturbed Person. Suspicious Circumstance.* And even a few *Assaults* where Larisa was listed as a *Suspect Chargeable.* Meaning she was lucky she hadn't been thrown in jail.

This alarmed him.

One of the assault charges was against one of the police psychologists, a man Larisa had worked with during her time in the Victim Services Unit. The charges had been dropped for compassionate reasons, further stating in the Remarks section that 'Mental Health Issues were involved'.

Striker felt himself deflate; the news was depressing and hard to believe.

He closed the laptop and felt overwhelmed by the information. Larisa Logan. His friend. The woman who had helped him through so much after Amanda's death. It just couldn't be true, and yet . . .

And yet here they were.

When he finally found the words, his voice was hard and full of grit. 'This woman helped me through the darkest hours of my life,' he said. 'I'm going to help her through hers.'

Felicia rubbed his arm. 'She's out there somewhere, Jacob. We'll find her.'

Striker did not return the smile. 'We have to – and not just out of compassion.'

'What do you mean?'

He turned to face her. 'Think about it, Feleesh. Her connection to the victim. Her open access to medications. Her history of mental illness. And over the last year, the willingness to resort to violence . . . I hate to think this way, but it's something that has to be considered. Something we have to be prepared for. Larisa Logan is one of our prime suspects.'

'Do you believe that?'

'No, but it's not about what I *believe*. We have to find her and get her professional treatment – but we also have to rule her out as a suspect first.'

He headed for the front door. The night was already cold and quiet, but it felt darker now than it had before.

Deeper, thicker. *Blacker.*

And he feared it was only going to get worse.

Twenty-Six

Across the way from Larisa Logan's place, beneath the overhang of a porch, the Adder stood in the total darkness. He stood tall in the night, completely still. Watching. Waiting.

Assessing.

Know thy enemy. These were words to live by. And how correct they were. For the cops had now found Larisa Logan's place. He had no idea how they had done it, but it was impressive nonetheless.

It was not totally surprising. There were trails everywhere in today's world. Physical. Audible. Electronic. Biochemical. No matter how hard a person tried to cover their tracks, there was always a trail. *Always.*

Somehow, some way, everyone was track-able.

The Adder watched both detectives enter and search the house, then the front and back yards. When they finally left, the woman carried a brown bag full of evidence. What it held, the Adder had no idea, but he assumed it was newspaper clippings and bills and whatever else they thought important.

Whatever the evidence, it was bad news for him. In fact, there was plenty of bad news to go around. *Very* bad news.

Larisa was gone.

The police knew of some part of her involvement.

And they would surely be coming.

The Adder frowned. The Doctor was going to be very unhappy with this news. There would be serious ramifications. Plan alterations. New strategies. And even worse problems if the cops – or the Doctor, for that matter – ever discovered *why* Larisa was so important.

This was most disconcerting for the Adder. The thought should have made him frown. Or squint. Or flinch. Or . . . something. He should have had *some* kind of physical reaction to it. At the very least, he should have worried for the future.

But he did not. He could not. All he could do was stand there and *smile* as the excitement built up within himself.

It was happening.

The game was on.

Twenty-Seven

It was well past midnight by the time Striker and Felicia pulled up to his house on Camosun Street. It was an old house, a small sleepy home on the corner lot. A tiny front yard with a maple tree stood out front. Most of the lights were off inside.

Striker looked at it with weary eyes. So many memories of Courtney and Amanda were here. After the suicide, he'd wanted to move out, but Courtney had freaked, so he'd abandoned the idea. There'd been good times and bad times here over the years, so many that it usually left him feeling awash in emotions whenever he looked upon the place. But now as he took everything in, all he could feel was a weary happiness to have arrived.

Home sweet home.

The day was done. He was done. Damn well depleted. And it was time for some much-needed shut-eye because tomorrow was undoubtedly going to be another wild day. He killed the engine and opened the door. When he started to get out, Felicia grabbed his forearm.

'Hey,' she said. 'The keys?'

He stopped getting out of the car, hesitated, then dropped back into the driver's seat. He looked at her. Felt a flood of disappointment. 'You're not coming in, are you?'

When Felicia didn't respond, he looked at her face – at her dark eyes and warm lips – and he wanted more than anything to have her come inside with him, so he could snuggle up next to her in his bed. Feel her warm flesh. Have her long hair spill all around him. Smell her in the sheets. Wrap himself around her . . . They had done all this in the past. But that was just a distant memory now.

'I really have to go,' she said.

'The door is always open for you.'

'Jacob—'

'Even if you just want to sleep on the couch, right?'

She looked over and met his eyes. 'The couch? Really. Come on, Jacob. It won't end there and we both know it.'

'And is that such a bad thing?'

'No. Yes. You know what I mean.'

'Feleesh—'

'I can't do this any more, Jacob. Courtney hates my guts. And then there's the whole thing with Amanda – I can't compete with a memory.'

'I never asked you to.'

'You don't have to ask – it's always there no matter what you say, and it always will be.'

He only shrugged at the comment; he didn't get what she was saying.

'This just isn't working out,' she finally said. 'Our relationship . . . it changes too many things. Especially at work. It's altered our whole dynamic. We're good partners, Jacob, and good friends, too. I don't want to lose all that.'

'And what about when we're not at work?'

She laughed. 'And when are we *not* at work?'

He searched for a response and came up short. And to be honest, he was too tired to argue the point. This was a conversation he was growing progressively weary of, and yet it was the same one that always seemed to pop up again and again at the end of every long day. He was beaten down by it, and he let it go.

He looked at Felicia's face, took it all in, and felt so many emotions that they over-spilled. He wanted to tell her how much he missed her. How much he wanted her there with him every day. How they should always be together, and that all the little problems just didn't matter.

But he didn't say any of that. He just sat there and said nothing, and, eventually, he handed her the keys and stepped out of the car.

Felicia took a long look at his face and her expression softened. 'I do love you, Jacob, if that means anything any more.'

'It means everything,' he said. 'Which is why none of this makes sense.'

Felicia made no reply. She just moved to the driver's side and closed the door. The transmission let out a loud clank as she put the car into Drive. And moments later, she was gone, speeding off down the road. Just a pair of tiny red tail lights growing smaller in the distance as the darkness thickened all around her.

Striker stood there in the cold and dark night, and stared at the empty road. Thinking, thinking, thinking. When it was more than Striker could take, he turned around and walked up the old porch steps.

Alone.

Inside, the house was dark and quiet. Only one light was on, coming from far down the hall, and Striker knew it was from Courtney's bedroom. Ever since the incident last year, she'd had problems with the dark. And confined areas. And who could blame her for that? He let the light be. She had enough on her plate with therapy; he wasn't about to push it.

He tiptoed down the hallway to his daughter's room and peered inside. Crashed out on the bed in a soundless sleep was Courtney. Her thick auburn hair swept over her creamy cheeks and hid the rest of her face. Striker took a long look at her, watching her chest rise with every breath. Then he looked at the crutches leaning against the far wall.

More bad reminders.

He closed her door and let her sleep. He went into the kitchen and grabbed a beer – a Miller Genuine Draft – and then walked into the den. It was cold and dark, so he flicked on the gas fire. He crashed down on the sofa and felt the hardness of the cold leather. As the room warmed up, he went over everything in his head.

The day had been long and hard. A good woman had died. And now another was missing. His world had been turned upside down. Twice in one day.

'Where the hell are you, Larisa?' he asked aloud.

The words sounded weak in the open space of the room. For all intents and purposes, Larisa Logan had disappeared. She had become a ghost. A Missing Persons file.

It made no sense.

His eyelids felt heavy. Bed was calling.

Striker glanced at his iPhone one last time to see if Larisa had called and he'd somehow missed it. There were no missed calls, but there was a big red number 1 on the email notification. He hit the Email button and saw one message on the screen. He read the header:

From: *Unknown*
Subject: *Snakes & Ladders*

At first, Striker almost hit the Delete button, but something about the message bothered him. He put down his bottle of beer and leaned forward in his seat. Then he opened the message.

It was short, simple, and to the point:

You won today, Detective Striker. You climbed up while I slid down. Good play. But tomorrow it's my turn to roll the dice, and it's only fair to warn you, I always get doubles. ;o)
Game on.

Yours truly,
The Adder

Day Two

Twenty-Eight

The world was still dark when Striker got up, and the room seemed to move on him in his half-asleep state. He kicked the blankets off his legs and stood up in the darkness, the hardwood floor feeling cold on his bare feet. He grabbed his robe from the hook on the wall, wrapped it around himself to ward off the chill, and stepped out into the hall.

Dim light flooded the far-away kitchen area and the sound of fingers tapping on a keyboard filled the air. It was Percy Wadsworth, Striker knew – *Ich*, as everyone called him, due to his uncanny resemblance to Ichabod Crane from the *Sleepy Hollow* fable. When Striker called him with news of the email message, the tech had come right over.

He was a godsend.

Striker walked down the hall and stopped in the kitchen doorway. The electronic blue light from the computer screen gave the corner where Ich was sitting an artificial look. Striker reached up and turned on the overhead light.

When the room brightened, Ich didn't even react. He sat at the kitchen table, slumped like a scoliosis victim with an arthritic spine. His eyes stared out from behind large wire-rimmed glasses, and the shirt he wore was two sizes too big for his skinny build. On the table in front of him were several empty cans of Irish coffee Monster energy drink and a few Snickers bar wrappers.

'Any luck?' Striker asked.

Ich finally stopped typing. He looked up, pushed his glasses back up the long thin bridge of his nose, and let out a heavy breath. 'Not much,' he said, and the words were a let-down to Striker. Among other things, Ich was the department's internet specialist. If he couldn't trace the source of the email, then no one could.

It was just that simple.

The acidic smell of stale coffee filled the air, and it was a welcome aroma. Striker walked over to the machine, grabbed a cup from the sink, and poured some old Nabob. It had been made sometime during the night – who knows when – and the brew was as black as motor sludge. He pulled a package of pastries from the cupboard – raspberry Danishes and lemon rolls. He threw it on the table.

'There you go, Ich. Breakfast of Champions.'

Ich looked over. 'Freshly baked, I'm sure.'

'Good hydrogenated pureness,' Striker countered. 'With a hint of trans fats.'

Ich grinned. 'Felicia would kill you if she knew.' He took a raspberry Danish without looking and bit off a chunk.

Striker came up to the table. 'So . . . we even know how this guy found me? I mean, this message came from my own personal email account.'

Ich swallowed a mouthful of Danish. 'Actually, that was the easy part. It's called having a sixteen-year-old daughter.'

Striker didn't like the ring of that. 'What do you mean?'

'Courtney's listed on a social-networking site called MyShrine.'

'So?'

Ich gestured for Striker to come around the table. Then he turned on Firefox and clicked on the MyShrine tab. Already pre-filled on the page was the login name and password. Ich hit Enter, and Courtney's homepage loaded:

Name: The Court.

Striker watched the screen as Ich navigated through different profile sections. He couldn't help but feel they were invading his daughter's privacy. It was like reading someone's electronic diary, and he self-consciously looked down the hall at her bedroom door.

'Right here,' Ich said. He clicked on the profile pictures and paged through them. As he did so, Striker saw several photos of himself among them – some of them in uniform. It was surprising. In some ways it made him feel good to know she had included him; in other ways, he didn't like it. He'd been in the newspapers and on TV enough times over the years – always when working a big case – for the general public to know who he was. And that was one thing.

But this connected his career of policing to their home.

It wasn't good.

'I want these pictures removed,' he said.

Ich nodded. 'The message this guy left you is right here.' He clicked on the Message Wall and brought up the veiled threat. 'Courtney has all her privacy rules set to minimum – she really should change that. She's got message forwarding clicked on, so all her messages are automatically relayed from here to your home email. And since you have email forwarding set up on your phone, you got it, too.'

Striker thought this over. 'But I don't get *all* her MyShrine messages, just this one.'

'That's because of the filter settings. They were altered the moment the email was sent. Which means that somehow he's been playing with your settings.'

Striker frowned at that. It was all technical mumbo-jumbo to him. 'Is this guy on her Friends' list?' he asked.

'Naw, she's never included him in that. He just sent a message to her wall – a post, like anyone can do. Normally, everything would be filtered to only Courtney. The weird thing is, this guy knew you would get it.' He searched through the forwarding options and unchecked Striker's email address. 'There. Fixed again . . . But that doesn't explain how he got into your email options in the first place. What are your security settings on your computer?'

Striker shook his head. 'I don't know. You tell me.'

'You need to know this stuff, Shipwreck. It's the computer age, remember?'

'That's Felicia's role. I shoot people.'

Ich laughed softly. He worked his way to the internet settings and shook his head. 'Your firewall is down, man. Anyone can get in here.' He made a few clicks, then saved the changes. 'There. It's secure now. But for all we know, this guy could've been rooting around in your computer for months. If he's good enough, that is – and I think he is.'

Striker said nothing. He was not a social-networking-savvy guy, nor was he technologically up to date. Every day, he just turned on the computer and it worked; that was about as far as his skills went. Felicia was the technological master of their partnership. He wished she was here right now.

For many reasons.

'What about the original sender?' he asked Ich. 'Can we find him?'

'Untraceable.' Ich grabbed a can of Monster drink from the table and slurped back the rest of it. He then wiped his mouth with the sleeve of his shirt and continued. 'First off, you need a warrant for this stuff.'

'That's not a problem, I can get one in two hours.'

Ich shook his head. 'Don't bother, that's not the point. I got a contact with MyShrine, and I already used him. He gave me the account info – off the record, of course. The message is being sent through a proxy server. Which isn't good for us.'

'Why not?'

'Because most of those companies wipe their data every hour on the hour. And ninety-nine per cent of them are set up offshore. The chance of getting anything back is abysmal, much less something useful. Plus, if this guy's smart enough to do this, he's probably using other hide-ware programs as well.' Ich gave Striker a hard look. 'Be careful with this guy. This shit ain't easy to do.'

'Point taken.'

Striker read the message one more time. Analysed it. There was no actual threat in the words, only insinuation. But that was enough. And the sender had signed the message with no real name, only *The Adder* – a name Striker had never heard before.

It was typical. In a time when internet sickos were cyber-bullying people, opening paedophiliac chat rooms, and defacing online memorial sites like creepy electronic trolls, not much surprised him any more.

He swallowed back the rest of his cup of coffee. 'Thanks for your help, Ich. Really, I owe you one.'

The techie just shrugged. 'Any time, Detective.'

Striker put a hand on his shoulder. 'You've done enough. Go home and get some sleep.' He smiled. '*My* day's just starting.'

Ich nodded and stood up from the computer. 'If this guy sends any more messages, don't delete them. Don't open them. And don't turn off the computer. Just leave it alone and call me – ASAP. I'll come right over.'

Striker nodded. He walked Ich to the front door, thanked him again for his time, and watched as the police car drove off into the grey darkness of the winter morning.

Ich had no sooner left when another police car came roaring down the road. An unmarked. A Ford Taurus. It came to a sliding stop on the icy road and almost hit the kerb. The sight of it made Striker smile.

Felicia had arrived.

She got out gingerly, balancing two coffees in her hand. Tim Horton's coffee. The Best. She walked up the sidewalk, kicked open the gate, climbed the steps, and handed him one. In the yellowish light of the porch lamp, she looked pretty. Rested. Like she'd slept well and was ready to go for another day.

'Good morning, Sunshine,' he offered.

She stepped right past him. 'Where the hell's this message?'

Before he could even answer, she walked into the house, kicked off her boots, and crossed into the kitchen. By the time Striker had shut the door and caught up with her, she was already paging through MyShrine.

'The Adder?' she asked.

'It's a type of snake,' he explained. When she gave him one of her annoyed looks, he added, 'A poisonous one.'

'I know it's a poisonous snake, Jacob. I didn't grow up in a friggin' commune. Who is this guy?'

Striker shrugged. 'It's untraceable.'

Felicia put down her coffee and shook her head. Her eyes stayed heavy on the screen and her jaw was tight.

'I don't like this,' she said.

'No one does. But there's no real threat here, just a wise-ass message. And that's the way I'm taking it for now. He's just another loon.'

'Or he could be our guy.'

Striker nodded in agreement. 'I realize that. I understand the coincidence and timing. But the more you go over things, the more you realize that's a pretty big could.'

'How so?'

Striker joined her at the table. 'Well, for one, the message was sent *after* we'd been seen on TV. If it had come in before the news segment, I would have given it a little more credit, but now, well, it could have been anyone in close proximity to a television set.'

Felicia thought this over, but her face remained hard. 'Still, we should take some precautions. I mean, what if it is him? We just go around doing our job like a pair of sitting ducks?'

'No, we watch our backs. Like we always do.'

She said nothing for a moment. She read the message once more, then twice, and frowned. 'It's like this is a game to him,' she said. 'He's a sick fuck. And he's *bold*. Who knows, he might even come after us.'

Striker smiled at that.

'If only we could be so lucky.'

Twenty-Nine

It was just after six a.m. when Striker and Felicia decided to leave his little bungalow on Camosun Street and head for the downtown core. Courtney was still fast asleep in her bed, and Striker had considered waking her up to say goodbye. He missed her, as always, and he felt like they never had enough time together. Felt like he was failing her as a father.

That thought was always with him, clouding his thoughts.

In the end, he had opted to let her sleep. The girl had been depressed lately, upset over her injuries and the lack of progress in her rehabilitation. This morning, she seemed to be getting some much-needed rest.

He didn't want to disturb that.

He left a note on the computer, telling her not to touch it because of police-related reasons, then left the house with Felicia by his side. As they stepped into the Ford, Striker took a long last look at his cosy little rancher.

Felicia noted this. 'Holy Jeez, she'll be fine, worrywart.'

Striker frowned and she laughed at him. He climbed inside the car, started the engine, and they headed for police headquarters. Not the downtown one, but the building on Cambie Street. It was their next best step in finding Larisa Logan.

It was where Victim Services was located.

*   *   *

Cambie Street was not far from the Dunbar area, so they made it there in less than ten minutes. When they arrived on scene at 0615 hours, the parking lot out front was unusually empty. Echo shift had already gone home for the night, Alpha was out on the road, and Bravo had not yet arrived.

Striker ditched the car and headed into the foyer. The building here on Cambie was owned by the Insurance Corporation of BC, not the Vancouver Police Department, and this pissed off a lot of the cops. Underground parking was shared with ICBC civilians – and, therefore, insecure – the elevators broke down every second week, and the entire building had a ramshackle, compartmentalized feel to it.

It made sense why. The building had been designed for the nine-to-five business crowd, not the twenty-four-hour/seven-days-a-week needs of a police department. Talks of relocating to a newer address out east were forever ongoing, but for now this was all the Vancouver Police had. Insufficient premises to go with an insufficient crime budget.

It was typical for the City of Vancouver.

In the end, Striker didn't much care. The Cambie building was mostly patrol. He spent most of his time down at the 312 station, and a lot more of it out on the road. All he cared about with regards to the Cambie building was that it housed Victim Services.

That was Larisa Logan's unit.

Sargheit Samra, the old bear, was the sergeant in charge of the Victim Services Unit, and had been for just over a year now. Before being transferred to the VSU, he'd spent damn near eight years working Alpha shift, so he'd become something of an early riser – the crazy hours were something he never could readjust from. For this reason, Striker hadn't bothered to call ahead; he was betting on the fact that Samra would already be on scene.

Even at six o'clock in the morning.

Once inside, Striker and Felicia crossed the foyer and turned right, heading away from the elevators. The Victim Services office was located on the southwest corner of the foyer, surrounded by a transparent wall of tinted glass. By most accounts, it was a tiny section. Six desks, and sometimes not enough workers to fill them. Most of the counsellors were usually busy, called out to the worst crime scenes and at all hours of the day and night. Every shift was filled with stress and anguish.

Striker didn't envy them their job.

He gave the glass door a solid rap with his knuckles, then turned the knob and went inside. Seated behind his desk with his police boots off, reading the Vancouver *Province* sports section was a fifty-ish East Indian male. Sargheit Samra.

The Sarj, as everyone called him.

He was a thickset man. Clean shaven. And even though he was carrying some extra cushioning these days, the thick underlying muscle bulk made his uniform fit well. Made him look like a force to be reckoned with.

Despite the fact it was a No Smoking building – a bylaw, in fact – a cigarette dangled precariously from his lips, and a steaming-hot cup of Starbucks coffee sat in front of him. Black as night, and in a paper cup, like always.

Upon seeing them, the Sarj looked up from his newspaper and a sly grin spread his thick lips. 'Well, holy Shipwreck, look what the cat just dragged in.' He spoke with no accent. He looked over at Felicia and smiled genuinely. 'You still hanging out with this loser? He'll get you a bad rep, you know.'

'Damage is already done,' she replied. 'How's life, Sarj?'

He folded up his paper and dropped it on the desk. 'Slow this morning – and happily so.' He gave them a dubious look. 'Why? You two lookin' at changing that?'

Striker closed the door behind them. 'We're here about one of your former counsellors. Woman who helped me out, in fact. Larisa Logan.'

The grin stretching the Sarj's lips slipped away, and he took his feet off the desk. He sat up like he was getting ready for serious business, took a long drag of his smoke, and then spoke. 'You really know how to kill a mood, Striker. Jesus Christ. What you want to know about her?'

'Everything. Like why she's messaging me, saying she has information on one of my cases.'

'She did?' The Sarj raised an eyebrow and stubbed out his cigarette in the plastic lid of his coffee cup. He rolled the butt thoughtfully between his fingers, as if debating something in his head. After a long moment, he gazed up at them, and suddenly he looked a whole lot older. *Tired.* 'You know she left here, right?'

Striker nodded. 'We're aware.'

'And not too long after I got here. So I didn't have a whole lot of time to get to know the woman.'

'Larisa didn't spend too much time in the VSU?' Felicia asked.

'She'd been here for quite a while when I got transferred in. Bout three years, I guess. And by all accounts, she was one of the good ones.'

'Good work ethic?' Striker pressed.

The Sarj nodded. 'The best. Had to be to work down here. Back then, the Victim Services Unit was really a hoppin' place – as busy as it is now, but with only two girls working it. Now we got five. So Larisa and Chloe were really moving. Hell, they were overworked. It burned them out good.'

'Chloe?' Felicia asked.

'Chloe Sera. Moved to one of the crime analyst areas. Burnaby South, I think.'

Striker nodded. 'Did you two get along?'

'Me and Larisa?' The Sarj spoke the words like the question surprised him. 'For sure. *Everyone* did. Larisa was a peach. Always happy, never moody. She did her work and she kept her mouth shut. Never gossiped, never complained. Hell, I wish I could say the same for the new girls – everyone feels so fucking *entitled* nowadays . . . I miss her.'

Striker crossed his arms, leaned against the wall. 'So what happened then? What made her leave?'

The Sarj opened his packet of Lucky Strike unfiltered. Thumbed one out. 'Bad times,' he said. 'Real bad. Stuff happened with Larisa.'

'*Stuff?*' Striker asked. 'Jeez, don't be so technical, Sarj, you're losing me.'

The old bear just grunted. He lit his cigarette, sucked deep, and blew out a trail of smoke that clouded the small office. When he spoke again, his voice was gruff. 'Her parents were killed. Her sister, too.'

Felicia made a surprised sound. 'My God, how?'

'Motor vehicle accident. Larisa was never the same after that. She wanted stress leave, I gave it to her. Shit, the tragedy aside, she had earned it. It was a bad, bad time for the girl.'

Striker thought that over.

A bad time. That seemed like an understatement.

On the far wall across the room hung a series of photographs, one for each of the counsellors in the Victim Services Unit. Larisa's face was still up there. Dark brown hair with reddish highlights. A warm stare. And a big wide smile that was captivating, exactly how Striker remembered it.

He missed seeing it now.

He turned and met the Sarj's eyes. 'You talked to her at all lately?'

The Sarj looked at the picture with a lost look distorting his face, as if he had forgotten the photograph was even there.

'No,' he said after a long moment. 'No, I haven't.' When Striker asked nothing else, the Sarj closed his desk drawer. Let out a tense sound. Continued speaking. 'I'll be honest with you, Shipwreck – and don't go spreading this around – but Larisa got a little . . . *weird* on us there.'

'Weird? How so?'

'It's kind of hard to explain, really. She got private. *Fiercely* private. And to some extent, I can see why – I mean, the way people gossip round here, it's like a goddam high school some-times. But after the tragedy with her family, she became really closed-off, really detached. Didn't come to the social functions. Didn't talk to anyone at the office – and it wasn't from a lack of trying. We called her all the time, sent out condolence packages, and we each took turns dropping by her place to make sure she was okay.'

Felicia asked, 'Did it help?'

The Sarj just furrowed his brow and sucked on his Lucky. 'Did it help? Who the fuck knows? The more we tried to keep contact with her, the more she stayed away. One time, I remember going out there and knowing she was home – and I mean *knowing* she was there. But no matter how much I knocked, she just stayed inside the doorway there, pretending to be away. It was really, really odd. After that, I sent an email to Human Resources about her. Thought maybe they could check into it. Do some follow-up on her. See if maybe they could get Larisa some professional help for her problems.'

'And then what?'

'And then she left.'

'You mean *quit?*' Felicia asked.

'Yeah, she quit. As in sayonara. End of April, I think. Maybe

May. I'm not sure, exactly, but it was long after she'd fallen off the social ladder.'

Striker thought this over. 'She give you a letter?'

'Nope. Just sent an email, telling everyone how sorry she was, but that she could no longer do the job – and you know what? I don't blame her for that, especially after what she'd been through. This place never gave those girls enough training and support for the job they did.'

'What do you mean, training?' Felicia asked.

'On how to deal with all this stuff.'

'But I thought they were all psychologists,' she said.

The Sarj shook his head. 'Psychologists? Fuck, no. That's a common misconception around here. As of this last year, yeah, *now* they're all psychologists – and that was done mainly for liability reasons to protect the department – but back then the counsellors were just a couple of young girls offering a shoulder to cry on. They got almost no training and even less support. Took the Union to get some changes on that.'

Felicia nodded as she thought this over. 'The stress obviously took a toll on Larisa. And she broke down.'

The Sarj said nothing.

Striker agreed with Felicia's analysis. He spoke with the Sarj some more and got all of Larisa's last-known details – her address, phone numbers, email addresses, and contacts. But the information he received was no different from what he'd already found in the PRIME database.

In the end, it did nothing to help them.

'I do have a photo of her on file,' the Sarj offered. 'Jpeg. Give me your cell and I'll Bluetooth it to you.'

Striker handed him his iPhone and the Sarj sent him the photograph. 'This is the latest picture we have.'

'It's appreciated,' Striker said. Before leaving, he met the Sarj's stare one more time. 'This is a really delicate issue for us. You call me if you hear anything about her, okay, Sarj? And I mean *anything*.'

He nodded. 'You and you alone.'

The Sarj stood up from the desk, rounded it in his socked feet, and started for the door to usher them out. At the wall, he stopped and stared at the photograph of Larisa Logan. 'She was such a good person,' he said. 'And we all miss her. But over time, she just kind of . . . faded away. It's not right.'

Striker just nodded and left the office.

On the way back to the car, the Sarj's words bore into him. The man was right. Larisa was a good person, and she had suffered a terrible tragedy. At a time when everyone should have stood up and been counted, they had all stepped back into the shadows. In essence, they had all failed her.

Him included.

Felicia looked over as they approached the car. She offered him a soft smile. 'You okay there, Big Guy?'

Striker barely met her stare. 'She became a goddam missing person, and no one noticed. Not even me.'

He climbed inside the vehicle and slammed the door shut.

They headed for Car 87 headquarters, the Vancouver Police Department's Mental Health Team. Striker was determined to see if they had any files on Larisa Logan.

He was betting they had.

Thirty

'That's odd,' Felicia said as she read through the computer reports.

Striker drove eastward into the fast lane of West Broadway Street and turned south on Main. 'What's odd?' he asked.

'Larisa Logan's already been run through the system this morning. Real early, too. Actually, there's a CAD call for her from yesterday. And Mandy Gill as well.'

This piqued Striker's interest. 'Run? By who?'

She read through the electronic pages. 'Car 87.'

'Who's in the car today?'

'Hold on, it's slow in coming . . . okay, here it is. Well, that figures. Just your favourite person in the whole wide world – Constable Bernard Hamilton.'

'Bernard, huh.' The words left a bad taste in Striker's mouth. 'So he gets off work real late last night, and already he's out this morning, running people. Our victim and Larisa, no less.'

'We worked late last night, too,' Felicia replied. 'And we're out early this morning.'

'That's not the point,' Striker explained. 'We *need* to be out this early. We're in the middle of an investigation here. Car 87 works regular hours unless something big comes up. So the question here is, what's going on that made Bernard get off his lazy ass for once?'

Felicia made no response, and Striker thought about it as they drove on. The question felt heavy in his mind.

As they passed 29th Avenue, Striker looked at his watch. It was quarter to seven now, and the Thursday morning rush-hour traffic showed it. Cars were already lined up bumper to bumper all along the main drive, but at least they were moving. The sun was rising in the east, barely breaking up the heavy darkness of the night with a slash of light grey.

They sped up and drove down 41st. When he reached their destination, Striker pulled over and stared at the old house in front of him. It was an old heritage home, three levels, and beautiful with big white shutters and a double door in the front. To most people, it looked like a private residence. But anyone in policing knew the truth. This was the headquarters of Car 87 and the rest of the psychiatric nursing team. They had arrived.

Striker parked the car. Without a word, he climbed out and made his way towards the front door. Bernard Hamilton was somewhere inside the house, and Striker wanted to speak to the man.

Bernard had a few questions to answer.

The double front doors of Car 87 headquarters were always locked for security reasons, so Striker had to be let inside. His knock was answered by the very man he was looking for. Bernard Hamilton pulled open the door, saw them, and put on a wide smile that didn't move the rest of his face.

'Striker,' he said. 'Felicia. Good morning. You're certainly up early.'

'Same can be said of you,' Striker replied.

He gave Bernard the once-over. As usual, the man had dressed with flair. The dress shirt he wore was made from pastel red silk

– a hideous floral pattern – and the accessory band he used to braid his ponytail matched.

Striker stepped inside the foyer without an invitation, and Bernard automatically stepped back. As Striker turned around, he bumped into a pile of boxes on the floor. Each one had a label and a date on it. He looked at them.

'Macy's Day Sale?' he asked.

'We're relocating,' Bernard said. 'Out east with everyone else.'

Striker nodded. He recalled hearing something about that. He turned the conversation to more immediate matters. 'You research Dr Ostermann yet, like we asked?'

Bernard said nothing for a moment, but looked uncomfortable. He cleared his throat and then turned his head towards the den area where three women – all psych nurses Striker had never seen before – were having coffee and going over files from the previous night. 'Perhaps we should take this discussion elsewhere.'

Striker didn't much care. 'You got an office?'

'Right over here.' Bernard showed them the way, then ushered them inside. 'I'll get us some coffee.'

Striker didn't argue the point, and Felicia nodded eagerly. When Bernard turned the corner and was gone from view, Striker shut the door and gave Felicia a hard look.

'Good old Bernard doesn't seem too happy to see us,' he noted.

Felicia agreed. 'You see that smile he gave us at the door?'

'More plastic than a Ken doll.'

Felicia laughed at that, and Striker looked around the office. On the wall was a picture of James Dickson – a well-known cop who had received the Officer of the Year award for his work with the sex-trade workers in the Downtown East Side. Next to the computer, which was locked, sat a pen and clipboard. On it was a piece of white paper with two lists written down. On one side were Bernard's accomplishments and commendations. On the other side was a list of all James Dickson's achievements, leading up to his Officer of the Year award.

Felicia saw this, too, and laughed.

'He wants to be cop of the year,' she said.

Striker nodded. 'No big secret there. Bernard always has. Too bad the guy doesn't get it.'

'*Get* it?'

'Yeah, get it.' Striker turned to face her. 'The cops who win that award are never *trying* to win it. They get it, 'cause they're good cops and they do a good job, and eventually they get recognized for it. It's not a checkbox list.'

Felicia looked at the list one more time. 'You never know. Bernard might get it; he is pretty ambitious, after all.'

'Well, let me know when he does. I'll start playing Russian roulette with six bullets.'

The door opened, and Bernard Hamilton walked in. He handed them both a cup of coffee, each with sugar and powdered cream, and they both thanked him for it. Felicia sipped hers; Striker just held the cup.

'So: Dr Erich Ostermann,' he said immediately.

Bernard let out a heavy breath. 'Look, I tried to dig up some stuff on the man, but the file's gone.'

'Gone?'

Bernard nodded. 'Like I said, they got rid of most of the personnel files a while back, after the leak. Department shredded every single one of them.'

Felicia stepped forward. 'But there should still be a copy of Dr Ostermann's employee record,' she said.

'Exactly,' Bernard replied. 'That was what I was looking for, but I can't seem to find it.' He looked around the small office and gestured to the boxes at each corner. 'It's probably here somewhere, but with the move going on, everything seems to be everywhere. Half the boxes are already in storage. I'll keep looking though, and I'll call you if I find something.'

'*When* you find something,' Striker said.

'Sure. When.'

Striker watched Bernard avoid eye contact, and had little faith in ever receiving a phone call from the man. 'So Ostermann's out. What about this Dr Richter?'

Bernard shrugged and raised his hands. 'Same thing. I can't find any of the files right now, not with all this mess around here. For all I know they've already been taken out east.'

'This isn't helping us,' Striker said.

Bernard sighed. 'Look, I know Dr Ostermann well, and I have the utmost respect for the man. He's a good man and he's connected to management – he donates quite heavily to the PMBA, you know. As for this Dr Richter though, I've never heard of him.'

Striker nodded. He took out his notebook and wrote this information down – for the sole purpose of showing Bernard that everything he did was documented. 'We're trying to find Larisa Logan. You ever deal with her?'

For a quick moment, Bernard looked lost. Frozen. His fingers tightened on the Styrofoam cup he was holding. Then he blinked and sipped his coffee.

'The name is familiar,' he said.

'It should be,' Striker said. 'You ran her this morning.'

Bernard said nothing, but his face turned red.

'I know, Bernard. I saw the call.'

'Well, so what if you saw the call?' Bernard threw his cup into the garbage and moved around to the other side of his desk.

'That call should never have been put on the board in the first place. It was *private*. Goddam dispatchers.'

'So what's going on?'

'Nothing's going on.'

'Then why all the sensitivity?'

Bernard sat down at his desk and wiped his brow with the sleeve of his shirt. His long drawn face looked even longer at that moment, and the muscles beneath his sagging skin looked tired and flaccid. 'I can't say too much on this one.'

'Can't, or won't?'

'Both,' he finally said, and the irritation in his voice was audible. 'There are rules, Striker. Privacy issues. *Sensitive* ones.'

'I'm aware of the legal issues.'

Bernard laughed bemusedly. 'Not just legal ones. And not just departmental policy. There's also the Mental Health Board to consider.'

Striker said nothing; he just looked at Felicia, saw the hard expression on her face, and knew that she wasn't falling for the stream of bullshit either. She stepped forward, came right up to the desk, and looked down at Bernard.

'We've gone through all the PRIME files,' she explained, 'and all the CAD calls, too. We know you've been running the woman through the system. But there also seems to be something missing here. Something happening *behind* the scenes. We were hoping your file could connect the dots.'

'Our file?' Bernard said. 'What file?'

'She's had depressive issues,' Striker said. 'Surely, the Mental Health Team—'

'There's nothing here,' Bernard said. He brushed his hand over his ponytail, as if making sure the braid was still in place.

Felicia turned to Striker and frowned. 'The woman's got to have a mental health file,' she said. 'Given what's happened. But

I've been through the database three times. There's nothing there to be seen.'

To be seen.

Her words clicked something in Striker's mind, and he smiled at Felicia.

'I know why,' he said. 'You can't find the file in PRIME because the system won't let you. The file has been hidden. It's *privatized*.'

Thirty-One

There was much to do. Plans – *good* plans – always took time. Preparation. Rehearsals. Risk management.

The Adder took nothing for granted.

The morning sky was finally turning blue when the old clerk from Home Depot shuffled up the walkway in his bright orange work apron and unlocked the front doors. The Adder watched him go, then waited for a few minutes until other customers entered the store. When at least ten had gone in – a high enough number to blend in with as an ordinary shopper – he adjusted his hat, put on his glasses, and entered the store.

He made his way under the harsh artificial lights of the warehouse as the PA system broadcast details of all the great sales that were available today. Something to do with bathroom renovations. He wasn't really listening; his mind was focused on the supply list.

He found Aisle 6: Building Materials, and bought himself one hundred ten-inch wood screws and six steel brackets.

He found the lumber yard and grabbed himself three two-by-sixes, cutting each one into six-foot lengths. Then he found a solid oak door. It was heavy as hell and by far the most expensive item on his list.

Lastly, he picked up five large canisters of Steinman's wood varnish – this was essential.

On his way to the checkouts, he passed the power tool section and stopped. A thought occurred to him. Sound; it was ever so important. He steered his buggy of lumber and supplies into the area and found the cordless drill section. There were many brands to choose from – Bosch and Milwaukee and Ridgid – but each unit was not what he was looking for.

A young sales clerk came over and spoke to him uninvited. 'The DeWalt there has the most power, if that's what you're looking for – 450 unit watts of power. But the Makita has the longest battery life.'

The Adder picked up each of the screw guns and hit the triggers on each, one at a time. He heard the loud, high-pitched whirr of the motors and shook his head. 'No good,' he said. 'I'm looking for one that's *quiet*.'

'Quiet?' the clerk asked.

'Ear problems.'

'Oh, we have hearing protection in Aisle—'

'I'll look through them myself, thanks.'

The clerk nodded, then walked down the aisle to assist another customer. With him gone, the Adder turned back to his task. He took his time, testing each one of the drills. It was the seventh one that made him smile. A simple Black & Decker. Less power than some of the others, but still plenty enough for the task that was required. But most important was the noise level. The Adder hit the trigger and listened to the soft whirr of the motor.

It was almost negligible.

He threw it into the buggy, walked to the checkout and rang his items through. Excluding the door, the cost came to one hundred and ninety-eight dollars and ninety-seven cents. The Adder smiled at that. Less than two hundred bucks.

Not bad for a murder kit.

Thirty-Two

Striker left the mental health office of Car 87 feeling angry and frustrated with the whole situation. Ever since he had joined the Vancouver Police Department, he had noticed that there had been a lack of communication between all of the health emergency services – the police, the paramedics, the fire fighters, the hospitals and psychiatric wards. Although a damned nuisance, it was understandable.

But how in the hell were they supposed to do their job when even their *own* department hid files from them?

It was maddening.

Felicia spoke out loud as she thought it through. 'Larisa was hired by the Vancouver Police Department, not directly by the City. If they've privatized her file, then there's something in it that's obviously considered sensitive.'

Striker agreed with this. Making a file privatized was not out of the ordinary at the department, especially if it concerned a fellow employee. Most of the time it was done out of a matter of respect – the person in the file didn't want co-workers knowing the innermost details of their private life. Making the file privatized locked everyone out from reading it.

At times it made sense.

But Larisa Logan's file had been taken one step further. Not only had the file been privatized, but it been rendered invisible on the system, meaning that only the people with previously granted authorization could even see that the file existed. For all others, it just plain didn't even show up.

This was a process rarely done, and it made Striker wonder: what exactly had happened to Larisa over the past year?

'I've never dealt with one of these files before,' Felicia said. 'How do we even bring it up then?'

'We don't.' Striker gave her a quick glance while driving. 'Management really doesn't like to do that – it brings up a whole lot of privacy issues with the Union and Human Resources. Labour law stuff.'

'Well, someone must have access.'

'They do.'

'Inspector Laroche?' she asked.

Striker laughed at that. 'Are you kidding me? Laroche would do everything in his power *not* to let us see the file. He'd bury it the first chance he got. Last thing he's gonna do is sign off on anything that might open a can of worms on him.'

'Then how are we ever going to see it?'

'We need a higher power than Laroche for this one. Superintendent Brian Stewart.'

Striker headed for 2120 Cambie Street to speak with the superintendent. Stewart was their only hope of gaining quick access to the file. Otherwise, they'd be forced to deal with one of the deputy chiefs.

And that always took time.

Superintendent Stewart's office was on the seventh floor of the Cambie Street headquarters and faced out over the North Shore mountains. When Striker and Felicia knocked on the door, the sun was just cresting the far-away peaks and the entire skyline was awash in a wintertime blue.

It was eight o'clock.

When they entered his office, the superintendent was sitting behind his desk with a pile of ledgers on one side and a stack of handmade notes on the other. In front of him sat a cup of coffee and an empty plate with some leftover pastry on it. He pushed the plate away from his big belly and wiped his moustache for crumbs.

'Morning, sir,' they both said.

'Shipwreck,' he said. 'Wow, it's been a while.'

Felicia gave Striker a surprised look, one the superintendent caught. He explained: 'Your partner and I worked together in our Patrol days. For what – two years?'

'Seemed like two thousand.'

Stewart let loose a deep belly laugh. 'Then Mr Hotshot here went to Homicide.'

Striker gestured to the man's lapels. 'I'm not the one wearing pips.'

Stewart raised an eyebrow. 'Yeah. Well, maybe you were the smart one. God, look at this mess.' He gestured to the mass of paperwork on the desk. 'It's all CompStat. All of it! Goddam meeting after meeting. *Stats* for City Council.'

Striker could have cringed at the thought. He'd been to one CompStat meeting before when he was an acting sergeant for the day. It had been a morning of drudgery as much as trickery. And as Striker soon learned, statistics could be played one way or the other. Some of the inspectors were wizards at it.

Well, they can have it, he thought. As far as Striker was concerned, there were three rooms in hell – the room with lava, the room with knives, and the room where they held CompStat meetings.

Superintendent Stewart stood up from his desk and extended his hand to Felicia. As he did so, his full girth became more noticeable. His belly hung down over his belt, making his hundred pounds of excess body weight apparent and offering an explanation for the ruddiness of his cheeks.

Felicia shook his hand, then took a seat next to Striker.

'So what brings you up to the seventh floor?' Stewart finally said.

Striker explained the whole story, holding nothing back. With every detail, the superintendent's expression hardened. When Striker was done, the jovial mood had completely left the superintendent and he looked every bit the man who suffered from high blood pressure and cholesterol issues.

'Can you bring up the file?' Striker asked.

Stewart rubbed his fingers down the sides of his greying moustache and nodded slowly. 'I can,' he said carefully, but made no move to do so. He looked at the computer screen for a long moment, thinking, then looked back up at Striker and Felicia. 'This normally requires paperwork. How are you planning on using this information?'

'You mean, are we seeking charges?' Striker asked.

'Exactly.'

'No. We're only trying to find Larisa. For her own welfare as much as anything else. So far we're coming up blank. We're hoping that her history will give us something to help track her down – or at least understand what's going on in her head right now. Because otherwise, we're pretty much at a standstill here. And to be honest, I'm worried she might be in danger – if not from something in our investigation, then from herself.'

Stewart nodded. He logged into the system and brought up the file. He then printed it out, slid it into a legal-sized envelope, and handed it to Striker. When Striker grabbed it, the superintendent did not let go.

'I don't have to remind you this is *extremely* sensitive.'

Striker nodded. 'It'll be shredded the moment we're done.'

'You shred it yourself, Shipwreck.'

'Understood, sir.'

Stewart finally let go of the papers, but even as he did, his fingers seemed reluctant. Striker handed the envelope to Felicia, then stood up to leave the office. 'We were never here,' he said.

'I heard nothing,' Stewart replied.

Striker grinned and left the office with Felicia by his side.

Once back in the cruiser, Striker drove a few blocks away from the station and parked beside Jonathon Rogers Park on Manitoba Street. Felicia opened the envelope, removed the papers and read through them. She did so silently, and the waiting made Striker anxious. He got out of the car and used the moment to call home.

Courtney answered on the first ring.

'Hey, Pumpkin.'

Her tone was stilted. 'Were you going through my MyShrine profile?'

Striker frowned; he had expected as much. 'Yes, well, no – it wasn't me. Ich from work had to do it—'

'Oh my GOD, Dad, a guy from your work! I've got my personal stuff on there! I can't believe you did that. It's, like, totally *private*.'

'Look, I'm sorry, but we didn't have a choice.' He explained to her how he had received the message, and it seemed to placate her a little. 'Do you know this guy? This *Adder*?'

'No. I've never heard of the guy before.'

'Well, I don't like it.'

'It's no big deal, Dad. You get tons of people sending you messages all the time and requesting to be your friend. I only add the people I know.'

Striker still wasn't happy with the situation. 'You had your security levels set to minimum, so anyone there could see your pictures.'

'So?'

'So I'm on there. And whoever looks at those photos can connect me to you – I don't want you exposed like that.'

She let out a soft laugh. 'After what happened last year, everyone knows you're my dad.'

Striker nodded as he thought that over. In last year's case, both of their pictures had been plastered all over the internet, on TV, and in the papers. It had been a full-blown media nightmare. Something few people in this city were likely to forget.

'Maybe so,' he finally said. 'But there's no point in making it any easier for them. When this is all done, I want you to remove my photos from your site and keep your privacy settings at maximum.'

'Dad—'

'I mean it.'

'Oh my God, fine – but you're being paranoid.'

'You're sixteen years old and I'm your father – it's my job to be paranoid. Besides, you would be, too, if you knew how many creeps are out there.'

'Like I said, paranoid.'

'What time is it anyway – shouldn't you be on your way to school right now?'

'It's a professional day.'

'Like last week?'

When she didn't answer, Striker forced a laugh, but the tension never left his chest. He reminded Courtney not to touch the computer, to get her ass to school, and to make sure she was on time for her occupational therapy appointment. Then he said goodbye. When he hung up and returned to the car, Felicia had already finished reading the report.

'Well?' he asked. The waiting was eating away at his patience.

She brushed her long dark hair out of her eyes and sighed. 'It's all here in black and white, Jacob. Larisa had a total breakdown.'

'How? Why?'

'There was a motor vehicle accident,' Felicia said. 'Both her parents and her sister were killed in the crash – their car skidded on the ice and went into the oncoming lane. Happened two days before Christmas.'

'The poor girl,' he said.

Felicia met his stare. 'It gets *worse*. Her younger sister was burned badly as a result, and held on for nearly three weeks before succumbing to her injuries. Third-degree burns to eighty per cent of her body.'

Striker thought this over and felt so bad for Larisa. 'No wonder she broke down. So much grief. All three of them.'

'Not just grief. Guilt.'

'Guilt?'

'Larisa was the one driving the car. And she escaped without so much as a scratch. CIU said it was a miracle she lived, much less escaped unharmed.'

CIU. The Collision Investigation Unit.

Striker let this thought settle in, and he felt a tightness spread all through his core. Such a tragedy. He looked over at Felicia. 'Please tell me she wasn't drinking and driving.'

'Not a drop. Stone-cold sober.'

'Thank God.'

'But the report does say that speed was a factor. Larisa was driving too fast for the road conditions. It was wintertime, after all. Icy out. And dark. Happened around eleven o'clock at night, after she'd already worked a long shift.'

'She fall asleep?'

'No one knows – not even Larisa. She couldn't recall anything about the accident. Who knows, maybe that was the beginning of her breakdown.'

'I'll bet it was. Let me see that.'

Striker took the bundle of papers. The words were harsh and it felt like he was being sucked into a real-life nightmare. It was all there, police statement after police statement. Ambulance crew reports. Medical reports. The file was *thick*. And at the end was an addendum from the assistant to the police psychologist.

The name was Richter, and at the top of the page was a stylized MVC:

Mapleview Clinic.

'There it is again,' Striker said. 'Dr Richter. That's the same doctor that gave the prescription to Mandy Gill. That message Larisa left might not be entirely off the mark. She might actually have known Mandy then. The connection is there.'

Felicia shrugged. 'That's not too surprising. The police psychiatrists and psychologists deal with all sorts of mental health problems. And both Mandy Gill and Larisa Logan suffered from depression. They might have met through the counselling sessions at the clinic.'

Striker nodded. 'It just seems awfully coincidental to me. I mean, what are the odds? Mandy Gill is our first file, and we know from her medication that she was given prescriptions by Dr Richter at Mapleview Clinic. Then this whole thing with Larisa goes down, and she was seeing Dr Richter, too.'

'It's not odd,' Felicia said. 'In fact, it's quite the opposite – it makes perfect sense. It's not that they both needed the police because they went to Mapleview; it's that they had mental health problems that Mapleview was dealing with, and those same mental health problems were what brought them police attention.'

Striker said nothing back, he just thought things over.

'The message from Larisa,' he finally said. 'She said she knew Mandy had been murdered.'

'And once again, her message came *after* we'd been seen on TV; she probably saw us, right? Just like you said about the message from this Adder loon. He saw us on TV after the incident occurred, and then reacted. It's standard.'

Striker thought over her logic; she was right about that. And for the first time, he wondered: was his connection to Larisa clouding his judgement?

'Read through the police psychologist report,' Felicia continued. 'It also says that Larisa suffered from paranoia. Some of the medications she was on were to counter that.' She reached out and touched his arm. 'I know you don't like to think this, Jacob, but Larisa isn't the same person you remember. Seeing her family killed like that, it obviously put her over the edge. She had a breakdown. The woman is *sick*.'

Striker nodded. 'I won't deny that. But just because she's sick doesn't mean she doesn't know something. She might have evidence on Mandy's death – it is possible – and if that's the case, then we need to know what. Keep reading through the files. Run every alias and associate the woman has. See if you can find a connection somewhere. Nothing is too small.'

Felicia let out a tired sound, as if she was sick of reviewing the same reports over and over again, but did as requested. Meanwhile, Striker got the phone number of Dr Richter from the details page and called it. The phone rang once then went straight to a standard pre-recorded computer greeting: *The person you are trying to contact is not available . . .*

Striker waited for the beep, then left a message, telling the doctor who he was and that he needed to speak to him about a particular patient. When he finally hung up, Felicia was also finishing reading the reports. She made a *hmm* sound.

Striker looked over. 'What do you mean, hmm?'

'There was an actual CAD call created for Larisa's place, just this morning.'

'This morning, or yesterday morning?'

Felicia looked up. '*This* morning.' She read through the call. 'It was made by Car 87. Bernard Hamilton. So not only did they run her but they went right out there to Larisa's place.'

'They actually attended the residence?'

'Yeah, they're listed as On Scene.' Felicia scanned the call. 'The narrative is basically a shell. There's no information in it. Just a time arriving on scene and then clearing.'

'What kind of call was it?'

'A Check Well-Being.'

'Does it actually show them arriving on scene? By GPS?'

'Yeah, the time was logged.'

Striker frowned. That was the second CAD call created by the mental health car for Larisa Logan. And in just two days. It bothered him, mainly because Bernard Hamilton was not that dedicated a man. If he had attended Larisa's place twice in two days – and at such an early time this morning – there was a good reason for it.

He considered just calling Bernard and asking him outright, but the man could be a snake. Striker wanted to do some of his own digging first, and he wanted to speak to the man in person, not over the phone. Face-to-face meetings always told cops more.

So much communication was non-verbal.

'Where to?' Felicia asked.

Striker cranked the wheel and hit the gas. 'Burnaby,' he said. 'We're going back to Larisa's house. I have a feeling we've missed something.'

Thirty-Three

'I'm liking Bernard Hamilton less and less,' Striker said as he drove across the Boundary Road perimeter and entered the City of Burnaby. 'And I never liked him in the first place, so that says a lot.'

'Maybe he's just respecting Larisa's privacy,' Felicia suggested.

Striker cast her a hard glance. 'Don't kid yourself, Feleesh. Bernard Hamilton does nothing that doesn't serve his own purpose. We're out here trying to save this woman, and he knows that. Yet he's done nothing to help us. If anything, he made things harder.'

He drove up Willingdon, turned east on Parker Street, and made his way down to Larisa's rancher. Seeing it felt odd. The last time he'd been here, it had been night, deep and dark. Now, in the soft hue of the nine o'clock morning light, with pale blue sky backing the lot, the entire place looked different. The vinyl siding was actually painted a dark blue colour, not grey, and the slab of stucco above the vinyl was an off-cream colour, dirtied and worn from time. Inside the front room, the window drapes were pulled shut.

Striker looked at this and frowned.

'Did Car 87 make entry?' he asked.

Felicia skimmed the computer. 'The call says no.'

'Then she's been home.'

He climbed out of the car and felt his shoes slip on the frosted asphalt. When he reached the sidewalk, Felicia got out, too. They hiked up the cement walkway to the front alcove, where Striker hesitated.

The door wasn't closed, like he'd originally thought; it was open a crack. Before leaving last night, he had made sure the door was closed and the entire place locked.

'Be ready,' he told Felicia.

When she nodded and took her position on the left, Striker knocked on the door. Three solid knocks.

'Larisa!' he called out. 'It's Detective Striker from the Vancouver Police Department. It's Jacob. Are you home?'

When no one answered, he pushed the door open and looked inside. The moment he did, the winter wind picked up and pushed the door all the way open. What he saw surprised him.

The place had been torn apart. Looked damn near ransacked. All the coats had been removed from the closet and were lying on the floor, pockets pulled open. All the drawers to the hutch had been pulled out, with the contents of each one dumped on the kitchen floor. And in the living room, all the cushions from the sofa had been torn off and the underside felt cut away.

'*Someone* made entry here,' Striker said. He drew his pistol and stepped inside the foyer; Felicia did the same. Three steps later, he stopped.

'Take the rear,' he said.

'Outside?'

'Yeah. If someone's in here, they're going to fly.'

An uncertain expression formed on Felicia's face. 'We should get another unit here, Jacob. A dog, maybe.'

'There's no time.'

'But—'

'I can clear the place, Feleesh, just take the rear.'

'No,' she said. 'You need two people. It's not safe.'

Striker said nothing for a moment, he just met her stare, saw that her mind was made up, and he nodded.

'Okay, together then, but now.'

She nodded.

They moved throughout the house, calling out police presence as they went. What they found in the kitchen and bedroom was no different to what they'd found in the living room. It had been torn apart – drawers opened, cupboards searched, and everything dumped on the floor. Left on the ground was everything from money and jewellery to papers and underwear.

In the office, the filing cabinet had been emptied. Everything had been rifled through, yet nothing had been damaged.

It was a *search*, not a mischief.

Striker made a mental note of what they saw, room by room.

They cleared the entire place. Made sure no one was still there, hiding in one of the closets, or in the crawl space. They even checked the attic. Then, when they were certain no one was left in the house, Felicia called Dispatch and had a call created for a Break and Enter.

She hung up and looked around at the mess of the living room. 'It doesn't look like anything's been taken,' she noted. 'You know, this might not be a Break and Enter. This might be more of Larisa's mental breakdown.'

Striker met her stare. 'You think Larisa did all this?'

She shrugged. 'Maybe. Who knows what her state of mind is right now? The house was a pigsty when we got here yesterday. Cupboards were open then. Papers left lying about. Clothes everywhere. Today is the same, only worse.'

Striker shook his head. 'Not this. This is different.'

Felicia just looked around and studied the room. 'I'm playing devil's advocate here. But you've got to admit, she's been doing a lot of weird stuff lately.'

'Someone else was here, Feleesh. And whoever they were, they were looking for something *important*.' He moved through the living room and studied the contents dumped out of the drawers. On the carpet, in the middle of the floor, was an open DVD case. It caught his attention.

It was empty.

He looked around, saw no disc, then moved back to the office. On the floor in the office were more empty cases. He looked all around the room and again could not find the missing discs.

'He took the DVDs,' he said. 'The DVDs are the only thing I can see missing.'

Felicia looked around the place, then frowned. 'Lots of things don't add up here, Jacob.'

'Like what?'

'Like Larisa running, for one. I mean, I can see her running from a home invader, or even the psychiatric ward, but not from *us*. Think about it. You're her friend; she was calling you. Asking for your help. So why not just come forward to the police if she knows something? Why run?'

Striker put his pistol back into its holster as he thought this over. Larisa running. Bernard acting all strange. Coming to her place. Twice, in fact.

A sinking feeling hit him in the chest.

'I got an idea why,' he finally said.

Thirty-Four

Despite the bad traffic and icy road conditions, they made the drive from Larisa's house in Burnaby all the way down to the Main Street headquarters in less than twenty minutes. Once on scene, they parked out back in the east lane – only rookies parked out front; that was where every complainant waited for the next poor patrol guy to appear.

They walked past the annexe and into the main building, then took the stairs up to the third floor. The concrete walls were painted a God-awful yellow colour. It was supposed to make the building brighter, more cheery, but there was no colouring up this place. It was one huge, depressing slab, and the paint looked like piss.

Striker had always hated it.

He reached the third floor. This was the primary information area. Records. Crown Liaison. CPIC – the Canadian Police Information Center. Transcription. And of course, Warrants.

Striker fished the key from his pocket. All the other doors in the building had been upgraded with the swipe-card system, but not here. This door still used the old-fashioned lock and key, and half the time, the lock was buggered. Striker slid the key in, fiddled with the lock, then yanked the heavy door open.

Inside, the floor was covered with brown threadbare carpet. Matching this were tinted brown windows on every wall. Above their heads, bare fluorescent tubes hummed in the cold winter air. Felicia squinted against the glare of one of them and cursed. 'The quicker they demolish the building, the better,' she said. 'Why the hell are we here anyway?'

'To see Lilly.'

'Lilly? That old battleaxe? God, why?'

'Confirmation.'

Before she could ask more, Striker walked ahead, circling Records and bypassing the other units, most of which were nothing more than ramshackle cubicles with inkjet-printed signs: TRANSCRIPTION. CPIC. CROWN.

As always, the entire floor was busy with people running this way and that, and the never-ending sound of keyboard clicks and phone trills filled the air. The floor was run entirely by women, and the high-pitched chatter of female voices was like backdrop music.

When they reached Warrants, Striker spotted Lilly. As always, her hair was brushed too high and she had plastered on too much make-up – a common occurrence that seemed to be worsening with every new-found wrinkle on her face.

They reached her cubicle, but Lilly ignored them and kept typing. When Striker cleared his throat and asked, 'Still happy as always, Sunshine?' she looked up with a pissed-off expression covering her face. Then, as recognition filled her eyes, she stopped typing and smiled.

'Well, I shoulda known trouble was coming. Got my period first thing this morning.'

'So I'm off the hook then?'

Lilly snorted more than laughed, and Striker moved up to the cubicle. He pushed the drop-off bins out of the way and leaned his arm on the top of the counter. Lilly glanced at the drop-off bins and scowled.

'Knock those off and I'll knock you off,' she said.

Felicia crossed her arms in irritation, but Striker just smiled, amused.

Lilly was an old-timer up here. Pushing sixty-five, she had long since passed the eighty-factor quota required in order for her to retire with a full pension. Still, she hung around in this dingy office, chugging away like an old diesel engine that refused to break down.

In the harsh, artificial light of the office, her face looked tired. Her eyelids drooped down over her cold blue eyes and her hair, which was sometimes dyed brown or even red, had grown long enough to show grey roots.

'What do ya want, Shipwreck?' she asked.

'Warrants. The freshest you got.'

When Lilly gestured to the bin, Striker made an *uh-uh* sound. 'The freshest, Lilly. And not just the criminal ones – I want them all.'

She made a weary sound, then struggled to her feet. 'You're always work,' she said. 'Wait here.' She grabbed her cane – required ever since her hip surgery – and wandered off down the hall.

Striker watched her go and smiled; Lilly never changed.

'God, she's a miserable old witch,' Felicia said.

'Hey, be nice. That's just Lilly.'

'No, that's just you – making excuses for everyone. Like you always do. She's a hag, half the time. And she's well past her retirement factor. Why doesn't she just quit, for God's sake?'

Striker turned to face Felicia. 'Because she has nowhere else to go in her life. No kids. No family. And her husband died six years ago. Lilly doesn't even have a dog. This is it for her. If she ever left here, what would she do?'

'Get a life maybe. Take some personality classes.'

Striker said nothing back. Felicia was right, in part; Lilly could be grumpy and annoying and even overbearing at times. But the woman had a good heart. You just needed to know how to melt the layers of ice around it.

He was about to say more when Lilly came hobbling back. Her face was tight and her hip looked to be paining her. When she reached the cubicle she muttered, 'Here,' and slammed the pile of papers down on the counter. 'Any fresher and I'd have to slap it.'

Striker picked up the pile and started paging through it.

'What are you looking for?' Felicia asked.

'Larisa Logan.' He handed her half the stack. 'Get looking.'

'In warrants? She may have issues, but she's no crook, Jacob.'

'I know that, Feleesh. Just look.'

Felicia said nothing more. She licked her thumb, then started paging through the different warrants. They were both halfway done when she made a surprised sound and held up one of the papers.

'I got it. She's right here.'

Striker put down the stack of papers he was sifting through and moved closer to Felicia. He scanned the top of the warrant and found the words he was looking for: *Form 21.*

He pointed this out to Felicia.

'A Director's Warrant?' she said.

He nodded. Now it all made sense.

A Director's Warrant was the medical equivalent of an arrest warrant. Essentially, it gave police the legal right – and the *duty* – to apprehend someone under the Mental Health Act. A Form 21 meant that a psychiatrist had ordered one of their patients to be returned to their care for further mental health assessment. Which, half the time, was politically correct jargon for imprisoning and medicating the hell out of them.

To Striker, the Form 21 signified one thing. It was proof that Larisa had gone over the edge – so far, that her own doctor believed she was now possibly a threat to herself or to others.

It made him deflate a little.

'This is why she's run away from us,' he said. 'She knows about the medical warrant. It's why she wants our help but won't come forward.'

Felicia nodded. 'Because the second we see her, we have to apprehend her and take her back to the hospital.'

'Not just any hospital,' Striker corrected. '*Riverglen.*'

'The insane asylum.'

'Mental Health Facility,' Striker corrected. 'Gotta be PC nowadays.'

Felicia raised an eyebrow. 'New term, same old shit.'

Striker agreed, even if he didn't say it. 'No matter what route Larisa takes, she loses. And she obviously realizes this, otherwise she'd come in to see us.'

'It also means she's unstable, Jacob.'

Striker took the warrant, photocopied it, and returned it to the fresh warrants bin. When he turned around, Felicia had a lost look on her face.

'What's wrong?' he asked.

'I ran her in the car,' she said. 'None of this came up.'

Striker nodded. 'Because it hasn't been entered in the system yet. CPIC can be up to six weeks behind at times.'

'Six *weeks?*'

Striker gave her an irritated glance. 'Yes, six weeks. Sometimes more. Jesus Christ, Felicia, get your head in the game. You should already know this. What are you, a homicide detective or some piss-kid rookie?'

Felicia said nothing back, but her cheeks flushed red. 'You need to seriously chill out, Jacob,' she finally said. 'Take a pill.'

Striker barely heard her. 'Most warrants aren't walked through the courts,' he continued. 'Only when there's been a history of violence. And Larisa hasn't tried to hurt herself or anyone else, so it won't be expedited.'

'She hasn't tried to hurt anybody *yet.*'

Striker turned and said goodbye to Lilly, then gave Felicia a curt nod and headed back down the narrow corridor of brown threadbare carpet. Before heading out through the exit, he ran right into Bernard Hamilton. The man stopped hard, looked surprised to see him, then put on his usual waxy smile.

'Striker, Santos. How goes the battle?'

Striker didn't bother to step out of his way. 'I know about the warrant, Bernard.'

Bernard Hamilton kept the smile on his face, but his expression tightened. 'What warrant?'

'The Form 21. Which tells me *why* you were out at Larisa's place last night and this morning. And why you created the CAD call. You want to apprehend her yourself – even though you know what we've been doing here. You're trying to pad your goddam stats.'

The smile fell from Bernard's lips. 'What I'm trying to do here, Striker, is locate one of our patients – for her own well-being.'

'Her own well-being? Really? You gonna seriously hide behind that?' Striker took a step closer to the man. 'Tell me, Bernard. Why didn't you inform us of the warrant when we saw you this morning? You knew we were looking for her.'

'I . . . I didn't know at the time—'

'The warrant came out last night. Car 87 gets first knowledge of anything related to mental health. So you of all people would have known *first.*'

Bernard's face reddened. 'There's privacy issues here.'

'Since when do privacy issues supersede protection of life?'

'I'm not getting into this.'

'No, you wouldn't, would you, Bernard? What does a woman's life matter when compared to your apprehension statistics?'

Hamilton's eyes darkened. 'Larisa Logan has a warrant out for her. She needs to be taken into custody. It's as simple as that.'

'Which would have happened already if you hadn't screwed us.' When Bernard's face took on a confused look, Striker grew angry. 'Larisa Logan was waiting to see me when you tried to nab her. Now she thinks I called you there. She thinks I screwed her. And she's out there on the fly because of it. Good job, Bernard. Top ten as always.'

'I . . . never knew—'

'You would have, if you had even bothered to ask.'

Bernard offered nothing back, and Striker just stared at the man. After a short moment, Felicia touched Jacob's arm to get him moving. He shrugged her hand away.

'One more thing, Bernard. Anything happens to Larisa, and I'm going to make damn sure that everyone in this department knows just how badly you screwed this. How you put your stats ahead of her protection. You got that? We'll see how far your bid for Cop of the Year goes after that.'

Bernard's eyes widened at the comment, and Striker finally moved out of his way. Without looking at Bernard, or even Felicia, Striker stormed down the hall, kicked open the door, and made his way down the stairs.

Everything had just gotten a whole lot more complicated.

Thirty-Five

Time was important, the Adder knew. Everything was progressing quickly. The items were prepared, all packed away and ready to go. And the van was filled with gas, the keys already in the ignition. It was parked, unseen, under the overhang of a weeping willow tree, at the end of a nearby dead-end lane.

He went over his checklist.

Leather mask. *Check*. Leather gloves. *Check*. Latex gloves. *Check*.

Video equipment ... *No*.

The thought caused a frown to form on his face. How could he forget that? The camera was the most important thing.

He returned to his dwelling, opened the hatch in the floor, and climbed down the ladder into his home. When he reached the concrete below, he beelined for the east side of the room. On the wall hung a print of M.C. Escher's *Relativity* – where people walked up and down stairs in all directions, in a world where gravity made no sense.

The Adder loved the image. However, his taste in art was not what made him buy the piece. What made him buy it was the size of the lithograph.

He reached out, grasped hold of the frame, and removed the picture from the wall. There behind it was an odd-sized door, two feet wide and three feet tall. Thin, made from wood.

An old dumbwaiter. It had been built God knows how long ago, and had long since been boarded up.

The Adder opened the door. Inside was the passageway leading up between the floors. It went all the way to the top of the house. Up there, the Adder knew – for he had rebuilt the system himself – were two strong platforms, each one less than one foot wide and two feet deep. The base of each was built on rollers, which rose and fell when the cords were pulled.

The Adder reached inside and grasped the cord. When he pulled it, the first unseen platform descended silently from above, revealing the array of electronic equipment. He removed the items he needed for the job.

Camera.

Relay.

Computer box with digital receiver.

And, of course, the back-up external hard drive. He *always* had a back-up drive. Because the thought of losing even one precious moment of the Beautiful Escape was horrifying and left him cold.

He took all the equipment out, placed it in the black leather duffel bag, and dropped it by the door. Then he raised the dumbwaiter once more, closed the door, and placed the painting back over it.

Almost set.

He crossed the room to the west side, to the only other door the room owned, and opened it. Inside was a small bathroom with a toilet and a shower but no bath. The Adder took off his clothes, revealing the marks on his back and legs – the unsightly welts he had received as part of his punishments – and turned on the water.

It was cold. Freezing cold – there was no hot water down

here; never had been – but that was okay. He took the bar of soap from the rack and vigorously brushed it through his hair and across every inch of skin. Then he grabbed the horsehair brush and did the same, pressing hard, scraping it against his skin until the flesh turned pink.

He did this every time in preparation for a job. It was a necessary part of the routine.

By the time he was done, some twenty minutes later, he was chilled to the bone and his welted skin stung like it had been sandpapered raw. He climbed out of the shower, dried himself off, and redressed in a brand-new pair of unworn black jogging pants and a matching black hoodie.

One more thing.

And perhaps the most important of all.

He crossed the room to the cabinet where his computer sat, and logged on. He started the Private Search program, then navigated to his MyShrine site. Once he had logged on, he began typing. The message was brief, direct, and aimed well:

. . . I saw them first in Afghanistan and Kandahar. In human form. They came in rows, wave after wave of masks.

But I KNEW what they were. The other soldiers may have been blind, but not me. I saw through the shells. And I took them all down. A soldier. An emissary. The HAMMER OF GOD!!!

Then I was, as I am today.

There is only one way to kill a daemon. A goddam Succubus. And that is through the heart.

You're moving downward. Into the mouth of hell, Hero. Can you kill your daemons?

I know I can mine . . .

The Adder

The Adder stopped typing. Read the message over.

And was content.

He hit the Send button and then logged off. Sometime today, Detective Striker would receive the warning. But would he get it soon enough? And would he make use of it?

It did not matter. Not in the end.

The Adder set up the KillDisk program. One wrong password and the entire hard drive would be deleted and then formatted. He logged off the computer and shut it down. Got up from the chair and headed for the ladder to the hatch above. The day may have been young, but there was still much work to do.

Thirty-Six

The Form 21 – the medical warrant sent out by a director, who was almost always a psychiatrist – was signed at the very bottom. Striker sat in the driver's seat of their vehicle and tried to make out the name, but it seemed damn near impossible. He would've had a better chance of reading hieroglyphics. He handed the warrant to Felicia.

'Can you make any sense of this?'

She took it, scanned it over, then shook her head. 'Chicken scratches. I think it's a prerequisite to being a doctor – the inability to write legibly.'

'It's a joke is what it is,' Striker said. 'Can you imagine if we submitted court notes like this? Defence would *freak*. What's the point in having someone sign a warrant if you can't even make out their signature? I can't tell if it's Ostermann or Richter.'

'Or Dr Phil.'

'Should be Kevorkian, the way I'm feeling now.'

Felicia let out a soft laugh.

Striker started the car and got the heat going. 'I'm sick of hearing the names Ostermann and Richter,' he said. 'I left a message for Richter, but as for Ostermann, he still hasn't gotten back to us on this whole Billy patient of his. What time is it?'

Felicia checked her watch. 'Ten.'

'That's late enough,' he said.

He dialled Dr Ostermann's cell number and got the message system. Then he tried Riverglen and was told that Dr Ostermann didn't start until noon on Thursdays. Finally, he dialled the home number. Again, he got voicemail.

'Screw it,' he said. He put the car into Drive and hit the gas.

They headed for the Endowment Lands.

Rush hour was still going strong, but the worst of it was thinning. The drive from 312 Main to Point Grey usually took about twenty minutes. They were only ten minutes into the drive when Felicia spoke up.

'Stop by 'bucks, will you?'

'Starbucks? What if we miss Ostermann?'

Felicia shook her head. 'The guy doesn't start till twelve; we got lots of time.' She gestured to the long stretch of West 4th Avenue. 'Besides, if he's going to go to work, he's got to come down this stretch of road. We'll see his X5 a mile off.'

When Striker said nothing and kept driving, Felicia gave him a jab in the arm. 'Really, Jacob, just a quick one to go. I'm dying for some caffeine.'

'Fine,' he relented.

When they reached the twenty-two hundred block of West 4th Avenue, he pulled over and Felicia darted across the road. He watched her go. As she crossed in the morning sun, she glanced back at him and smiled.

He couldn't help but smile back. When she disappeared through the glass doors of the coffee shop, a sense of gloom came over him, and he felt bad for giving her hell back in the Warrants section. He wondered if he had really been mad at her for not knowing the time-delay issues with CPIC, or if he was really just mad about her not staying the night.

Now, he wasn't so sure.

He sat and thought about that.

Five minutes later, when she returned with a latte for herself and the usual Americano for him, Striker took it and thanked her. He cast her a quick glance. She had vanilla milk foam on her upper lip, and he reached out and wiped it away.

'Look, I'm sorry,' he started.

She looked back with a lost expression. 'Sorry? For what?'

'Back there. At 312. I shouldn't have given you shit about the warrants. Calling you a piss-kid rookie. I was out of line.'

She met his stare. 'You've been testy all morning. I thought maybe it was Bernard.'

'It was. I guess. I dunno.'

'Then why take it out on me?'

'I wasn't trying to take it out on you.'

'Sure felt that way.'

'Well, I can't help the way you *feel*, Feleesh.'

'Obviously.'

Striker frowned. What had started out as an apology was fast turning into a tense moment. He put the car into Drive, did a quick shoulder check, and pulled back out into traffic. When Felicia added, 'You don't know how I feel sometimes because you're not exactly sensitive to it,' Striker felt his frustration growing.

He cast her another glance while driving. 'And you know what, Feleesh? Sometimes you're not sensitive to the fact that I'm the lead on our cases. In fact, you outright begrudge it.'

'I do not.'

'You *do*. Yet the reason I am the lead is because of things like what happened back there in Warrants – I'm senior here not only because I've got more time on the road than you, but because of the experience that comes with it. That's why I know things. Like the delay with the Form 21s.'

Felicia's eyes had a flash of fire. 'I don't ever *begrudge* you being the lead in our partnership, Jacob. What I begrudge is you having a condescending attitude sometimes. I begrudge you assigning me to menial tasks instead of having me assist you in the real meat of the investigation. And I begrudge you talking *at* me instead of *to* me.'

'I do not talk *at* you.'

'You do, and you don't even see it. You often treat me like I'm some civilian here to take statements for you and drop your evidence off at the lab. Well, I'm not a civilian, Jacob. I'm a *cop*. A homicide detective, no less. And when you don't treat me like one, yes, I do begrudge it.'

Striker turned on to Northwest Marine Drive and continued west. 'I guess we'll agree to disagree then.'

'What else is new? Once again Jacob Striker has the final say.'

He gave her a hot look. 'Well, you know what I begrudge? You uprooting my life. One minute, you're close and with me, the next moment you're gone and running.'

She looked back at him for a long moment with a look of shock on her face, then her expression hardened. 'Are we talking about our professional life here, or our personal life?'

'Is there a difference any more?'

'And you wonder why it failed,' she said.

'Yeah. Well, just don't run out on me *professionally*, if things get too hard one day here, too.'

'That's not fair.'

'You're right. It's *not* fair.'

He made a hard turn at Belmont Avenue, so hard the tyres slipped on the frosty street. He drove a half-block down. On the right-hand side sat a huge lot, gated, with tons of maple and Japanese plum trees.

The Ostermann house.

The front gate was already open. So was the front door.

Striker pulled the car inside the gate and parked on the roundabout. When he shut off the engine and stepped out of the car, the girl with long black hair and pale skin walked out of the front door. She spotted them and stopped short, her face turning hard.

She said nothing to them.

'Good morning,' Striker offered. 'It's Dalia, right?'

The girl said nothing at first, she just looked back at him with a cold empty stare. Striker didn't like it. Her eyes seemed damn near vacuous. Disconnected. He gave Felicia a quick glance, which she returned.

'Yes, Dalia,' the girl finally said, her voice low and neutral.

She bundled up her coat, a long black lambskin number that came down to her knees, then tied the accompanying sash. After looking back inside the house, she turned around and fixed them with a stare that suggested she was surprised to see them still standing there.

'Is your father home?' Striker asked.

'The Doctor is out.'

Striker found her wording odd. Not *Dad* or *my father*. It was *the Doctor*.

He moved up the walkway to be closer to the girl, and Felicia joined him, flanking Dalia from the opposite angle. At this closer distance, the girl looked different. For one, she had tons of make-up plastered all over her face. Her skin was pale, no doubt. Practically ghostly. But the concealer made her look one step away from being a modern-day vampire. When Striker took a closer look, he saw that beneath the white make-up, there were blemishes – as if her skin was marred in some way, bruised. Below her right eye. And near her chin. Like she'd been smacked a few times.

She caught his stare and turned away, hiding her face.

'I will tell him you came by,' she said over her shoulder.

Felicia was the first to speak. 'Where is your father?'

'At work.'

Before they could ask more, Lexa Ostermann walked out through the front door. She was buttoning up the long coat she wore, and upon seeing them, she stopped. For a moment, her face remained expressionless, but then her natural graces took over once more. She looked past Felicia, directly at Striker, and smiled.

'Well, it is a good morning, I see.'

Striker smiled. 'Good morning yourself, Mrs Ostermann.'

'It's *Lexa*, for you,' she said.

'What should I call you?' Felicia cut in. Her voice was dry, business-like.

Lexa only smiled at her, said nothing, then turned her attention back to Striker. 'Please, from now on don't be so formal.'

'I'll try to remember that,' he said.

She stepped right into his personal space and stared into his face. When she smiled, she looked ten years younger, Striker noticed, and that magnetism pulled at him.

'How are you?' he asked. 'Last night you seemed a little . . . tense when we left.'

The smile on Lexa's face remained, but her lips tightened and her eyes got a faraway look in them. 'So what brings you out my way, Detective Striker?'

Felicia stepped forward. 'Sorry to break up this scene from *The Bridges of Madison County*, but we're here to speak with your husband.'

Lexa's cheeks reddened from the comment. 'Oh. I'm . . . I'm sorry. You missed him.'

'Missed him?' Striker asked.

'Yes, he had much to do today, I'm afraid. He left far earlier than usual. Around six o'clock, I think. Didn't Dalia tell you?'

Dalia, who had been standing there silently, said nothing. She then took the opportunity to make herself scarce. Without so much as a word, she slipped in between the group, crossed the driveway in front of the undercover police car, and hopped into the passenger side of a green Land Rover.

'Quite the chatterbox,' Felicia noted.

Lexa said nothing. She looked back at Striker and put on her best smile. 'I will tell Erich you came by the moment I see him, Detective Striker.'

'And when will you see him?' Felicia persisted.

Lexa's eyes never left Striker's. 'In a few hours. I'll see him at the clinic.'

That made Striker blink. 'What clinic?' he asked.

'Why, Mapleview, of course.'

'Mapleview? I didn't think your husband worked there. You mean, you work together?'

She nodded softly. 'Yes. Well, now we do. It's how Erich and I met, actually – through our professions. Long ago, before Erich even started the EvenHealth programme, I was a psych nurse at Riverglen.'

Striker thought this over. 'Riverglen, huh? Interesting. But you no longer work there?'

'No, now I do more private than public work. The pay is better, the hours are less and, more importantly, it's all day shifts now. I stopped pulling nights after I turned forty. It was just too hard – though, with your profession, I'm sure I don't need to tell you that.'

Striker raised an eyebrow. 'I know nights.'

'I bet you do.'

Felicia stepped forward to get Lexa's attention. 'When *exactly* are you going to see your husband, Mrs Ostermann?'

'Well, when he gets to the clinic.'

'Which will be?'

'Sometime this afternoon, I would guess. Erich usually does his paperwork in our home office Thursday mornings. The rest of the week, he spends the mornings at Riverglen. He avoids the worst of the rush-hour traffic that way – coming back from Coquitlam at the end of the day can be a real grind.'

'But he did end up going to Riverglen today?' Striker asked.

'Yes, but he should be at Mapleview after two or so.'

'We can't wait till then,' Striker said to Felicia. 'We'll have to head out there to see him.'

At hearing this, Lexa made an uncomfortable sound. She took in a deep breath and her face turned hard. She looked directly at Striker. 'Erich doesn't like being disturbed when he's in the middle of his work – he takes it very, very seriously.'

'So do we,' Felicia said dryly. 'Suicides and missing people are generally rated fairly high on our list.'

Lexa Ostermann didn't so much as acknowledge the comment. She kept her eyes focused on Striker and continued speaking. 'I only ask that you don't . . . *upset* him right now. Erich is under a lot of pressure with his caseload at Riverglen, not to mention all the private work he's doing with EvenHealth. He's very tired. And he's stressed out. He hasn't been sleeping well of late, so he upsets rather easily.'

'I'll do my best to keep things on the level,' Striker assured her.

Lexa nodded as if she was grateful for this, but her expression remained one of concern.

Striker felt for the woman. He said goodbye to Lexa, and they returned to the car. They climbed inside, backed out of the driveway, and then reversed so Lexa and Dalia could drive their Land Rover out of the front gate.

The last thing Striker saw before leaving was the look on Dalia's face through the windshield. Her expression was as hard as rock and her eyes were cold and empty and seemed very far away.

'Something's wrong with that kid,' Felicia said.

Striker knew it, too. He felt it deep down in his chest.

Thirty-Seven

The mental health centre known as Riverglen was old, having been built in the early nineteen hundreds. Fresh layers of white paint had been added to the old wood trim of the windows, and the crumbling blocks of surrounding red brick had been spray-washed clean. But no matter how much work the government put into the hospital, no matter how hard the politicians tried to make the facility look like a modern-day, healthy and happy place to live, an air of despair cloaked the facility, as visible as the storm clouds that were sweeping in from the north.

This was Riverglen – an institution for the mentally ill. It was listed under the government's Mental Health and Addiction Services, for those who bothered to look for it.

Felicia pointed to the belfry high atop the central roof. 'Gives me the creeps, this place,' she said.

Striker nodded. 'Right below that is where they gave people the shock-treatment therapy.' The moment he said the words, he regretted them. Felicia already had a problem with these places, he didn't want to make it worse.

'I hate this place,' she said softly. 'My grandmother was brought here, way back in the days when everyone called it The Hallows. The things they did to make her *better*. Christ. They drugged her, strapped her down, gave her electric shocks. I don't remember much of it – I was so little then – but I remember enough. Like her hair falling out from the stress, and her body turning rake thin.'

'I had no idea,' Striker said.

Felicia looked over at Striker and her eyes were hard. 'She was a lot better off before ever going in here. And once she was committed, she never left. It was a tragedy.'

'Psychiatry's gotten a whole lot better since then,' Striker offered.

But Felicia didn't seem moved by the comment. She glared at the building before her, then shuddered. Striker parked the car, gave her a nod and they climbed out.

Outside, the wind from the Pitt River funnelled into the hospital grounds and caused the bushes flanking the walkway to flap and flutter. Felicia bundled up her long charcoal coat and marched ahead. Striker joined her. Together, they hiked up the old stone steps of the entrance and stepped between a giant pair of freshly painted white pillars before entering the foyer of the mental hospital.

Riverglen.

They had arrived.

Inside, the place was no different. An aura of despair filled the halls. Once past the front security station, Striker and Felicia were led by a guard to the east wing of the facility, then down a long narrow corridor towards the office of Dr Erich Ostermann.

Striker took note of their surroundings as they went. The walls were high, easily ten feet, and the windows were small, allowing little natural light to break the gloom and offering absolutely no view of the land outside. Just being there was depressing.

'This place is fucking barbaric,' Felicia said.

The guard, a short fat guy who looked to be in his mid-fifties, gave them a queer look when he heard the comment, but Striker just nodded at the man, and they all kept going.

The office of Dr Ostermann was located in the corner of an L-shaped hallway. In the east wing, leading off the hallway, was an entirely separate room – a common area where several patients were sitting, dressed in pale blue gowns.

Striker looked into the room. It was small, rectangular and, unlike the halls, had natural light and even a few windows over-looking the mountains to the north. Some of the patients were playing backgammon. Some were reading books and talking in pods. But most of them were huddled around an old tube TV in the far corner of the room. On the TV was a cooking show.

The whole scene reminded Striker of an old folks' home. As they waited for Dr Ostermann to return, Striker watched the patients.

In the nearest corner, a group of four people were playing cards. One of the participants, a tall thin white guy who looked like he hadn't shaved in days, suddenly stood up from the table and yelled out, 'Fuck you, you FUCKERS!' He ripped off his shirt and threw it on the floor.

Striker looked at Felicia, saw the tense look on her face.

'Strip poker?' he asked.

Before she could even respond, one of the security guards stood up from his station in the corner of the room and called out, '*Henry!* You'd better calm down over there. I mean it!'

The man was unafraid. 'He's got a knife at the table!' he cried out. 'A knife! Can't have that – it's against the rules, it's DANGEROUS!'

The guard looked over at the table, saw the paper plates and bran muffins, the squares of butter and plastic knives. 'It's okay, Henry. It's all fine. He's allowed to have that one. It's plastic. So just *relax.*'

'It's DANGEROUS!'

'Just be good and I'll give you some of your favourite snacks again.'

'M&Ms?'

'I promise,' the guard said.

'Peanut?'

'Of course.'

Henry didn't respond at first; he just gave the guard a hot stare, stuck out his jaw, and then finally put his shirt back on. He left the other patients playing their card game and hung out by himself near the room entranceway. He turned his eyes towards Striker and Felicia, and caught their stares.

'What the fuck you two lookin' at?'

Striker said nothing; Felicia just grabbed his arm and turned him away.

'Don't provoke him,' she said. 'He's mentally ill.'

Striker wasn't planning on it. Before he could respond, a woman behind them asked, 'Can I help you two?'

They both turned to face her.

Seated at the reception desk in front of Dr Ostermann's office was a woman dressed in an all-white hospital uniform. She looked thirty or so, and harsh, with her hair pulled back into a tight bun and little to no make-up on her face. She did not smile.

With Henry still ranting behind them, Striker approached the desk. 'Detectives Striker and Santos,' he explained. He showed the woman his badge and credentials. 'We're here to speak with Dr Ostermann.'

She still did not smile. 'Did you book an appointment?'

'For an asylum?' he asked. 'No, we didn't.'

The woman's face tightened – her first sign of any emotion. 'We don't call it that any more,' she corrected. 'This is a mental health facility.' She leafed through a ledger on her desk and made an unhappy sound. 'Dr Ostermann is in session for another twenty minutes. Until eleven. And after that he has to be at his personal practice by twelve . . . I don't know if he'll be able to fit you in today.'

'He can and will,' Striker said. 'He knows we're coming. I talked to him yesterday.'

'I was never informed of this.'

Felicia's face darkened. 'So there's some things in this world you don't know?' she asked.

Striker offered the woman a smile. 'I'm sure it just slipped his mind.'

The woman showed no reaction to the words. She just gestured to a row of seats along the far wall. 'Sit there. I'll let the doctor know you're waiting for him.'

Striker looked over at the door to Dr Ostermann's office. He walked across the room, grabbed the handle, and opened it.

'Sir! Sir! *Detective!*' the receptionist called.

Striker played ignorant. 'Yes?'

'Out here, please.'

'Oh, sorry. I thought you wanted us to wait inside his office.'

'No.'

Striker sat down next to Felicia, who craned her neck and grinned at him.

'Nice try, Sherlock.'

He said nothing back. He just sat next to her, breathed in deeply and smelled the vanilla perfume she always wore. The scent filled his head with other memories, enjoyable ones, and he tried not to think about it. He focused instead on a way to get inside the office.

They waited for another five minutes, until the receptionist got up from her desk. 'I'll be back in a moment,' she said. She offered no further explanation, and disappeared down the hallway. Striker waited for her to disappear around the corner. Then he stood up.

'What are you doing?' Felicia asked.

'Magic,' he said.

He walked over to the wall, leaned against it, then made a soft whistling sound. In the common room, Henry was still muttering to himself about the knives being too dangerous. He heard the whistle and looked over.

This time, Striker did not look away. Instead, he smiled at the man, winked, and whispered, 'Look at what I got.' Then he brushed the tail of his jacket to the side, revealing the pistol holstered beneath. 'I *snuck* it in here.'

Henry let out a loud gasp. 'You can't have that in here!'

Striker thumbed the release button and slid out the magazine. He popped out a bullet, reloaded it, then slid the magazine back into the gun. He looked back at Henry.

'Got three full mags.'

'You can't have those – they're *dangerous!*'

'Real dangerous.'

'It's against the rules!'

'I don't follow the rules.'

Henry's face darkened and he started to tremble all over. 'YOU CAN'T HAVE THAT IN HERE – IT'S DANGEROUS!' he bellowed. He stepped forward and kicked one of the chairs, just as the receptionist returned. She let out a gasp and dropped her coffee cup as the chair went sliding across the floor and slammed into the door, rattling the safety glass.

'Henry, calm down!' she ordered. '*Calm down!*'

'HE CAN'T HAVE THAT IN HERE! CAN'T HAVE IT! IT'S FUCKING DANGEROUS!'

The guards came rushing over, took custody of Henry, and

quickly escorted him back to his room in an effort to maintain calmness in the area.

But the damage was done. The other patients were already leaving their card games and backgammon tournament, and the TV had lost its appeal. Striker turned to face the receptionist.

'I'm sorry,' he said. 'I stood up to stretch and I guess he saw the gun. He just *freaked*.' He glanced around the area. 'Jesus, they all look angry now.'

The receptionist looked at the spilled coffee on the floor, then at the mass of patients mustering near the doorway. 'Perhaps . . . perhaps it would be best if you did wait inside the office, after all.'

Striker smiled at the woman and held up his hands.

'Whatever you think is best,' he said.

Thirty-Eight

The moment the receptionist allowed them inside Dr Ostermann's office and shut the door behind them, Felicia looked over at him and a grin spread her lips.

'That was terrible,' she said.

Striker just shrugged. 'I know, and believe me I'm not proud of it, but we had no choice. We needed to get in here before Ostermann got back. We *need* to know who this Billy guy is. It's as simple as that.' He looked at his watch and saw that it was ten-fifty now. 'What time she say his session ended?'

'Eleven – and that's if he doesn't finish early.'

Striker frowned at that. Ten minutes wasn't a lot of time. He looked around the room. To his surprise, the office was fairly barren. He'd expected to see medical diplomas hung on every wall. Plaques and certificates and awards. Maybe some pamphlets for the EvenHealth programme. A row of books, at the very least.

But there was none of that.

All that occupied the office was a large oak cabinet in the far corner, a big sturdy wooden desk, and a pair of comfortable-looking leather chairs sitting opposite the desk.

On the walls hung nothing but standard pictures. A sailor looking out over the sea; a little boy at the doctor's office; and a Native Indian-style wolf head. Aside from this and a few plants decorating the room, there was nothing of interest. No shelves, no books at all.

Striker moved over to the desk. He tried to open the drawers but they were all locked. On it was nothing but an ink blotter, a computer and a keyboard with mouse. The computer screen was blank, and when Striker moved the mouse, the logon screen appeared.

'Needs a password,' Felicia said.

'EvenHealth?' he asked.

'Lots of luck,' she said.

He knew she was right, and didn't even venture to guess. Instead, he moved over to the cabinet on the far side of the room and opened the doors. Inside was a small TV set with built-in DVD player. A Samsung. On the shelf below was a row of DVDs, each one with a name on the side. Striker searched for any with the names Larisa Logan or Mandy Gill, but found none. Instead, he found one labelled *Billy Stephen Mercury*. And in brackets were the words: *Kuwait. Afghanistan. PTSD.*

PTSD – Post-traumatic Stress Disorder.

He turned and looked at Felicia. 'Our Billy?'

'Write down the details. Hurry. Before Ostermann gets back.'

'I'll do more than that,' he said. He flicked on the TV and grabbed the DVD case. He opened it, slid out the disc, and slipped it into the tray.

Felicia gave him a nervous look. 'Jacob, what are you doing?'

'Just watch the door.'

'Watch the door? It's five feet away from you.'

'Then just stand by it and listen. Let me know if you hear him coming.'

'Ostermann's due back *any minute*. And what if I don't hear him? What then?'

Striker smiled. 'Then sit back and pull up a chair because there's gonna be some fireworks.' He leaned forward and pressed Play, and the disc loaded.

Seconds later, the screen came to life.

The video quality was surprisingly good, damn near high def, though the sound was slightly muffled. The camera was angled from the left side, with Dr Erich Ostermann sitting opposite a young man. Between them was an ordinary wood desk with nothing on it.

A different room.

Striker took note of the walls – there was absolutely nothing on them – and then of the male being interviewed. He was Caucasian, and terribly thin, emaciated, yet he looked wiry, strong. He could have been in his late twenties or early thirties – it was hard to tell. His hair was dark brown, but greying, and the stubble on his face was almost entirely white.

'He looks young, but old,' Felicia noted.

Striker made no reply. He just studied the patient on the feed.

The skin of Billy Mercury's face had few wrinkles, except around his eyes, where there were many. The man looked *tired*, as if he hadn't slept well in years, and the paleness of his skin amplified this look. Perspiration dampened his skin, and when he breathed, his chest rose and fell heavily, unevenly, as if he were hyperventilating.

Dr Ostermann sat in his chair, then turned it slightly to the left to allow the camera a better angle for recording. He stated the date and time of the interview – it was just two weeks ago – and then briefly introduced himself, humbly giving the most basic of his credentials.

Last of all, he introduced his patient.

'And this person opposite me is Billy Stephen Mercury,' Dr

Ostermann said to the camera. 'Billy is a soldier who spent time in Afghanistan. First Class with the 7th Regiment. Coming back from the war, Billy suffered from extreme depression and night terrors, making it difficult to sleep and cope with the normal activities of daily life. He was subsequently diagnosed with Post-traumatic Stress Disorder and has been doing sessions with me here and at EvenHealth for the last seven months. Billy is making significant progress, and if all goes well, will be returning to his life outside the facility very soon. His independence is our first and foremost priority.'

Striker studied everything on the screen. During the entire introduction, Billy Mercury had said nothing. He just sat there and barely moved, staring at nothing in the room. His body trembled. His skin sweated. His breath came in fast and uneven gulps of air.

'So Billy,' Dr Ostermann continued. 'Last session, we ended with you speaking of your time in Afghanistan. More specifi-cally, the enemy engagements. You were talking specifically about Kandahar. This was a very bad time for you, as I understand.'

Dr Ostermann paused to give Billy Mercury a chance to speak; when the patient didn't, Dr Ostermann continued.

'When we last left off, you were telling me how one of your company – a Colonel Dylan – was killed by a roadside attack and how you had been separated from your party in the back roads of the town. Would you care to continue the story?'

For a long moment, Billy Mercury said nothing. He just sat there, shaking and sweating, letting the silence envelop them. Then, with a start, he came to life. He began looking all around the room, his eyes shifting rapidly, as if seeing things in the room that no one else could see.

'They were *everywhere*,' he finally said. 'In the streets of the

village. In the doorways of the homes and in the open markets
and in all the crevices . . . but in the shadows. Always in the
shadows.'

'And this was . . .'

'The enemy.'

'The resistance soldiers?' Dr Ostermann asked. 'The people of
the town? Who exactly were they, Billy?'

'Who?' he asked, and suddenly he let out a high-pitched laugh
that turned into a cry. '*What* is more important.'

Dr Ostermann's face tensed, though only for an instant.
'Billy, we've been over this before—'

'I saw them over there. In *Farah* and *Herat* and *Kandahar*. I
saw them many times. They were everywhere. Pretending to be
soldiers. And citizens. Children, even. They lived in the darkness. Came out of the shadows. They're *born* in the blackness,
made from blackness. It seeps right out of their eyes, their
mouths.'

'Billy—'

'Made of fucking hellfire!'

'*Billy*, we've discussed this before. It's psychosis, it's
delusions—'

'NO! You don't understand, Doctor. You weren't there, so
you can't know. It's not like here. It's another world. Another
place. They can live there, they can grow. And they're getting
stronger. They'll be coming here soon. They'll get inside the
clinic. Come for me. Come for you! *Come for everyone!*'

Dr Ostermann's face took on a disappointed look, but he said
nothing. He just stood up slowly from his chair and shook his
head.

'I think we need to revisit the medications,' he said.

'NO!' Billy said. 'You don't understand. You think I'm crazy.
But you don't know. I can hear them at night, whispering.

Always whispering. They're coming for me. For us all. *You can't fucking KNOW!'*

Dr Ostermann reached for the door, and Billy suddenly jumped up. He up-ended the desk, grabbed hold of the doctor, and Dr Ostermann began to scream for security. Within seconds, three large men dressed in white pants and shirts burst into the room. They grabbed Billy Mercury, but he fought them. Raked his nails down the first man's face; hammered the second orderly with a vicious punch to the throat.

'Daemons!' he screamed. 'Fucking *daemons* – THEY'LL GET US ALL!'

Thirty-Nine

Striker stood in the centre of the room, mesmerized by the video footage before him. The man on the screen was completely delusional. And dangerous. Striker could feel it. He was so engrossed in the interview that it took him a few seconds to hear Felicia's whispered warning from beside the door.

'. . . coming, Jacob. Dr Ostermann – he's *coming*!'

Striker finally clued in. He hit the Stop button on the DVD player, powered off the television set, and walked back across the room. He was just nearing Felicia when the door opened and Dr Ostermann walked into the office.

The doctor gave them both a careful look, then nodded. 'Detectives. Good to see both of you again, though rather unexpected, I must say.'

Felicia said, 'It's good to see you as well, Doctor.'

Striker felt less inclined for the bullshit. 'We said we'd be in contact, Dr Ostermann. So this is anything but unexpected. In fact, the way I remember it, you were supposed to call us.'

Dr Ostermann's face took on a faraway look, and he nodded. 'Oh yes. Yes, I believe that is correct. And I planned on doing so. But it has been a very busy morning indeed.'

He stepped further into the room and closed the door behind him, locking out the receptionist and patients. In his hands was a dark green file folder with some black writing on the tab.

Striker could not make it out.

Dr Ostermann walked over to his desk, slid open the drawer, and dropped the file inside. As he turned to face them, closing the drawer, his eyes caught the open cabinet, and he stopped what he was doing and just stared at it. Without saying a word, he walked across the room, stopped facing the DVD player, and looked at the DVDs. He picked up the empty case marked Billy Mercury and opened it. When he saw no DVD inside, he turned to face them and the skin of his cheeks was slightly pink.

'Were you . . . *watching* this?'

Felicia said nothing.

Striker stepped forward. 'Stop answering my questions with ones of your own, Doctor.'

Dr Ostermann's face turned from pink to red, so deep that even the top of his thinning hair showed blush. The contrast made his eyes look like green ice. 'I beg your pardon, Detective Striker?'

'Beg nothing. You heard what I said.'

Dr Ostermann snapped the DVD case closed and put it away. 'There was never any question *asked* of me.'

'It was implied.' Striker stepped up to the desk so that he was within arm's reach of the man. 'I didn't come all the way from Vancouver to Coquitlam for a social visit, Doctor. And I think you know that. You were supposed to call us this morning; you didn't.'

'I just told you, it's been a very busy morning. I've had many things on my mind. Many patients to tend to. They come first.'

Striker steeled his voice. 'I wish I could say the same for Mandy Gill.'

Dr Ostermann froze, and silence filled the room. Striker was happy to wait it out. He gave Felicia a quick but casual glance to make sure she kept quiet, too.

He wanted Ostermann to sweat on this one.

'The reason I haven't called back,' the doctor finally explained, 'is because I haven't yet been able to reach my patient. And I'm not about to give out this person's *personal and private* information until such time that I do. It's as simple as that.'

Striker nodded. 'That's fine then, Doctor. And here's my response to you: you can either fess up this guy's name, or I will head down to the court house, bang up a warrant, and then come out here and take your whole office and Records Section apart.'

Dr Ostermann's face paled. 'No judge would allow that.'

'Actually, I think they would. And think of how the media would eat that one up: "*Dr Ostermann, psychiatrist for the poor, refuses to help the Vancouver Police Department's investigation on the possible murder of a poor mentally ill woman – a patient of the EvenHealth programme, no less.*" Man, I can just see the headlines now.' He looked back at Felicia and smiled. 'Or we could just seize any files and be done with it.'

Dr Ostermann stepped back. '*Seize* my files? Under what grounds?'

'Exigent circumstances,' Felicia said.

Striker nodded. 'Exactly. You have a patient who we think might have been murdered – not committed suicide, as previously thought – and there's a connection to one of your other patients. A man who might also pose an extreme risk to others. That's exigent enough for me. Hell, it's one of our prime duties as police officers – Protection of Life.'

'That would never stand up in court.'

Striker shrugged. 'Maybe not. But I'm more than willing to fight that a year or two down the road – after I seize your files here and at EvenHealth.'

'EvenHealth?'

Felicia stepped forward. 'Work with us, Doctor.'

Dr Ostermann's face paled even more and he leaned back against the desk. 'I wonder. What would your Inspector say to all this? Or perhaps your Deputy Chief. He and I know each other, you know. I am a well-known contributor to the Police Mutual Benevolent Association, and have been for many years.'

Striker grinned. 'The chief would care as much as the media would if, say, this thing got leaked and they learned we were seizing your patients' files.'

Dr Ostermann said no more, and a distant, horrified look filled his eyes, as if he was picturing the nightmare that could unfold.

Striker gave Felicia a quick glance, saw the concern in her eyes, and knew she would give it to him later. But for now, he had the upper hand, and he knew it. He met Dr Ostermann's stare and said, 'So what's it going to be, Doctor? Are we going to help each other out, or not? We are on the same team, after all, right?'

Dr Ostermann's posture sagged and he let out a tight breath. 'Same team. Yes. Yes, of course.' He moved gingerly around his desk and sat down in the high-backed leather chair. He opened the drawer. Pulled out the green file folder he had been carrying when he entered the room. He flipped wearily through the pages, then dropped the whole thing on the desktop.

'His name is Billy Stephen Mercury,' he finally confessed. 'As I am sure you well know. He has been a patient of mine for quite some time now, ever since his return from overseas.' His eyes flitted to the DVD player, then back at Striker. 'We are off the record here?'

'Of course.'

He nodded. 'Billy was a soldier, suffering badly. Post-traumatic Stress Disorder, just like the DVD says. Barely sleeping. And self-medicating to deal with the pain. Delusional. One step away from being psychotic. When he was here, he was a very hard patient to deal with at times.'

Felicia asked, '*When* he was here?'

'Yes, when. The medications helped greatly. And Billy did progress. He was released because of this – as part of the outpatient programme. And for a while, he was doing quite well on his own. We always kept tabs on him, of course. He had to see one of our psychiatrists regularly. But that was mostly to reassess the medications and make sure they were working. Make sure he was taking them as prescribed. The majority of his healing came through one of the EvenHealth programmes.'

'Which particular programme?'

'We called it SILC – Social Independence and Life Coping skills. The programme was designed to help some of our more stable patients gain their independence through what we called the trinity approach – regular counselling, group therapy sessions, and home visits. For some – for *most* – of the patients, SILC worked quite well. But for Billy, well, there were setbacks.'

'What kind of setbacks?' Striker asked.

'Medication-related, mostly. Which sounds simple enough. But the medication was the only thing controlling his delusions. The group therapy sessions . . . these were aimed at the depression.'

'And where exactly is Billy now?'

Dr Ostermann splayed his hands. 'That's the problem. I can't get a hold of him. He is supposed to call into the office daily, but I'm afraid to say he hasn't done so for quite some time. Almost a week.' The doctor shook his head sadly. 'This . . . *unreliability* was one of the reasons why he was removed from the group.'

'Removed from the group, but not from the entire programme?' Striker clarified.

'Of course not, this is a rehabilitative programme, not a punitive one.'

'You said, *one* of the reasons?' Felicia noted.

Dr Ostermann nodded slowly. 'Well, yes, there were other reasons as well.'

Striker pressed the issue. 'What were they, Doctor?'

'Billy had certain . . . obsessions.'

'With what?'

'More like with who,' Dr Ostermann replied. He looked away from them for a brief moment and his lips puckered. 'Billy was obsessed with Mandy Gill.'

'Jesus Christ,' Striker said. 'You're only telling us this now?'

Dr Ostermann raised his hands in surrender. 'It was never in a violent way,' he insisted. 'These were completely non-violent obsessions, I can assure you of that. Billy was never a . . . violent person.'

'He was a soldier,' Striker pointed out. 'He is at least familiar with violence.'

Dr Ostermann tilted his head as he spoke. 'Billy may have been a soldier, but he was a communications officer first,' he explained.

'Communications officer or not, he is still trained for violence,' Striker replied.

'Did he have obsessions with any of the other patients or staff?' Felicia asked.

'Well, yes. There was another, yes.'

Striker felt his blood pressure rising. 'Names, Doctor. *Names.*'

'She was another one of the patients. Her name is Sarah Rose.'

The surname meant nothing to Striker, but the first name made him pause. *Sarah?* Wasn't that one of the names written down on the large piece of paper back at Larisa's home? He looked at Felicia, and she nodded; she too had made the connection.

'Sarah was the only one who really looked out for Billy,' Dr Ostermann continued. 'The only one who genuinely cared for him. I guess she was Billy's only, well, *friend.* They became close. Too close. A romantic relationship, I believe – which was strictly against the rules of the therapy. I was forced to remove them from the group. It was for this very reason Sarah broke off their relationship.'

Striker couldn't believe his ears.

'Broke off their relationship?' He swore out loud. This was more than a mental health nightmare, it was a possible drug-fuelled *domestic.* He calmed his mind down and focused on the basics.

'Were Sarah and Mandy close?' he asked.

The doctor seemed perplexed by the question. 'Yes, I believe they were. As close as anyone could get to Sarah – she was quite introverted, you know. Almost a recluse. It was all I could do, at times, to have her attend the counselling sessions. One time, I even had to get my receptionist to—'

'Hold on a second,' Striker said. 'Sarah Rose isn't one of the *in-house* patients?'

'Oh dear lord, no. Sarah's depression is quite treatable.'

'So she's not actually here? She's out there on her own?'

'Yes, of course.'

'Give me her telephone number.'

'Sarah does not have a telephone, but I do have her address.'

'Then give me that, and a photograph of the woman if you have one.'

From his desk, Dr Ostermann pulled out a file and removed a photocopy of a picture of the woman. He also pulled out an old-fashioned Rolodex, found the address, then wrote it down on a yellow Post-it note. 'This is the most current information we have on Sarah.'

Striker took the photocopy of the woman's picture as well as the Post-it note. 'We can finish this discussion later,' he said. 'Right now, we have to check on this woman's welfare. You had better hope, Doctor, that she's okay.'

Dr Ostermann's face took on a tight expression, but he said nothing back.

Striker turned and gave Felicia a nod, and the two left the office and made their way down the long dark corridors of the Riverglen Mental Health Facility. They returned to their car, got inside, and headed towards Vancouver. Destination: the Oppenheimer area. More specifically, the violent slums of Princess Avenue.

It was time to see Sarah Rose.

Forty

The Adder sat in the driver's seat of a plain white van. A GMC with double back doors and no rear windows. It could have been a work van. It could have been a delivery van, or any one of the old privately owned heaps around town. There were a million of them.

And that was why he had picked it.

Next to him on the centre console sat a small black Nokia cell phone. It was an old model by today's standards. No camera. No touch-screen. Hell, no screen at all. No nothing. Just a plain-Jane model that was pre-paid through a 7-Eleven cash card. It was untraceable. And when the job was done, he would break it into pieces and discard them at the other end of town.

He was always overly careful. He had to be. The results of carelessness could be detrimental.

His legs jittered, and he began to fidget. The waiting was always the hardest part. Especially in a van that stank of old dampness and stale coffee. He looked at the paper cup of old Tim Horton's decaf in the tray holder – the cup so old the writing had faded. He grabbed it, unrolled the window, and threw it outside.

Cold wind blew into the cab. Hit him like an invisible hand, slapping his skin. Far above, the sun shone almost white. All at once, it hit him, and he was slip . . . slip . . . slipping away. Back in time.

Back to *then*.

'No, not now,' he whispered. 'Not again.'

His hands started to shake, and all at once he could hear the laughter all around him, as if it was happening right now, right here in the cab of the van. And then the sounds of the snapping started. Those terrible, thunderous *crashing* sounds.

He reached out, fiddled with the radio, and turned the knob to a station that didn't exist. Cranked the volume and let the static sound fill his ears. That heavenly, heavenly *noise* . . .

It overpowered the old ghosts.

For now.

Still sweating, still shaking, he looked down at the cell again. As if sensing his desperation, it finally went off and relief flooded him. Only one person had this number. The Doctor. And so the Adder picked up on the first ring.

'Yes.' His voice was rough, weak.

'He's coming. There isn't much time.'

The Adder nodded absently as if the Doctor could see him. 'I am already here.'

'Be careful, you can't be seen.'

'No one will know.'

The Doctor started to say more, but the Adder couldn't listen. He hung up the cell and dropped it into the pocket of his black Kangaroo jacket. Zipped the pocket. Then pulled up the hoodie. Fighting the daemons of the past, he shouldered open the door and left the van.

The target suite was to the east, down the snaking, icy slope of Hermon Drive; the Adder knew this because he had already performed his recon of the area, and he had hauled all his gear inside the command room.

'*Those who plan will live; those who don't life-give.*'

An old soldiers' rhyme. The cadence brought him some comfort. Made him feel an ounce of control in a world where no control existed.

When he reached the west side of the road, at the top of the hill, the Adder moved inside the nearest apartment complex. Hermon Heights was a standard project slum – a dilapidated building, screaming of neglect and falling down all around him. But it was no doubt cheap on rent and, even better, Hermon Heights had no onsite manager.

Inside the slum, the air was just as cold as out. The halls were dim and the walls felt uneven, giving the corridor a slanted feel. In fact, everything felt off-kilter, warped.

Or was that just him?

The Adder walked down the eastern hall of the main floor and opened the door to the last room. Unit 109 was unoccupied, and the residents of the other units were smart enough to leave each other alone.

One of the unwritten rules of the projects.

Once inside, he closed the door behind him, then turned to face the room. Straight ahead was his collection of electronic equipment, already set up and ready to go.

The computer with external drive and signal receptor.

The monitor all hooked up with a colour feed of the target suite.

And, of course, his *supplies.*

He grabbed the cans of varnish. Four for the job; one for the police. Then he snatched the can of Coke from the table, popped the cap and chugged some down. The sweet caustic liquid burned his throat wonderfully. Outside, the sky was so big and so clear and so icy pale blue. It made the sounds of laughter invade his head once more, and the Adder could feel tears welling in the corners of his eyes. He picked up the screw gun. Gave the trigger a squeeze. And listened to the soft steady *whirr* of the motor.

He closed his eyes and listened to it for a long moment. Until the laughter faded and he could think again.

It was time to get to work.

Forty-One

They were halfway to Sarah Rose's address when Felicia gave him a jab.

'We need to make a pit stop first,' she said.

'Where?'

'Ladies room. Any place.'

Striker was concerned about getting there. 'Can you hold it?'

'I wouldn't ask if I could.'

Striker just nodded. A few blocks later, at the corner of First Avenue and Rupert, he pulled into the Chevron lot. The owners of the gas station were police friendly and gave cops free coffee. More importantly, the bathrooms were normal – clean, tended, and free of black lighting and discarded needles.

Felicia hopped out and ran inside.

As Striker watched her go, he felt his cell buzz against his side. Hoping he was receiving another text or email from Larisa, he immediately pulled out the iPhone and read the screen.

It was an email:

. . . I saw them first in Afghanistan and Kandahar. In human form. They came in rows, wave after wave of masks.

But I KNEW what they were. The other soldiers may have been blind, but not me. I saw through the shells. And I took them all down. A soldier. An emissary. The HAMMER OF GOD!!!

Then I was, as I am today.

There is only one way to kill a daemon. A goddam Succubus. And that is through the heart.

You're moving downward. Into the mouth of hell, *Hero*. Can you kill your daemons?

I know I can mine . . .

The Adder

Striker frowned on reading it. More riddles, more gibberish. Though when compared to the last, more stable message, the sender seemed to be spiralling out of control.

He got on the phone and tried to trace the message. Within seconds, the tech provider told him exactly what he expected to hear – the email was untraceable, most likely sent through an offshore proxy server. Striker nodded absently as he listened to the man. He hung up, called Ich, and the VPD tech said he would look further into it.

Moments later, Felicia returned to the car. She brought with her a pair of gas station sandwiches – egg salad – and a couple of chocolate milks. She dropped a sandwich in Striker's lap, gave him a quick look and knew something was up.

'What now?' she asked.

Striker showed her the message, and she read it through slowly as she tore the wrapper from the sandwich. Striker did the same.

'Friggin' creep . . . How did he get your number?' she asked.

Striker shrugged. 'Who knows? Probably through the work directory.'

'But this is your *personal* phone.'

'My work phone forwards to my personal one, and the work phone is listed.'

Felicia thought this over, then swore. 'I don't like this.'

'The sooner we get Mercury, the sooner this entire nightmare can end,' Striker said. 'But first we have to make sure Sarah Rose is safe.'

He tore a bite out of his sandwich, put the car into Drive and hit the gas. He wanted to get to Sarah Rose's place. Suddenly, it seemed like they were running out of time.

Forty-Two

The address for Sarah Rose – the one Striker got from Dr Ostermann – was in the two hundred block of Princess Avenue, and the building was aptly named Princess Place. It was essentially a social assistance-funded, outpatient programme for the drug addicted and mentally ill, with assisted living and onsite medical staff. The exterior was made from faded pink stucco that was now reinforced with white smears of spackle that looked like scars on skin. Dark iron bars lined every window.

Princess Place.

Where no princesses lived.

Felicia got out of the car first. She looked for a long moment at the building in front of them, then met Striker's stare. 'Last time we were here, Thunderchild tried to stab you with a sword.'

Striker smiled. 'Ah, the memories. We could reminisce forever, but hey, duty calls.' He headed across the road to Princess Place. Before he reached the sidewalk, the front door of the facility flew open and crashed into the wall with such force that all the windows rattled. A small woman, terribly thin with red-dyed spiky hair, came stomping out, turned south and then marched on towards East Hastings Street.

'Stole my fuckin' ROCK!' she screamed, and gave the building the finger.

Striker barely gave her a glance; this kind of behaviour was all par for the course in the Oppenheimer area. Before partnering up with Felicia, he had spent three long years here, during his time in Patrol, dealing with everything from the never-ending clumps of passed-out drunks to the cocaine-psychosis stabbings that were commonplace in any one of these slums.

He gestured to the building ahead. 'You ready for a walk down memory lane?'

'I'm still trying to forget my last time here.'

Striker smiled at that. He pulled open the front door and walked through the opening into Princess Place. He took in a deep breath, and winced. As always, the place smelled of body odour and piss.

The foyer around them was busy with crackheads and crazies – all of whom were one step from life on the street. Princess Place was the end of the housing line for most. It was cluttered and dirty and never seemed to hold a moment's peace. And the angry screams from the floor above were a testament to that.

'Fight up there,' Felicia said.

Striker didn't hesitate. He bounded up the stairs to the second level, then found his way down the hall to unit 212. Sarah Rose's room. When he reached the unit, the door was wide open and the room was empty. Completely. Not even a chair was left inside. The place smelled of bleach, like it had just been cleaned.

'Another dead end,' Felicia said.

'Let's talk to the staff,' Striker said. 'Maybe she's changed rooms.'

They headed down the stairs again. By the time they reached the bottom, the sounds of another fight had erupted – this time, sounding much higher. Maybe third floor. Striker stopped and listened to the yells.

'Too much self-medication,' Felicia said.

'What do you expect? We're in Crack Central.'

Striker was still concentrating on the noise up above when the wiry redhead returned from Hastings Street, still yelling about someone stealing her rock. Striker turned to keep an eye on her. As he did, he caught a glimpse of the old brick building across the road, on the other side of East Cordova, a half-block down.

The Social Assistance office.

He nodded to Felicia. 'You still got your contact at the welfare office over there?'

She nodded. 'It's been a few years, but, yeah, he might still work there.'

'Well, if Sarah Rose has ever lived here, then she's definitely picked up her cheques from that office before. You go over there while I talk to the staff here. See if you can work some magic on your man. Find out where they're sending her welfare cheques.'

'You mean, if they're going anywhere at all – Sarah's records indicate she was in Riverglen for quite some time. So she might not even have an outside address yet.'

'Hey, it's worth a try. Zero plus zero still equals zero.'

Felicia thought this over, then nodded. She headed for the door, stopped and looked back.

'You sure you're gonna be okay here all by yourself?'

Striker looked through the safety glass of the onsite nurse's office and spotted a tall blonde woman. She was over six foot and large. Striker knew her, and he smiled. 'I'm not by myself.' He jabbed a thumb over his shoulder. 'I got Nurse Ratchet here to protect me.'

Felicia gave the nurse's office a long look, apparently still uncomfortable with leaving him. 'Be careful,' she finally said, and left the building.

Striker watched her cross the road and walk through the tinted front doors of the Social Assistance office. Once she was gone from view, he blinked, snapped from his thoughts, and turned towards the nursing station.

Inside the protected area, behind the locked door and safety glass, was the nurse. Striker couldn't recall her name, but upon seeing him, she smiled, got up from her desk and opened the office door. She leaned against the door frame and crossed her arms, and Striker noted that they looked strong across her chest.

'Constable Striker,' she said. 'Or is it Corporal by now?'

'Detective.'

'*Detective?* Well la-dee-daa,' the woman said. She extended her hand to him, and he took it. 'Janice, in case you forgot. I'm the onsite nurse here. You helped me out a few years back when one of our patients was delusional – Johnny Thunderchild.'

'Thunderchild.' Striker nodded. 'How could I forget?' He looked around the foyer and all its connecting halls. Already, many of the live-ins were gawking at him. 'Maybe we should take this into the office,' he suggested.

Nurse Janice agreed.

They went inside.

'Coffee?' she asked right away.

Striker declined. 'No time. I'm here to speak to one of your patients,' he explained. 'A woman named Sarah Rose. I thought she was up in 212, but apparently not.'

The nurse immediately shook her head. 'Sarah? God, she hasn't lived here full-time for close to a year now, I bet. Nine months, at least. And that was probably before her stint in Riverglen. She did come by here for a few days – on a part-time temporary basis just a few weeks back. Stayed a half week or so, then was gone again.'

'You know where she went this last time around?'

The woman made a *who knows* face and approached the coffee

maker. The brew looked thick and it smelled burned. Striker watched her pour herself a cup, then add a healthy dose of cream to it.

'We have no idea where Sarah went,' she finally said, then sipped and tested her drink. 'The woman just took off on us one day. Which is too bad because who knows where she ended up. We tried to get her into Belkin House, but she said no to that. And then we tried the Lost Ladies shelter on Marine. But Sarah refused that, too. She was very . . . particular about where she would go. In the end, she left of her own accord and, to be honest, we were thankful for it. We just wanted to get her out of here. And *quick*.'

Striker frowned. 'Out of here? Why?'

Her response was telling: 'Because of Billy.'

'Billy *Mercury*?'

The nurse nodded. 'That guy had a strange thing for Sarah. Just wouldn't leave her alone. He was delusional. Psychotic, really. And not just about her. He was paranoid about the doctors, too – kept telling everyone who would listen to him that they were giving him experimental medication. Stuff the army had used overseas during the war. That they were all in bed with the pharmaceutical companies and using patients as test subjects – *guinea pigs*, were the words he used.'

Striker took out his notebook. 'Billy has a history of paranoia. Delusions, too.'

Janice sipped her coffee. 'You don't gotta tell me that. He was always in here, talking about demons and the devil and evil ghosts. And he was always off his meds. One day, for no reason at all, he punched right through the window over there. Tore his hand up really bad. Needed over seventy stitches to close the wounds.'

'Bad cut. Was he high?'

She shook her head. 'That's the scary thing – he wasn't. We'd just had his blood work done as a favour to Triage. And he was absolutely clean . . . You should've seen the blood; it just *poured* from his hand. I thought we had an arterial bleed for sure. And Billy, he just stood there and stared at it. Like it was the most beautiful thing he'd ever seen . . .'

Striker wrote this down, then looked up. 'Any other strange stuff?'

'With Billy? Lots, sure, always. He seemed to get even worse after that. Really *obsessive* with Sarah. Kept saying he knew she was whispering to him at night. Creepy stuff like that. Said he heard noises.'

'What kind of noises?'

The nurse shrugged. 'I dunno. He never really said and I never really asked. I just wanted Sarah to move out of here because of him. For her own safety. And to be honest, Billy scared the hell out of me and the rest of the staff, too. When they committed him to Riverglen, we all breathed a sigh of relief. He's gonna kill someone one day. Her, or one of us.'

Striker stopped writing and met her stare. 'Well, watch yourself, Janice, because he's out.'

Her face tightened. 'Are you fucking kidding me? They let him out again?'

Striker nodded. 'Outpatient care.'

'Christ Almighty.'

Striker looked at the room keys hanging on the board. 'Did Billy actually live here, himself?'

Janice almost spit out her coffee. 'Here? No, never. *Sarah* did. She was why he always came by. They were part of that EvenHealth programme, you know. For all the good it ever did them.'

That got Striker's attention. 'Not a fan of the programme?'

She waved a hand. '*Please*. It's all fluff – just like the doctor who created it. Everything is image. Stats. That's how he makes his money, you know. By getting people out of government care so it costs the taxpayer less money. He gets a percentage of costs saved.'

'You got proof of that?'

'It's what people in the profession say.'

Striker said nothing. He just made a note of this, then flipped through the pages of his notebook. So many of the words seemed to jump out at him. *Billy Mercury. EvenHealth. Dr Ostermann* and *Dr Richter.*

Medications and mental illness – it was becoming a common theme.

He finally looked up and refocused on Sarah Rose. 'No forwarding address?' he asked.

Before Janice could respond, Felicia knocked on the door. Striker let her in. She was breathing hard from running and her eyes looked like dark fire. 'I got it,' she said. 'Sarah's latest res. It's out east. The one place we should've looked in the first place.'

'Where?' Striker asked.

'Where you think?' she teased.

The sour tone of her voice gave it away.

'Hermon Drive.'

Forty-Three

Hermon Drive was a complex of communal housing, situated in District 2, far out east in the North Renfrew area. Although dilapidated in its own right, the complex was one step up from the shit of the skids and the concrete jungles of the Raymur Street slums, but that was as far as the sugar-coating went. The road was a short slope, composed only of low-income box apartments built in the fifties. Only the poor lived here.

And that included Sarah Jane Rose.

Striker and Felicia had been here too many times to remember over the years. For all the bad calls. Anything related to drugs or mental health.

They drove towards the area. They took East Broadway all the way out, then parked a half-block away and walked in on foot. Far above, the sun did nothing to ward off the cold, and the wind blustered hard against them.

As they made their way down the sloping crest of asphalt, Striker saw several groups of kids hanging out and watching them. Teenagers, for the most part. Fewer than half of them would see Day One of grade twelve, but they were street smart. Had to be to survive around here.

A few pointed and a couple called, 'Six up.'

Street slang for *cops nearby*.

Felicia smiled. 'I think we got them fooled.'

Striker smiled at that. The only people who were ever fooled by the undercover cruisers and suits were the normal folk living in middle and upper-class areas. Criminals and the poor always knew the cops with a single glance. Criminals because they were always being arrested, and the poor because they were so often the victims.

They located 3103 Hermon Drive, and Striker slowed his pace. Half the buildings were covered with scaffolding and old green tarps from where they were repairing water damage. Striker took note of all this. The place looked ready to fall down all around them.

They found Sarah Rose's address. It was located in a set of row-homes. The windows were all barred, and the paint was flaking and dirty. Sarah Rose's unit was situated at the east end, beside a playground where children rarely played. Inside the townhome, the lights were all on, but there was no movement inside.

'Want to call for a second unit?' Felicia asked.

Striker shook his head. 'Not yet. Just put us out.'

Felicia did. She got on her cell, called Dispatch, and let them know the address. 'Put us already on scene,' she added. By the time she hung up, they were walking in between the two bushes that flanked the front walkway.

Striker reached the front alcove and studied the door. It was made from solid wood, lighter in colour than the frame. When he looked at the hinges, he realized that the door actually opened *outwards*, which was unusual for these places. He took a moment to study the next-door neighbour's doorway and saw that it was quite different. The wood looked darker, older. He turned to face Felicia.

'Was there anything in the computer about a break-in here?'

'No, nothing was listed in PRIME.'

He didn't like the answer. The door had been fortified for some reason. Why? Was Sarah Rose afraid of something?

Or someone?

He reached out and rapped on the door. It was hard and let off a solid-sounding *thunk-thunk-thunk*. As they waited for a response, Striker took a quick look behind them at the building that was in a state of disrepair. Probably another leaky condo. On the other side of the road, in one of the ground-level suites, someone was watching them. A lone figure standing just behind the sheers and drapes. Striker nodded at the man, but received nothing in reply.

It was typical for the area. Police unfriendly.

'No one's home,' Felicia said.

Striker rapped harder. He leaned over the railing and tried to look through the kitchen window, but the lower portion of the glass was bevelled, and the upper portion was too high to see through. He tried the front door, found it locked.

'Any phone number for this res?' he asked.

Felicia shook her head. 'None listed. Tried Info, too. They got nothing.'

'Hold the front then,' he said.

When Felicia nodded, Striker made his way around the building, cutting through the empty playground. Once there, he frowned. The rear of the townhome belonged to a separate residence altogether. The buildings faced back to back, which meant there were no windows facing south.

And no rear entry.

The front was the only way in.

When he returned to the front, Felicia nodded to the adjoining row-home. 'No one's home there, either,' she said. 'Actually, it looks like it's unrented right now.'

'Big surprise.' Striker removed a folding knife from his inner jacket pocket and opened the blade.

Felicia took note. 'What are you doing?'

'Making entry.'

'On what grounds?'

'Exigent circumstances.' He assessed the lock. It was made from steel and appeared strong, but the wooden frame of the doorway was bowed and old. 'Mandy Gill is dead. Billy Mercury is clearly off his rocker. And now Sarah Rose isn't answering her front door.'

'Which means she could be out getting groceries, for all we know. We haven't even checked Billy's place yet.'

'This is more urgent.'

'We don't even know if Sarah lives here,' Felicia said.

Striker just smiled at her. 'Well, we're about to find out.'

Striker angled the knife in between the lock and the frame, put pressure medially, and a loud *crack!* filled the air. The door popped open and swung lightly outwards.

Felicia swore, then drew her pistol. 'This'll never hold up in court.'

'My evidence, not yours,' he said, then stepped inside the foyer.

The first thing Striker noticed upon making entry was the smell – a strong burned stink. Directly ahead of them was a long narrow stairway leading down, and that confused Striker momentarily as he tried to understand the layout. There was no upper floor, no main floor – that belonged to the back suite. All Sarah Rose's apartment owned was the lower floor. And this looked like the only way in and out.

'This suite should be illegal,' Felicia said.

Striker said nothing. He just studied the way ahead. Down the stairs, which descended directly in front of him following the small foyer, there was light. Artificial, not natural. Everything looked dim and hazy.

'There's smoke down there,' Felicia noted.

When Striker's eyes adapted, he saw it, too. A thin veil of smoke floated through the air. Looking down the stairs into the murky darkness of the lower floor gave him a bad feeling. The smoke seemed heavier to the right, in what appeared to be a small kitchen area. But from this upper angle it was difficult to tell.

'Hello?' Striker called out. 'It's the Vancouver Police! Is anyone home?' When he received no answer, he gave Felicia the nod. 'Stick together on this one. There's no cover.'

'Keep close to the wall,' she said.

He agreed.

They started down the stairs. Striker took them two at a time, until he felt his shoes touch the hard concrete of the bottom floor. The burned smell was stronger here. He immediately looked around and could see an empty living room and kitchenette to his right, a hallway leading left, and another room at the end of the corridor ahead. No matter which way they walked, they would be exposing themselves to some degree.

He didn't like it.

He looked around the area. In the living room, the TV was turned on, the sound muted. On the table sat a container of box wine, some prescription pill bottles, and a bag of Miss Vickie's Sea Salt & Vinegar chips.

'Watch the hall and our backs,' Striker told Felicia.

'Got it.' She moved up behind him, using the wall as poor cover.

Striker stepped inside the living room and adjoining kitchenette. On the stove was a cast-iron pan with the element below it glowing red. He looked at the switch and saw it was set to High. He moved up to the stove and looked inside the pan. In it was the source of the burned smell. It made him frown.

'Coffee granules.'

'Oh fuck me,' Felicia said.

Striker felt her concern. There was a reason for it. In the old days, before the influx of proper breathing apparatuses, the burning of coffee granules was sometimes used by cops – as well as murderers – to hide the smell of a dead body.

To see them burning in the pan was not a good sign.

He turned off the element.

With the kitchen, bathroom and living room both cleared of threat, he made his way down the hallway towards the lone bedroom. The door was half open, the light also on. When he reached the archway, he peered inside the room.

The bed was messed, piles of clothes spotted the floor, and the bureau was covered in old newspapers. Some pill bottles, too. The drawers were left open. Everything was a mess, but the room was empty. The closet, too.

Striker picked up one of the prescription bottles from the bureau. Most of the writing had faded, but the name was readable.

Sarah Jane Rose.

'We're definitely in the right place,' he called out. 'She lives here.'

He rejoined Felicia in the hallway, then took the lead. Gun at the low-ready, he made his way towards the final corridor to the left. There, all the lights were turned off, and Striker didn't like it. After a few more steps, he liked it even less. The burned smell of the coffee grounds faded and was replaced by a new stink. One all too familiar.

'Shit, we got us a DB,' Felicia said.

Striker nodded. 'Don't lose focus.'

He stared ahead and let his eyes adapt to the gloom. The corridor was long and narrow with no room to move. There were no doors on either side, just a single room at the end. An office, or a second bedroom maybe.

Regardless, it was a bad place for entry.

'Hold back,' he said to Felicia.

'What?'

'Just hold here.'

'No way, I'm coming with you.'

Striker never took his eyes from the darkness ahead. 'It's a fatal goddam funnel, Feleesh. If someone starts shooting we'll both be screwed. At least from back here you can cover me.'

'But—'

'But nothing. Just *hold.*'

Felicia said nothing more. She repositioned herself in the doorway of the living room for better cover, and Striker made his way down. With every step, the darkness thickened and the smell got worse. Dirty, foul . . . *oily.*

He reached the doorway of the last room, peered slowly around the corner, studied the room. It was dim. At the far end, near the top of the wall, was an iron-barred window. It was small, less than a foot high and two feet in length, built obviously to give the room a trace of natural light.

And it did, just barely.

Within that cone of natural dimness, Striker could see a recliner positioned in the very centre of the room. Seated in it, with her feet up and facing the opposite way, was a woman. Her hand dangled off the armrest, her fingers clutched tightly into a fist.

Striker scanned the room one more time to be sure there were no threats. When he saw none, he made entry into the small room and slowly rounded the person in the chair. When he reached the front and studied her face, his stomach tightened.

It was the woman from the photocopied picture Dr Ostermann had given him. It was Sarah Jane Rose. And judging from the amount of rigor on her face, she'd been dead for quite some time. They were too late again.

Another woman was dead.

Forty-Four

When the two cops went inside the building, the Adder tied the long laces of his leather mask and pulled up the hoodie of his kangaroo jacket, fully hiding his face. He left the Command Room by cutting through the sheers and drapes, and climbing out of the front-room window. The frozen blades of grass crunched beneath his feet.

He hurried down the slope, then raced across Hermon Drive, the cold wind blowing through the eye slits of the mask; the screw-gun dangling from his tool belt. In his hands, he carried a burlap sack, filled with the metal brackets, a package of thirty ten-inch wood screws, and the four cans of Steinman's wood varnish.

The fifth can he kept separate.

When the Adder was close enough, he opened it, then threw both the can and the lid into the bushes that flanked the front walkway of Sarah Rose's townhome.

Up ahead, the front door was slightly open.

The Adder took note of this. He rounded the lot and came in from the side; no point in being seen just yet. When he was close enough to the doorway to smell the burned coffee grounds inside the unit, he slowed down. Reached the entrance. Peered inside.

All he could see was a dark stairway leading down.

Somewhere down there were the cops. Deep inside the trap. Oblivious of his presence. Unaware of the danger.

And so the Adder initiated the plan.

The front door was heavy, built of solid oak – he knew this for he had installed it himself – yet it shut smoothly and silently as he pushed on it, thanks to the heavily oiled hinges he had screwed into the frame. He pushed the door all the way closed until the lock clicked in place. Then he put the key into the slot and locked the door from the outside.

A sense of excitement blossomed in his chest.

The critical part was done.

He put down the burlap sack, removed the metal brackets, and began fixing them alongside the frame. There were six brackets in total – a pair for each of the three two-by-six beams. As the almost-inaudible whirr of the screw-gun filled the air, the Adder smiled beneath the thin, cold leather.

It was happening,

It was *really* happening!

The Beautiful Escape was almost here.

Forty-Five

'The place is clear,' Striker called to his partner.

Felicia marched into the room. The moment she saw the body slumped back in the chair, a hard look took over her normally pretty features.

'Sarah Rose?' she asked.

Striker nodded and handed the photocopied picture to Felicia.

She gave it a quick glance, then handed it back. She cursed and place a hand against her forehead as if disbelieving what they had found. She moved around the room for a better look at the body. After a brief moment, she asked, 'How long?'

Striker shrugged. 'Judging by the smell, I'd say more than two days. Judging by the rigor, I'd say less than three.'

'So before Mandy,' Felicia said.

'I would think so. It's hard to tell. We'll leave that to the medical examiner. The question here is *why*. Why kill Sarah and then Mandy? Did they both know something? Was it an act of jealousy? A love triangle or something to do with the sessions at the clinic?'

'Or was Mandy murdered next because she knew Sarah?' Felicia suggested. 'Because she knew what had happened to Sarah?'

Striker paced the floor and thought this all over. After a

moment, he stopped talking and craned his neck. Somewhere behind them – back from the way they'd come – there was a soft whirring noise. Like a drill.

Felicia heard it, too.

'What is that?' he asked.

'Sounds like they're working on the building again,' she noted. 'Leaky condo.'

Striker nodded. 'We'll talk to the workers afterwards – see if they saw or heard anything.'

The sound of the drill faded, and Striker focused back on the investigation.

He removed a pair of latex gloves from his pocket. As he put them on, Felicia got on the phone with Dispatch and had them create a Sudden Death call at this address.

Striker looked over at her. 'Tell them to put an APB out on Billy Mercury while you're at it – arrestable on sight. Armed and Dangerous. Possible suicide by cop.'

Felicia nodded and kept talking to the dispatcher.

Satisfied, Striker tuned out her voice and fiddled with the gloves. Once they were on tight, he took out his flashlight. He was about to examine the body of Sarah Rose in greater detail when something else caught his eye: along the edge of the coffee table in the far corner of the room was a row of pill bottles. White labels, blue caps.

He crossed the room and picked them up. Read the labels. All of them were the same medication.

Lexapro.

Striker thought this over. Then he recalled seeing more pill bottles elsewhere. He returned to the kitchenette down the hall and stood in the doorway, letting his eyes take in every detail. All along the countertop were more pill bottles, just like he'd seen on the bedroom bureau.

All of them were empty.

He moved up to the counter and read them. Many of them were marked: Lexapro. But there were others, too. Mainly Effexor.

Just like Mandy Gill's.

He opened his notebook, wrote down the type and number of bottles he'd found, then looked at the dosage. He frowned. It was the exact same as Mandy's medications – and again, the same prescription number, ending with MVC.

Mapleview Clinic.

Striker closed his notebook and examined the area. Unlike the filthiness of Mandy Gill's unit, Sarah Rose's townhome was clean and orderly, for the most part. Sure, it was messy in some areas – dirty dishes in the sink, unwashed laundry in the basin, a vacuum cleaner left out in the centre of the room – but nothing beyond the realm of normality. Mandy's apartment slum had been chock-a-block full of trash and old food, old newspapers and old mail. Sarah's was not.

Striker thought this over, comparing the two. And something else occurred to him. While clearing this place, he had seen medications and newspapers and even some flyers – but no mail.

None of any kind.

He looked around the townhome, going through the drawers and cupboards and closets. Eventually, on the top shelf above the fridge, he found what he was looking for – a small plastic organizer. He pulled it down, opened it, and flipped through the contents.

Inside the folder were all sorts of bills, and all of them marked *paid* in thin red pen. There were receipts for the electric company and the phone company and even separate listings of Visa and MasterCard payments. In the back of the folder, there was one section for bank records, another for insurance papers, and one for miscellaneous details.

Striker noticed one thing: the bills were all *old*, outdated by at least six months. The oldest went back two years. The most recent bill he could find was one for the cable company, and that had been paid in July of the previous year.

After that, there was no mail.

'Keep your eyes open for another mail organizer,' he said.

Felicia nodded and began snooping around the other rooms.

After another fruitless search of the kitchen, Striker put the organizer he was holding back on the shelf, then returned to the den where Felicia was making a list of the medications.

'You find anything?' he asked her.

She looked up. 'No. Maybe she just gets rid of the stuff.'

'She *doesn't*. Her old stuff is all still there. And it's all categorized. This woman was anal about it.'

Felicia thought it over before speaking. 'Well, according to my guy at the welfare office, she just moved here two months ago. Maybe she hasn't done a change of address yet. Either way, I don't think it's something to be concerned over.'

'I do,' he said. 'It's more than missing mail. It's a broken pattern in the woman's daily routine. And if you look at the way she kept track of everything before, something here has changed.'

Felicia said nothing in reply; Striker made a mental note of the issue. He gloved up with fresh latex, then returned to the body of Sarah Rose.

Even in death the woman looked troubled. Her face was sad, and in the dim light of the room, her long blonde hair looked like brittle straw. Her flesh seemed more like sculptured wax than human skin. It was tight across her bloated tissue, stretching her mouth open and deepening the wrinkles near her brow.

Striker shone his flashlight on the woman's face. Her icy blue eyes stared at nothing, and the pupils did not change. They remained milky, lost-looking, and seemed to stare right through him – as if accusing him of being too late to save her.

He looked away. Took a moment to collect his thoughts. He tried to re-set his viewpoint. To think of Sarah Rose not as a person, but as just another body. Another sudden death.

One of the thousand he had seen.

But he could not. Ever since the death of Mandy, everything had felt more personal to him. These weren't just sudden deaths, they were lost lives. There was no ignoring that fact.

The thought was depressing, and he tried to vanquish it by keeping busy. He shone the flashlight all over Sarah Rose's body, looking for any trace evidence. The white blouse she wore was distended over her breasts and belly, and the buttons looked one gas bubble away from popping. The body was bloating profusely. Evidence of this could be seen in the swelling of her cheeks, and of her fingers too, where the rings all appeared to be three sizes too small. The one on her ring finger was so tight, the gold looked melted into the flesh.

Striker noted this ring, and turned to Felicia. 'Did you research her fully on the way over?' he asked.

'Of course.' Felicia said the words like she was offended; research was always the passenger's job.

'Was she married?'

Felicia nodded. 'According to PRIME, she was married. Years ago. To a man named Jerry something. I can't remember the details, but he died of an overdose. I'll read up more on it when we get back to the car.'

Striker looked back at the ring on her finger. 'Guess she never let go of him.'

He used a gloved finger to pull away the soft material of her blouse, exposing the neck and upper sternum regions. Using his flashlight, Striker inspected the skin. On the right side, there was nothing out of the ordinary, just paleness and bloating. On the left side, a very small area of the skin looked different to the rest. A tiny red dot.

A puncture mark?

With all the bloating of the body it was difficult to tell, but the mark was in the same area – lateral to the base of the neck, over the first rib area – just like Mandy Gill's injury.

Thoughts of injections again filtered through Striker's mind. He took out his notebook and made a crude drawing of the neck and the position of the possible puncture mark. He then drew a diagram of the room, and noted something critically important – the positioning of the body.

Mandy Gill had been seated in her easy chair, facing the window.

Now so was Sarah Rose.

Striker turned slowly around and looked at the window with bad thoughts filling his head. He put away his notebook and approached it. The window was small – much too small for an intruder to fit through, especially with iron security bars blocking off the inside.

But that wasn't what he was concerned about.

As Striker got closer to the frame, he could see that the panes of glass were quite dirty. As if they had never been cleaned since the townhome had been built. The dirt was so thick, the outside world was difficult to make out.

Except in one place.

A small portion in the bottom right corner. There, the glass was sparkling clean, as if someone had cleaned it today.

Striker leaned closer for a better look. What he saw made him reach for his pistol. Positioned on the other side of the glass was another camera.

They were being filmed.

Forty-Six

The Adder finished covering the front door with the wood varnish, then threw the last of the empty cans into his burlap sack. He removed his leather gloves and snapped on a fresh pair of latex, covering up the red rash of his skin.

Smiling, he stood back and examined his work. The door was so wet it glistened in the cold winter sun.

It was beautiful.

Unfortunately, there was no time for enjoying his work. He grabbed the lighter from his pocket – a long, ten-inch one for lighting barbecues. With his fingers trembling from the excitement, the Adder took a half step back. Raised the lighter. And pulled the trigger.

The entire front door exploded with a soft *whoooosh!* sound, and white-hot flame crawled up the front of the building like a living beast.

It was beautiful, the Adder thought again.

So undeniably beautiful.

Mesmerizing.

He fought to pull his eyes from the blaze. With the operation complete, he regained his focus, grabbed his burlap sack from the ground, and hurried back across the road to the Command Room. Minutes were critical now. He needed to be out of sight when the cops and fire crews arrived. And more important than that, he needed to be sure the video feed was being properly transmitted and recorded.

That was essential.

He climbed back inside the ground-level apartment and pulled the drapes closed. The moment the outside light was blocked, a sense of relief spilled through him.

It was done.

The job was complete.

He glanced over at the computer screen, saw that the video was recording – saw the two detectives moving through Sarah Rose's suite – and an excited sound escaped his lips. Outside, smoke was already flowing strongly from the fire – the dark angry tail of the beast snaking around the west side of the building. The sight filled the Adder with a sense of heavenly calm.

It was here. It was here. It was here . . .

The Beautiful Escape had arrived.

Forty-Seven

Striker whirled away from the camera.

'Someone's here!'

He drew his gun and scanned the area all around them. As if on cue, four tiny red lights turned on, one at each corner of the ceiling. Like the glowing red eyes of some angry creature. Striker raised his gun to fire, then stopped as he realized what he was looking at.

More cameras.

'There's smoke!' Felicia said.

Striker saw it, too. He searched through the black haze that was unfurling. At first, in the dimness of the basement area, he had thought the smoke was leftover residue from the burned coffee grounds in the kitchenette. But now as he looked at the thickening mass unrolling around them, he realized the truth of what was happening.

The place was on fire.

They'd walked right into a trap.

Gun out, he hurried back into the hallway that led to the stairs, and then the front door. All he could see down at the far end was a smear of puffing blackness. A crackling noise now filled the air. And it was growing louder.

'Come on!' he screamed to Felicia. 'We have to get the hell outta here!'

She ran to his side and they moved back down the long narrow corridor together. The closer they got to the stairs, the more the blackness thickened – to the point where it was difficult to breathe. The air was hot, irritating Striker's eyes and choking his lungs. Felicia began coughing, and raised her arm to cover her mouth.

When they reached the first step of the stairs, Felicia tripped and almost fell, but Striker snagged her. He pulled her with him, up the stairs. When they got halfway, Felicia tugged at his jacket.

'It's too hot,' she yelled above the noise. 'We're running right *towards* the fire – we have to turn back. Find another way.'

Images of the floor layout flashed through Striker's head; the entire apartment was below ground level, and the only windows he had seen were small and barred.

'There is no back,' he yelled. 'This is the only way out!'

Without waiting for a response, he pushed on up the stairway, pulling her with him. They reached the small alcove of the inside foyer. Here, the heat from the fire was immense, palpable through the front door. Without thinking, Striker reached out and grabbed the doorknob—

And yanked his hand back.

The knob was *blisteringly* hot. He quickly stripped off his jacket, wrapped it around the knob, turned it and pushed hard.

The door wouldn't budge.

Felicia shone her flashlight on the door. With the thick smoke billowing all around them, it was almost impossible to see.

She pointed at the plate. 'It's a one-way lock!'

Striker said nothing. He just stepped back and gave the door a couple of solid kicks, once at the bottom and once in the middle. The door barely budged. He shoved hard at the top, then stepped back, coughing.

Smoke was flowing heavily through the cracks now. Like

something liquid. Soon the air around them would be too thick to see anything, and they'd be scrambling in darkness.

Blind.

There was no time.

Striker aimed his gun. 'The lock! Shoot out the lock!'

Felicia said nothing; she just raised her pistol and pulled the trigger. *Bang!-bang!-bang!-bang!* – rapid fire on the door. She shot all twelve bullets, until she had emptied her entire magazine. Then she reloaded.

Striker did the same, concentrating his fire on the lock and plate. By the time his clip was out of ammo, over twenty-four bullets had punched through the oak. Breaking it. Splintering it apart.

He stepped back and gave the door a few hard kicks. The lock and wooden frame surrounding it broke outwards, but the door remained strong. Intact.

'Make the hole bigger!' Striker yelled.

Felicia was already firing before he finished his sentence. She blasted eleven more rounds into the wood, then reloaded her last mag. Striker did the same, then gave the door a few more hard kicks.

This time the entire middle of the door broke outwards.

At first, Striker felt a sense of relief, and Felicia let out a cry. But then smoke billowed through the hole, and the cracking and popping sounds of the fire became amplified.

Flames curved inside the hole of the door.

'Get back, get back!' Striker yelled.

The smoke was hot with specks of burning ash. It burned his skin and throat. Made it difficult to see.

Striker grabbed Felicia, pulled her close. 'The frame!' he screamed. 'Shoot six inches above the lock! One spot so we can kick it through. *Shoot!*'

Felicia opened fire with her last clip, the explosions of the rounds overpowering the roar of the fire. Striker followed suit, emptying his last magazine.

'I'm out of ammo!' Felicia yelled.

Striker said nothing. All in all, they'd put a total of sixty-eight rounds through the door. Trying to weaken one area enough to create a hole and expose the beams behind.

It had to be enough.

He leaped forward and kicked the door with everything he had. The entire structure rattled and something wooden let out a snapping noise.

Felicia began kicking the door, too.

They hit the door again and again and again. Eventually, after what could have been twenty or forty kicks – Striker would never know – something gave way. The door broke outwards and came toppling down with a loud shrieking *snap!* Striker saw smoke and ash and flame – and a glimpse of blue sky.

Felicia ran forward, but Striker hauled her back. Yanked off her jacket. Shoved it into her stomach.

'Use this!' he screamed. 'Over your hair and face!'

She took it and held it over her head, and Striker pushed her forward. In one quick movement, she dived through the doorway and disappeared from view.

Striker did the same. Head down, he tightened his grip on his coat, held his breath, and searched for an inch of blue sky. He saw none, but took his chances anyway, for there was no other option.

He plunged forward into the fiery blackness of the blaze.

Forty-Eight

By the time Striker escaped through the hole in the door and made it past the lawn to the safety of the sidewalk, Felicia was already on the cell, calling for assistance.

Striker turned his eyes from her to the building; the entire front of Sarah Rose's complex was *engulfed*. Bright orange flames crawled all over the west side of the building, up the roof, and were now spreading northward towards the next unit.

'We got to get everyone out of there!' he said to Felicia.

He raced across the lawn to the next unit and kicked in the door with one try. Felicia ran to the next home and did the same. Once done, he ran around the rest of the building, clearing all the units. By the time he was finished and had returned to the front lawn, the sky above the complex was a mass of black angry churls.

The sting of his hand stole his attention. He looked down and saw red swollen skin. When he tried to contract his fingers, it hurt like hell. It hurt to do nothing. Somehow, somewhere he'd burned it in the fire. Maybe when he'd tried to turn the doorknob.

His gun was empty, and that was never good. So Striker returned to their cruiser, opened the trunk, and got some more ammo from the munitions box. He loaded up all three mags, then gave one to Felicia on the way back.

'Load up,' he said.

Off in the distance, the high-pitched wail of fire trucks could be heard, coming from the south. Someone had called in the fire, and Striker was thankful for it.

He looked back and studied the blazing fire, then focused his stare down at the iron-barred window. No hope in hell of reaching the camera now. The entire building was aflame and the camera would undoubtedly be incinerated.

Striker studied the fire. The roof and sides were a bright reddish-yellow hue. But the doorway where he and Felicia had escaped was different from the rest – it was a bright yellow-white. And the smoke from there was darker than the rest, an oily black colour.

An accelerant had been used. There was no doubt about it.

He took a moment to examine the area. In less than a minute, he found an empty can in the bushes flanking the front walkway. He gloved up, knelt down, and picked it up. Read the label.

Steinman's Wood Varnish.

The warning label showed a bright red flame and a caption that read: *Flammable.*

'Collect this,' Striker told Felicia. 'It's evidence.'

With his hand stinging, he took out his notebook and scribbled down the time and where the can had been found. As he looked back up, he spotted several pods of looky-loos coming out from the projects. Some of them were brave enough to creep out on to the sidewalk, but most of them stayed inside the safety of their own yards to watch the show. The sight of them reminded Striker of the figure he'd seen watching them when they'd first arrived.

He looked across the road to the suite where he had seen the mysterious figure; the drapes were now closed. Odd, since everyone else had come out to see what was going on.

He put away his notebook and started back across the street.

Felicia walked over and looked at him. 'Where you going?' she asked.

He barely glanced back. 'I'm checking something out.'

'Jacob—'

'Just stay there, Feleesh. We need to let the bucket-heads know we cleared the other townhomes. Otherwise they'll head into the fire themselves.'

She looked ready to say more, but Striker didn't give her the chance. He hightailed it across Hermon Drive towards the apartment where he'd seen the person watching them. At the time, he had deemed him one of the neighbourhood busybodies.

Now he wondered.

Striker drew his pistol and hiked up the small crest of hill, keeping to the side of the suite, out of the line of fire. When he reached the window, he took out his flashlight and shone it through the glass. It was difficult to see. The only area visible was between the hanging drapes, and there were still sheers blocking his view.

He was about to circle the building and try the front door, when he noticed something. The window was open a crack. He reached out, pulled on it, and the window opened fully.

'Vancouver Police!' he called. 'Is anyone inside?'

No answer.

He tried again: 'Vancouver Police! Is anyone home?'

Again, nothing.

He drew the curtains and sheers aside, and shone the flashlight inside the apartment. Everything there was quiet, and still. The place appeared as vacant as the townhome unit across the road. Keeping his gun aimed into the darkness ahead, Striker climbed inside the window, felt his feet touch the vinyl surface of the floor, and looked around the area.

On the floor by the window was the female end of a long electrical cord. Striker swept the flashlight along it to find the other end. The cord ran all the way to the entrance of the apartment, then under the door into the communal hall. Striker reached out for the light switch. He flicked it on, and nothing happened.

The apartment had no power.

Keeping his gun at the low-ready and his flashlight aimed ahead, he searched the entire apartment, starting with the main room he was in and then finishing with the lone bathroom and bedroom. Both were empty. Anyone who might have been here was now long gone.

Striker opened the front door and peered into the hall. At his feet, the extension cord ran down the wall to an electrical outlet, where it was plugged in. He nodded absently. The room had had no power, and whoever had been in there had obviously needed some.

Why, he wondered.

Thoughts of the camera relay system he had seen flashed through his mind, and made his fingers tighten on the gun. He returned inside the apartment and shone his flashlight all around the front window looking for prints. What he found was a plastic package. He picked it up and read the label.

Wood screws. Ten inchers.

Perfect for mounting steel brackets and beams to a front door.

'He was right here all along,' Striker found himself saying. '*Fuck!*'

He looked out of the window and studied the scene across the road. Out there on Hermon Drive, the entire row of townhomes was a mass of flame. Two fire trucks now occupied the block, their red flashing lights as bright as the fire. Felicia was down there, speaking to the Fire Captain and pointing to the series of units they had already cleared.

The captain seemed relieved by this.

Striker turned his eyes past them to the front of Sarah Rose's apartment. This window was the perfect vantage point. The perfect spot for recon. And Striker began to wonder how the Adder had come across it. Was it by chance? Or was the whole thing planned?

He hoped the former.

But experience told him otherwise.

He looked at the window where he had seen the video camera, tucked down in the lower left corner of the window. That area was now completely engulfed in flame, with two firemen hosing down the wall to no avail.

With his hand stinging and his frustration growing, Striker left the apartment through the window he had come in. Mandy Gill was dead. Sarah Rose was dead. And any evidence inside the townhome was likely lost in the flames.

It doesn't get much worse, Striker thought.

He thought wrong. A white unmarked Crown Victoria pulled up on scene and a short man in a pristine white dress shirt climbed out. It was Car 10. The Road Boss.

Inspector Laroche had arrived.

By the time Striker made his way back down the slope of lawn to street level, an ambulance and two patrol cars had arrived on scene. So had two news crews – a van from British Columbia TV News and one from the Canadian Broadcasting Corporation. It was standard practice in the City of Vancouver. Word spread fast among the media. Nothing was sacred and no story was too small – so long as human lives were in jeopardy.

Striker watched them with disdain. One of the reporters was

a short blonde woman he recognized from a previous nightmare call. She'd distorted every fact of the case and ended up jeopardizing his investigation. The memory of it was still raw. She stepped out of the van and began raking a brush through her long blonde hair in preparation for the shoot.

'I want tape up *now*,' Striker said to one of the patrol cops.

'Don't anyone say one word to them,' a deep voice ordered.

Striker turned around and spotted the Road Boss. Inspector Laroche stood with his hands on his hips, assessing the carnage all around them. His deep voice seemed wrong for his diminutive body. As always, his uniform was impeccable. His pants were as black as his hair and pressed to equal perfection, and his white dress shirt was without wrinkle.

It was hard to believe he'd been sitting in the car.

The inspector saw Striker and marched over. 'What the hell is going on here?' he demanded.

'It was the Adder,' Striker said.

Felicia came over and joined the conversation. 'Billy Mercury,' she clarified.

Striker nodded. 'It would *appear* so. We have to check his place right now. Get him on CPIC. Broadcast it on every channel.' He made a fist as he thought this over and winced.

Felicia took notice. 'You're hurt.'

'It's nothing.'

'Your hand . . . Jacob, it's *burned.*'

Striker gave her an irritated glance. 'It's fine.'

Laroche shook his head. 'An on-the-job injury? No, you need to go to the hospital for that. And make sure you fill out the Workers' Compensation Board forms.'

'It's nothing. A light burn. First degree at best.'

'Department liability,' Laroche said. He spoke the words like a speech he had memorized. 'According to Workers' Compensation

Board rules, you have to attend the hospital and be assessed by a physician. Either you go, or I remove you from the road, effective immediately.'

Striker felt his hands balling into fists again. This time he ignored the pain.

'Someone needs to go after Billy Mercury,' he said.

'Someone already has,' Laroche said. 'Your All Points Bulletin worked well. Billy Mercury just got taken down by a pair of patrol cops, not ten minutes ago. He's in custody as we speak.'

Striker thought of the timeline. 'Ten minutes ago? *Where* did this happen?'

Laroche looked north. 'Not five miles up the road. Hastings and Kootenay. Just outside his residence. He was screaming about demons and hellfire. Cops took him down right there in the bus loop.'

Striker said nothing as he thought this over. The timeline fit. As did the proximity of the location. As did the man's crazed actions.

'He had his laptop with him when they took him down,' Laroche continued. 'And they hit the mother lode. Everything was on it. All his MyShrine pages were up and running, along with a million other chat rooms and blogs – Twitter, MySpace and LinkedIn.'

'And?' Striker asked.

Laroche nodded. 'Pretty much what you'd expect – talk of demons. Rants about the Middle East and the war. Accusations about the validity of the medications he's on. And, of course, the threats. They were all in there – even the email he sent you. The man is clearly delusional, and highly volatile. He's being taken back to Riverglen as we speak.'

'Riverglen?' Striker asked. 'You mean he's being sectioned?'

'Yes.'

'What about charges?'

'Can't charge him. He's being pinked,' Laroche explained – a term used in lieu of *institutionalized*, due to the bright pink colour of the medical health warrant. 'By order of his very own doctor.'

Striker gave Felicia a dark glance. 'And which doctor would that be?'

'Why, Dr Ostermann, of course.'

Striker swore. 'This is bullshit. We should charge Mercury with attempted murder, then hold him for a Psych Doc.'

Laroche glanced back at the various camera crews that were setting up at the top of Hermon Drive. There were more of them now. As many as six. It was quickly becoming a media nightmare. They were here because of the fire, no doubt. But eventually the whole story would leak. It always did. Soon enough they would know about Billy, and then the real blitz would begin.

Laroche shook his head. 'Billy can't be charged criminally with anything – he's been pinked.'

'But—'

'It's not gonna happen, Striker.'

'Why? Because of how it will look on the news? The man tried to kill us!'

Laroche was unmoved. 'Mental illness supersedes criminal charges.'

Striker just glared at the man; the medical-versus-criminal debate had been going on for decades in Canada, and he knew it would never end. It was a black hole in the system, an area where bad people slipped through and criminal charges were lost.

'This is wrong, and you know it.'

'It's *reality*,' Laroche replied. 'Don't make it personal.'

Striker almost laughed. The man had just tried to kill them – how could he not make it personal?

He looked all around the area. He found it hard to breathe. His lungs still felt burned from the hot ash of the smoke, and the flesh of his fingers throbbed. He placed his good hand against the passenger-side door of Laroche's unmarked cruiser and stabilized himself.

The world was spinning.

Laroche took notice, and his voice took on a softer tone. 'It's over, Striker,' he said. 'You can relax now.'

'It's *not* over – Larisa is still out there somewhere. She was connected to Dr Richter and the Mapleview Clinic, and so were Billy, Mandy and Sarah. Now Mandy and Sarah are dead, and I can't find Larisa . . .'

The inspector nodded slowly, taking it all in. 'I understand all that. But with Mercury institutionalized, the woman is out of immediate danger. We'll find her. In time.'

'In *time*?'

Laroche turned and they met face to face. 'Yes. When you're in a better frame of mind. And in the meantime, I expect you to lay off Dr Ostermann.'

'What?'

'Are you even aware he is a yearly contributor to the Police Mutual Benevolent Association?'

'I'm well aware.'

'And that he is good friends with the mayor?'

Striker felt his jaw stiffen. 'Again, your point's lost on me.'

'I'm just saying be careful with the man. Dr Ostermann has a good reputation in this city and he has powerful friends in all three levels of government. The last thing this department needs is more melodrama.'

Striker said nothing for a moment as he sized up the man.

Then he realized: 'You're worried about a law suit.' He shook his head in disgust. 'I need to interview Mercury.'

He started to turn away; Laroche stopped him.

'You can interview him later, Striker.'

'Now. Before—'

'Do I have to put you on mandatory leave?' Laroche asked, and now there was a hardness in his tone.

'Mandatory leave?' Striker repeated. 'Why? Because of the injury to my hand – or because of Dr Ostermann's prized reputation?'

Laroche's face darkened and his voice deepened. 'You need a breather, Detective. Your way, or mine.'

Striker looked back at the man, saw the seriousness in his stare, and knew that this was one battle he was in no position to win. He took in a deep breath, shrugged, and gave in.

'Fine,' he said. 'But this is a mistake.'

He took a long look at the swarm of media at the top of Hermon Drive, then glanced back at the raging fire, which had taken over the neighbouring row of townhomes. It was a beast of a blaze, and there was little doubt that the entire building would be nothing more than a blackened shell by the time the fire crews got everything under control.

With billows of hot ash and black oily smoke blotting out any trace of blue sky, Striker turned away from Felicia and Laroche and headed for the waiting ambulance. This wasn't over. He knew it. Something was wrong. And because of Laroche, there was nothing he could do about it.

He was being taken from the road.

Forty-Nine

The visit to Burnaby General Hospital went fast, thank God. The doctor who treated Striker was one he had dealt with before on a few occasions. Dr Alison Montcalm was as friendly as ever, making light of the situation, yet also warning him of the risk of infection.

It was the standard speech.

The burn was worse than Striker had originally thought – first degree to the skin of his left-hand fingers, but second degree on the base of his palm. It hurt like hell.

Dr Montcalm gently cleaned the wound with a cold solution that stung. 'Are you left-handed?' she asked.

Striker winced. 'No. Right.'

'I'm surprised you grabbed the doorknob with your left hand then.'

'I had my gun out at the time.'

Dr Montcalm nodded as she listened. She dressed the wound with antibiotic ointment, then taped a light dressing around the area to keep it clean. Striker looked at it and frowned. The blister that had formed was dead centre at the base of his hand, and it stung every time he so much as flexed it.

'I wouldn't worry too much about it,' Dr Montcalm said. 'I'm sure you'll survive.'

Striker smiled at her. 'Yeah. I have a way of doing that.'

He left Burnaby General as quickly as he came. Felicia had asked him to wait while she finished tidying up the crime scene back on Hermon Drive, but he couldn't stay there a second longer. He hated hospitals. Always had, always would. Too many bad memories. It wasn't until he was free of the front doors that he felt good again.

It was half-past noon, and he needed a mental break from it all, so he hailed a taxi and headed to the one place that ever gave him any solace.

He headed for home.

Once home, Striker climbed out of the taxi and paid the man. Far above, the sun was still out and glowing a strange, pale white colour in the frosty sky. It reminded Striker of the fire.

He killed the thought and started up the sidewalk. Despite the fact that it was lunchtime, frost still covered the gate. The air was so cold he could see his breath, even in the daylight. Winter was still here, no doubt, keeping the grass of his lawn frozen and brittle and the front porch steps slippery.

He unlocked the front door and went inside. The first thing he noticed was the flickering glow of the flames in the fireplace. It warmed the room with a gentle, welcoming heat. The soft lighting of the den made everything feel cosy and safe. And as Striker looked around the room, he smiled despite his pain and weariness.

Be it ever so humble, he thought.

He took off his coat, being careful not to catch the dressing of his hand on the cuff of the sleeve, and hung it up on the coat rack. Then he moved into the den and crashed down on the couch. Kicked off his shoes. Put his feet up on the table and enjoyed the heat.

A second or two later, he heard a door open down the hall, and Courtney came out.

'Dad?' she called.

'Hey, Pumpkin.'

She shuffled down the hall on her crutches, then stopped at the entrance to the den. 'I thought you were at work,' she said.

'I thought you were at school.'

A surprised look spread across her features, as if she realized she'd just been caught. 'It's a professional day.'

'Hmm. Just like last Friday.'

Courtney's blue eyes turned shifty, then they focused on his hand and turned hard. 'What happened?'

'Rough game of Rock-Paper-Scissors.'

'I'm serious.'

He let out a long breath. 'There was a fire in the projects. The burn is minor.'

She looked at the bandage, as if she could see right through all the gauze. 'It gonna heal?'

'It's only first degree,' he lied, 'so yeah, in time.'

For a long moment, the two of them turned silent, Striker enjoying the heat of the fire and being home for the moment; and Courtney moving around the room and gathering her things.

Striker caught himself watching her. She was so much like her mother at times. A carbon copy of Amanda. The way she looked at him, the way she pursed her lips when she was thinking, the way she made soft clicking sounds with her teeth when she got stressed.

And the temper, too. The moodiness. In that, she was *definitely* her mother's daughter. Sometimes, when Striker looked at her, he felt like he was staring at Amanda all over again, and it made him feel anxious and regretful for all that had happened in the past.

He tried not to think about it.

When Courtney put on her runners and started lacing them up, he took notice. 'Going back to school on a Pro Day – wow, you are dedicated.'

'I have other things to do.'

'Like rehab,' he reminded her.

She rolled her eyes. 'Yes, Dad, I'm going to my appointment, okay? God, you're always riding me. What, does it make you happy or something?'

'What would make me happy is if you would stop skipping your therapy sessions. You *need* them.'

'And I'm going!'

Striker nodded. 'Good. Say hi to Annalisa for me. And get her to check out your braces again, make sure they're the right level.'

Courtney's eyes narrowed and she shook her head. 'They're crutches, Dad, okay? *Crutches* – not braces. I keep telling you that.'

'Crutches, braces – it makes no difference.'

'It makes a difference *to me*,' she said, and her eyes suddenly looked wet.

Striker saw this, and he felt his heart clench. 'I'm sorry, Pumpkin, I didn't mean to upset you.'

'You never mean to do anything.'

'I'm sorry,' he said again.

Courtney offered no reply. She finished tying her laces, then stood back up. When she reached the door, she opened it and stepped outside without saying goodbye.

'I can drive you,' he said.

She looked back at him and her blue eyes were ice. 'Why don't you drive yourself, Dad. Take a trip down Sensitivity Street. Might do you some good.'

'Courtney—'

She slammed the door behind her and was gone.

For a moment, Striker considered going after her, but then reconsidered. It would do no good. In fact, it would probably only make things worse. Courtney was just like her mother; when she got into one of her moods, nothing would fix it but time and space. And now he wondered what he'd done to set her off this time. He went over their conversation in his head, trying to figure out where it had all gone wrong, then finally gave up. His hand hurt. His head hurt. And he was damn tired.

In the medicine cabinet was some Extra Strength Tylenol he'd bought for Courtney last year. It was old, probably past its due date, but he took some anyway. Then his mind returned to work, like it always did. He plucked his cell from his pocket and read the screen in hopes of finding voicemail.

There was none.

It pained him. Larisa was still out there somewhere, and here he was, taken off the road – forced from the job on injury reserve. He could have fought the issue, battled the doctor and Laroche, but then they would have been forced to fill out the Compensation Board forms right there and then. And once that was done, no one got back on the road without seeing the specialist.

The way it was now – so long as the forms were not filled out – Striker could play with it.

The thought pinballed around in his head as he sat there, trying to relax but not managing it. Too much had happened, and too much still had to be investigated. Mandy and Sarah. Larisa Logan and Billy Mercury. Drs Ostermann and Richter. Mapleview and Riverglen. And then there was the whole EvenHealth programme and the SILC sessions.

There was just so damn much – and that was outside of the problems he had with Courtney and Felicia. The more he thought about it, the more his head hurt. He leaned back on the couch, closed his eyes, and tried to clear his mind.

It was only one o'clock in the afternoon, and already it seemed like a long, hard day.

Fifty

When the front door swung open and a cold draught of winter air blew inside the den, Striker opened his eyes. How much time had passed, he wasn't sure. He felt halfway between wakefulness and sleep. He sat up on the couch, took his feet off the table, and stretched. Standing at the entrance to the den was Felicia. Her long dark hair was brushed back over her shoulder, and her warm eyes were fixated on him.

'Feel free to let yourself in,' he said.

'You were supposed to wait for me at the hospital.'

'Had to leave. Nurses kept hitting on me. You would have flown into a jealous rage.'

'You could at least have phoned me.' She closed the door and walked into the room. 'How's your hand?'

'It's fine.'

'Fine. Sure. Just like everything else.' She threw her coat on the chair, then shivered as if cold. She walked across the den, her dress shoes clicking on the hardwood surface, and sat down next to him. She kicked off her shoes, grabbed the blanket from the corner of the couch and wrapped it around herself.

'It's one-thirty in the afternoon and it feels like midnight,' she said. 'Crank the fire, will you? It's freezing in here.'

Striker got up and turned the dial to High. Then he went into the kitchen and made a pot of coffee. He warmed a couple of mugs as the brew percolated, then added some cream and sugar to each one. When it was done, he filled both mugs and brought them to the den.

'Here.' He handed her one.

She took it. 'Thanks. You're a dream.'

'A nightmare?'

Felicia ignored the comment. She looked at the bandage covering his hand and wrist. 'What degree of burn?'

'Second.' When Felicia made a face, Striker added, 'We're lucky that's all it is, we could've died in there.'

She said nothing back, but her dark eyes took on a distant look. 'Well, at least Mercury's being institutionalized,' she finally said. 'And we can put an end to all this.'

Striker made an unhappy sound. 'I'm not so sure we can.'

'Why not?'

He put down his mug and turned on the couch to face her. 'The psychology is all wrong.'

'And since when did you get your doctorate?'

'Don't got to be a doctor to figure this one out, Feleesh. Think about it. You read the first message he sent. *The game is on*, and all that shit. He was basically challenging us, taunting us. Very direct and logical.'

'So?'

'So, the next thing we know he's putting stuff on MyShrine, and it's all crazy-ass shit. Stuff about the war in Afghanistan and demons and him being the Hammer of God – it's all paranoid delusions.'

'Which shows he's been spiralling out of control.'

'Fine. Then tell me, how does a guy who's spiralling out of control maintain enough logic and sanity to lure us into a trap like that? Make no mistake about it – that was set for us, and

Sarah Rose was the bait. Those cameras were meant for our deaths, too. There couldn't have been a better location for it – almost as if he somehow directed Sarah Rose to be there.'

'Directed?' Felicia smiled at him. 'I think you're giving this guy too much credit.'

'Am I? There was only one way in and out of that place, Feleesh, and the moment we went in, he trapped us. Ten-inch screws. A solid oak door. Combustible material to accelerate the fire. And through it all he was recording us – does that sound like a man who's so delusional? Who's seeing demons everywhere?'

'He's a soldier, Jacob. He's broken from the war.'

'I don't buy it. If he came after us, shooting like a madman, fine. But not like this. And that's to say nothing about the injections. Who knows what he's been pumping into his victims.'

'You're assuming they were injected,' she said. 'We have no proof of that yet. No tox tests back. No syringes left on scene. Just a strange mark on Mandy Gill's neck.'

'And Sarah Rose's, too.'

She gave him a tender look. 'Are you sure about that, Jacob? One hundred per cent sure? The place was dim as hell, and there was a haze in the air, too. Not to mention how distended her body was – she'd been there for over a day, for sure. Maybe two. Then the fire starts and all hell breaks loose. We never really had a chance to assess the body properly.'

'Then let's go do it now,' he said.

She gave him an uncertain look. 'You didn't hear?'

'What?' he asked.

'Burned completely,' she said. 'You won't be discovering any needle marks on that flesh, even if there were some there for you to find.'

Striker cursed. He looked at the screen of his phone again, saw that there were no more messages from the Adder. And also no message from Larisa Logan. He sat heavily back against the couch. Rubbed his eyes with his one good hand. Scratched at a half day's stubble on his face.

'We're missing something,' he said again.

Felicia reached over and touched his face. 'The only thing we're missing here, Jacob, is some *sleep*. Some rest. Last week we put in over eighty hours. And we've put in more than thirty the last two days. We're exhausted.'

He looked back at her, and even though he didn't agree with everything she said, he knew there was truth to parts of it. He reached out to touch her, forgot his hand was injured, and raked his burned hand against the side of the couch. He flinched.

Felicia looked down at his hand. 'It must hurt.'

'It was a stupid thing to do, grabbing the doorknob like that.'

Felicia gently touched his fingers, where there was no bandage. 'If you hadn't done something, we would never have made it out of there.'

He said nothing back, he just looked at her, and before he knew it, her lips were on his lips – soft and wet and warm. He kissed her back, felt her mouth open, felt her tongue on his tongue.

He eased her back on the couch, and she let him. With his good hand, he pulled down her dress pants, tore them from her legs, then reached down and slid off her panties. She let out a soft sound as he felt her warmth and wetness, and she shuddered beneath his touch.

'I want you, Jacob.'

He kissed her again. Breathed in the soft vanilla of her perfume. Listened to the moans that escaped her lips with every thrust of his body. And he lost himself in the moment.

Felicia was there. In his home. And they were together again, if only for the moment. The world outside may have been cold and harsh, but the mood in here was warm and inviting.

He wished it would never end.

Fifty-One

A while later, at almost two-thirty in the afternoon, Striker lay back on the couch and watched Felicia walk out of the washroom and return to the den. As she went, she adjusted her shirt, then began smoothing out the wrinkles of her dress pants. She looked beautiful in the soft glow of the fire. Her straight black hair spilled all around her shoulders and her dark eyes were warm and magnetic. She stepped into the den, in front of him, then met his stare and let out a sigh.

'I can't believe we're here again,' she said.

Striker smiled. 'You mean in the den?'

'Stop it, Jacob. You know what I mean.' She gestured towards herself and then him. 'This. Us. I didn't want it to happen again.' She reached up to adjust her earring and closed her eyes. 'Oh *God*, how did this happen again?'

Striker sat up. 'Well, first you touched my shoulder, then you looked into my eyes—'

'Stop.' She gave him a hard look, cutting him off. 'Just knock it off, Casanova.'

He laughed, then stood up. He stepped forward, into her personal space. When he went to put his arms around her, she stiffened a little, so he let go. She looked up at him, and there was conflict in her eyes. Tenderness, yet stubbornness. Nothing changed.

'What?' he asked.

'We're back to square one. All over again.'

'Is that really so bad?'

'Well, no. Yes. *Shit.*'

Striker just looked at her and didn't know what to say. Their relationship had been complicated from day one. Had it just been them, everything would have been fine. But it wasn't just them. There was work. And Courtney. And everything in between.

And they both knew that would never change.

He wanted to say something. Felt he *had* to say something. But, like always, he couldn't find the words.

'So what now?' she said softly. 'Where do we go from here, Jacob?'

He met her eyes, felt the heaviness of her stare, and gave her the only honest answer he could think of:

'Back to the case.'

Fifteen minutes later – after another failed attempt at reaching Dr Richter and getting only voicemail – Striker drove them out east. More than anything he wanted to interview Billy Mercury, but in order to do that, he had to do one of two things first – either arrest the man on charges of arson and attempted murder, or gain permission from the man's psychiatrist.

Who was none other than Dr Erich Ostermann.

They had come full circle.

He drove towards Riverglen Mental Health Facility, where Billy Mercury had been sectioned to. When they were nearing the east end of Vancouver, Felicia let out a long hard breath.

'Inspector Laroche is gonna freak when he sees you're not on medical leave.'

Striker scowled. 'Laroche . . . who the hell cares what he thinks?'

'*I* will when he suspends us.'

Striker gave her a hot look. 'Okay, first off, Laroche never put me on leave. I took myself off the road in order to deal with the injury to my hand – and I never filled out the Workers' Compensation Board papers yet.'

'Semantics. You can't be back on the road again until you're cleared by one of the doctors at Medicore.'

Striker said nothing back. Felicia was right about that one – she was always right about stuff like that. She knew the *Rules and Procedures* manual better than anyone, and she was the only cop he knew who had actually read the damn thing from beginning to end.

The Medicore Health Center was the primary health insurer the Vancouver Police Department contracted. Once an officer was off duty from an injury, they could not return until cleared by Medicore – not even if another specialist had already been consulted.

It was all to do with insurance claims, and, therefore, *money*. So nothing about the system was overly surprising.

Striker gave Felicia a quick glance. 'I won't argue that point, but don't forget, the whole Medicore thing is just policy, not the law. And it's not even *our* policy, it's a Workers' Compensation Board thing. If I make the injury worse, they'll just fight me on it in court. Well, no big deal. I'm fine with that.'

'You oversimplify everything.'

'I wish I could do that with you.'

She gave him a hard look, then let it go. Striker was happy with that. There were other larger issues to deal with here than injury compensation.

When they reached the corner of Broadway and Nanaimo Street, Striker pulled over to the kerb.

'What?' Felicia asked.

He looked at her. 'What time did Ostermann say he worked at Riverglen until?'

Felicia looked at the clock, and was surprised to see it was already going on three o'clock. 'Shit, you're right. He'll be gone by now. Maybe we can intercept him somewhere on the way back into town.'

'Or maybe he'll be staying longer today because of Mercury.'

Striker took out his cell and called Riverglen. The call was answered by the main switchboard who then transferred him to the receptionist they had dealt with earlier in the day. She was less than friendly.

'Dr Ostermann only works here in the mornings,' she said, offering nothing further.

'I understand that,' Striker said. 'But I thought he might be putting in some extra time this afternoon because of what happened today with Billy Mercury.'

The woman made a weary sound. 'Mr Mercury is not Dr Ostermann's only patient, I'm afraid, though he does seem to take up the bulk of his time. Dr Ostermann will be seeing him at the clinic.'

Striker cast Felicia a disbelieving glance. When he spoke again, it was difficult to keep the agitation out of his voice. 'Hold on a second, are you telling me that Billy Mercury is not already at Riverglen? I thought he'd been institutionalized.'

'He has been, and he will be here – *after* Dr Ostermann is finished seeing him.'

'In a private clinic? I'm not comfortable with that.'

The woman let out a long breath, as if to express how tired she was of the conversation. 'We have armed guards, Detective.

We deal with a lot of violent patients. We do it all the time. And we do it quite well. There is nothing for you – or anyone else, for that matter – to be concerned about.'

Striker felt his fingers tighten on the cell. 'You might think differently if it was your house he just burned down. Now which clinic is Dr Ostermann seeing Billy at?'

'That's confidential information.'

Striker had had enough. 'I'll put it to you this way: right now I'm dealing with an important investigation and I need to speak to Dr Ostermann as quickly as possible. If you don't tell me where he is, I'll charge you with Obstruction. And I'll take the time to drive out there right now and arrest you myself. You got that? Now where the hell is he?'

The receptionist's tone didn't change, but she coughed up the information. 'Dr Ostermann is where he always is on Thursday afternoons. He's working with the EvenHealth programme.'

'Which branch?'

'It's at Boundary and Adanac.'

Striker hung up the phone. When he turned to face Felicia, he saw a dark curiosity in her expression.

'Well?' she asked. 'Where the hell is he?'

'Mapleview,' Striker said. He put the car into Drive, hit the gas and drove down Broadway.

The clinic was only twenty minutes away.

Fifty-Two

Striker and Felicia drove down Broadway. East Pender Street was less than five miles away, so Striker expected to be on scene in minutes. But he had barely gone five blocks when the emergency tone went off on the radio. The dispatcher, Sue Rhaemer, came across the air, and it was the first time in Striker's memory that he had ever heard the woman rattled:

'All units, all units, we have an officer down. Repeat: an officer down. Thirty-six hundred block of East Hastings Street.'

'Jesus Christ,' Felicia said.

Striker said nothing; he just hit the gas. Before he could respond verbally, the road sergeant, Mike Rothschild, came across the air.

'Who's calling this in?' Rothschild demanded.

'We're getting it second-hand from Ambulance,' the dispatcher replied.

'Where is the nearest unit?'

Striker grabbed the radio and gave their location. 'Detective Striker, Broadway and Nanaimo.'

The moment he let go of the plunger, another unit came on the air: 'Charlie-21, we're already at Hastings and Windermere. Ten blocks out.'

Felicia looked at Striker. 'They're way closer,' she said, relieved.

Sgt Rothschild gave the order: 'That unit is authorized. Code 3.' Then he directed his question back to the dispatcher. 'Which unit is supposed to be riding with the ambulance?'

The dispatcher paused for barely a second. 'Alpha-13 . . . but they're not answering their radio and their emergency button's been pressed.'

Rothschild: 'Do we know the nature of the injury?'

'Unknown,' the dispatcher replied. 'We can't raise the ambulance crew either.'

Striker pressed the radio plunger one more time. 'Mike,' he said. 'They were transporting Billy Mercury, the war vet who just tried to burn us down in the complex.'

Rothschild heard that and wasted no time. 'Does Burnaby have any units closer?' he asked.

'Burnaby is negative for units,' the dispatcher replied.

'We're on scene,' Charlie-21 broke in. 'Mercury has escaped. Repeat: Billy Mercury has *escaped*.'

Rothschild made a frustrated sound. 'Give them the air. Charlie-21, update their status when you can.'

The radio went quiet for almost a half-minute; the seconds were excruciating. And when Charlie-21 got back on the air, the man's voice was jittery.

'Jesus, we got two paramedics down on scene. And two officers, too. One of their guns is gone!'

'I want more units there now,' Rothschild ordered.

Bravo-15 broke in: 'We're already on scene, Mike. So is Bravo-73.'

Charlie-21 took control of the air one more time, and the voice was fast and frantic:

'Oh Christ, both cops . . . both medics . . . they're dead, they're dead. *They're ALL DEAD.*'

Fifty-Three

Striker hammered the gas and raced north on Boundary Road. By the time they'd passed 1st Avenue, the Taurus was nearing one hundred and forty kilometres per hour. By the time they reached Napier Street – and Striker heard there were now more than *six* patrol units on scene – he hit the brakes and slowed down. Far up the road, a mass of blue and red emergency lights flashed in the daylight.

'Go,' Felicia said. 'What are you doing? *Go.* Let's get there!'

But Striker did the exact opposite. He pressed his foot even harder down on the brake and swerved over towards the grassy meridian. Once there, he drove into the middle of it and stopped.

'Jacob, what are you doing?'

He ignored her question and grabbed the radio mike. 'Do we have a direction of travel?' he broadcast.

When units on scene replied, 'Negative' and dispatch also replied, 'Negative,' Striker scanned the road ahead of them. The intersection where the ambulance had crashed was only a mile or two up the road. Striker's heart told him to race to the scene with every kilometre of speed the cruiser was capable of.

But his instincts told him otherwise. Billy Mercury was fit. And their location was within running distance for the man.

'Jacob?' Felicia asked again.

'They got tons of units on scene,' he explained. 'Mercury was being escorted by police and ambulance back to Riverglen. So when he escaped, there's only two places he's gonna run to.' He pointed ahead, northwest. 'Mapleview Clinic is right there on the left side. And six blocks behind it, in the north lane of Pender, is where Mercury lives.'

'That close?'

'That close. We need to cover both of them. If Mercury's got any brains, he'll run in the opposite direction, but I doubt that. Not in the state of mind he's in. My bet is he ran right for his nearest place of comfort – and that would mean he's barricaded himself in his apartment.'

Felicia already had her gun in her hand and was scanning the roads ahead, looking for any sign of movement. 'He's awfully close to the clinic, too,' she worried. 'The doctors need to be warned; the place needs to be shut down.'

Striker agreed. He hit the gas and peeled off the meridian, tearing up the earth and sending waves of dirt and grass into the air.

Destination: Mapleview.

Even though the address of the Mapleview Clinic was in the thirty-six hundred block of Adanac Street, the only entrance to the facility was off the main stretch of Boundary Road. The building sat way back from the roadside, nestled behind a large cement roundabout, which was filled with flowers and barren trees. Flanking the facility grounds was a wooded park to the south and an old folks' home to the north.

Another place of possible escape.

Another place of vulnerable victims.

Striker spotted the facility and slowed his speed. He scanned the road ahead, then the entranceway, and finally the entire lot. Safety was his foremost concern right now. *Their* safety.

Billy Mercury had just killed two cops and two ambulance attendants.

He would surely kill again if given the chance.

From the east side of Boundary, the lot appeared empty of people. Unfortunately there were tons of hiding spots: a passenger van sat by the roundabout, its side door open, its interior lights off. Just ahead of the van, an outdoor patio area was sunken and fenced off, providing additional cover. And opposite that, the trees of the park offered numerous spots of concealment. All in all, it was a bad place for police entry. Had time not been so pressing, he would have waited for some extra units and a dog.

But not today. There was no time.

Billy was gone. Billy had killed. And Billy would kill again.

Striker gave Felicia a quick glance. 'Be ready for anything,' he said. Then he drove into the entranceway of the compound.

Straight ahead sat the three-level facility that was Mapleview Clinic. It was a relatively new building, with lots of tinted glass and clean beige stone. With the fountain and garden centred out front, the place looked more like a spa retreat than a clinic.

Striker reached the roundabout, considered driving around it, then opted not to. Any further ahead and they'd be dead centre between the park, the old folks' home, and the medical clinic.

A perfect target section for any sniper.

At least now they were behind the cement wall and the foliage of the roundabout.

Striker rammed the steering column into Park, opened the door and hopped out. Getting free of the car felt good. When Felicia did the same, Striker pointed to the old folks' home. 'Lock it down,' he said.

She raced across the lot without so much as a word.

With her gone, Striker turned back towards the clinic. He

kept his gun at the low-ready, passed the concrete roundabout, and ran up the stairs. He kicked open the front doors, and they banged against the wall, releasing a loud hollow *thud* in the high-ceilinged foyer of the entrance. The wired window glass rattled.

At her desk the receptionist let out a sharp gasp.

'Vancouver Police!' Striker announced. 'Has Billy Mercury been in here?'

The woman placed a hand over her heart. 'Well, yes, yes, yes . . . he has.' She looked at him in bewilderment, realizing something bad was going on. 'He left here not twenty minutes ago. With the other officers.'

'In the ambulance?'

She nodded emphatically. 'Yes, in the ambulance. He was sent to Riverglen. He's been . . . he's been *sectioned*.'

'Well, he's escaped,' Striker said. 'And he just killed two cops and a couple of paramedics.'

The receptionist's pale face turned even whiter and her mouth tightened into a straight line. She looked stunned. And then Dr Ostermann suddenly appeared from the back room. He walked up to the front counter and met Striker with a look of concern.

'What exactly is going on here?' he demanded.

Striker stepped forward to meet the man. 'Your patient has escaped.'

'Who? Not Billy?'

'Yes, Billy. He just killed two cops and the ambulance attendants.'

Dr Ostermann wavered where he stood. For a moment, Striker thought he might keel over in front of him. But then he placed his hands on the receptionist's counter and blinked.

'Oh God. Oh dear God,' he got out.

'Let's go,' Striker said. 'You're coming with me.'

This seemed to wake the doctor up. 'Go? But . . . but where?'

'Three blocks north. To Billy's place.'

Dr Ostermann took a full step back. 'Billy's place? But-but-but . . . why *me*?'

'Because you're the only one I know who has any kind of a rapport with the man. He's your patient, Doctor. Depending on how things go out there, we might have need of you.'

'But, but I can't—'

'You're coming, Doctor. End of discussion.'

Striker took Dr Ostermann by the arm and guided him out of the front doors of the facility. Before closing the door, Striker looked back at the receptionist and gave the order. 'Lock this place down. Every door, every window. And don't open up again until the police return.'

The receptionist nodded daftly, blinked, then got herself moving and hurried down the hall. With her gone, Striker turned to face the front and spotted Felicia racing back to their car. He pushed Dr Ostermann forward, down the building's steps. When they reached the cruiser, he gave the man an intense stare.

'Prepare yourself, Doctor,' he said. 'We're about to find out just how good a psychiatrist you really are.'

Fifty-Four

Billy Mercury lived in a rundown dump in the thirty-six hundred block of East Hastings Street. Safe Haven Suites. Striker knew the building well.

Safe Haven.

Nothing here was safe, and it sure as hell wasn't a haven. The place was a halfway house for people of all types who were trying to glue their life pieces back together again. Everyone from the mentally ill to the criminally minded lived here.

It had been that way for ten years.

The place was poorly designed. Having been constructed and reconstructed several times over the years in order to create more and more suites, the layout was now a maze. All the even-numbered suites faced on to the front side of the building, which was Hastings Street. All the odd-numbered suites – like Billy's unit, number 103 – backed out on to the north lane of Pender. Knowing this, Striker dumped his vehicle at the east end of the laneway, then got out on foot.

A few blocks north and east was the primary crime scene, where Billy had killed two cops and two paramedics. There were more than six units up there now, and Striker considered calling a few of them away to block off the north side of the building. Even though Billy had no exit there, it was always good practice to have the place contained.

In situations like this, surprises were generally bad.

Striker got on the radio. 'We need a few more units to this location,' he said.

The dispatcher's response was blunt. 'There are none. I've got some coming from District 4, but they're gonna be a while.'

Striker thought this over. 'Send the first one here to cover the north side of the building. I don't want this guy running on me.'

The dispatcher said she would, and Striker opened the trunk. Inside were a shotgun and two bulletproof vests. He took out Felicia's vest and handed it to her. He then gave his own vest to Dr Ostermann.

'Put it on,' Striker ordered.

The doctor said nothing, and quickly draped it around himself. Once he had his arms through the openings, Striker readjusted the straps so that the trauma place was properly centre. He gave it a hard rap with his knuckles.

It was good.

Felicia took notice. 'You need a vest, Jacob.'

'Just keep your eyes up,' he told her. 'Billy could be anywhere right now.'

'Which is all the more reason you need some Kevlar.'

He gave her a hard look. 'We only got two.'

'Then take Ostermann's vest and keep him here out of trouble.'

'The doctor comes.'

'But—'

'He's the only one Billy trusts and connects with. We might need him, and if we do there won't be time to come back to the car. The doctor comes.'

Dr Ostermann cleared his throat nervously. Back in the safe setting of the clinic environment, he had offered a powerful and impressive aura; now he looked as scared as a field mouse. 'Billy has never been an especially close patient of mine,' he said. 'He's generally resistant to my suggestions.'

Striker ignored the man. He took out the shotgun and slammed the trunk of the car. The heavy black steel and rubberized grip felt good in his hands. Like a little piece of heaven. He racked a round, then gave them both a nod.

'Game on.'

The alleyway was narrow and long.

Striker led them down it, creeping westward slowly. He went first, with Felicia at the rear, bracketing the doctor between them.

Lining the right side of the lane were the back entrances to the numerous small shops that opened up on to East Hastings Street – Bridal Dreams wedding gown and dress shop; Dario's Italian meats; and the Italian Bakery. Above these shops, along the top floor, were more rented suites. Their extended balconies were perfect spots for a sniper.

'Watch the balconies,' Striker told Felicia.

'Copy,' she said. 'I got the balconies.'

They moved on.

To the left, the backsides of houses lined the lane – all the homes from East Pender Street. Each one was a carbon copy of the next. Standard lot. Square back yard. Small unattached garage.

Another perfect place for an ambush.

Striker relaxed his fingers on the shotgun. The black steel of the trigger guard was cold against his skin, but it felt good. Felt like reassurance. Like protection.

They reached the parking lot to Safe Haven Suites.

Striker stopped at the beginning of the fence and used it as concealment. He took the moment to slow down their pace

– which was always a good thing in moments like this – and reassess how things might unfold if they got into a gunfight in this area. The key was to never lose control over yourself.

Calmness equalled precision; and smoothness equalled speed.

'You see his suite?' Felicia asked from behind.

'Hold on,' he said.

Striker leaned around the edge of the fence and studied the parking lot and rear of the building. The lot was small, barely able to hold five or six cars, and the pavement was sloped. Immediately behind the parking lot was a tall wooden fence, the paint chipped and muddied. Rising up out of the fence, dead centre, was an old wooden staircase that led to the upper floors.

Striker pointed to the top, west side.

'That should be Billy's unit.'

'But he's unit 103,' Felicia said. 'Shouldn't that be the ground floor?'

Striker nodded. 'Should be, but it isn't here. This entire place is ass-backwards.' He glanced at Dr Ostermann. The man's face was white, tense. His breathing was too fast. 'You ever been here for a home visit?'

Dr Ostermann shook his head. 'No, never. I always saw Billy at the clinic. And, of course, at Riverglen.'

Striker frowned. He had been hoping for a layout of the suite. Not knowing was never good. For a moment he considered looking at one of the other suites – this was always good practice in apartment blocks where, floor after floor, the layout was the same – but he soon killed that idea. Safe Haven Suites was too much of a mishmash. It wouldn't help.

Like it or not, they'd be going in blind.

Before moving in, Striker took one last look at the buildings flanking Safe Haven – at the empty balconies and then at the open garages. He saw no signs of threat, but that didn't alleviate his concern. He didn't like the idea of climbing the staircase before clearing the yards – it left them clustered together and in the open.

Completely unprotected.

'I'll do it myself,' he finally said.

Felicia shook her head. 'What? No way – you need cover.'

'You can cover me from down here.'

'And what if he comes barging out up there?'

'Then he'll have two targets to shoot at instead of one. If we're all bunched up together he can mow us down with a single shot.'

Felicia still didn't like the idea. 'Let's wait for a dog,' she said.

But Striker shook his head. 'They're both out tracking him now.'

'Then let's get more units here.'

Striker felt his frustration growing. 'There are no units, Feleesh. They're already all taken up with containment and the crime scene and transport. The only other units are the ones coming from South Burnaby, and I'm not waiting for them to arrive. The longer this takes, the more chance we have of losing him. Billy's too dangerous for that. We can't let him escape again.'

'Jacob—'

'I'm going in, Feleesh. Cover me – from down here.'

He purposely avoided her stare and left his position of concealment.

The parking lot was empty for the most; just a single four-door Toyota Tercel in the first stall and a plain white van in the far one. Both were older models. Late eighties or early nineties. *Junk.*

Keeping the shotgun at the low-ready, Striker moved up to the Toyota. All the windows were clear, and there didn't appear to be anyone inside. He tried to lift the trunk, failed, then moved on to the white van. When he got near it, he slowed his pace. There were no rear windows in the van. Just a pair of solid rear doors and one sliding side door, which faced the building. Striker tried them all, found them locked, and moved on.

When he reached the bottom of the stairway, he climbed up to the first turn and scanned the yards to the right and left. They were barren. Just empty slabs of patio concrete.

Seeing they were clear, he moved up to the next level. The stairs were old, made of wood, and they creaked loudly beneath his feet. Each groan of wood felt like someone screaming out a warning to those above, and it made Striker's guts tighten.

Still he continued. He'd turned the next bend, made it to the second floor of the building, and started for the third. He'd barely put his foot on the next step when the shot rang out – a sharp, hard *crrAACK!* in the cold winter air. But it wasn't coming from the apartment above, it was coming from street level.

The garages behind them.

'Gun! Gun! GUN!' Felicia screamed.

Striker spun around and raised the shotgun. In one fleeting moment, he saw it all:

From the garage directly across the lane, Billy Mercury came sprinting out of the darkness. His face was twisted. His mouth open and screaming. And he was firing as he came: Ka-POW! Ka-POW! Ka-POW!

But not at him.

At *Felicia.*

The first shot flew past her and slammed into the fence, sending splinters of one-by-six cedar flying in all directions. The second bullet hit the cement by her feet, sending chunks of concrete exploding into the parking lot.

Dr Ostermann screamed out in horror and dropped to the

ground, covering his head with his hands; Felicia got moving. She got into a twenty-foot gun battle with the man—

And she lost.

The third bullet Billy Mercury shot took her square on. It knocked her back off her feet. Sent her reeling on to the pavement behind her. Left her helpless.

'BILLY!' Striker screamed.

Without aiming, Striker fired from the hip – a diversionary shot to distract Billy from Felicia. He then raced back down the steps, racking and firing as he went.

Billy Mercury didn't so much as move. He stood there, out in the open, and returned fire. Bullets rained through the staircase above and below Striker, some of them shredding the wood, others plunking heavily into the stucco walls behind him.

Striker reached the first turn of the stairway. Stopped. Took quick aim.

And blasted off a shot.

A loud thunderous BOOM! filled the air, and double-odd buck exploded across the lane. Part of the spray took Billy Mercury in the legs. He spun around like a yanked puppet. The gun flew from his fingers, and he dropped forward on to the pavement.

Striker leaped off the staircase and landed on the concrete below. Gun still aimed, he raced across the parking lot to the far corner, where he used the white van for cover.

Already Billy had crawled to the gun. Reached it.

Striker took aim on the man. 'DON'T DO IT, BILLY!'

But it was too late.

'Fucking demons!' the man screamed. He raised the gun—

And Striker pulled the trigger. He blasted off another round of buckshot, then racked and fired another. The first one took

Billy in the shoulder; the second one tore through his chest and came out of his back.

The gun fell from his hands and landed with a soft click on the asphalt. His head dropped, then he fell. His body shuddered for a moment, then became still.

Striker raced forward and kicked the handgun far across the road, away from Billy. It was a black pistol. Not police issue. With the gun out of the way, Striker dropped one knee on top of Billy's back, pinning him to the ground. He searched for more weapons.

All he found was a constant flow of blood.

'. . . daemons . . .' the man said one last time, but his voice was soft and faraway.

He was dying.

Striker jumped back to his feet and searched out Felicia. She was lying half on her stomach, half on her side, trying to get up. Her hair was draped across her face and her gun was two feet ahead of her.

She was crawling for it.

'I got you!' Striker yelled.

He raced over to her side. Grabbed her by the shoulders. Pulled her on to her back. And readied himself to stop the flow of blood.

But none came.

'My ribs,' she breathed. 'My fucking *ribs*.'

He looked down at her chest, at the torn fabric of the Kevlar. He saw the twisted steel of the trauma plate, and let out a sigh of relief.

'He tagged me,' Felicia said in disbelief. 'The fucker actually *tagged* me.'

Striker said nothing for a long moment, he just stared at her with a horrible sense of desperation flooding his chest. With Dr

Ostermann proned out on the ground and sobbing, and Billy Mercury lying dead behind them, Striker pulled Felicia close and held her tight.

'I thought I lost you,' he said. 'Jesus Christ, I thought I fucking lost you.'

It was all he could think of to say.

Fifty-Five

Twenty minutes later, Felicia sat in the back of an ambulance with two paramedics and Dr Ostermann. The initial assessment was not as bad as Striker had feared it was going to be: her ribs didn't appear to be broken, but without an X-ray, there was no true way of knowing. Without a doubt they were bruised. Deeply.

As one of the paramedics palpated Felicia's ribs, Dr Ostermann leaned back in the seat beside her. His eyes were closed and his breathing was still far too fast and uneven. He wiped his sweaty brow with his forearm. 'I feel . . . *ill*,' he said softly, then vomited into the bag the medic had given him.

Striker assessed the man. He appeared so different to how he had looked before. Weaker. Older. *Fragile.*

'It's over,' Striker told him.

When Dr Ostermann did not respond, Striker turned to Felicia. She winced as the medic touched her ribs, but still managed to smile at him.

'Are you okay?' Striker asked. It was the tenth time he had asked her this.

She frowned. 'Go check out the crime scene or something.'

'I will when you're—'

'Really, Jacob. Please. Just go check out the crime scene.'

He didn't move at first. He just stood there and looked at her.

Lost her. The notion was unthinkable, yet true. He had almost fucking lost her.

Finally, he moved back. 'I'm gonna go check out his place,' he said.

Felicia looked relieved. '*Go.*'

Striker closed the ambulance doors. Before moving, he turned his head and stared at the body of Billy Mercury, lying in the very centre of the laneway. Blood had pooled all around him in a distorted, oval shape, and the skin of his face and arms looked terribly pale. Bloodless.

Striker moved up to him. He bent down on one knee and studied the man's face. Even in death, Billy Mercury looked ill. More than ill, he looked downright *insane*. His lips curled back, exposing uneven yellow teeth, and his pupils were black and way too large. Like a doll's eyes.

Demons, the man had said.

Striker shook his head at this. It was a sad statement on the state of this world that Billy Mercury was a war vet. He'd been through combat. And he had broken down because of it. The numerous mental health problems he suffered were in no way his fault. Demons; there had been many of those in Billy Mercury's life.

But it was all over now.

Striker looked up at the cop guarding the body. A young woman who looked no more than twenty-three.

'Who took the gun?' he asked.

'Sergeant Rothschild, Detective.'

He nodded. Rothschild had seized the shotgun, too. Good. That meant they were in good hands.

Striker looked back at the woman. 'When Jim Banner from Ident gets here, tell him I'm already up in the suite.'

The cop said she would, and Striker left the dead body of

Billy Mercury lying in the middle of the lane. He walked to the parking lot and took note of the licence plates of the vehicles left in the lot – the Toyota Tercel and the old van. Neither came back to Billy Mercury, and within minutes, both the owners were located as living in one of the bottom suites.

Disappointing, Striker thought.

He had hoped for a lead.

He left the vehicles behind and slowly started back towards Safe Haven Suites. The wooden stairs creaked loudly as he walked them, as if warning him once more. But he continued on.

Pandora's Box had already been opened. He might as well see what was inside.

The door to Billy Mercury's unit was painted dark brown and had been labelled not with a proper sign but a thick smear of white paint:

103.

The door was already open, though just a few inches.

Striker stopped in the entranceway and took out his flashlight. This was one part of the investigation he was not going to rush. Billy had been excessively paranoid, and Striker was worried about encountering IEDs – improvised explosive devices – in the suite.

Booby-traps.

Without opening the door any further, Striker shone his flashlight inside the apartment. He looked all around the edge of the door and saw no signs of tampering – no wires or snares or flip-switches. Satisfied, he gloved up with fresh blue latex, grimacing as it snapped against his burned hand. He pushed on the door lightly. It glided open effortlessly and soundlessly, revealing the apartment inside.

All the lights were out. Only the rear window offered some natural light. Striker scanned the suite. What he saw was surprising.

The place was damn near empty. The apartment owned nothing but two wooden chairs and a small table in the far corner of the room. On it was an old desktop computer and a mouse with keyboard, along with some papers and pill bottles.

Striker turned his eyes from the computer to the rest of the tiny apartment. Like any Single Room Occupancy dump, it was an all-in-one – a kitchen, washroom, and a common room, which also served as a bedroom.

The place was almost empty of furniture. No bed sat in the corner, just a blanket and a pillow on the ground. But at least the floor was clean. The blanket had been spread out into a perfect creaseless rectangle. Billy Mercury had made his bed after getting up in the morning.

Striker found that odd. It didn't seem to go with his psychosis.

In the same corner of the room was a pile of clothes. Striker inspected them. All were freshly laundered, ironed and folded precisely.

Striker noted that, too.

He looked briefly around the kitchenette. The plates had been washed and set in the drying tray; the counters were clean; and when he opened up the cupboards and fridge, there was plenty of food. Basic stuff. Peanut butter and jam. Bread. Coffee and cream. Some Raisin Bran cereal.

None of it was expired.

Striker checked out the washroom and saw that there was deodorant, toothpaste, dental floss and soap. The only towel in the room had been hung up to dry. So had the floor mat.

Everything was clean and well cared for.

Striker took out his notebook and wrote down the details. When he put it away, he looked up and saw that the far wall was covered by two large maps. One of Kandahar, and one of the Lower Mainland – which constituted Vancouver and all the surrounding subsections. All across the Kandahar map were small red X-marks and the word: *Daemon. Daemon. Daemon. Daemon.*

Striker turned his eyes to the second map – the one of the Lower Mainland. On it were no scribblings, only a series of X-marks. Striker looked at them all and felt a cold sensation spread through his core.

Union Street and Gore Avenue. Hermon Drive and East 5th. The thirty-eight hundred block of Adanac Street in Burnaby – they matched the residences of Mandy Gill, Sarah Rose, and Larisa Logan.

The thought made Striker check his iPhone again, to see if there were any more messages from Larisa. But once again he was let down. None had been received.

He looked at the torn-up notebook pages on the table. All were the same, filled with barely legible scribblings. Words like *Daemons*, and *Shadow men*, and *Succubus*. Next to the collection of papers was a row of pill bottles. They were lined up perfectly.

Striker looked at them.

The bottles were all from Mapleview Clinic, and they each had Dr Ostermann's name and what appeared to be a prescription number on the label. There were three different types of medication: Effexor and Lexapro were medications Striker was familiar with, but the last one – Risperidone – he had never heard of before. He took out his iPhone and Googled the medication. When he found a webpage listing, one word caught his attention:

Antipsychotic.

He put his iPhone away, moved up to the computer and grabbed the mouse. The moment he moved it the black screen of the monitor disappeared and was replaced by the white and blue page of MyShrine:

I saw them first in Afghanistan and Kandahar. In human form. They came in rows, wave after wave of masks.

But I KNEW what they were. The other soldiers may have been blind, but not me. I saw through the shells. And I took them all down. A soldier. An emissary. The HAMMER OF GOD!!!

Then I was, as I am today.

There is only one way to kill a daemon. A goddam Succubus. And that is through the heart.

The words made Striker pause.

A daemon – evil.

A succubus – the *female.*

Through the heart – the target area where the bullet had struck Felicia.

Striker leaned back against the wall as he realized this. 'He warned me,' he said softly. 'Jesus Christ, he fucking warned me, right there in the wording. And I never saw it.'

Thoughts of Felicia taking that bullet flooded him and left him nauseous. He should have known. He should have seen it coming. But he hadn't, and it had almost cost Felicia her life.

He would never forgive himself for that.

The thought remained heavy in his head, even when he turned away from the computer and spotted the landline telephone on the kitchen counter. He walked over and picked it up. Hit Redial. The call was picked up by a woman.

'EvenHealth,' she said. 'How may I direct your call?'

'Sorry, wrong number,' Striker said, and hung up.

He scrolled back through the incoming calls and saw that the most recent two calls were blocked. Blocked calls were nothing out of the ordinary, but Striker didn't like the timing. He called up his contact at the Bell, a guy named Clyde Hall, and asked him to run the incoming calls for Billy Mercury's telephone number.

'Off the record, of course,' Striker added.

Clyde got back to him in less than thirty seconds. 'Only two calls exist for today.'

Striker nodded as if the man could see him. 'Numbers and times, Clyde.'

'No problem.'

Clyde gave him the information, and Striker took it down. After thanking the man and hanging up, he looked at the data and frowned.

There was a correlation here.

Someone had called Billy Mercury's telephone from an untraceable prepaid cell at exactly 1517 hours. This matched the time they left Mapleview Clinic. And then someone from the same untraceable cell had called again, just three minutes later – the time that they had arrived on scene at Billy's.

A warning? Striker thought. A tip-off?

Or someone giving instructions?

He looked at the crazy writings on the table and at the delusional message on the MyShrine page, then he looked over at the folded clothes on the chair and the smoothed-out creaseless blanket in the corner of the room. Everything in this place spoke of madness and yet logic, delusions and yet clear, concise thought. And no matter where he looked, he saw no video recording equipment.

He didn't like it. A bad feeling hung heavy in his chest. His instincts kicked in, and they were the one thing Striker never ignored. Something was wrong here.

They were missing something.

Fifty-Six

When Striker walked down the old wooden staircase to the north lane of Pender Street, directly behind Billy's apartment, he saw that Car 10 had arrived. It was hard not to notice the man. Inspector Laroche was being his usual overbearing self.

Striker stopped at the bottom of the stairs and looked around the scene. Both ends of the block had been taped off with big yellow smears of police tape, and news crews had already huddled at each end – BCTV to the east; CBC to the west. They had probably all driven up after the Hermon Drive fire. High overhead, the Chopper 9 news crew floated about beneath the clouds, its omniscient eye taking in the full scene.

Striker refused to look up.

Already, Noodles had arrived and was standing centre stage in this drama, by the body of Billy Mercury. The Ident technician had already taped off the surrounding area, set up cones, and was busy taking photographs. *Click-click-click.*

Striker approached the man, got to within twenty feet, and was cut off by the inspector. Laroche's normally pale face was flushed red and his hands were balled into fists and resting on his hips.

'Jesus Christ, Striker,' he said. 'What the hell were you thinking?'

Striker blinked. 'What? What was I *thinking*?'

'You're damn right, what were you thinking. You just gunned down a mentally ill man – and you're supposed to be on medical leave!'

Striker couldn't believe what he was hearing. He felt his jaw tighten. Billy Mercury had just killed two cops. And two paramedics, too. Mentally ill, he might have been. But so what?

'He was a *cop-killer.*'

Laroche's face remained tight. 'He was a man who thought he was saving the world from *demons.*' Laroche threw his hands in the air. 'Oh Christ, it's all over the radio, every thirty seconds: a mentally ill man, who was in our custody, is now dead along with four emergency workers.' Laroche looked around the area, then shook his head as if bewildered. 'You should have waited for cover, Striker! For the Emergency Response Team. And the mental health car. A negotiator. Christ, you didn't even have a less lethal unit on scene!'

Less lethal – a beanbag shotgun or a Taser. Or, if the Emergency Response Team was around, an Arwen gun.

Striker frowned at that. He stepped forward into the inspector's personal space and lowered his voice. 'All other units were already searching other areas or stuck in containment. ERT was out at the range and too far away. And the doctor *was* our negotiator,' he said. 'I also had a Taser on the way. They just didn't make it here in time because there was no time. *He ambushed us.*'

Laroche was unwavering. 'Of course he did. What did you expect? You corner a dog and he'll bite, Striker. Every single time.'

'I did what was necessary.'

'No, what you did was create a situation here where there was no way out for anyone involved – not unless someone got shot. It's called Officer-Created Jeopardy. And make no mistake about it, that's exactly how the press will view this thing. Every goddam newspaper and newsreel's gonna have the Big Story, and it'll go on for weeks, if not months. It's gonna rain down on us now.'

Striker looked down at Laroche and felt like grabbing him and twisting him into a pretzel. 'You think I give two shits about the friggin' media?' he asked. 'Felicia took one in the chest, and you're worried about how this will look on the friggin' news?'

Laroche raised a finger and pointed it in Striker's chest. 'No one would've been shot period if you had followed proper procedure.'

'It was a dynamic situation.'

'Because you made it that way. You're just lucky that Dr Ostermann wasn't hurt or killed in the process.' Laroche shook his head. He took in a long breath, then seemed to deflate a bit. 'Look, don't get me wrong, Striker. I'm glad you're okay. And Felicia, too. But you guys royally fucked this one. And I'll be sending my findings to the Police Board for review.'

'You do that,' Striker said. 'Be sure to include the part about how I warned you this would happen back on Hermon Drive, when you refused to charge Mercury and send him to jail. When you let him be transported in an ambulance instead of a police wagon, despite the fact he had just tried to burn up two cops. Make sure you include all of that – because I most certainly will when I write up my response through the Union.'

For a moment, Laroche seemed even smaller than his five-foot-seven frame. Moments later, a camera crew from one of the unaccredited news groups was caught trying to sneak in between the houses from the south side of the laneway. Laroche went rushing over, and Striker turned and spotted Sergeant Mike Rothschild entering the strip.

'How you holding out?' Rothschild asked.

'I need to check on Felicia.'

'Burnaby General. Go there. I'll take over the scene here.'

'Thanks, Mike. I owe you one.'

The sergeant grinned. 'Just get out of here before Hitler there knows you're gone.'

Striker didn't have to be told twice. He walked back to Kootenay Street where they had dumped the wheels, and climbed inside the cruiser. Moments later, he was headed down Boundary Road for Burnaby General Hospital. Where Felicia and Dr Ostermann had been taken.

It was less than ten minutes away.

Fifty-Seven

The Adder was shaking. Shaking so hard he could hardly hold on to the rungs of the ladder as he made his way deeper and deeper into his room. When his feet touched concrete, he raced across the room and slid the disc into the player so hard and fast he nearly jammed the machine.

The DVD began playing and the screen came to life.

On it was the woman cop. Standing in the laneway. Watching the big detective move slowly up the stairs. She was beautiful – the Adder could see that in his analytical, separated way – with her long brown hair draping down the caramel skin of her neck. She was in her prime, no doubt, bursting with beauty and energy and radiance. Like a star going supernova.

The Adder watched her, standing there, completely unaware of the hidden threat. Then the bullets came.

One – a miss.

Two – another miss.

And then three – the most perfect, wonderful shot he had ever seen. A lightning bolt from an *angel.* And suddenly Detective Felicia Santos was reeling. She arched backwards, landed hard on the pavement, and lay there with a stunned look in her pretty eyes.

The camera angle was bad, and the Adder had to zoom in to

see the expression on her face. And that was when he discovered the God-awful truth of what had happened. She opened her eyes, and touched her chest . . .

The *vest*.

The goddam Kevlar vest.

'NO!' he screamed. 'NOOOO!'

Shaking all over, uncontrollably, he took the disc from the tray and snapped it in half, slicing his hand as he did so. Then he stepped forward and kicked the cabinet. Hard. The entire thing swayed back and forth, as if it would tip over and come crashing down on the concrete.

The Adder could not have cared less.

His moment of pure, untainted beauty – *stolen* from him in an instant.

'*No*,' he said again, though softer this time. And now there were tears leaking from his eyes. Big salty drops rolling down his cheeks.

It was unfair.

So terribly unfair.

Soon his head began to pound, to *throb*. It was as if there was a worm inside his skull, eating away at his brain tissue. And then the sounds came back, flooding him, deluging him, drowning him in great, awesome waves.

The laughter.

Then the snapping and cracking.

And then the silence. That horrible, horrible *silence*.

With unsteady hands, the Adder scrambled for his iPod. Jammed in the headphones. Hit Play. And listened to the white noise. Turned it up to full volume.

But this time, it did little good.

The sounds of the outside world did not matter now, for they were overpowered by the ones that echoed inside his head. All

he could hear was the loud cracking sounds of ice and that coldness washing all over him again.

Relax, he told himself. You have to *relax*.

But it did little good.

He was unravelling.

Fifty-Eight

By the time Striker made it to Burnaby General Hospital, his heart was racing and his mood was darkening quicker than the five o'clock skyline. No matter how many times he tried to erase the memory of the MyShrine taunt the Adder had left him, the image remained.

He parked the undercover cruiser out front in the Police Only parking, climbed out, and walked in through the Emergency Room front doors. Inside, the hospital was packed. A line of weary-looking patients snaked along the hall, and another group lined up all the way to the entrance doors. It was busy, but still nowhere near the chaos that ruled at St Paul's.

Striker made his way down the hall to a patient room that consisted of six beds, separated only by hanging drapes. Felicia was in the sixth one. Striker was surprised to see her already in the process of tightening her suit belt, and wincing from the pressure. She looked up and spotted him. A look of relief fell across her face, and she smiled.

'Hey, Tiger.'

Striker walked over and helped her with her coat. 'You're *done?*'

She nodded. 'Yeah. Fast Track – it pays to be the police.'

'And what did they find?'

'The body of a twenty-year-old woman,' she said with a grin.

'Hell, *I* can find one of those.'

She smiled at his comment and when she did Striker felt something tug at his heart strings. At thirty-two years of age, Felicia was almost ten years his junior. It was not a lot of time, but enough to feel the difference. Sometimes she seemed *generations* away from him. And then, at times like these, time didn't even exist.

'How are you?' he asked, the humour all gone from his voice. 'Really, Feleesh.'

She shrugged carefully. 'Some of my ribs are bruised, especially around my breastbone, but nothing got broken. Not even a hairline fracture. Trauma plate took the full brunt of it. I think I'll have the thing framed and put on the wall . . . I got lucky this time.'

'Not as lucky as me,' he replied.

She reached out and touched his face. Striker grabbed her around the waist and gently pulled her close and gave her a long soft hug. He buried his face in her hair. Breathed in. Smelled that familiar vanilla scent.

She felt so, so good. He never wanted to let go.

Felicia pushed him back softly. 'Jacob, people are looking.'

'Let them look,' he said. 'Hell, let's give them a show.'

She laughed at that, then winced. 'My ribs.'

When he finally pulled back from her, her cheeks were slightly red from blushing and she stood there looking awkward. Striker wanted to kiss her. Right there in the hospital.

But something else broke into his mind. He turned his eyes from Felicia to the rest of the unit and saw that each and every bed was already filled with someone he didn't recognize. He frowned.

'Where the hell is Dr Ostermann?'

Felicia frowned. 'The good doctor checked himself out as

quickly as he could. I told him to wait here for us, that we would need a written statement from him and all that, but he kept saying he was worried about his staff – it seemed like a line to me.'

'A convenient one.'

'Either way, he took off outta here once he was done. When the nurse was checking me over. He left.'

Striker didn't like it. Honest men didn't run. And he didn't buy the fact that Ostermann was worried about his staff. For one, he didn't seem like that kind of boss. For two, they'd already told him everyone was fine. He was about to comment on it when his cell went off. He looked down at the screen and saw the name *Jim Banner* displayed. He picked up.

'What you got for me, Noodles?'

'How's Felicia?' he asked.

'She's okay, she's right here with me.'

Noodles let out a relieved sound, then got right down to business. 'I managed to pull another print off the fridge in unit 305,' he said. 'A *palm* print.'

'It comes back to Mercury, right?'

'Actually, it comes back to *no one*.'

This startled Striker. Mercury was a soldier. His prints were on file. 'You mean the print wasn't good enough?' he asked.

'No, I mean the print doesn't belong to Billy Mercury.'

Striker felt his mood darken a little further. 'Anything else?' he asked.

'That's it.'

'Then I'll get back to you later.'

Striker hung up the phone and relayed the information to Felicia. She didn't seem concerned one way or the other. 'A thousand people might have been in that suite,' she said. 'We never knew for sure if the print belonged to the suspect. Obviously, it doesn't.'

Striker said nothing; he wasn't so sure. He stood there, brooding, and thought of everything from the bad print to the way
Ostermann had run out of the hospital. And the more he
thought about it, the angrier he got. After a long moment, he
met Felicia's stare again.

'You done here?' he asked.

'I was twenty minutes ago.'

'Good, then let's go find Dr Ostermann . . . The man has a
lot of explaining to do.'

The moment they were back in the cruiser, Striker started the
engine and Felicia turned on the heater. The sun was still out,
but just barely. It was half-past five, and the oncoming winter
evening was invading everything in its path.

While the car warmed up, Striker brought Felicia up to speed
on everything that had happened while she was being escorted
to the hospital – everything from Laroche's accusations of
Officer-Created Jeopardy to the conflicting evidence he'd found
inside Billy Mercury's apartment. When he was done with the
debrief, his mind felt more settled. More focused.

And specific facts stuck out.

He looked at Felicia. 'So with the exception of the Risperidone
– which is an antipsychotic, by the way – every other medication
Billy was on is the exact same as those for Mandy Gill, Sarah
Rose, and Larisa Logan.'

She nodded absently as she thought this over. 'But is that
because they're cookie-cutter referrals, or because each one
of those patients suffered from the exact same disorder?
Maybe those medications work most effectively in that
combination.'

Striker bit his cheek as he thought. 'That's not what bothers
me. What does is the *preference* of the drug type.'

'I don't follow.'

He explained. 'There's over a thousand types of mood stabilizers out there, but our victims and our bad guy were on the same type. And the same type of antidepressant as well.'

'So? They were also all in the same programme.'

'And therein lies the problem,' Striker said. 'Dr Ostermann is the one who runs the therapy group, this SILC or whatever the hell it's called. And yet, with the exception of Billy, the one who's providing all the medications is Dr Richter. Why is that?'

'Is it really all that important?'

'Maybe yes, maybe no. But this much is certain: Dr Richter is one of the main connections here – to Mandy and Sarah through their medications, and to Larisa through the counselling.'

'And Billy?'

'Indirectly through the Mapleview Clinic. With Ostermann. And all their rehabilitative programmes.'

Felicia nodded. 'And no callback from Richter yet?' she asked.

'No, and I've left several messages. But in reality it's only been twenty-four hours.' Striker thought this over. 'Maybe, in the end, there's a logical answer to Richter and Ostermann being involved.'

'There is. It's called counselling,' Felicia said.

Striker raised a hand defensively. 'I'm not completely discounting their validity here, I'm just . . . analysing things. Carefully.' Striker looked out of the window, at the sun which was now slowly falling in the west, into a darkening blue skyline. 'There's something else, too.'

'What?'

'The gun Mercury used. Dispatch broadcast that it was taken from one of the fallen officers.'

'The unit on scene said that.'

Striker nodded. 'Well, that was a mistake. It wasn't even a SIG Sauer. Maybe a nine mil.'

Felicia nodded. 'Then let's trace it.'

Striker agreed. He got on the phone and called Noodles, hitting Speakerphone as it dialled. The technician answered on the second ring. 'Shipwreck,' he said.

'The gun,' Striker replied. 'You have a chance to check it yet?'

'Sure. It's been almost two hours since the shooting, so the entire scene has been photographed, the body autopsied, the gun tested for ballistics – and oh yeah, I also discovered the cure for cancer.'

Felicia laughed at this; Striker did not.

'I need the results on that gun, Noodles. And I need them quick.'

The man just laughed sourly. 'Can't run it through the registry anyway, if that's what you're thinking – there's no serial.'

Striker cursed. He should have figured as much. 'They filed it off?'

'Filed *and* acid burned.'

'Really?' Striker thought this over. He said goodbye to Noodles and hung up the phone. Then he turned in the seat to face Felicia. 'Doesn't that seem a little strange to you?'

'What part?'

'The whole thing. Billy somehow obtains a gun—'

'Nothing surprising there. The guy was in the army. Did time overseas. He could probably get a rocket launcher, if he wanted one.'

'Fine, fine, I'll give him that. But then he files off the serial numbers *and* acid treats the metal.'

'So?'

'Two questions: one, would someone as delusional as Billy Mercury be focused on doing something like that in his current mental state? And two, why would he bother getting rid of the serial numbers in the first place? Did he think we'd never guess his identity? It was a suicide mission. He went toe-to-toe with us in a gun battle. Does it make sense from a psychological perspective?'

Felicia shrugged. 'I don't know, I'm not a psychiatrist.'

'Exactly, and the one we wanted to talk to skipped the hospital the moment he got a chance.'

Felicia nodded. 'He really hightailed it.'

Striker turned back in his seat. He put the car into Drive, hit the gas, and pulled back on to the road. But instead of heading west, he headed north. Felicia cast him a questioning stare.

'Where we going?' she asked.

'Back to Mapleview. I'm seizing Mercury's medical files.'

Fifty-Nine

Striker and Felicia parked directly in front of the Mapleview Mental Health Center, and got out. The wind was strong, blowing in from the park to the south, and it was cold. Felicia bundled herself up and got moving; Striker walked by her side.

With the sun now dipping behind the rising cloud banks to the west, the building was cloaked in purple-grey. In this dimmer light, it looked less like a modern-day mental health clinic and more like a retail store.

Striker said, 'First we get Billy Mercury's file, then we find Ostermann.'

Felicia was in agreement.

They reached the front steps, and Striker stopped. He got on his phone and called up Sue Rhaemer at Dispatch. He got her to send a message to the Coquitlam police. He needed a patrol unit to attend Riverglen immediately; they were to seize Billy Mercury's file, and any other seemingly related files the officer stumbled upon.

When he hung up, Felicia frowned. 'I know you don't want to hear this,' she said. 'But we really should be getting a warrant first.'

'There's no time for that.'

'The court will disagree. They'll say there was nothing but time. After all, with Mercury dead, why rush? If we don't do it right, some judge will throw out anything we find in that file. It will never be admitted as evidence.'

'Like I said, Feleesh, these are exigent circumstances.'

'*Exigent?* How? The man is dead.'

'And we have doubts he was acting alone.'

She gave him one of her sceptical looks. 'We do?'

'I sure as hell do.' He explained. 'Those two phone calls back at Billy's place make me wonder. They were made right when we left Mapleview, and the moment we entered the block – as if someone was doing recon on us. I don't like it. So when you break it down, we don't know yet if anyone else was involved. But if someone else was involved, you can bet your ass the first thing they would do is start getting rid of any evidence pertaining to the case or the patient involved. I'm seizing the file. *Now.*'

Felicia's sceptical look never faltered. 'Nice speech, Martin Luther King. You just want to see what's in that file.'

Striker only grinned. 'Six of this, a half-dozen of that – it's all the same.'

Felicia made no response, and Striker started up the stairs. It was cold out, and the wind was blowing worse with every minute. He pulled open the double glass doors and stepped aside.

'After you, Princess.'

Felicia smiled. 'Well, at least you've learned your place.'

She walked through the front door, and Striker followed.

Stepping in through the front doors brought Striker a strange sense of déjà vu. A lost feeling. It had been only, what, two hours since he'd rampaged through here, ordering the receptionist to lock all the windows and doors, and then kidnapping Dr Ostermann and dragging him up to Safe Haven Suites to deal with Billy. Now, it all felt like a bad dream.

And in some ways, it was.

Striker slowed down walking, looked at the clock, then leaned on the banister of the stairway. A wave of mild dizziness washed over him, and he felt like his blood pressure had just skyrocketed through the roof.

Felicia took note. 'Hey. You okay?'

'I just need a second here,' he said, but he made no move to walk on.

After a few more seconds, Striker ignored Felicia's worried stare, and looked around the place. Everything felt darker in here now. The walls seemed higher, the corridors narrower. Straight ahead was the receptionist's desk, and behind it was a room fronted by a large glass pane. Through the glass, Striker could see an entire wall of file folders.

The records room.

He pointed to it, if only to divert Felicia's lingering look, and said, 'The file we want will be in there – unless someone has already gotten rid of it.' He got himself moving again. He walked on through the foyer and reached the front desk. As he did so, the receptionist he had spoken with earlier in the afternoon exited the records room. The muscles of her face were tight beneath the skin and her eyes looked tired. She looked up and spotted them, then came to a hard stop, her shoes almost slipping on the white tiles of the hospital floor.

'Oh. Detective.' She looked from Striker to Felicia and back again. 'I heard about what happened out there. With Billy. And, well . . . I'm sorry.' As she spoke the words, her fingers tightened on the file she was holding, her long red nails digging into the white cardboard.

Striker read the label on the tab. It was the one he had come here for:

William Stephen Mercury.

'What are you doing with that?' he asked.

The nurse blinked as if coming out of a bad dream, then looked down at the file in her hands. 'This? Oh yes. Well . . . Dr Ostermann wanted it. He wants to review the history. See what went wrong. See if there were any warning signs he might have missed – he's quite upset over the whole matter and he blames himself. He's always so . . . *protective* of his patients. He's taking this quite hard.'

Striker nodded. 'I completely understand. Unfortunately, him seeing it won't be possible just yet. We're actually here to seize that file.'

The woman said nothing back. Felicia stepped forward and took the file from her.

'Oh dear,' the woman said. 'Dr Ostermann—'

'Can speak to me whenever he needs to,' Striker finished.

As if on cue, Dr Ostermann came marching around the corner of the west corridor. His skin was covered in a fine sheen of perspiration. His eyes looked dark and large behind the glasses, and when he caught sight of them they grew even larger. He stopped walking, looked at them for a brief moment, then continued across the foyer.

'Detectives.' He looked directly at Felicia. 'I trust you are well?'

She bumped her fist over her chest. 'Heart's a Timex. Keeps on ticking.'

Dr Ostermann licked his lips, almost nervously. 'Well, that is so very good to hear, Detective Santos. After what happened out there . . . when the shot went off and the way you fell down . . .'

Felicia nodded. 'It's all over now.'

Dr Ostermann's eyes fell from Felicia's face to the file folder in her hands and his expression darkened.

'Is that my file?' he asked.

'It's our file now,' Striker said. 'We're seizing it.'

'Seizing it? But . . . I still need to go through it. Review our sessions. See what went wrong.' He gave them both a desperate look. 'Detectives, you must understand, I'm *mandated* to—'

'I'm not unreasonable,' Striker said. 'We can make you a copy.'

This seemed to placate the doctor. He nodded slowly to the receptionist, and she then led Felicia into the back room. Moments later, Striker could hear the loud hum of an old photo-copier working. As they waited for the copies, Striker studied Ostermann's posture and expression. The man seemed highly strung and fidgety.

It made sense, given all that had happened.

'Why did you leave?' Striker asked.

Dr Ostermann blinked. 'I'm sorry?'

'Burnaby General. The hospital. Why did you leave? You knew we needed to talk to you.'

Dr Ostermann splayed his hands. 'I knew you could find me here any time you desired – a man of my position cannot hide from anything, as I'm sure you well know.' He gestured to the area around them and raised a finger, as if sermonizing. 'Look at this place. Mapleview. My clinic. It was in absolute *chaos*. Everyone was traumatized. I had to return here as soon as possible to rectify the situation.'

'That sounds a tad melodramatic,' Striker said.

'I had my staff to consider, Detective. And the other patients. Appointments were scheduled. Medications due. The entire clinic was in an uproar over what had happened. I simply had to be here.'

'What about Dr Richter?' Striker said.

'I have left messages,' was all he said. His face took on a tired look, and he absently rubbed his brow.

Striker just watched the man and said nothing more. When Felicia and the receptionist returned, he took the file from them and casually flipped it open. It was thick, compartmentalized. And as he paged back through the entries, he noticed one more thing.

The file was incomplete. Huge periods of time were missing.

He looked up and met the doctor's eyes. 'Where's the rest of it?'

'The rest?'

Striker smiled. 'You like doing that, don't you?'

'Doing what?'

'Repeating my questions. Is that a practised technique of yours? A way to delay time and think your answers through?' When Dr Ostermann said nothing back, Striker continued. 'Huge chunks of time are missing in this file. So I will ask you one more time, Doctor, where is the rest of the file?'

Dr Ostermann's face tightened. 'There is no *rest of the file*, Detective. Any parts that are missing are unfortunately somewhere in the system.' He adjusted his glasses, and continued. 'Before coming out west, Billy was also being seen by army psychologists in Ottawa. He went back there several times. Not much is known about these sessions. I've requested copies of that file many times myself, but have never received so much as a response from the military. Which is not surprising. It all comes down to financial liability in these matters. And you know how secretive the army is with all their records.'

Striker leafed through the folder. There were *many* gaps in time. 'What about the rest of the missing patches?'

Dr Ostermann shrugged. 'Billy bounced around the system

for quite some time before finding me. A few years at least. I began seeing him just under three years ago – and all our time is documented precisely in this file or the one we keep at Riverglen. There are two, after all; he was unfortunately sectioned for some time.'

Striker and Felicia shared a glance at hearing this. Then Striker spoke again. 'So Billy saw another doctor around here?'

'Well, yes. Before me, Billy saw *many* different doctors. I'm not privy to all that information. And to be perfectly honest with you, I don't even know what other files exist. Billy was something of a ghost in the system. I did the best I could for him. And I failed terribly.'

The words seemed to take a toll on the doctor, and his posture slumped. Behind him, the receptionist worked hard at trying to look busy, but the blush of her cheeks gave away her discomfort with the situation.

Striker said nothing for a long moment, waiting out Dr Ostermann to see if the man would say more. When he did not, and instead remained completely silent, Striker gave Felicia a glance, and she spoke up.

'Did Billy ever see Dr Richter?' she asked.

This seemed to surprise Dr Ostermann, and he blinked. 'Dr Richter? Well, yes. But only when I was unable to attend the sessions – which was a rare occasion indeed.'

'But there were times?' Striker pressed.

Dr Ostermann nodded. 'There were. A few.'

'Well, we've tried to get hold of this Dr Richter several times—'

'Dr Richter is away,' Dr Ostermann replied. 'On leave for *personal* reasons I am not allowed to divulge. I have no other contact information, other than the cell-phone number you were given. I would suggest you leave another message like I did.'

'I have left a message,' Striker said. 'In fact, I've left many.'

Dr Ostermann frowned. 'Well, I'm sorry. I wish there was more I could do for you.'

The words rang empty to Striker.

'One last thing,' he said. 'Before the shoot-out with Billy, what were you doing here at Mapleview?'

Dr Ostermann looked at Striker in confusion. Like he didn't understand the question. 'I was sorting through the clinic records. We are in the process right now of archiving the older files. It is quite a bit of work, I can tell you.'

Striker nodded. 'I find that interesting. Yesterday, when I asked you if you worked here, you said no.'

'I said no?' Dr Ostermann replied. He calmly removed the spectacles from his face, withdrew a silk cloth from his front suit pocket, and cleaned the lenses as he explained. 'That is not quite true, Detective. What I said to you the other day, is that I *no longer* work here – I have, however, worked here in the past. Quite a bit, in fact. Now, I more or less just oversee things. Mapleview Clinic is, after all, a branch of the EvenHealth project.'

'You're saying this is semantics?'

'Precisely.'

'My mistake then,' Striker replied.

He turned to Felicia, gave her the nod to leave, and they said goodbye to Dr Ostermann and his receptionist. When they were out of the front doors, back into the darkness of the pressing night and the cold gusting winds, Striker gave Felicia a hard look.

'Semantics?' he asked.

'Bullshit?' she replied.

He agreed. 'Something just isn't right with Dr Ostermann,' he said. 'I think it's time we started making him a top priority.'

'Surveillance?' Felicia asked.

Striker flashed her a smile. 'Yeah. Time for a little game of I Spy.'

Sixty

It was getting late now, six o'clock, and the rush-hour grind was thickening still. When the traffic came to another stand-still, Felicia reclined her seat a little and looked at him. 'I'm starving,' she said, and gave a smile. 'Getting shot will do that to a girl.'

Striker forced a grin, but said nothing. They drove down Boundary Road and cut through the McDonald's drive-thru for a couple of burgers: a Big Mac and a coffee for Striker, a Filet-o-Fish and an eggnog shake for Felicia. Striker looked at the combination and scowled.

'Nice mix of flavours. What next – steak tartare and caramel sauce?'

'Hey, relax. Be festive.'

'It's January. Christmas ended four weeks ago.'

'Scrooge.'

They parked behind the Harley-Davidson motorcycle shop on Boundary, away from the rush of the street. As they ate, they went over what they had to work with. Striker took out his note-book and paged back through the notes. He also read through the pages of the Billy Mercury file. In it was a copy of unpaid billings to the government. The session notes were written and signed by Dr R. M. Richter, yet the name on the billing sheet was Ostermann.

'That's odd,' he said between bites. He took out his cell phone and called up Mapleview Clinic. When the receptionist answered and learned it was him again on the phone, she sounded nervous.

'Oh hello, Detective,' she said. 'Dr Ostermann is busy at the moment—'

'That's perfectly all right. I'm not calling to talk to him.'

'Then how may I help you?'

'I have another question,' Striker explained. 'How come all the billings for Billy Mercury's treatments are done under Dr Ostermann's name when it looks like Dr Richter was the one who did the sessions?'

The receptionist was straight to the point. 'Dr Richter works nights. After-hours private work.'

'I don't follow,' Striker said.

'All the doctors here pay a portion of their income to the clinic, so the money comes through EvenHealth first – under Dr Ostermann's physician number – then the clinic deducts the percentages owed and delivers the rest of the income to the attending psychiatrist.'

Striker nodded. That made sense.

'Any return calls from Dr Richter?' he asked.

'None, Detective.'

'And you have no idea when the doctor will be back?'

'Next Monday, the book says.'

Monday. That figured.

Striker had had enough of waiting for doctors. He asked the receptionist for Dr Richter's billing number. When he wrote it down in his notebook he saw that it was indeed the same number as on all the prescription pads. He thanked the receptionist for her time and hung up. He immediately called up the College of Physicians and Surgeons of BC, gave his badge number, and asked them to verify that the physician number did, in fact, exist. The clerk got back to him within seconds. 'Yes,' he said. And the name corresponded.

Dr Riley M. Richter.

There was no permanent clinic listed with the College of Physicians and Surgeons. No home address either. Just one contact number – the pager he already had.

Frustrated, he hung up. Frowned. Pinched the bridge of his nose. Another goddam headache was coming; he could feel it, right behind his eyes.

'Tylenol?' Felicia asked.

He ignored the offer. 'Mandy Gill and Sarah Rose were both taking their SILC class—'

'Social Independence and Life Coping skills.'

Striker nodded. 'Yeah. Under the EvenHealth programme. I got that. Point is, they were both doing sessions there, along with Billy. Now the three of them are dead. Larisa was also taking therapy sessions at Mapleview, and from Dr Richter, who was writing all the prescriptions. Larisa is one of the links in all this. We've got to find her.'

Felicia touched his arm. 'And we will find her, Jacob. I promise you that. But don't lose focus here. This case is done. And it looks pretty straightforward.'

'Does it?' Striker asked.

'It does to me. Billy Mercury was a delusional psychotic who had an obsession with Mandy Gill first, and then Sarah Rose. We don't know all the details involved but we do know this – both women are now dead.'

'And what about Larisa's message?' Striker asked.

'We've already been over this. Larisa said she knew it was murder, yes, but her warning came *after* we'd been plastered all over the TV news. And even if she does know something about the murder, what she probably knows is that Billy was responsible. And that's why she wanted to come forward. Now that she's gone into hiding because of this mental health warrant, it's kind of thrown a monkey wrench into everything. But it makes perfect sense – she doesn't want to be institutionalized again.'

Striker thought this over before speaking. 'And what about the palm print found on the fridge at Mandy Gill's crime scene – it doesn't match Billy's.'

'It doesn't match *anyone's*,' Felicia reminded him. 'And it's just a partial print at that. It could belong to the former tenant, a guest of the former tenant. A squatter, even.'

Striker listened to every word she said.

'It all makes sense,' he admitted.

'It does make sense. You're just too close to Larisa to see that. You don't *want* to see that. That's why you're having problems with closing the case.'

'Not because of Larisa,' he said, 'but because there's *holes*.'

'What holes?'

Striker counted them off. 'The videos, for one. Both Mandy Gill and Sarah Rose had their deaths filmed. I know it, you know it. And yet there was no video equipment inside Billy's apartment. I looked for it.'

This didn't sway Felicia one way or the other. 'He's obviously kept it somewhere else. We'll check into it. Maybe he's got a storage locker somewhere. Or a second pad. A safety deposit box. There's a million places. We'll do some foot work.'

Striker just nodded, but he didn't like it. He couldn't help feeling like this was just too easy. Too convenient. And more than that, he was worried for Larisa. Billy Mercury and the whole case aside, the woman needed professional help.

He was determined to get her that.

He took out his iPhone, logged into his Gmail account, and

sent her a message. In the subject heading, he typed: URGENT!!!
Then he worked out a few sentences:

> Larisa, I know about the medical warrant. And the murders.
> We may have caught the person responsible. Can't say more.
> You and I need to talk. Now. Please call me or email back
> ASAP. I'm here for you.
> Striker

He sent the email, then put his iPhone on top of the dashboard
and grabbed the remainder of his burger. He brought it to his
mouth, found he couldn't eat, and threw it in the bag. He sipped
his coffee and watched the sky slowly turn a darker shade of
purple. He wished to God there was something else he could do
for the woman. He wished she would just get back to him.

But the minutes passed and his cell never rang.

Felicia finished her Filet-o-Fish and looked over at him. 'Hey.
You okay?'

Striker said nothing. He just looked at the world beyond the
windshield and frowned. It looked like a cold and dark place out
there. And to Larisa Logan, it was. He blamed himself for that.
For not responding to her calls until it was too late.

It had been a terrible mistake.

Sixty-One

Sweat dampened the Adder's body. He could feel it as he lay there on the cold hard concrete of the floor. Drips of sweat, sliding down his cheeks. Drips running down his neck. Down his back. Everywhere.

His heart was racing. And the more he thought of the woman detective surviving the attack, the worse his heart pounded.

No more, he thought.

Please, no more.

As if on cue, the bell rang. The *high* bell. Not the one that was low and resonated all through his chamber like the call of some ungodly demon – that was the one that summoned him to the Doctor's office. No, this one was the sound of the angels. The chimes. And it told him he had done well today.

The Adder struggled to sit up. Wiped his brow with the sleeve of his shirt. Looked daftly around the room.

Broken in two in the middle of the floor was a DVD. Try as he might, the Adder could not recall breaking it. His memory failed him. All he knew now was the lost feeling that filled his insides.

That terrible, terrible feeling of grieving.

The bell chimed again, this time twice. And the Adder knew it was time to go. The Doctor was alerting him, and as always it was best not to keep the Doctor waiting.

He climbed to his knees. Then to his feet. And made his way towards the ladder. He climbed the rungs numbly, mechanically, until he reached the hatch. As he undid the latch, a sense of surreal awareness came over him. It was time to play the part again. To put on his outer-world face. His mask. To become one with the facade of the upstairs world.

His reward was waiting.

Sixty-Two

When Striker's iPhone went off on the car's dashboard, he snatched it up like it was a bomb ready to go off, and read the screen. He was hoping to see Larisa's name, or an email notification. Instead he saw the name *Jim Banner* across the display.

Striker hit the Talk button and put the phone to his ear.

'Noodles,' he acknowledged.

The technician sighed. 'God, I hate that nickname.'

'Just be happy you didn't choke on Fish Balls. Now what do you have for me?'

'How about another partial print, for starters?'

Striker leaned forward in the seat. 'Where?'

'We recovered one from apartment 109 in Hermon Heights – the suite across the road from Sarah Rose's place, the one you thought this guy might have been watching you from.'

'I knew it,' Striker said. 'And?'

'Nothing earth-shaking, but we got some relatively interesting findings. I dusted all the areas you wanted – the electrical outlets, the window and frame, the plug end of the extension cord – and we got something. One single print on the inside of the front window. When I was doing it, one of the neighbours came by. Told me that suite's been vacant for over six weeks, ever since the last renter moved out.'

'And the print – you run it?'

'Can't. It's just a partial,' Noodles replied. 'Nothing good enough to send through the database. But I did use it for a comparison.'

'With whose?'

'Billy Mercury's. And once again, it *doesn't* match.'

Striker thought this over. Just because the print was on the inside of the window, and just because it didn't belong to Billy Mercury, that didn't prove anything. Anyone could have been in that suite over the last six weeks. A squatter. Some neighbourhood kids. The landlord. Anyone. Or it could belong to the previous tenant.

They needed corroboration.

'Did you compare it with the prints found on the fridge at the Lucky Lodge?' he asked.

'There's the key,' Noodles said. 'The print might not match up with Billy Mercury's prints, but it's a perfect match with the one I found on the fridge at the Lucky Lodge.'

Striker felt a bolt of energy surge through him. What were the odds of finding two partial prints at two separate crime scenes that matched?

The answer was *zero*.

'What about the can of varnish?' Striker asked.

'We got a good print there too. But it's not the same.'

'*Not* the same?'

'Doesn't match the print on the window, doesn't match Billy's.'

Striker frowned. There was no doubt that the varnish had been used as an accelerant on the door. 'Run the print through the databank when you get time and let me know the results either way. For all we know, it could come back to a checkout girl. And swab everything for DNA. We need something here, Noodles. Gimme some magic.'

'The only tricks I know involve a bottle of Jack Daniel's and a pair of air stewardesses.'

Striker smiled into the phone. 'Just call me the moment you know.'

He hung up the cell and relayed the entire discussion to Felicia, paying particular attention to the fact that the partial print from the fridge back at the Mandy Gill crime scene matched the print from the window at the Sarah Rose crime scene.

The news seemed to shock her.

'It has to be connected,' she admitted. 'The odds are too high.'

'Which means that there's a very good chance Billy Mercury wasn't acting alone.'

'Jesus.'

Felicia rubbed her face, massaging her temples. She brushed her hair back over her shoulders and shook her head as if she just couldn't believe it. Without warning, she opened the car door.

Cold wind swept into the car, sucking away the heat.

'I need some air,' she said.

She climbed out, and Striker got out with her. He took his coffee cup with him. They walked down the long stretch of Kootenay Street, just below the highway overpass, where it was dark and quiet. They talked. After going over everything from beginning to end one more time, Felicia stopped walking and turned to face him.

'Only two people stick out to me – Dr Ostermann and Dr Richter.'

Striker agreed. 'Dr Richter is nowhere to be found. And I don't like the way Ostermann is constantly avoiding us and skirting around our questions. There's more going on here. You can bet your pay cheque on that.'

Felicia shivered, but nodded in agreement. She bundled up her coat, then snagged the coffee cup from his hand and slurped some back. She kept the cup.

'Ostermann has proximity to everyone involved,' she noted. 'The timelines also correlate; he was seen driving like a madman through the area five minutes after you got into a fight with the suspect at Mandy Gill's crime scene. He's been resistant to our questions from the beginning. He had a sharp pain in his side that first night we spoke with him – maybe from a high fall. And last of all, we've caught him lying to us about working at Mapleview. Which is odd. Why lie about something so trivial?'

'He says it was all a misunderstanding,' Striker said, and they both laughed. After the moment had passed, he continued speaking. 'This is all excellent insight, but it's also all *circumstantial*.'

Felicia shivered and took another sip of Striker's coffee. 'Circumstantial, fine. But how much do we need?'

'What we need here is *motive*.'

Felicia nodded. 'That's what interrogations are for.'

Striker didn't disagree. 'You're bang-on right about that – but not just yet.'

'Why not? Now's as good a time as any.'

Striker only smiled at her. 'You don't go big-game hunting with a mag that's half full of bullets.' He took back his coffee cup and sipped it, then let out a long breath that fogged the air under the street lamp. 'No, we'll finish our investigation first, gather as much evidence as we can on Ostermann, and then we'll go after him fully loaded.'

'Guns a-blazing,' Felicia said.

Striker smiled back.

'I never fire blanks.'

Sixty-Three

The Adder entered the Special Room. He had been in here over a dozen times in his life. And every time for his reward.

The room was different from the others. Certainly different from his own dwelling. Thick silk drapes, blood-red in colour, framed the bay window at the far end of the room. The glass of the window was tinted – easy to see out, impossible to see in. Flanking the window was a pair of high-backed leather chairs, red-brown in colour, matching the mahogany bar that was set at the opposite corner. On the countertop of the bar were several bottles of booze. Twenty-five-year-old Bowmore. Fifteen-year-old Grey Goose. Forty-year-old Rémy Martin. And types of hard liquor the Adder did not even recognize. There were also several bottles of mineral water, all for him.

He touched none of it, just as he never had.

Sitting in the centre of the room was a king-sized bed. A four-poster, covered with thick heavy sheets of high-count cotton thread and big puffy pillows that were so deep, you fell right into them.

The Adder stepped into the room and closed the door behind him. His eyes flitted to the old bronze lamp on the desk, then the luxurious chandelier above, and then the mirror on the far wall. These were all beautiful items.

And all perfect for secretly hiding a camera.

He looked around the room but found none. He never did.

He unbuttoned his shirt and let it fall to the thick white carpet below. Then he did the same with his jeans and underwear. When he saw the image in the mirror before him, it was bony thin and terribly white. There were scratch marks all down its arms – from the well, he knew – and two of the fingernails from the left hand were broken off.

The sight was interesting, and for a moment it stole his attention.

Then the door behind him opened and shut. And the Adder knew that she was there. She came up behind him, wrapped her soft hands around his ribs, and his body automatically tightened.

'You're cold,' she said.

Then her body pressed into him from behind. He could feel her firm breasts against his back. Her flesh on his flesh. Her warmth invading his body.

He turned around and met her eyes, and was sucked down deep into their stare. She kissed him with an open mouth, her tongue slipping on his. Touching, tickling, caressing. And then she gently pushed him back to the bed.

He let her. He fell back on the thick cotton sheets. And then she climbed on top of him. Her hips straddled his, her long dark hair spilling all around him like heavy thread. She stared deep into his eyes.

'Did the Doctor put you in the well again?' she asked.

'Yes.'

'You're cold.'

'Yes.'

'Let me warm you.'

She reached down between his legs and grabbed hold of him, squeezed him, made him stiff. Then she lowered her hips and took him inside her. And the Adder did what he thought he was supposed to do – though his thoughts were still far away, where they needed to be. Not here, not now. But on Larisa Logan.

'Warmer now?' she asked.

He closed his eyes and tried to focus on the immediate.

The Girl let out a soft sound, a moan that escaped her thin bluish lips. And she tightened down on him; he could feel it. A throbbing sensation was pulsating through him. Because of her. She was warm and wet and wonderful.

'I love you,' she said, again and again.

The Adder did not reply. Did not even try.

I love you . . .

He wished he understood that.

Sixty-Four

Striker and Felicia went to meet Noodles at the Ident Lab at 312 Main Street. As always in this city, there was no parking to be found, so Striker left their car on Cordova Street in the Patrol Only parking – an action which always drove the road cops crazy, but Striker couldn't help it.

Things had to get done.

He and Felicia walked down the laneway which divided the main building from the annexe. Once inside, they made their way to the Ident Lab. The unit was old and run-down and screamed of makeshift necessity. On the left side of the hall sat the Blood Drying Room, where all soaked materials were tagged before being swabbed. Up ahead they saw the chemical lab, where Noodles had undoubtedly applied the ninhydrin to bring up the print.

To the right of the chemical lab was the main Ident office, where most of the paperwork got done. In this area, it wasn't all that different from Homicide. Rows and rows of thrown-together cubicles cluttered the office, each one seeming far too small for the amount of clutter the desks owned.

In the last one was Noodles.

The portly Ident tech was sitting far back in his chair with his feet up on the desk and a frozen gel pack laid across his eyes. When Striker got close enough to him, he gave his chair a kick.

'Trying to get rid of the wrinkles there, Princess?'

Felicia laughed at this. 'Botox works better.'

Noodles just removed the bag from his eyes and blinked a few times while trying to get used to the light. He threw the cold-pack on the desk, sat forward in his chair, and rubbed his eyes.

'Been reading prints all damn day,' he said. 'My eyes are seeing stars.'

'Any news on the print you found on the can of varnish?'

'It's being sent through the database as we speak. I'll let you know if there are any hits.'

'And the DNA?'

'Swabbed from the gun, the can, the pill bottles, the windows – God, you name it. I'll let you know if we get any hits on those too, but that'll take a few weeks, as I'm sure you already know. As for the palm prints, well, take a look for yourself.'

Noodles pushed his chair out of the way and showed Striker the two samples. Both were palm prints, and only partials at that. One from the Mandy Gill crime scene, one from the apartment across the street from Sarah Rose's unit.

The first print, from Mandy's crime scene, was well detailed, with lots of good ridge detail and areas where the bifurcation and endings were easily apparent. But the second print, the one from Sarah's crime scene, was indistinct, blurry – as if the hand had been dragged across the window surface, catching only the barest bit of skin.

Striker stood back and changed the subject. 'Any news on the gun?'

'It's a Browning 9-mm pistol.'

The news made Striker's hopes drop. The Browning nine-mil was standard issue in the army. Good for close-quarters combat; quick and easy to draw. Plus the mags held thirteen rounds. All in all, it meant the same damn thing to him.

Another dead end.

Felicia saw the frown on Striker's face and asked, 'What? What does that mean?'

'It means that, in all likelihood, Billy Mercury stole the gun from the 7th Regiment when he got discharged – it means it will probably lead us nowhere but back to the army. And a stolen pistol at that.'

'I'll look into it and let you know what I find,' Noodles said.

Striker appreciated it.

He was about say more when his cell vibrated against his side. He picked it up and read the screen, expecting to see Laroche's or Courtney's name. But what he saw made his heart skip a beat. He had received an email from: *Larisa*. He opened up the file and read the message.

> I trusted you and you sent the Mental Health Team after me.

'Oh shit,' Striker said.

He immediately thought of Bernard Hamilton from Car 87, and anger rose in his chest. He looked at Felicia, then showed her the message. 'What did I tell you – she thinks we sent the Mental Health Team after her.'

He typed back:

> Not true. They were there on their own separate call. We never knew till later.

He sent the email and waited. But there was no immediate response. He added:

> Where are you? We will meet you.

He hit Send. But again, there was no response. And he waited for what seemed like an eternity. Finally, just when he was about to close the email program and stuff the phone back into his jacket pocket, it vibrated again. He opened the email, read the screen and was disheartened by the words:

I trusted you, Jacob.

After that, nothing else came back. And after another long moment, Striker knew the discussion had ended. He closed off his email program and put his cell away. He leaned back in the chair and felt like screaming. Partly because he was frustrated, but partly because of the guilt. What Larisa had written was not entirely untrue. She had trusted him, reached out to him, and he had failed her.

'She won't listen to me now,' he realized. 'The trust is gone.'

Felicia nodded. 'I'm not surprised. Don't forget, Jacob, she's paranoid right now. She thinks the whole world is out to get her. We need to ping her number and find out where she is.'

'That's the problem. She's not sending it from a cell phone; she's at a computer terminal somewhere. Using email. Who knows where?'

'I have a contact with Shaw and some other service providers. Let me see if we can trace it for an IP address. Then maybe we'll get a location of that terminal.' Felicia grinned and stuck out her hand. 'Come on, baby. Give momma the phone.'

Striker hesitated while looking at the message. After a moment, he relented and handed the cell to her. Felicia opened up the email program, pressed the Details button, then looked at the email sender's address:

L.Logan@gmail.com.

'It's a Gmail account,' she said. 'I have a contact there.'

Before Striker could reply, Felicia was on the phone to her contact. Striker spent the time going over the prints with Noodles one more time, making certain there was nothing they had overlooked. Ten minutes later, when she finally hung up, she had a smirk on her face. She said nothing.

'Well?' he asked.

'Whenever you need something, you just come to momma, baby.'

Noodles laughed at this; Striker did not.

'Come on, Feleesh. What you got?'

'She's at a coffee shop in the Metrotown Mall. A place called Arabic Beans.'

Striker swore. That was Burnaby. 'We'll never get there in time.'

Felicia agreed. 'We need to send another unit.'

Striker shook his head. 'Absolutely not. She sees one of their cruisers and she'll freak.'

Felicia's eyes stayed on his. 'We have no choice in the matter. She may be delusional, Jacob, but Larisa knows *something*. You said that yourself. And if you're right – if there is more than one person involved here – then she's in a lot of danger, too. She could get herself killed before we have a chance to catch her again.'

Striker said nothing as he thought it over.

'I agree with Felicia,' Noodles said. 'And you're running out of time.'

Striker shook his head and gave in. 'Fine. But a plainclothes cop only. No goddam uniforms. I mean it. She sees one of them, she'll bolt on us. Even worse, she'll know we sent it and she'll never trust me again.'

Felicia grabbed Noodles's portable radio, then went over the air, asking if there were any plainclothes units out east near the

Boundary border. When the answer was negative, she switched over to the Info channel and asked them to see if there was a plainclothes unit in Burnaby South, near the Metrotown Mall. There was one, and Felicia relayed the message to them.

'Be discreet,' she said. 'This woman is *super* heaty.'

'Copy,' the unit replied.

Striker cut in. 'Give me your cell-phone number and I'll send you a photo of the target.'

The Burnaby South cop gave Striker his number, and Striker flipped through his iPhone photos till he found the one of Larisa the Sarj had downloaded from her personnel file back at the Victim Services Unit. He brought it up and sent the attachment. Moments later, when Felicia handed the radio back to Noodles, she looked at Striker and smiled.

'It's done,' she said.

Striker didn't smile back. He couldn't – he was sick to his stomach. If Larisa spooked on this one and got away from them, there was no telling what might happen. Thoughts of suicide even crossed his mind.

He stood up from the chair and grabbed his keys from his jacket pocket.

'Come on,' he said to Felicia. 'We're going there, too. *Code 3.*'

Sixty-Five

Normally the drive from Main Street to Burnaby's Metrotown Mall took a good twenty minutes. With Striker driving lights and siren the entire way, they made it there in less than ten, and ended up intercepting the plainclothes cops from Burnaby South.

Striker spotted their undercover cruiser turning off Kingsway and driving into the underground parkade. It made him shake his head; he had hoped for an undercover operative, not a plainclothes cop in an unmarked Ford. A white Crown Victoria stood out in the parkade like a lighthouse at sea. It was no good. If anything, it was detrimental. And to make matters worse, Larisa had spent three years working for Victim Services. She knew what an undercover police sedan looked like. Hell, she used to drive around in one of them while en route to calls.

'Just get them the hell out of there,' Striker said to Felicia. 'Larisa will make them in a second, if she sees them.'

Felicia agreed. She got on her cell, called Burnaby South Dispatch, and had the unit pulled. Less than a minute later, the Crown Vic peeled out of the underground, leaving in its wake a loud squeal of tyres and a patch of rubber on the parking lot surface a foot long.

It was a *fuck you* from the other unit.

'That idiot,' Striker said. 'Get their unit number. I want to deal with them later.'

While Felicia got the number from Dispatch, Striker drove them into the central part of the parkade and dumped the wheels behind a tall support pillar, hoping to blend in with the grey concrete. When Felicia got out and stared at the size of the parkade, a worried sound escaped her lips.

'We got our work cut out for us on this one,' she said. 'This mall is huge. If she's left the coffee shop, we'll never find her in here.'

'All the more reason to get going,' Striker replied. He pointed to the escalator. 'Arabic Beans is on the northwest side of the mall, below the movie theatres – the older ones, not the new Cineplex. You go round the Skytrain ramp and come in from the south; I'll cut through the mall and come in from the north.'

'And if I find her, then what? Take her down right there?'

Striker thought it over. 'No. Don't let her see you. Call me on the cell, and let me approach her on my own. If she runs, then take her down. We have to. It's for her own good.'

Felicia nodded. Without a word, she spun about and hurried for the escalator. When she reached the top and disappeared from view, entering the first floor of the mall, Striker turned around and ran for the north-side elevators.

He hoped they weren't too late.

Despite the fact that Christmas and Boxing Day sales were long over, and all the New Year's Day sales had ended three weeks ago, the mall was jam-packed with people. Gangs of teenagers with their baggy pants and skateboards hung out near the McDonald's alcove, and adults with their children flooded the Gamespot counter. Everyone was making exchanges and new purchases. It being seven o'clock and dinner time for the late crowd, the Food Court was jammed.

Striker took a moment to scan the area.

Larisa Logan was Caucasian. At five foot seven and one hundred and forty pounds, she blended in well with most crowds. The last time he saw her her dark brown hair had been shoulder length and straight though it could be worn many ways. As if to make spotting her even more difficult, she also wore glasses and, sometimes, he recalled, coloured contacts.

She was a hard target.

Striker saw no sign of her in the Food Court, so he made his way down the east–west walkway. He found the mall doors, exited the building, and began rounding the building along the Kingsway boulevard.

Outside, the night was as dark as a day-old bruise. The side-walk was frosted over. Only the street and walkway lamps illuminated the area, turning everyone more than twenty feet away into silhouettes.

Striker passed a few clusters, making sure he saw the face of each person and paying even closer attention to any lone indi-viduals that sneaked off the path. When he rounded the bend and came within sight of the coffee shop, Arabic Beans, his heart clenched and his hopes evaporated.

Sitting outside Arabic Beans was an unmarked Crown Victoria sedan. A Vancouver Police car. Its red and blue lights were flashing and its spotlight was turned on.

'What the fuck?' escaped his lips.

Before Striker knew it, he was running. Racing down the long strip of corridor towards the coffee shop. He passed the Happy Gate Sushi shop and the Muffin Inn, and finally the Save-on-Foods store.

When he came to within fifty feet of Arabic Beans, he spotted Felicia coming the other way. The hard look on her face told him that she felt the same confusion. What the hell was going on? And just as importantly, *who* the hell was in Arabic Beans?

Striker got his answer less than ten steps later.

The tinted glass door to the coffee shop slowly opened and two figures emerged. The first one was a short Asian woman Striker recognized but could not place. The second figure was easily distinguishable, and the sight of the man made Striker's blood *hot*. With his long ponytail hanging down from his balding head, and wearing a bright red dress shirt with matching tie, was Bernard Hamilton of Car 87. The Mental Health Team.

They were here for the warrant.

Striker ran right up to the man. 'What the hell are you doing here?' he demanded.

Bernard Hamilton smiled. Smiled like he wasn't surprised in the least to see them. 'We're looking for Larisa.' He winked. 'Got a tip she might be here.'

'A tip? From who?'

Bernard just kept smiling. 'Never identify a source,' was all he said.

Striker looked around for Larisa, did not see her.

'Where is she?' he asked.

'Not here,' Bernard said. 'I checked out the entire place. She left long before we got here.'

Striker looked at Felicia, whose face appeared as tight as his chest. 'Watch the front,' he told her, and headed into the coffee shop.

The place was small and dark with a mirror behind the front bar that reflected back the blue lights of the Arabic Beans neon sign in the window. Behind the bar stood a tall thin black man. He was washing mugs.

Striker approached him and got his attention. 'You see a

white woman in here? Five foot seven. A hundred and forty pounds. Brown hair?'

The man put down the mug and frowned. 'I see lots dem people in here,' he said. His voice was deep and smooth, and he spoke the words slowly, with all the patience in the world. His accent reminded Striker of the Hondurans he'd dealt with in the skids so many times during his time in Patrol. 'Dis is Metrotown, man. Always real busy.'

Striker fished out his iPhone and opened up his photos folder. He scanned through the pictures, found the one of Larisa and showed it to the man. The barista took a long look, then shook his head.

'Never seen da girl.'

'You got video surveillance?'

'Naw, the owner's too cheap for dat, man. We's lucky to have lights on in dis place.'

Striker cursed. Without another word, he left the front counter and began searching through the shop. He started in the rear, checking both washrooms and finding them empty. Then he began making his way among the patrons. There were fewer than ten in total, and only four of them were women. Two Asian, one black, and one white woman. She was over six foot.

Striker tried to contain his temper.

Larisa was gone; they had missed her.

Again.

He was about to leave Arabic Beans when his eye caught the row of monitors along the far wall. There were five in total, and the first four all faced towards him, each displaying a stark white Google screen from the Firefox web browser.

The last terminal was turned to face the wall.

Striker walked over to the area. He searched the chair and floor for anything that might have been dropped. A purse. Some

ID. Anything to show that Larisa had been here. Anything to lead them to a new location.

But he found nothing.

He reached out, grasped hold of the monitor, and turned it so he could see the screen. What he saw was alarming. The screen was white, just like the others, but the application running wasn't Firefox, but Microsoft Word. Typed across the screen was one brief message. When Striker read it, his heart plummeted:

Car 87?

Betrayed me again!

I can't believe it.

You were my only hope, Jacob.

My only hope.

Sixty-Six

When the reward was over, and after the Girl had left him, the Adder left the soft comfort of the bed and approached the bar. From it, he took a bottle of sparkling mineral water – Sémillante, from France – and uncapped it. As he drank some down, the bubbly fluid tingling the back of his throat, the Adder thought of the Girl. He could still feel her warmth against his body. Her wetness all around him. Her tender sweet taste on his lips. Now that she was gone, he felt like something was missing.

It was very, very odd. He could not understand it.

He got dressed and exited the Special Room. He found the hatch in the floor, opened it, and started down the rungs of the ladder. He'd made it less than a quarter of the way down when he heard the Doctor and the Girl, speaking somewhere above him.

'Did you please him?' the Doctor asked.

'I think so.'

'You *think?*'

'Well . . . yes, he seemed pleased.'

'Did he ejaculate?'

Pause.

'Answer the question, girl.'

'He doesn't . . . he doesn't always—'

Slap!

Then . . . crying.

'Come here,' the Doctor ordered.

'Please . . .'

'Lift up your skirt.'

There was another moment of silence, and then the Girl let out an uncomfortable sound. 'Please, you're hurting me—'

'Shut *up*! . . . Look, there – he ejaculated.'

The Girl made no reply, only another uncomfortable sound.

'Do not make me do this again. Do you understand?'

'Yes, Doctor.'

There was silence. No more conversation. Just the sound of footsteps walking away down the hall.

The Adder did not move from the ladder. He stayed there, rooted to the spot like a gargoyle, and replayed the dialogue in his head. Over and over again. And a strange feeling rose up inside him. One he didn't like. The Doctor was stirring things up. Old things within him. Bad things. *Feelings.*

It was the Doctor's fault.

Like a distant, growing thunder, the laughter started in the Adder's head. And he closed his eyes, as if this would somehow shut out the sounds. Before they could expand on him again – before they could crash down on him like cold lightning – he climbed back down the ladder, opened up the dumbwaiter, and grabbed his recording equipment from the shelves. He shoved it all into a burlap sack, along with a drill, screw-gun and some screws.

Then, with the burlap sack slung around his shoulder, the Adder crouched down low and climbed inside the dumbwaiter. He then began climbing up the old chute, one bracket at a time. He headed for the second floor.

For the room that was forbidden.

Sixty-Seven

Striker and Felicia spent the next half-hour checking out the rest of Metrotown Mall, but Striker knew in his heart it would be a wasted effort. Larisa had seen Bernard Hamilton of Car 87, and she had hightailed it as far from Burnaby South as her legs would carry her.

Their one big chance, destroyed.

While Felicia did another run around of the main level, Striker attended the security office and spoke to the two guards inside. He emailed the office a copy of Larisa's picture and told them to scour the footage and see if they could find her.

He had little hope of success.

By the time he was done and leaving the small office, Felicia was already outside waiting for him. She had two cups of Tim Horton's coffee in her hands and a tired but determined look on her face. Striker took one of the paper cups from her, said thanks.

'Any luck?' he asked, already knowing the answer.

'She's gone,' was all Felicia said.

Striker could not help but scowl as they headed back to the car. 'This is such bullshit,' he griped. 'That fuckin' Bernard. He's royally screwed it for us on this one.'

Felicia nodded. 'I wonder who his source is.'

Striker took a sip of his coffee. It was too sweet. As usual, Felicia had put sugar in it. 'There is no source,' he said. 'Never was.'

'Then how—'

'Hamilton was eavesdropping on our conversation when we went over the air,' he said. 'He heard you on Dispatch, then he listened in when we switched to Info and requested a Burnaby unit to attend here. He caught on. Figured out we were coming for Larisa.'

'You really think? That's pretty devious.'

'I know it is, and I know Bernard.' Striker thought of how they had also coincidentally run into Bernard at 312 Main Street when checking for warrants. There were too many coincidences with the man. He turned to Felicia. 'Run a history of Bernard's unit status. I'll bet you a hundred bucks he was closer than we were when we made the call to Burnaby. It's how he got on scene so fast.'

Felicia grabbed the computer and ran the Remote Log. After a few seconds, she nodded. 'You're right, he was already out here at the same time we made the call. He put himself out at Boundary and Adanac Street.'

Striker glanced over at her. 'Recognize the location?'

'Mapleview,' she said.

'Exactly. He was probably there looking for Larisa. Or trying to get information.'

'But why? Why would he care so much?'

Striker gave her a bemused look. 'You still don't get it, do you? Bernard *doesn't* care. When was the last time you saw him put in this kind of work for any other mentally ill patient?'

'Well, never.'

'Exactly. Bernard just wants to be the one to *save* Larisa. Think about it. She's a former employee of the Vancouver Police Department. A Victim Services worker, no less. And she's been through hell and back. Now Bernard Hamilton – caring community cop and all-around godsend – comes along and rescues her from her mental illness. Think of how he'd spin that one.'

Felicia nodded. 'More glory in his bid for Cop of the Year.'

'Exactly. The worst part is he knows he's actually putting her in greater danger – and ruining our chances of getting her back safely. But he doesn't care. Because he wants to be the one who scores on the arrest.' Striker felt his entire body grow tight with anger. 'He'll never get that award. Not ever. Because everyone knows what he's all about. He doesn't care about Larisa or any of them.'

'He cares about the publicity,' Felicia said.

'He wants publicity, I'll make sure he gets some,' Striker said. 'Starting off within the department.'

Felicia gave him a curious look, and he smiled at her darkly.

'Later,' he told her. 'When the time is right.'

A half-hour later, at exactly eight o'clock, they drove back over Boundary Road municipal border and entered the City of Vancouver.

'We're looking at this the wrong way,' Striker said. 'Let's stop trying to find out *where* Larisa went and find out *why*.'

Felicia gave him an odd look. 'We already know why.'

'Do we?' he asked.

'The medical warrant.'

He shook his head. 'There's something else she's running from here, something besides the medical warrant. There has to be. Think about it. The woman emailed me and told me she believed Mandy was murdered. She also had Sarah's name written down in her place. At the time, we thought it was all part of her mental illness. But now I wonder.'

Felicia nodded. 'It was almost like she had proof.'

Striker thought of all the opened DVD cases they had found on the floor of Larisa's ransacked rancher.

'We need to find out what that proof was,' he said.

Felicia opened up the laptop with a renewed sense of energy about her. 'Let's go over everything one more time.'

Striker pulled over to the side of the road. He opened up his notebook, then the file folder of all the evidence he had collected back at Larisa's rancher. There was a ton of stuff. Stories. Articles. Newspaper clippings.

One thing stuck out more than all the rest. It was the article from the Vancouver *Province* newspaper about the man who committed suicide at the Regency Hotel. Someone had used a thick pen to write *LIES! LIES! LIES!* across it.

Striker read through the article, saw that the victim's name was Derrick Smallboy. The man was said to have suffered from depression, addiction and fetal alcohol syndrome.

A hell of a trio.

Striker found the article intriguing, in a dark sort of way. 'Run this name,' he said to Felicia. 'Derrick Smallboy. Age twenty-eight.'

She did, and after a moment the feed came back.

'He's deceased,' she said.

'I know that; he's the guy from this article. Read up on him, tell me what you find.'

Felicia did. After a long moment, she looked up with a shocked look on her face. 'Holy shit, Jacob, look at this. Says here that Smallboy suffered from depression, FAS, alcoholism, and schizophrenia. This guy was really messed up. He ended up throwing himself off the top of the Regency Hotel.'

'I know all that.'

'Be patient,' she told him, and read on. 'Says here he was enrolled in the EvenHealth programme, and was taking SILC classes.'

That made Striker take notice.

He leaned over and scanned through the report. As he learned the basics – that Derrick Smallboy had plummeted from the top of the Regency Hotel with no witnesses and no evidence of foul play – something else caught his eye.

A Lost Property file where Smallboy was listed as a complainant.

'Bring up that one,' he said.

Felicia exited the current report and brought up the Lost Property page. The synopsis was brief. Smallboy had lost several pieces of ID, namely his BC driver's licence, his status card, and his birth certificate. He believed they had been stolen, but the author of the report hinted at paranoia.

'Go back into Larisa's main page again,' Striker said.

When Felicia did, he pointed to one of the reports Larisa had made in August last year. It was listed as a Lost Property report, and when Felicia brought up the synopsis, he saw the same basic facts.

All of Larisa's ID had been taken. Just like Smallboy's. She also thought it had been stolen. But there was no proof of this. Not even a possible suspect. In the end, the report had been cleared as Unfounded.

Striker looked at Felicia. 'You still have your contact at Equifax?'

'You bet. TransUnion, too.'

'Call them. Find out if there were any credit problems with Smallboy and Larisa.'

Felicia got on the phone and got hold of her contact at the credit bureau who could search both TransUnion and Equifax databases. The process was slow and cumbersome, but after almost twenty minutes, she hung up the phone with a curious look on her face.

'Bad credit reports?' Striker asked.

'The worst. Non-payments. R3s. You name it. And it gets

worse than that,' she said. 'Smallboy and Logan were both victims of identity theft. Full frauds. It's all documented with the bureau. Someone damn well bankrupted them. Took out credit cards in their names, emptied their bank accounts – everything.'

Striker felt the energy of a new lead.

'Awfully coincidental,' he said.

'That's not the half of it,' Felicia continued. 'I also got him to check on Mandy Gill and Sarah Rose. Exact same thing. They *all* had their IDs stolen and they were *all* victims of identity theft.'

'Did Larisa report the physical theft of the identification, or that someone was using her identity to obtain more credit?' he clarified.

'Both.'

Striker looked down at the date when Larisa Logan had reported the identity theft.

'Larisa made a report of this on August third of last year,' he noted.

Felicia nodded. 'And three days later, she was committed.'

'To where?'

'Riverglen.'

'By whose order?' Striker asked.

'Dr Riley M. Richter.'

Striker leaned back against the seat, his head swirling with information. Four victims of identity theft. All connected through the doctors of the EvenHealth programme. And now three of them were dead, one was missing.

The odds were astronomical.

'It all comes back to the doctors,' he said. 'To Ostermann and Richter.'

He'd barely finished speaking the words when his cell phone

rang. He picked it up, stuck it to his ear, and said, 'Detective Striker, Homicide.'

The voice responding was smooth and soft. *Feminine.*

'This is Dr Richter. Apparently you've been looking for me.'

Sixty-Eight

The address Dr Richter gave Striker was for a road named Stone Creek Slope in West Vancouver, Canada's most expensive area of real estate. Within ten seconds of driving off the Trans-Canada Highway and entering the district, Striker could see why.

The lots became large and more secluded. Driveways were flanked by tall rows of old-growth cedars, and most of the mansions were barely visible behind the gated driveways and high stone walls. Every house had a veranda that stared out over the cold deep waters of the strait below.

Striker looked out over those waterways. They appeared like polished black stone, matching the cloudless night sky. Beyond them was the city of Vancouver, all lit up and busy. Just another weekday night in a city buzzing with night life.

He drove slowly down the long swerving slope of hill, until he spotted the address they were looking for on the left. A small driveway compared to the others, almost hidden by the trees.

'It feels so secluded out here,' Felicia said. 'Like we're out in the middle of nowhere – yet the city's just a ten-minute drive away. It's beautiful.'

'And costs a fortune. That's why only doctors and lawyers and celebrities live here.'

He turned the car up the driveway and stopped on a small, round parking area. They got out. The house before them was not as plush as the others but, in this neighbourhood, 'not plush' still meant worth millions.

Out front, the alcove lights suddenly turned on and the front door opened. Standing in the doorway was a woman of maybe thirty years, dressed in a sombre black dress jacket and matching skirt. She had soft brown hair that was long, but tied up in a bun. A strong but pretty face. And confident eyes that held Striker's gaze without a moment's nervousness.

'Good evening,' she said. 'I'm Dr Richter. I've been expecting you.'

Moments later, after they were all inside and introductions had been made, they moved into a small sunken den that overlooked the pool area outside and, beyond that, the cliffs over the strait. On the coffee table was a bowl of ripe mandarin oranges. The smell of them filled the room.

Striker sat down in a leather EZ Boy recliner, directly across from Dr Richter, who took the loveseat. In between them, on a matching sofa, sat Felicia.

'Nice place,' Striker offered.

Dr Richter tucked one leg under the other and smoothed out her skirt. 'It's my uncle's,' she replied. 'The rent is good and he lives just across the street, which is perfect for me since I'm away much of the time. He keeps an eye on things for me.'

'Were you away yesterday?' Striker asked. 'I left you several messages.'

'Yes, and I apologize for not getting back to you sooner. I hadn't bothered to check my messages since the day before. And then, all day long, I was flying back from New York.'

'Conference?' Felicia asked.

Dr Richter shook her head. 'I have family out there. I visited a little bit, did the mandatory social thing. But I was really there to assess the area. I'm considering opening a private practice there. The money is triple what I can make here, and the taxes less than half.'

'That's quite a difference,' Felicia remarked.

'It's a difference of fifteen years – retiring at fifty versus sixty-five.' Dr Richter gave them both a quick look, then spoke again. 'I didn't get into this profession for the love of psychiatry,' she said bluntly. 'I entered this field to make a lot of money, to retire young and still enjoy life.'

'And yet you choose to work for EvenHealth,' Striker pointed out.

'Yes,' she admitted, as if not making the connection.

He explained. 'They're government subsidized, and Dr Ostermann has built his reputation on helping out the poorest of patients. I'm sure the government don't pay anywhere near what the private practices pay – especially in this area.'

'They don't,' Dr Richter replied. 'I'm not working at EvenHealth for the money, I'm there for the experience. Dr Ostermann's name reaches to far places. Plus, I wanted to see how he had put together the programme. My goal in New York is to start my own private programme with doctors working *for me*. That's where the money is.'

Striker found the woman interesting. Blunt and brutally honest, but interesting. Charming, even. He pulled out his notebook and leafed back through the pages until he came to what he was looking for.

'You prescribed medications to some patients,' he began. 'Exact same kind and dosage.' He reached out to show her what he had written in his notebook; she read the names and medications listed on the page.

'These patients, were they part of EvenHealth?' she asked.

'Yes. Enrolled in the SILC classes.'

Dr Richter made an *ahh* sound. 'The group sessions. Social Independence and Life Coping skills.' She smiled. 'One of Dr Ostermann's ten-step programmes. It is aimed primarily at bipolar patients, for the most. A few of the patients have Generalized Anxiety Disorder. Lexapro and Effexor are common treatments for this. They more often than not work extremely well, especially when taken together. For any more detail than that, I'd have to check my files.'

'You don't recognize your own prescriptions?' Striker asked.

Dr Richter laughed bemusedly. 'Detective, please. Between my work with EvenHealth and the other clinics, I've treated over seven hundred patients in the last year. Each one of them is on as many as ten different medications. That's *seven thousand* medications in total. Do you honestly think I remember them all?'

'Sounds like mass production.'

'It sounds like *money*,' she said brazenly. 'I've already told you, I never joined this profession for the long hours and the constant lack of progress, I joined it to make money. Cold, hard cash. And I intend on being retired on a beach in Jamaica by the time I'm forty.'

Striker ignored that. 'I'm less concerned about the medication types and more concerned about the patient names,' Striker said. 'Mandy Gill, Sarah Rose, and Larisa Logan, in particular.'

Dr Richter said nothing for a moment. Her eyes took on a faraway look and her face remained expressionless. In that moment, she looked older. And much more experienced. *Clinical.*

'I have a vague recollection of the group,' she finally said. 'And I'm not overly comfortable discussing them, especially not without perusing the file first – remember, I was only a fill-in for the group when Dr Ostermann could not be present.'

'Larisa Logan,' he pressed.

Dr Richter gave him a cold look, but then spoke anyway. 'Her, I do remember. She was a Victim Services worker, if I recall correctly.'

'She was,' Striker confirmed. 'Her family was killed in a car accident. She suffered a breakdown.'

'Yes, I remember Larisa Logan. She was a kind and genuine person. I felt for her.'

Striker doubted that, but said nothing.

'Larisa is missing,' Felicia interjected. 'And we're desperate to find her – not for any criminal reasons, but for her own safety.'

Dr Richter's face took on a confused look. 'I don't understand, why are you here talking to me?'

Striker blinked. 'Are you not her doctor?'

'No. Not at all. As I already explained, I was only an *interim* doctor for the SILC classes. I never worked with any of the patients during private sessions – there's no money there.'

'Then who was Larisa's doctor?' Felicia asked.

'Why, Dr Ostermann, of course.'

Striker leaned forward in his chair. 'Let me get this straight here. Other than the odd fill-in day here and there, you never worked with Larisa?'

'Of course not. She was Dr Ostermann's patient, and his alone. He was quite ... possessive of her, really. His own personal project.'

Striker looked at Felicia and saw the tightness of her expression. He steered the conversation back to other matters – whether Dr Richter had ever used any experimental medication on the patients, whether she had any connections to the army, and whether she ever did any work at Riverglen Mental Health Facility.

The answer to all three questions was a resounding *no*.

When they were done with the interview, Striker stood up and put his notebook away. He shook the woman's hand, and thanked her for her time. Then, with Felicia at his side, he walked to the front door.

'Keep your phone nearby,' he said to Dr Richter. 'I have a feeling I'll be calling you again.'

'Any time,' she replied.

But no smile parted her lips.

They drove back out of the cedar-covered hills of West Vancouver and took the highway to the downtown core. During the drive, Striker tried to relax his mind and let everything fall into place. But Felicia was unusually wired.

'We have the connection,' she said. 'Dr Ostermann was seeing *all four* patients – Gill, Rose, Mercury and Larisa Logan – and he was seeing them not only during group sessions but one-on-one.'

Striker nodded. 'I agree. He's also about the same size and stature as the man who attacked me back at the Gill crime scene – but it's all still circumstantial at this point. Everything.'

Felicia scowled. 'Which means what, he gets a free ride?'

'No. Which means we see the man.'

Felicia nodded, but her face took on a concerned look. 'Just be careful you don't tip him off on anything.'

Striker gave her a quick glance as they headed over the Lions Gate Bridge. 'I said *see* him, not speak to him.' He took out his cell phone and dialled Hans Jager – *Meathead*, to anyone who knew him. Meathead was one of the breachers for the Emergency

Response Team. The man answered, they talked, and a few minutes later, Striker hung up the phone and headed for the Cambie Street bridge.

There was some equipment they needed to pick up.

Sixty-Nine

The Adder had no idea what time it was when he finished the set-up. It could have been eight o'clock at night, it could have been well into the morning hours. He did not know. He did not care. Time held little importance to him, and he only took careful note of it when on a mission. All that mattered now was that the set-up was complete. And that it was done well.

It was.

The bulk of the camera's body sat within the steel bracket, which was screwed securely to the two-by-four beams of the dumbwaiter. The lens poked through the small hole in the wall, coming flush with the other side – just a one-inch lens that focused on the centre part of the Doctor's private room.

The forbidden room.

The Adder turned on the camera and looked at the LED screen. The image displayed was angled perfectly. It captured the oak bureau across the room. The four-poster king-sized bed in the centre of the room. The locked cabinet in the far corner.

The camera took in *everything*.

As if scripted, the Doctor returned, and not alone. At first the Adder reared from the camera and started to make his way back down the long and narrow chute of the dumbwaiter. But something made him pause.

A dark curiosity.

He climbed back to the top and stared at the camera's LED screen. Already the motion sensor had been triggered and the recording had been started. The two people in the room were beginning. The Adder had heard the act before. He had seen the results. He had known it existed.

But he had never actually *seen* it.

Now, as he stood in the darkness and watched the Doctor unlock the cabinet, a strange feeling invaded his chest. And it only got worse when he saw what the Doctor pulled out.

He should have felt shock. Fear. Revulsion. He should have felt all of these things, he knew, but he felt none of them. All he experienced was a growing tension in his chest, one that spread all throughout his core as he watched the LED screen in near disbelief.

When the screams began and the first glimpse of blood appeared, the Adder wanted to leave the chute, but he did not. He stayed there, fixated, immobile. A statue in the dark.

He just could not take his eyes away.

Seventy

The traffic was surprisingly bad, so they were later than antici-
pated. Striker half expected Meathead to be gone by the time
they reached the north end of the Cambie Street bridge. But
within seconds of reaching the bottom of Nelson Street, Felicia
spotted a group of big men clad in black jump suits. In the heavy
darkness of the night, they blended well. Most of them were
climbing into a white van that was parked kerbside.

They were ERT. The Emergency Response Team.

Canada's answer to SWAT.

The cluster of cops were Red Team, and Striker knew most of
them: Reid Noble, who everyone called Jitters. Davey Combs,
who was only five foot six but over two hundred and twenty
pounds of muscle. And Victor Santos, who was a crazy-ass
bastard and – thank God – no relation to Felicia. Their sergeant,
Zulu 51, was Tyrone Takuto, a top-notch Eurasian cop Striker
had known and respected for years. He would be Chief one day.
Striker knew it.

All the men looked tired from training, but happy to be going.
It was Miller time.

Striker parked on Nelson and scanned the street both ways.
'You see Meathead anywhere?'

'Just in my nightmares,' Felicia said.

Striker laughed at that. She had barely spoken the words

when they looked up at the nearest skyscraper and spotted the man. Meathead was rappelling down the south side of the building. He was three storeys up and still looked massive. At six foot four and two hundred and seventy pounds, he was a force to be reckoned with.

He saw Striker from the second storey level and gave a holler. When his eyes found Felicia, a large smile spread his lips and he yelled out, 'Hey, honey-cakes, can I come down there and butter your muffin?'

'Butter *this!*' she called back.

Meathead let out a hoarse laugh, then rappelled down to ground level. He tried to lever down, did it a bit too fast, and accidentally unclipped before his feet were fully planted. He fell awkwardly, landing half on his ass, half on his hands.

'Smooth,' Felicia said.

Meathead looked up and grinned. 'I always fall for the hotties.'

She made an *ugh* sound.

'I was referring to Shipwreck.'

Meathead let out a hyena laugh and climbed to his feet. Striker was six foot one and two hundred and twenty pounds. No small man. And yet next to Meathead, he felt undersized. He moved up to the breacher, and the two bantered about their old partnership days for a few minutes. Then Meathead packed up his gear and started placing it in the transport van.

'About the gear,' Striker said.

Meathead nodded. 'Yeah, yeah. I got what you need right here, but you got to get it back to me tonight or Stark will have my balls in a sling.'

Striker nodded. James Stark was the inspector in charge of the Emergency Response Team. He was a by-the-book guy and would never have allowed Striker the gear he wanted without the proper paperwork – and even then, probably not. ERT was his baby, and he liked to keep it separate.

Meathead was sticking his neck out for them on this one, and Striker appreciated it.

'Scout's honour,' he said.

Meathead just gave him a look like he didn't fully believe him. Still he grabbed two pairs of night vision binoculars from his gear bag. He handed one to Striker, and Striker took it. When Felicia reached for hers, Meathead held them up to his eyes, looked at her chest, and said, 'Yummy.'

'Give me the goddam binocs,' she said.

When Meathead held them out again, she snatched them away from him. She gave Striker a hard look and said, 'I still think we should be getting SF for this.'

SF. Strike Force. The Vancouver Police Surveillance Team.

Striker frowned. Felicia had already brought up the topic in the car and, as usual, she was refusing to let the issue go.

'We can do this ourselves,' he said.

'We're not trained for it.'

'Trained?' He laughed. 'We're not going mobile, we're just setting up a stake-out. Like a drug buy. God, how many of those have you done?'

Felicia just shrugged. She'd probably done over a hundred in her time.

'We're just making observations,' Striker said.

'SF is still the best way to go.'

'And SF will take *time*,' he argued. 'Time to write up the forms. Time to make the requests. Time for them to be read over and approved. And you know as well as I do that Laroche does *nothing* out of policy.'

Felicia said nothing for a long moment, then looked at her watch.

'It's getting late,' she said.

Striker agreed. He looked at Meathead. 'I'll put these back in your locker when we're done.'

'Be sure you do,' he said. 'This is my ass on the line.'

Striker said nothing more. He took the gear with him and stuffed it in the trunk. When Felicia returned to the car, they hopped inside and got going. It was going on for nine o'clock now, and there was no time to waste.

The Endowment Lands were only ten minutes away.

The Ostermann house was on Belmont Avenue.

Striker parked a few blocks out and they went in on foot, coming in from the west. When they reached the lot, Striker slowed down. Inside the gated entrance, the house sat with most of the lights turned off. Only a few were left on – the ones in the library and kitchen, most noticeably.

'Looks like no one's home,' Felicia said.

Striker pointed to the Land Rover parked beside the house and the BMW in the drive. 'Someone's home.'

He assessed the house. The rooms that interested him the most – the master bedroom, the office and what appeared to be the study – were all located on the southwest side. That made the small grove of Japanese plum trees the best vantage point for surveillance. There was a small elevation there, near that corner of the yard, and the area was dark.

'Over there,' he suggested.

'I already see it,' Felicia said.

Striker looked at the neighbouring lot, the one to the east. There were no dogs. No sign of people. And all the lights in the house were off, as if the owners were away for the night.

It was the perfect place for entry.

Gear in hand, they made their way into the neighbouring lot.

All down the yard, a stone-and-cement wall separated the two properties. When they were a third of the way down, in behind the tall, bony Japanese plum trees, Striker stopped. He checked his cell phone to be sure it was set on vibrate, then looked at Felicia.

'Make sure your ringer is off.'

She did.

Satisfied, he assessed the wall. It was eight feet high, so he had to give Felicia a boost over. Once she was there, he took a running start, sprung up off the wall and pulled himself over behind her.

In the Ostermann yard everything was quiet and still. From the grassy elevation they knelt on, the entire south and east sides of the mansion could be seen. Between the trees to the north, Striker could see past the end of the floodlit yard to the cliffs beyond. Out in the strait, the moon shimmered off the waves and made the water look like smoked glass.

'We can see the bedroom, den and study from here,' Felicia noted. 'But the library and kitchen are completely out of view.'

Striker nodded. 'Then go around back. See if you can find a different vantage point for the kitchen and library. When you get one, call me. That way we'll have the whole house covered.'

Felicia climbed to her feet and slowly made her way down the east side of the house. When she turned the corner, she was blocked from sight by the barbecue area. With her out of sight, Striker took out his binocs and used them to focus in on the front of the house.

In the driveway was Dr Ostermann's BMW. Parked at the east side of the house was the Land Rover. Striker looked past it, past the stone-and-steel pillars of the driveway and the old-fashioned lanterns that lined the cobblestone walkways. He focused on the window to the doctor's study.

The blind was drawn, the drapes pulled shut behind it.

His cell vibrated against his side, so he snatched it up and brought it to his ear.

'I have a good position,' Felicia said. 'I can see the entire north and west sides of the house.'

'Anything of interest?'

Felicia made an unhappy sound. 'The place looks empty.'

'Just keep watching. And be ready to go at a moment's notice.'

He hung up and looked at the house.

For a long moment, he watched the study, staring at the blind as if it would suddenly pop open and reveal to him the secrets that lay behind it. It didn't, of course, and after a few more minutes, Striker placed his focus on the office below. It appeared vacant. All the lights were off. There was no movement inside.

He looked at the master bedroom. There the drapes were only half pulled shut, but with the telescopic lens of the binocs he could see inside.

Everything there was just as dark and still as the office.

He was just about to reposition himself to be more comfortable, when the bedroom door opened and the light flicked on. Walking in through the door was Dr Ostermann – although walking seemed an odd word for it. He moved gingerly, limping more than walking. And when he began to take off his shirt, the action clearly pained him. He slid the shirt off his body and let it drop to the floor.

As Striker watched the man, he noticed a few long reddish marks. Scratch marks maybe. One ran down the side of the man's neck and one trailed across the top of his back. He tried to focus in for a better look, but the doctor stepped out of view and remained hidden behind the partly closed curtains.

Striker remembered how gingerly the man had moved the first time he had met him – just hours after the suspect had fought with him and jumped out of the third-storey window of Mandy Gill's building.

Now, here he was, seemingly injured again.

It was strange.

The thought had barely formed in his mind when the front door suddenly swung open. From the house ran Dalia. She had her hands over her ears and her face was tight. She raced across the front yard, opened the gate, and then ran down Belmont Avenue to the west. When she reached the next lot, Striker lost sight of her.

Something was wrong.

Striker took out his cell and called Felicia. 'You getting anything back there?'

'Nothing. All dead.'

'Well, I got the doctor in view, and he looks like he's been in a fight again. Plus, Dalia just went racing out of the house like it was on fire. Something's going on here, Feleesh. I'm moving in for a closer look.'

'Let's get another unit here first.'

'This will just take a second.'

'There's something weird about this family, Jacob. I don't like it. It's not safe.'

'No police work is.'

'This is different.'

'Just cover me, Feleesh. Cover me and keep your radio turned on.'

He hung up the phone, got up from his prone position and made his way through the plum trees. As he reached the driveway and roundabout, he tucked the binoculars inside his inner coat pocket, then made his way up the steps of the front walkway.

The front door was half open, and everything inside the mansion was quiet and still. Down at the far end of the hall, the lights from the kitchen and library were on, flooding the area with bone-yellow light.

No one was there.

Striker stepped inside the foyer. The air felt hot compared to outside, and the soft hum of the furnace filled his ears.

'Hello?' he called out.

No response.

He leaned back outside and hit the doorbell. Loud chimes rang through the house, echoing in the foyer. Moments later, the sound of footsteps could be heard, stomping across the hardwood floor above.

Master bedroom, Striker deemed.

He waited patiently as the footsteps grew louder, until Dr Ostermann appeared at the top of the stairs. Even from a floor away, the beads of sweat on the man's skin were noticeable, as was the heavy breathing of his chest. His dark eyes were acute and flitted constantly around the foyer, even if his body moved lethargically. He took one step down the mahogany staircase and, upon seeing Striker, came to a sudden stop.

'Detective,' he said. He could not hide the surprise in his voice. 'This is rather . . . unexpected.'

'You and I need to talk.'

Dr Ostermann nodded slowly. 'Need to talk . . . Well, yes, of course. Why don't you drop by tomorrow morning and we—'

'Not tomorrow. *Now*,' Striker said.

He closed the door behind him.

Seventy-One

For some reason, the library was excessively hot and humid. Hot air blew in from the furnace ducts all around the room, strong and steady. Striker closed one of the vents with the toe of his shoe. As he looked around the room, he saw the Ostermann family's photographs on the mantel once more. Staring back at him were the pictures of Lexa and Dalia, Dr Ostermann and Gabriel. The first time Striker had come here, something about these pictures had bothered him. At the time, he didn't know what.

Now he understood.

It was the smiles. Each one near perfect, as if carved into their faces. But there were signs within those expressions of other emotions. The fear in Lexa Ostermann's eyes; the hollowness in Dalia's stare; and the way that Gabriel looked back, eyes acute and focused, the smile on his lips never causing a wrinkle near his eyes or brow.

It was all plastic.

Only the doctor looked truly happy, his smile stretching his goatee across his face. The rest of the family looked like they were all wearing masks. Striker wondered what was behind each one. As he considered this, Dr Ostermann stepped into the room behind him. His face looked tired and his slumped posture was no different.

'This is about Billy again, I would presume.'

Striker gestured towards the picture of Dalia. 'She's a beautiful girl.'

Dr Ostermann nodded, almost hesitantly. 'She is that. She is also stubborn and defiant and complicated.'

'How is her hearing?'

The doctor blinked. 'Her hearing? Why, it's fine, as far as I'm aware. Why do you ask?'

'Because she ran out of here like a bat outta hell, covering her ears. So I'm thinking either she's been hearing things she doesn't like, or there's a problem with her ears.'

Dr Ostermann's face turned slightly pink. 'What are you here for, Detective?'

'I came here to discuss some . . . *oddities* that keep popping up with Billy's case, but then when Dalia came racing out of the front door, I reconsidered.'

'I can assure you, Detective, you do not need to worry about Dalia.'

'I think I do.' Striker took a step closer to Dr Ostermann and gazed at the side of the man's neck. At the crimson bands in his flesh. 'Where'd you get those marks?'

Dr Ostermann's face reddened further. 'I hardly think that's any of your business.'

'Then we got a problem here, because I do think it's my business. In fact, I think it's my *duty*.' Striker took his hands from his coat pockets and explained. 'I got a girl racing out of here like the house is on fire, and I got you with marks up your neck and back, moving about with the sensitivity of a burn victim. All in all, it makes me ask myself: is everyone here all right?'

For a moment, Dr Ostermann's eyes took on a strange, panicked look, and Striker half expected the man to run. Or maybe even attack. But the doctor did none of this. Dr

Ostermann took a long look at him, as if to compose his thoughts, and then let out a jovial laugh.

'You think I'm abusing my family?' he asked.

'It crossed my mind.'

Dr Ostermann finally stopped chuckling, and when he did all humour left his face. 'You are quite the investigator, Detective Striker.' He pulled his collar away from his neck, so that Striker could better see the marks. 'It's called *shingles*.'

'Shingles?'

'Yes. Brought on by the herpes zoster virus. I'm sure you've heard of it before – the chicken pox virus.' When Striker said nothing back, Dr Ostermann continued. 'It usually only comes out when a person is at their weakest. Which, I guess, would make it my own fault. I've been working weeks of sixty and seventy hours for half a year now. Stress at Mapleview; stress at Riverglen – it's no wonder my body has become run-down. And then all the drama that was happening with Billy – well, I guess that was all it took to put me over the edge.'

'Shingles,' Striker said again.

Dr Ostermann nodded slowly. 'It's been a very unpleasant two days now. I have marks down my neck and back and waist – and I can hardly move. Even showering is painful.'

Striker said nothing back as he thought this over. 'And Dalia?' he asked.

Dr Ostermann sighed. 'Fighting her mother – as usual. Which is why I was upstairs in the first place. They're too much alike, those two, and when they get like that, it's best to just leave them alone. Retreat to a place of solace.'

'And where is your wife now then?'

'In the bath, I would think. She was drawing one when I heard the doorbell.' Dr Ostermann gave Striker a long look before sighing. 'If you insist, I can get her out of the tub to come down here and talk to you.'

Striker ignored the comment and focused the conversation back on other matters. 'How long were you treating Mandy for?'

Dr Ostermann raised an eyebrow. 'We're changing subjects, I see. How long did I treat Mandy Gill for? I'm not sure. A couple of years, I would think.'

'And Sarah Rose?'

'About the same.'

'What about Billy?'

'I've been treating Billy ever since he came back from Afghanistan and was recommended to my programme, which would be about three years ago – is there a point to all this, Detective?'

'What about Larisa Logan? How long were you treating her?'

Dr Ostermann's face took on a look of understanding, and he nodded. 'I see now. Larisa. I'm afraid I can say little about her.'

'I know you were treating her.'

'I will neither confirm nor deny that.'

'You don't have to,' Striker said. 'I already have confirmation. I know that you were seeing all four patients – Mandy, Sarah, Billy *and* Larisa. Now three of them are dead and Larisa is missing. Does that not seem odd to you?'

Dr Ostermann gingerly sat down in one of the library chairs, letting out a tender sound as he did. 'Unfortunately, Detective, it does not. All it tells me is that I should have seen how dangerous Billy was in the first place. It tells me that I failed at being his doctor and it cost two innocent people – maybe even three – their lives.'

Striker was unmoved. 'It tells me something else – that maybe I've been looking at the wrong person.'

Dr Ostermann's face had a lost expression; then it tightened and turned pink. 'I understand your insinuation, Detective, and it is *not* appreciated.'

'I wouldn't think so.'

Dr Ostermann stood up from the chair. 'I think it's time you took your leave, sir. And when you return next time I should hope you have a warrant, for I will surely have spoken to my own counsel – criminal *and* civil. It would appear our friendly conversations are over.'

Striker nodded. 'That choice is entirely yours.'

When Dr Ostermann gestured towards the library exit, Striker took a long look around the room, purposely taking his time, then walked down the hall towards the front door. When he reached the foyer, he ran right into Lexa Ostermann.

'Detective Striker?' she said, surprised.

'Mrs Ostermann.'

She looked down at herself – at the revealing kimono she wore – and her cheeks blushed. She gestured upstairs, to the west side of the house. 'I'm sorry . . . I was getting into the bath . . . I thought you were Dalia coming back . . .'

'Do not speak to him,' Dr Ostermann said, coming up behind them.

Lexa's face took on a confused look.

Striker ignored the man. He nodded to Lexa, then moved to the front door. Once there, he turned around and looked at them. Dr Ostermann stood in the forefront, his face hard as rock, his fingers curled into fists. Behind him, on the first step, stood Lexa. Her cheeks were rosy with blush and her deep brown eyes looked uncertain beneath the long, blonde curls of hair that fell across her brow.

Shingles? Striker thought.

He thought of how he and Felicia had almost burned up in that fire. And he remembered the camera set up outside the window, facing in through the iron-barred panes of glass, capturing their demise. It angered him, and he felt like grabbing the doctor right there. Snapping him in two. Instead, he gave the man a long, hard look and smiled. 'One last thing you might be interested in, Dr Ostermann . . . I know all about your videos.'

The angry, smug look fell from Dr Ostermann's face and was replaced by a pale sick expression.

Lexa looked at her husband. 'What videos? What is he talking about?'

Dr Ostermann said nothing. He reached out, and with a trembling hand opened the front door. 'Goodnight, Detective.'

'Not for you, it won't be.'

Striker walked through the front door and never looked back.

Seventy-Two

The Adder was sitting on the cold concrete floor, in his Place of Solace, thinking of nothing when he heard the loud angry *shrenk!* of the hatch being opened. Had he not locked it? He turned around oddly from his seated position, surprised by the familiar sound, and slowly slid the DVD – his most precious of all the precious videos – into the inner pocket of his coat. Then he looked back up towards the hatch.

Clambering down the ladder was the Doctor.

This surprised the Adder, for no one ever came down here. *No one.* Not in ten years. This room had always been his, and his alone. Having the hatch opened at all was an intrusion.

He climbed to his feet and turned around.

The Doctor reached the bottom of the ladder. 'You taped it? You taped it, didn't you? You stupid, stupid *fool!*'

'I don't know what you're talking about.'

'Don't lie *to me!*'

SMACK!

The Adder felt his head jolt to the left and he reeled backwards, his cheek hot and stinging. For a moment, he did nothing. He just stood there in the centre of the room and felt the air hum about him. Felt that feeling wash over him once more. And suddenly he was fading again. Melting away into that other place. And the sounds started to come back, starting with the high-pitched laughter.

'I need some space,' he found himself saying. 'I'm losing control.'

The Doctor paid him no attention and instead found the box of DVDs on the floor. With one quick swoop, they were taken away.

And just like that the Adder couldn't breathe.

'No,' he managed to get out.

'You can't have these.'

'They're mine.'

'I'm destroying them.'

'No, they're mine! They're *mine!*'

The Adder felt his entire body begin to shake, so hard the room wobbled and vibrated all around him.

As always, the Doctor paid him no heed. Just ignored him. Climbed back up the ladder. And took away the videos of everything the Adder held precious in life. Everything the Adder loved. Everything the Adder needed to calm the frantic voices in his head and keep himself rooted in the reality of this cold and horrible world.

The hatch slammed shut.

And then he was alone again.

Just him and the voices.

'No,' he said softly, and then there was a desperation in his voice even he could hear. 'NO!'

The voices came at him in waves. Thunderous, overpowering waves. And the Adder did the only thing he could do. He gave in and let the voices take him away. And after that he remembered nothing.

Seventy-Three

Striker exited the front walkway of the lot, rounded the corner on to the sidewalk and continued east until he was out of view. He then ran back down the side of the neighbour's lot, climbed the wall and dropped down next to Felicia under the dark shadows of the plum trees.

'I could kill you,' she said.

'I had to go in, we were getting nowhere.'

'You should have waited for me!' she whispered angrily. 'You always do this.'

'It wasn't planned.'

'Bullshit. Are we a partnership here, or not?'

Before Striker could respond, loud yelling noises came from within the residence. The words were impossible to make out, but the voices were definitely male and female. And Striker knew he had done his job well.

Dr Ostermann and his wife were fighting.

'What did you do in there?' Felicia asked.

He shrugged. 'I just cornered a dog.'

Felicia gave him a hard look. 'What else?'

Striker shrugged. 'I bluffed him. Told him we knew about the videos.'

'You *what?*'

'Let him think we have more than we have,' Striker said. 'It worked, Feleesh. It connected. Like a friggin' home run. You should've seen the look on his face. He damn near had a coronary right there in the foyer.'

'But at what cost? Now he might destroy the evidence.'

Striker shook his head. 'Never. If he's making videos, then you know as well as I do what they are – his goddam trophies. He'll keep them forever, even at the expense of being caught. But he will try to hide them.'

'Probably immediately.'

'Exactly, so get ready to motor.'

Striker focused back on the house. He'd barely lifted the binoculars to his eyes when a table lamp smashed out through a front-room window. Shards of glass littered the front lawn and driveway, and the lamp came crashing down on top of Dr Ostermann's X5, denting the hood and cracking the windshield. Almost immediately, the car alarm went off and the street was filled with long, undulating wails.

'Jesus Christ,' Felicia said.

They both got up. Striker got on his phone and called Central Dispatch. Sue Rhaemer told him they were already getting a call from a frantic neighbour.

'We're already on scene,' Striker told her. 'And we're going in.'

He hung up the phone and they headed for the house.

Felicia ran beside him. They crossed the lawn, reached the roundabout, and were just nearing the front door when Striker's cell went off again. Thinking Sue Rhaemer was calling back, he snatched it up. But instead of hearing Sue's scratchy voice, he heard the hardened tone of Jim Banner.

'Noodles, I'm going into a domestic here.'

'The Ostermann house?'

'Yeah.'

'Then be careful. We got the prints back on the can of varnish. And we got a perfect hit on them.'

'Who do they come back to?'

'Who do you think?' Noodles replied. 'None other than the doctor himself. Erich Reinhold Ostermann.'

Seventy-Four

When Striker and Felicia reached the front alcove of the Ostermann mansion, they each took sides. Striker glanced at the broken shards of glass that covered the front lawn and driveway, then at the table lamp that had broken apart when smashing into the BMW. Lastly, he looked at the room above, where curtains now hung out of the window.

'Watch our backs,' he told Felicia and gestured towards the window.

'Copy. You take the door.'

Striker did. He moved up to the front door and knocked hard.

'Vancouver Police!' he yelled. 'Dr Ostermann, it's Detectives Striker and Santos – come to the door!'

No response.

He pressed the doorbell and heard the chimes go off inside the house.

'Dr Ostermann! Lexa!' he called, then added, 'Dalia? Gabriel?'

But again there was no response.

'Fuck this,' he said.

He stepped back from the door and gave it a quick once-over. The door was made from solid oak with steel hinges, and the surrounding frame looked strong. It was going to be a bitch to kick in, but what other option did they have?

Striker turned around and gave the door three heavy donkey kicks, placing the heel of his shoe between the lock and frame each time. On the third kick, the frame cracked. On the fourth, it splintered. And on the fifth, the entire structure broke apart and the front door went crashing inwards.

Striker pulled out his pistol and used the broken frame as cover. 'Chunk out,' he told Felicia. '*Chunk out!*'

She nodded and drew her pistol.

And they headed into the house.

They swept into the foyer and quickly took sides; Felicia got the east, Striker took west. Striker strained his ears to detect anything besides the blaring car alarm out front, but heard nothing.

The house was dead silent.

'It's too quiet in here,' Felicia said.

'Just be ready,' Striker told her.

Together they cleared the bottom of the house, starting with the living room and den area, then carrying on into the kitchen, a sitting room and the library.

At the far end of the hallway was the last room, the office. Striker reached it, tried the doorknob, and found it locked. He didn't so much as hesitate. He simply took a step back, then swung his leg forward and kicked the door in with one try.

The lock snapped and the door broke inwards, revealing a small secluded office. There were no windows in the room. No closets. And no other doors. Just a huge old wooden desk with a computer on it, a pair of chairs on one side, and the doctor's chair on the other.

A place for private sessions? Striker wondered. The emptiness of the room seemed odd.

'It's clear,' Felicia said.

Striker nodded. 'Upstairs then.'

They spun about and made their way back down the hall. When they reached the foyer, they turned and started up the stairs.

Felicia spoke. 'We should have a second unit for this. Patrol cops will be here soon.'

'Not soon enough,' Striker replied.

He pressed on, up the stairs.

When they reached the landing, they stepped into a hallway that led in both directions. Striker paused. A strong smell filled the hall – clean, floral, earthy. After a moment, he figured it to be herbal additives from the bath Lexa had been taking. Lavender. Or juniper, maybe.

'Hold west,' he said. 'Make sure no one comes up behind us. I'll clear the east end first.'

'Got it,' Felicia said.

Striker made his way down the hall. He came to a bathroom, complete with shower and tub, but this was not where the smell was coming from. Once cleared, he made his way down the hallway, clearing two more bedrooms along the way. The smaller one belonged to Dalia, Striker presumed, for the clothes on the chair were almost Goth in style, dark and drab, and all the same. The pictures on the wall were equally morbid. Posters of Marilyn Manson and the like.

The second bedroom was the exact opposite. A guest bedroom of sorts that looked made for a queen. The bed was immense, a king-sized, four-poster number, covered with a thick burgundy quilt that matched the colour of the drapes, which now hung out of the broken window. In the far corner of the room was a pair of high-backed floral Victorian-style chairs, and opposite them was a small bar, complete with fridge and an ice-cube machine.

Striker cleared the room then made his way down the hall,

and came up beside Felicia. She still had her pistol aimed down the other side of the landing.

'It's all clear,' he said. 'You ready?'

'Just go.'

Together, they made their way down to the west end of the hallway. They passed an old storage room, which was empty save for a few piles of boxes and an older-style television set. Then they cleared a reading room with a huge bay window that looked north over the cliffs and harbour below. Out there, the night was black and the waters below looked deep and violent.

Striker had no time for the view, and he carried on. So far they'd cleared almost two out of three floors in the house, and they had yet to run into one member of the family.

Striker didn't like it.

When they reached the only other bedroom on this floor, Striker paused. It was the master bedroom. He knew this from the way Lexa had gestured to it during their earlier conversation in the foyer.

Through the door he could smell that strong, earthy scent.

He gave Felicia the nod to make sure she was ready, then pushed open the door. Inside, a king-sized bed owned the middle of the room, unmade. Next to it, the drawers of the credenza had been opened and dumped.

'It looks like the place has been ransacked,' Felicia said.

'Or like someone was getting ready to run away in the middle of the night.'

Striker stepped into the room. He cleared the walk-in closet to his left, then made his way towards the last door, which led to an ensuite. When he reached it, Striker readied his pistol and slowly pushed the door all the way open with his foot.

What he saw inside the bathroom shocked him.

The windows were fogged, and the air was hot and humid. Along the far wall sat a Jacuzzi tub, filled to the rim with hot foamy water. The foam was not white, however, it was a deep brownish-red colour – because in the centre of the tub lay Dr Erich Ostermann.

His eyes were like a doll's eyes, wide open and unfocused, and his skin was ghostly white. One of his arms lay beneath the discoloured water of the tub; the other draped over the side. One look at it and Striker saw the meaty razor gash running down the length of the forearm, on into the wrist and palm. There were several, in fact.

Deep, grooved lines that no longer bled.

'Jesus Christ,' Felicia said. 'He killed himself.'

'Just watch our backs,' Striker said.

He stepped carefully into the room and looked around the area. On the floor, by the foot of the tub, lay an old razor knife. The blade was brownish-red.

On top of the toilet-seat lid was a note and a key.

Striker moved over to it. The paper was folded, and on the face were the two handwritten words:

Detective Striker

He gloved up and picked up the note. Opened it and read. The message was brief and direct:

Dear Detective Striker,

I have spent over fifteen years perfecting the EvenHealth programme, dedicating countless hours of my time in the selfless service of others. I have sacrificed all for the lost and the ill, and would ask you only to consider this before destroying my legacy.

Before you act too rashly – before you tell the world what I have done – please consider this ... intimately. The videos. They are what they are. I am not proud of them. Or of my weaknesses. To be blunt, I simply couldn't help myself. I couldn't stop, no matter how hard I tried, or how bad I felt afterwards.

Please, do not show this letter to anyone. Please do not tell the world what I have done. Especially not the other members of my profession. This is my final request.

With this letter is the key to my study.

Sincerely yours,
Doctor Erich Reinhold Ostermann

Seventy-Five

A friggin' suicide, Striker thought. He couldn't believe it was ending this way.

He read the note three more times and felt a sense of frustration wash over him. This was the coward's way out, and it left him feeling empty. Like something had been stolen from him.

It also never told him where Larisa was located.

He gently folded the paper and placed it back exactly as he had found it. Sitting beside the letter was a key to the study. Striker picked it up, then returned to the master bedroom to join Felicia.

'Suicide note?' she said.

He just nodded.

'Let's clear the rest of this damn place,' he said. 'We still need to find the rest of the family.' There was a sense of worry in his words; he could not hide it.

The quicker they got moving, the better.

They left the bedroom, then made their way down the hall to the stairway and continued up to the final floor. At the top of the stairs, the landing went three ways: east, west and one short add-on to the north.

They headed east. Down at the end was another bedroom with the door wide open. Striker and Felicia went down there. The room was very clean and orderly, with all types of clothes hanging in the closet, and a standard-sized bed. Striker guessed the room belonged to Dr Ostermann's son, Gabriel.

From the bedroom they went back to the west side of the house. It turned into one giant loft. The room had been renovated into a movie room, complete with an overhead projector, movie-style seats with drink holders, and a surround-sound system built right into the walls. The room was impressive, and it made Striker wonder if Ostermann had watched his videos up here.

'Clear,' Felicia said.

'Clear,' Striker agreed.

He turned around and looked back into the hall. Every room had been cleared now. Every room except for one down the north hallway.

The doctor's private study.

They made their way back down the hall, then turned north along what appeared to be an add-on to the house. The hallway went on for about fifteen feet before stopping at a plain door. Striker touched the wood. It was solid oak. Strong.

Before opening it, Striker paused. He looked all around the area for wires or hidden switches. Dr Ostermann had been bat-shit crazy. No matter what he said in his letter, no matter how much he prattled on about his legacy and the welfare of his patients, Striker would never trust the man. There was nothing a madman loved more than taking a couple of cops with him.

Seeing no imminent danger, Striker turned to Felicia.

'Watch for traps.'

He reached out and grasped the doorknob. It refused to turn, so he stuck the key into the lock and gave it a twist. The lock clicked and the knob turned, and the door opened.

As it did, Striker scanned the room. What he saw surprised

him. He had expected to see another office, similar to the one downstairs. A large desk. Some reading chairs. Maybe even a file folder or two. A credenza.

He saw none of that. Instead, he saw a cabinet in the far corner of the room, composed of polished redwood and shiny brass locks. The doors to it were closed.

In the centre of the room, he saw what appeared to be a large wooden table, also made from polished redwood. It was covered with scuff marks and scratches. Opposite the table, on the wall, hung a brand-new LED widescreen with a built-in Blu-ray player.

Striker made his way into the room. When he closed in on the table, he noticed that there were heavy iron pins and hand-cuffs attached to each side. And chains. On the top right handcuff, brownish-red liquid coloured the steel. The floor below it was also stained.

'We got blood all over here,' Striker said.

Felicia looked under the table and her face tightened. 'We got torture stuff under here, too. Rods. Knives. Holy shit, a pair of pliers. Man, this guy was one sick puppy.'

Striker said nothing. He looked at the table with the bind-ings, then at the torture tools underneath it. A thought crossed his mind, and he made his way over to the redwood cabinet. Once there, he slowly opened the doors and looked inside.

Staring back at him was a black leather mask – the exact same type as the one he had seen on the suspect, back at the Mandy Gill crime scene. There were also two rows of DVDs. An exter-nal hard drive. And cameras – high-def tape, mini-disc and digital. The sight of it made his stomach tighten.

Felicia saw all this, too. 'The mother lode.'

Striker didn't reply. He was too busy taking it all in. He reached up to the top shelf and plucked up one of the Blu-ray discs. He took it over to the wall-mounted TV, turned on the Blu-ray player, stuck in the disc and hit Play.

The TV came to life.

On the screen was a man imprisoned in a cage. He was facing away from the camera, curled up on his side. His back and legs were bleeding and he was quivering.

'Please,' he whimpered. '*Please.*'

But his voice was weak, lost.

Barely a whisper.

Behind him, half in the shadows, was a figure. Dressed in a long dark cloak. The face was hidden, but in the person's hand was a long, thin rod. Sharp steel. The end of it glistened with wetness.

'Jesus Christ,' Felicia said. 'What a sick fuck.'

Striker took another look at the DVDs in the cabinet. One of the discs had no title but it displayed today's date on the label. Thoughts of Mandy and Sarah filtered through his mind and were replaced by the image of Larisa.

It left him sick inside.

He stuck the disc in the player, but the machine couldn't read it. Swearing, he took the disc out, cleaned it off, and tried again. But the machine displayed the same message:

Unreadable format.

'*Shit.*'

'You need a computer,' Felicia said. 'There was one in Ostermann's main office.'

Striker didn't hesitate. He took the disc with him down the two flights of stairs. When they reached the main-floor foyer, Striker could hear the sound of police sirens in the faraway distance, their sad wails slicing through the night. The sound felt good to his ears, and he continued down the hall.

They made their way into Dr Ostermann's office. As Felicia

booted up the computer, Striker took note of the throw carpet on the floor. It was a small rug, less than four feet wide and eight feet long, and it sat unevenly in the room, covering more of the right side than the left.

Why would the doctor leave it that way?

Curious, he walked across the room and stepped on it. As he did, he felt a little give in the centre. Some springiness. He stepped back, grabbed hold of the corner of the rug, and pulled it across the room.

Beneath it was a hatch in the floor.

'Look at this,' he said to Felicia.

She stopped fidgeting with the computer and came up beside him. 'Wine cellar?' she asked.

'We're about to find out.'

Striker slid his fingers through the iron handle and pulled; the hatch lifted with a metallic groan and Striker let it fall to the floor on the other side. He stared down the ladder, into what looked more like a concrete bunker than an old wine cellar.

The lighting down there was dim and appeared to be fluorescent. Weak, but it did the job. As Striker stared into it, something caught his eye. Stacked on the floor, near the bottom of the ladder, were some pertinent items.

A battery pack for a cordless drill.

A box of latex gloves.

And a half-dozen packages of relay cameras.

Striker drew his pistol and gave Felicia a hard look.

'The Adder,' Felicia gasped.

'Keep your gun ready and cover me,' Striker said. 'I'm going down.'

Seventy-Six

Striker aimed his SIG Sauer and scanned the area below as he prepared to descend. There was no movement down there, just a still, murky dimness. The room appeared medium in size. Maybe twenty feet by thirty. Lots of grey concrete. A bed that was messed up. A dresser next to it with a small widescreen TV and a Blu-ray player. And a cabinet, holding a computer.

It all seemed rather ordinary.

Striker stepped on the first rung of the ladder and looked below. It was a surprising drop. Over fifteen feet down to hard concrete. He kept his gun pointed below, ready for anything unexpected, as he made his way down.

From above, Felicia covered him.

When Striker's feet touched bottom, he turned around and stared at the room before him. From this vantage point he could see that the bed was actually an old futon, and the space beneath it was empty, save for a pair of old runners.

The room smelled strongly of disinfectant. Something like bleach. And as Striker made his way around the perimeter, he found the source of the smell. Sitting in the far corner, tucked behind one of the boxes of latex gloves, was an old can of varnish.

Steinman's.

The sight made him tighten his grip on the gun.

'What you got down there?' Felicia called.

'It's a friggin' *lair*,' he called back. 'The Adder's. No doubt about it.'

'I'm coming down.'

Thoughts of getting trapped back at Sarah Rose's place flashed through Striker's mind. 'No!' he called. 'Stay up there. We need you up there covering our backs.'

'Patrol's with me.'

Striker looked up and spotted a blue uniform behind her. 'Okay, fine. But get someone to guard the top there. I don't need us getting trapped in another burning building.'

Felicia got the patrol unit to cover them, then came down the ladder and joined Striker. The moment she looked around, her claustrophobia kicked in. Striker knew it; he'd seen it in her a million times.

'You can wait upstairs,' he said. 'You don't have to be down here.'

'Just get looking.'

He did. He started with the shoes under the bed. The label inside said size ten and a half. Same as the suspect's shoe imprints they'd found back at Mandy Gill's place, in the secondary crime scene.

Striker turned the runners over and analysed the tread. Checkered. And the wear pattern on the right toe was far greater than on the left shoe, suggesting an awkward gait. Maybe from a previous knee or hip injury. Maybe something congenital. Regardless, the pattern of wear matched the sole imprints from the crime scene.

'There's no doubt,' Striker said.

'I'm getting the creeps,' Felicia said.

'Just keep your guard up. There could be traps.'

Felicia turned away and started carefully searching through the bedding on the futon; Striker left her there and approached the cabinet. On the desktop sat a new computer case, three external back-up drives, and a mouse with keyboard. Lining the top shelf was a row of DVDs and Blu-ray discs. All of them were brand-new, unused, still covered with cellophane wrap.

Striker moved the mouse, and the monitor turned from black to blue. Across the screen was the Windows password request. A hundred different possibilities ran through Striker's head, but he opted to leave the computer untouched. One wrong attempt might be enough to lock them out or start a pre-programmed formatting application.

The Forensic guys could handle this one.

'We need Ich here,' Striker said. 'To unlock the computer and back everything up.' He pulled out his iPhone and tried to make the call, but from this deep in the bunker, surrounded by walls of concrete, he couldn't get a signal. He headed back for the ladder, put his foot on the first rung, and stopped.

To his left was a picture on the wall. A lithograph of some kind. It was a famous work. Striker couldn't recall the artist, but he knew the title.

Relativity.

It was a picture of people walking up and down different flights of stairs that defied all laws of gravity. Twisted, abnormal, unnerving.

Fitting for this place.

The print was huge, blown up, easily four feet by four feet. In a room that offered nothing else – no family photos, no posters, no knick-knacks of any kind – it seemed odd and out of place. But it was not just the picture that stole Striker's attention, it was the frame. The frame hung slightly out of kilter, the left side higher than the right.

Striker stepped towards it, pulled out his flashlight, shone it all around the wall. On the concrete, there were faint scuff marks, ones that matched the gold-black paint of the frame.

He reached out and took hold of the painting. With one heave, he lifted it from the wall and put it down on the ground. Behind it was a strange door, half the size of a regular one. Maybe two feet wide and three feet high.

After staring at it for a half-minute, Striker realized what it was.

An old dumbwaiter.

The perfect hiding spot or escape route.

He gestured urgently for Felicia to join him. She saw what he had found and drew her pistol. She aimed it at the door and waited for Striker to open it. When he did, then aimed his flashlight inside at the gaping darkness, all they found was an empty space.

Felicia deflated and holstered her SIG; Striker leaned down and shone his flashlight up into the hole. There was a passageway there, leading up. It was large enough for a man to stand in.

Striker angled the beam towards the upper floors and saw that the dumbwaiter went all the way to the top. Right to Dr Ostermann's locked study.

Interesting.

'Why have a built-in dumbwaiter all the way down here?' Felicia said, half to herself.

'They probably used this room as an old food or wine cellar way back when,' Striker replied. 'God knows it's cool enough down here.'

He studied the dumbwaiter.

On the left side, on the inside of the post, was a pulley system. Striker grabbed the rope and slowly lowered the dumbwaiter down to his level. On the tray was a video camera, a model he had never seen before, one with an LED screen. Instead of a disc or tape, the camera had a built-in hard drive. The camera also had a built-in motion sensor. So when Striker moved the camera, it began recording again.

He found the settings and turned off the motion sensor.

Felicia came up beside him. 'What's on it?' she asked.

'We're about to find out.'

Striker hit Play and the video began. On the screen were Dr Ostermann and Lexa, but dressed like Striker had never seen them. Dr Ostermann was naked, except for the leather collar and chain that hung around his neck; Lexa was tightly wrapped in a red leather corset, her breasts pushed up and outwards, almost falling out of the cups. Below, she wore a pair of red silk panties and stockings to match.

She tied Dr Ostermann down, face first, on the table, shackling his hands and feet to each post. Then, when he was all splayed out, she began caressing his body with a long strap of black leather.

Ostermann groaned in delight with every teasing lash. But within minutes, the lashings grew more strenuous. Fierce, even. The tail-end of the strap left huge raw red marks on the doctor's back and neck and buttocks and legs.

'Red,' he cried out. 'Red, Lexa. *RED!*'

But she acted as if she never heard their safety word and continued lashing the man. The expression on her face was one that Striker had not seen on her before – smug, controlled, *dark*.

The feed went on for another four minutes. Until Ostermann stopped moaning and groaning, and just lay there whimpering on the table like a tenderized piece of meat.

Lexa slowly approached the table, the smile on her lips stretching across her entire face. She moved slowly from corner to corner, unfastening each handcuff and setting her husband free. When they were all off, Dr Ostermann did not move. He remained on the table, his breathing laboured and his whimpers audible.

Lexa leaned over him. Kissed him gently on his neck. Reached down and squeezed his balls.

Dr Ostermann let out a frantic cry, and Lexa smiled once more.

'You *disgust* me,' she said.

Then she dropped the leather lash across his back, stripped out of her dominatrix lingerie, and dressed once more in her green silk kimono. Without so much as a glance back, she left the room.

Dr Ostermann lay in the centre of the feed, quivering but still, with only the sounds of his whimpers and cries filling the room.

Then the video stopped.

Striker looked away from the video camera display, back at Felicia, and couldn't hide the surprise from his expression. 'The office upstairs . . . it isn't a torture room at all – the Ostermanns are into S&M sex.'

'What a couple of sick fucks,' Felicia said.

Striker thought it over, pieced it together. 'The marks we saw on Dr Ostermann's back and neck make sense now. They weren't shingles, or an injury from a fall – they were friggin' *whip* marks.'

Felicia nodded. 'It would also explain his feeble movements.'

'And why he was so embarrassed about the videos. Jesus, when I was threatening him about the murder films – he thought I was talking about his S&M videos. His home videos.'

Felicia thought it over. 'Dr Ostermann, a masochist.'

'And Lexa, a *sadist*,' Striker finished.

The word seemed wrong as he spoke it, but he couldn't help thinking that. Lexa was the one constant here. And the image of her coming downstairs in her kimono, her skin dappled with sweat, her eyes wide and doe-like, came back to him.

'Lexa,' he said. 'Where the hell is she now?'

Felicia said nothing.

Striker placed the camera back on the dumbwaiter tray for Forensic Video to process. As he did this, thoughts of the Adder taping them returned. Striker turned from the dumbwaiter, took out his flashlight, and began going round the room, inspecting everything. There were no other cameras or microphones visible, or any other surveillance equipment, but that didn't mean none were there.

A sweep of the room would be necessary.

He shone the light under the bed and saw nothing of importance. He then shone it under the dresser and the computer cabinet. There, he stopped. On the concrete below the cabinet there were faint but visible brownish marks.

Scuff marks, just like with the painting.

'This cabinet's been moved,' he said.

He wrapped his fingers around the base of the cabinet and slowly swung it out from the wall. When he looked behind it, he saw a small hollow in the wall. About as long and high and deep as a small microwave. In it sat two rows of DVD and Blu-ray cases. Marked on all of them was the word *Back-up*, followed by different dates. Striker read through them.

One of them had been made just this morning.

He took it out and dropped it into the Blu-ray player across the room. When he turned on the TV and hit Play, the video started. What Striker saw made his blood turn cold; the video was of him and Felicia. Inside Sarah Rose's apartment. Right before the fire had started.

Felicia stepped forward. 'Jesus Christ, is that us?'

Striker said nothing. He just looked from the TV to the row

of DVD and Blu-ray discs in the nook behind the cabinet. All of them would have to be watched. Reviewed for any shred of evidence.

It would take *hours.*

He watched the feed continue until the moment when he and Felicia had managed to break out of the front door through the burning blaze. Then the video stopped—

And started once more.

The camera angle spun about, as if the camera was being picked up. And then, for one fleeting moment, the feed caught the image of a young man with wild, jet-black hair and eyes such a light green they looked transparent.

Felicia turned to look at Striker. Her face was ashen.

'The Adder isn't Dr Ostermann,' she said softly. 'It's—'

'Gabriel,' Striker said, and he could hardly believe his own word.

Gabriel Ostermann.

The boy.

The son.

And he was gone.

Seventy-Seven

The Adder walked slowly down Sasamat Trail, one of the bark-mulch pathways that snaked all through the Pacific Spirit Regional Park. When he reached the end of it, he stopped on a bluff overlooking the strait. Far below, the turbulent waters were black and deep and cold.

Like the well.

Memories of the front window of the house smashing apart after he'd thrown the lamp through it returned to him. In bits and pieces. In intermittent waves. Like a TV signal fading in and out. His actions would have attracted much attention, no doubt.

Another one of the Doctor's rules, broken.

As if sensing his thoughts, his cell phone rang and the Doctor's name flashed across the screen. The Adder looked at it for a long moment, listening to the rings, not wanting to pick it up.

One. Two. Three . . .

He finally picked up. 'I am here.'

'Have you managed to calm yourself down?'

'Yes.'

'Do you know what has happened since you left?'

'No.'

'Your father is dead, Gabriel. He committed suicide.'

The Adder said nothing.

'Come to the lake house. We will meet you there. We need to . . . *re-plan*.'

The line went dead and the Adder stood there motionlessly.

Father dead. It was a strange notion. And it made him feel somehow hollow and light. He could not understand it.

He walked to the edge of the bluff and sat down on a rotting log. As he stared out over the black waters, he took out a DVD and cradled it in his hands. This was the one. The one that had started it all. And the thought of it made his heart beat faster, made his throat turn dry.

The voices would start soon; he knew their pattern well. And so he took out his headphones and plugged them into the speaker port on his iPod. Moments later, the only file loaded, and the blissful release of the white noise began.

The Adder needed it to clear his head. To calm his nerves. And to *think*.

Clear thought was essential right now. There was no place for error. No excuse for acting hastily. He simply could not afford to. The most crucial of all moments was almost here. For Homicide Detective Jacob Striker.

That thought made the Adder smile.

The Big Surprise was coming.

He could hardly wait.

Day Three

Seventy-Eight

It was early morning when Striker awoke from the stinging of his burned hand, and the day felt every bit a Friday. The room was dark and cold. He was in that realm, still somewhere between wake and sleep, and a sense of desperation filled him. He reached over in the darkness, felt for Felicia, and could not find her. Then he remembered she was sleeping on the couch.

That bothered him, and it woke him up fully.

He sat up in the bed, looking around the drab greyness of the room and trying to sort things out in his head. Yesterday had been a constant whirlwind, and discovering Gabriel Ostermann's room and learning he was, in fact, the Adder had sent the investigation exploding in new directions.

So much had already been done, and so much was still required. Already, he had flagged the entire family – Gabriel, Lexa and even Dalia – on all the different systems: on PRIME, CPIC, and with even Customs and Interpol. He was taking no chances with this one.

The Adder could not escape again. He was a serial killer. And serial killers never stopped killing until one of two things happened – either they were caught, or they were killed.

Striker kicked the blankets off his legs and stood up. The first thing he did was grab his iPhone from the charger and read the screen. There were no new calls, and that was disappointing.

He'd been hoping for something – for anything – from Larisa Logan.

But nothing had come in.

He dialled the number for Central Dispatch and was pleased to hear Sue Rhaemer's voice: 'CD.'

'Shouldn't you be off by now?' Striker asked.

'I already was,' she groaned. 'Got called in early. We're short. The flu's going round again.'

'Anything on the file?'

'Did I call you?' she asked.

'No.'

'Then there's your answer.'

Striker ignored her testiness and nodded as if she could see him. 'Keep me informed, Sue.'

He hung up the phone, then left his bedroom and did the usual grind. He checked on Courtney, who was still fast asleep in her bed, then put on some coffee and swallowed some Tylenol for his injured hand, then he woke Felicia. By the time they had both showered and poured a cup, it was just after six a.m. and the morning was still dark.

'You ready?' he asked her.

She offered him an eager smile. 'We're gonna find him today. I can *feel* it.'

He hoped she was right.

A half-hour later – after picking up another coffee, this time a traditional Timmy's brew – they were back at the Ostermann mansion. The sun was still asleep, the air was cold and the morning sky a deep purple smear. To Striker, it felt like they had never left the crime scene. Only now there was a patrol guard posted outside the front and back of the house. He badged the guard – some young kid he had never seen before – and went inside.

They went straight to Dr Ostermann's office. The room had already been photographed by Ident, and during the subsequent search, all sorts of files and folders of interest had been boxed as evidence.

Striker pointed to the farthest row of boxes. They were all ready-made cardboard containers, each with the case number written in thick black felt on the sides.

'You take that row,' he said to Felicia. 'I'll take the one over there.'

Felicia sipped her coffee, then made her way over.

Striker opened up the closest box and leafed through the paperwork inside. There were mounds of the stuff. Everything from paid bills to case studies to back-ups of patient files. And Striker now wished they'd brought a thermos of coffee for the day.

They were gonna need it.

As Striker went through the boxes, he made sure he kept everything in order. Nothing was more frustrating as an investigator than realizing something you'd already read was now a critical piece of evidence, but you had no idea where you'd left it. It was a lesson learned once, and learned hard, and never repeated.

The process was slow and time-consuming. By the time Striker got to the fourth box, he considered running down the road to grab them both yet another cup of coffee. He was about to suggest it when Felicia made an interested sound.

He looked over. 'What ya got?'

'Look at this,' she said.

She held up a thin white file folder. On it was a printed label with the words: Jonathon McNabb. But when she opened up the file, there were no patient reports, only a list of credit cards and bank accounts. Attached to the inside back cover was an

envelope. Felicia opened it and pulled out several pieces of identification: a BC driver's licence, a social insurance number card,
even a birth certificate.

The picture on the driver's licence showed Gabriel Ostermann.

'Let me see that,' Striker said.

He took the driver's licence from Felicia and scrutinized it.
Everything was done in perfect detail, from the writing on the
front and back of the card to the authentic-looking hologram on
the front.

'Are they fakes?' Felicia asked.

Striker raised an eyebrow. 'These are pretty good. They might
be legit.'

'So then is Gabriel Ostermann's real name Jonathon McNabb,
or is he using someone else's identity?'

'Call your guy at the credit bureau. Will he be in yet?'

Felicia nodded. 'They're on eastern time.'

Less than two minutes later, she hung up the phone and gave
Striker the nod. 'Victim of identity theft,' she said. She pulled
another file out of the same box. The name on this file was
Eleanor Kingsley. When she opened up the folder, everything
inside was the same as in the last folder – credit card applications, bank accounts, gas cards, and more. Attached to the back
of the folder was another envelope. From it, Felicia took another
stack of identification cards. Only this time the face wasn't
Gabriel Ostermann's, it was Lexa's.

'Run the name with your contact,' Striker said.

She went through the process again. Two minutes later, they
had another confirmed hit. Eleanor Kingsley had reported over
seventy-eight thousand dollars in charges to credit cards she had
never requested or received.

Striker saw the pattern.

'They're stealing everyone's identities,' he said. 'And then taking them for every damn penny they can get from their credit. Bankrupting them.' He looked at the box Felicia was holding. It was thick with folders. Probably contained more than fifty.

'Look for Mandy Gill and Sarah Rose,' he said.

It took Felicia less than thirty seconds to find both, and when she took the IDs from the two folders, it was the same thing all over again – only this time Lexa was Sarah Rose and Dalia was Mandy Gill.

Felicia couldn't believe it. 'My God, they're a one-family crime ring.'

Striker looked at the row of boxes behind her and thought of all the file folders in each one. Eleanor Kingsley alone had been ripped off for more than seventy grand. Here they had boxes and boxes of file folders. *Hundreds* of victims.

The money count was mind-boggling.

Seventy-Nine

It was over two hours later, at quarter after nine in the morning, by the time Striker and Felicia left the Ostermann house. With them they took three cardboard boxes, jam-packed with file folders.

All possible victims of identify theft.

When they reached their vehicle, Felicia opened the trunk and Striker dropped the boxes inside. He closed the trunk, then took a moment to pull out his phone and call Courtney. She had an appointment booked with her OT this morning, and Striker wanted to make sure she attended.

The phone rang three times, then went to voicemail.

'Get up, Pumpkin,' he said. 'I'm already at work and you got an appointment with Annalisa this morning. Ten o'clock, and don't be late. I love you.'

He hung up the phone and went to put it away, but it vibrated against his hand. He looked down at the screen, expecting to see Courtney returning his call, but all he saw was a red number 1 over his phone icon.

A missed call.

He read the number and recognized it as Kirstin Dunsmuir's. Which piqued his curiosity. The woman was a pill, and colder than a popsicle enema, but no one could question her work ethic. She had probably been at the lab all night long.

Fitting for a Death Goddess.

'That was the medical examiner who called,' he said.

Felicia made an *ugh* sound. 'I don't do Kirstin Dunsmuir before lunch.'

'She might have something.'

Felicia offered no reply, but her scowl remained.

Striker ignored it and checked his voicemail. Dunsmuir hadn't left a message, so he returned her call. She answered with her usual grace and warmth, which meant one-worded and ice cold:

'Dunsmuir.'

'It's Striker. I saw you called.'

She skipped the small talk. 'I have the results of the autopsies. There are two things of importance. Mandy Gill had a needle-mark incision. Angled medially and inferiorly, just posterior to the medial head of the clavicle.'

'Left side?' Striker asked.

'Yes.'

'What about needle marks on Sarah Rose?'

'Far too badly burned to determine. Regardless, it does appear he's injecting them.'

'But with what?'

Dunsmuir made an uncertain sound. 'I'm not entirely sure at this point – there are numerous drugs in both the victims' systems. One of them we've managed to isolate is a powerful muscle relaxant. There was enough of it in Mandy Gill's system to eventually stop her heart. We're awaiting test results for an exact determination.'

Striker thought this over. He recalled how both victims had

been facing the windows, facing into the camera. Unable to move. Unable to call for help. Barely able to breathe. He hoped they didn't realize they were going to die at that moment, but somehow he thought otherwise.

'No idea on the kind of relaxant?' he asked.

This seemed to irritate the ME and her tone dropped. 'These things take time, Detective. It's not a movie, after all.'

'I know that. Otherwise we'd have a happier ending.'

Dunsmuir let out a bemused laugh. 'There are no happy endings.'

Striker had had enough of the conversation. He told Dunsmuir to call him with the results. Then he hung up the phone.

Felicia started to get into the car. When he did not follow her lead, she stopped. 'What?' she asked.

'Is Gabriel left-handed?'

'Why?'

'Just a thought. But look at the location of the needle marks. Left side, just posterior to the clavicle. And the angle of the needle – driven in at a medial angle. If the suspect came up behind his victims, this would be a hard angle to get with the right hand.'

'And why do you think he comes up behind them?'

'No defensive wounds. Depressed or not, they would still react in some way. But here, there is nothing. It makes me think they were surprised, hence from behind.'

Felicia nodded back but said nothing, and they both piled into the car. For Striker, the phone call with Dunsmuir had been emotionally draining. And he'd had enough of the Death Goddess to last him a lifetime.

He put the car into Drive and drove. There was still tons of paperwork and police reports to comb through. Already they'd been at it for more than three hours, and they'd barely made a dent in things. Neither one of them had gotten enough sleep the last few days, and he was feeling it.

It was going to be another long, hard day.

Eighty

The day had arrived and the sun was finally out – a piercing ball of whiteness in a sky so light it was barely blue.

Striker drove them down Main Street, then detoured on Terminal. He cut through the Starbucks drive-thru and ordered them a pair of egg-white breakfast wraps and a couple of coffees – an Americano, black, for himself, and a vanilla latte for Felicia.

Then they returned to headquarters.

Back in Homicide, the office was dead. Everywhere Striker looked, he saw empty rows of cubicles. Half the office was on their day off, the other half was out in the field, trying to write off leads and solve files. If any of them caught fire, they'd be back in before noon; otherwise, it would be an early weekend for most.

Once back at his desk, Striker set down all three boxes they had seized. There were still more boxes back at the Ostermann home, and due to the enormity of the task and their limited time, Striker had called in Clowe and Parker from Robbery to assist them. They were leafing through the files back at the Ostermann house even now.

Felicia came up beside him. She gave him an irritated look. 'We should be researching Gabriel,' she said. 'And Dalia and Lexa. We can go through all this stuff later.'

Striker shook his head. 'These folders are the reason all this is happening. Understand the victims and you'll better understand the Adder.' Striker thought it over. They still needed to access the Police Information Retrieval System and the Law Enforcement Information Portal. 'You research Gabriel through PRIME and PIRS and LEIP; I'll keep wading through the files.'

The suggestion seemed to placate Felicia. She went to take another long sip of her latte, found it empty, then threw it in the trash can. 'I'll make us a pot,' she said, and walked across the room.

Striker was glad to have some space. He pulled over the first box and started skimming through the files.

Each was important, because of the crime that had been committed. Identity theft had ruined many a person's life, and it was the fastest growing crime in today's white-collar society. But, collectively, the files said so much more. He was less than halfway through the first box – well into the *H*s – when he saw a pattern emerging.

One that twisted up his insides.

The folder he was reading was labelled: Jeremy Heath. It was divided into sections. The first section held pages upon pages of basic information. Everything from his date of birth and mother's maiden name to computer passwords and banking information. There were also forms from the Post Office for a change of address.

The next section of the folder had every type of insurance Jeremy Heath had ever taken out, ranging from medical insurance to life insurance to disability insurance. Jeremy Heath's file even had a soldier's recompense page from Veterans' Affairs.

The third section of the folder was all the avenues of income. Visa. MasterCard. American Express. Bank names and their associated account numbers. Even pages of stocks and bonds.

The fourth and final section was composed of spreadsheets, showing lists of income from each of these cards. There was also a column for how many times each credit card limit had been upped, and if and when that request had been declined.

Everything was precise, systematic, planned.

Last of all was the envelope attached to the back of the folder that housed all the various pieces of ID. As Striker looked them over, he realized why the ID looked so real. The answer was simple.

The ID was all legitimate.

The Ostermanns hadn't been creating fake IDs, they had been obtaining real identification from the original source. All the driver licences, social insurance number cards and birth certificates were legitimate issue. He had never seen anything like it, not on this scale.

He showed all this to Felicia. 'They've actually attended the motor vehicle branch and have had their own pictures implemented.'

'They're friggin' experts,' she said.

He nodded solemnly. 'And they're systematically destroying people's lives. Even worse, they're going after all the marginalized victims.' His own words triggered some darker thoughts, and he got on the phone with the Collins Group.

The Collins Group was a private company, run by ex-cop Tom Collins – a friend of Striker's from years past. Collins had worked primarily in Financial Crime during his twenty-year stint with the VPD, and he had carried that expertise with him into his new endeavours of investigating corporate insurance fraud. When Striker told the receptionist who he was, she transferred him without question.

'Tom Collins,' Striker said. 'How's my favourite highball?'

The man on the other end of the phone let out a gruff laugh.

'Shipwreck. Good to hear from you, man. I hear you had some problems last year over at St Patrick's.'

That made Striker pause. 'Yeah, memories better left forgotten,' he finally said. 'Look, I got some victims of identity theft here, and I was wondering if you could research them a bit for me.'

'How fast you need it?'

'Like yesterday.'

'I should have let it ring to voicemail.'

Striker just laughed and gave the man a list of the names he had accumulated from the boxes.

'And what exactly are we looking for?' Collins asked.

'You'll know it when you find it,' Striker said. 'I need this done fast. Today sometime.'

Collins let out a sour laugh. 'Your way or the highway, like always, huh?'

'What can I say? I'm particular.'

He hung up the phone, feeling better. He liked Tom. The man had been a good cop and a better friend. It had been too long since they'd seen one another.

Typical in the world of policing.

He looked back at Felicia, who had her head buried in the computer. 'What are you finding on Gabriel in PRIME?'

She looked up as if she was only now aware that his conversation with Collins had ended, and turned the screen to face him. 'With the exception of Dr Ostermann, there's not a whole lot on any of them,' she said. 'Gabriel is carded in a few of the police reports as a witness, but that was only due to car accidents. There's also a report here from almost twelve years ago. He must've been, what, eight at the time.'

'What does it say?'

'I can't bring it up, it's privatized, and it's a Burnaby file.'

'We still need it,' he said.

'Well, *duh!*' She laughed at the surprised look on his face. 'I've already left a message for the detective in charge. Get this: her last name is *Constable*. Can you believe that? Detective Constable.'

Striker grinned. 'Well, if she ever makes *Chief* Constable, the papers will have a field day with it.'

'Yeah, no kidding. I'm just waiting for her to get back to me.'

'What about Lexa?' he asked.

'In PRIME? Lexa is listed only once. Under a fingerprint file.'

'Probably for when she got her criminal record check done for nursing.'

'Bang on,' Felicia said. 'As for Dalia, she is a complete non-entity. Not in any of the systems. She doesn't exist.'

Striker thought this over.

'Run both their vehicles for tickets. Any infraction. Speeding. Red light. Parking. I don't care. Just run it all.'

Felicia didn't move. 'We already know Ostermann drove like a maniac.'

'I'm not interested in the offence, I'm interested in the locations.'

Felicia said nothing and turned back to the computer. After a few clicks, she made an interested sound. 'Hey, look at this. We know the X5 has streams of tickets, but the Land Rover, which is registered to Lexa, has only three tickets – all of them on the Trans-Canada Highway.'

This piqued Striker's interest. 'Where exactly?'

'One out near Furry Creek, and the other two just outside of Whistler Village.' She looked up. 'Maybe they have a cabin there, or something. I'll check it out.' She turned around and got on the phone to Whistler's registrar office; while she talked, Striker continued going through the boxes of files. When he finished the *K*s and started the *L*s, he found one file that made him pause.

Logan, Larisa.

'Holy shit,' he said.

He opened up the file, but it was empty.

Confused, he looked back in the box for any loose papers, but found none. The words on the tab stared back at him. Made him angry. He searched the next three files to see if Larisa's paperwork had accidentally slipped into the wrong folder.

None had.

He sat there, letting everything sink in and feeling sick about it. He picked up his desk phone and checked his voice messages. There were seven, but none from Larisa, and none relevant to the file.

No time for them now.

He archived the phone messages and looked through his emails. Again, there were tons of messages, but nothing pertinent to this investigation. Irritated, he brought up the email Larisa had sent him the previous day and made another reply to it:

To. L.Logan@gmail.com
Subject: Contact me!

Larisa,
Please tell me where you are! Or go to the nearest police station and call me. Dr Ostermann is *dead*. Gabriel and Lexa and Dalia are missing. They are very dangerous. Beware of them. Come in or call me. Please!
– Jacob

He looked at the message for a moment, hoping it was personal enough to make her respond. He hit Enter and the message sent. After that, he sat there for a long moment, waiting for a response.

None came. And after recalling the way things had gone down at the Arabic Beans coffee shop at Metrotown, Striker wondered if one ever would.

It was doubtful.

The woman no longer trusted him. She trusted no one. She was all alone and in hiding. And the longer she stayed missing, the worse their chances of finding her became. It was a cold, hard fact. But it was real.

They were running out of time.

Eighty-One

It was morning by the time the Adder reached his destination. He was tired. He had not slept all night. He was hungry. He was cold.

He rounded the cabin from the north in the mid-morning light, and stood on the back deck. As he breathed out, the warmth and moisture from his breath fogged the air. He stared out over the lake. The edges were still covered with a fine layer of ice, and the weeds and reeds were frozen in place. The air smelled strongly of pine and cedar. Morning sun broke the top of the mountains to the far east. It gleamed on the cold, calm waters of the lake.

It was the perfect day. The kind of morning every skier and snowboarder craved all season long. Crisp, clear, cold. It should have been beautiful.

But the Adder could focus on none of this. All he saw was one bad memory. And the images in his head. Ones that had once been terrifying but now seemed like faded stills from a different life. A different world.

And in some sense, that was exactly what they were.

The sliding glass door opened behind him with a soft rolling sound.

'Gabriel,' a feminine voice said. Soft, and with emotion. With *relief.* And the Adder immediately knew it to be Dalia. She was the only one who cared. The only one who had *ever* cared. She came up behind him and wrapped her arms around his chest, then let loose a gasp and shivered. 'You're so cold,' she said softly. 'Come inside. Later on, I'll help you warm up.'

He said nothing; he merely turned around and walked with her towards the cabin. Before entering, he stopped.

Thought.

He knelt down and removed the DVD from his pocket. It was Disc 1, the only copy he had left, and the only one that truly mattered. He slid it beneath the porch steps, far into the back where it was out of view. Then he stood up and moved into the warmth of the cabin. He'd barely stepped foot on the ceramic tile when the smell of green tea hit him. And then the Doctor came storming into the kitchen. Her eyes were set and dark, her face so tight it looked bloodless.

'It's about time – you fool,' she said.

Dalia stepped forward. 'Mother, please—'

'To your room, girl.'

'But Mother—'

'To your room!'

Lexa Ostermann stepped forward and gave the Girl a back-handed strike – a sharp, hard *SLAP!* that resonated like the crack of a whip. Dalia recoiled from the blow and grabbed her cheek. Sobbing, she spun from the kitchen and raced up the stairs to the second floor of the cabin.

The Adder watched her go, but did nothing. A strange tingling sensation was tickling the back of his mind. His heart. His entire body.

And he did not like it.

'You're a fool,' the Doctor continued. 'Everything, ruined. Years of work, ruined. Our family, ruined!'

'I did nothing.'

'Your *videos*,' she said, and there was ice in her words. 'They are what set everything off. Your father, dead. The police, hunting us down. Like animals, Gabriel. Like animals!'

He said nothing, and his silence only seemed to infuriate her more.

'Outside. Now.'

He looked out of the sliding glass door. 'There is no reason.'

'You know the rules.'

'But there is no well here,' he started, then he saw the lake.

'Outside,' the Doctor ordered. 'I will not tell you again.'

The Adder said nothing for a long moment, then he nodded absently and walked back out through the door. The moment he left the kitchen, the cold wind slapped his face. Sharp, stinging, burning his skin and eyes. He marched across the slippery wooden porch, down the steps and across the small back yard. The frozen blades of grass crunched beneath his feet. Then he was at the edge of the lake. Memories of the past *deluged* him. Memories of William.

He could not bear it.

'Take off your clothes,' the Doctor ordered.

Mechanically, the Adder did as instructed, folding them neatly and placing the articles one on top of the other. Shoes, then pants, then shirt. When he was completely naked – when the winter wind was cutting into him like an icy blade – the Doctor stepped closer.

'Into the lake.'

Without so much as a word, the Adder stepped forward until the soles of his feet touched the thin ice of the lake. The ice cracked, and broke beneath his weight, and the sounds of laughter grew in his ears and the image of William was suddenly there before his eyes. A little boy running and giggling on the lake.

He stopped moving.

'Into the lake,' the Doctor said again.

But this time, the Adder did not respond.

'I *order* you into the lake.'

The Adder turned. Faced her.

'No,' he said. 'I will not do this any more.' And for the first time in his memory – the first time since William's death – the Adder felt more than alive, he felt *awake*.

The Doctor's face took on a shocked look, and then she nodded slowly. 'I always knew this day would come, Gabriel. Very well then. You have finally left the past behind you. Pick up your clothes and join me in the cabin. We have much to discuss.'

The Adder nodded. He bent over to pick up his clothes and suddenly sensed movement beside him. He turned – but was far too slow. A sharp pricking sensation stung his neck, and he knew the needle had gone in.

He jerked backwards, stunned, and felt a strange hot warmth rush from his neck down his arms. The flow carried on through his body, down his legs, and even up into the top of his head – a strange numb warmth. Almost immediately, his muscles grew weak and he felt himself folding inwards. His legs trembled, then gave out, and he collapsed on the edge of the lake.

A strange, distorted sound filled the air, and the Adder realized it was the Doctor. She was laughing at him. One second there was only white sun and blue sky above him; the next moment, the Doctor was there, looking down at him with a dark smile on her lips.

'Mivacurium chloride,' she said. 'How does it feel to be on the receiving end, for a change?'

The Adder could not speak. He looked up at her melting face and tried to respond, tried to say something – what, he had no idea – but his lips would not move.

'There is a certain set order, Gabriel,' the Doctor continued. 'A *hierarchy*. And you need to remember your place within it.'

The mask she wore crumbled away in pieces, and the Adder saw her for everything that she was. Everything she had always been.

The monster beneath.

He felt her grab his legs. Felt his body being dragged along the ground. There was a wet, cold feeling surrounding his legs and hips, and he knew she had left him in the lake. Cold. So terribly cold. And the sky was black and growing blacker by the second. After a while, the sky faded. And eventually the sun burned out, leaving him with nothing but black.

Eighty-Two

Felicia hung up the phone. 'Nothing comes back,' she said.

Striker cursed. 'Nothing?'

'*Zilch*. The only address the registrar's office has on file is their house on Belmont.'

Striker thought this over. 'What about using EvenHealth as an entity?' he asked.

'Already one step ahead of you. EvenHealth as an entity comes back to every clinic the programme is associated with – and there's more than two dozen all across the city. Not to mention the rest of the Lower Mainland. How many clinics there are out there in total, I have no idea.'

Striker frowned. It left them with nothing. All they had was a house where Lexa and her children had fled from, and a pair of speeding tickets from the Whistler Village area.

He met Felicia's stare. 'If you were Lexa Ostermann and you needed somewhere to store some extra cash and ID, where would you go?'

'A PO box.'

'Agreed. But a post office box is only accessible during business hours. Normal people like you and me could always wait till the next business day, but someone involved in a scam like this would have to run at a moment's notice. So where else would you go?'

Felicia was quiet for a moment, then shook her head. 'There's only one other place I can think of – where she works. The clinic her husband owns.'

'Exactly,' he said. 'It's time to go to Mapleview.'

At exactly ten-thirty, Striker parked the undercover cruiser by the roundabout and stepped out. With the morning sun now rising high overhead, and backed by brilliant blue sky, the modern clinic of Mapleview looked pleasant enough. But all Striker could think of was when they'd come there to kidnap Dr Ostermann and intercept Billy Mercury. That had happened at three o'clock yesterday afternoon.

It felt like a lifetime ago.

'I'm starting to hate this place,' he said.

'You're preaching to the choir,' Felicia replied. She started up the old cement stairs, and Striker went with her. The moment they walked through the wired-glass double doors into the ante-chamber of the facility, the receptionist behind the desk looked up. Her face took on a pleasant look, and she smiled at them.

'Detectives,' she said. 'Good morning.'

Striker smiled. Obviously she hadn't heard the news of Dr Ostermann's demise and the family's disappearance.

'Good morning back,' he said. He approached the front desk, smiled at the woman, reached out and gently touched her hand. 'You know, in all the pandemonium yesterday, I never did get your name.'

She smiled at his concern. 'It's Pam,' she said. 'Well, *Pamela*. Pamela O'Malley.'

'I'm actually surprised to see you in here today.'

She looked around and shrugged. 'Everyone else called in sick, and someone has to be here for the patients.'

'It's very decent of you.'

'Yeah, good job,' Felicia added.

Striker met the woman's stare. 'How are *you* coping, Pam? If you need a card for Victim Services, I can give you one.' He looked around the room as if suddenly realizing where he was, and grinned. 'Actually, if you need some therapy, I guess you're probably covered.'

When the receptionist smiled and chuckled at his comment, Striker got down to business.

'I need to speak with one of your staff members,' he began.

'Dr Ostermann still isn't in yet.'

'Actually, I was looking for *Lexa.*'

The smile on the woman's face fell away. 'Mrs Ostermann isn't in yet either. She doesn't normally work till the afternoon.'

'You almost say that with relief,' Striker said. When the woman didn't know how to respond, he smiled at her and lowered his voice. 'It's okay. I've dealt with her only twice – and that's been enough for me. But duty calls, you know.'

The receptionist laughed softly. 'Yes, Mrs Ostermann can be a bit . . . *demanding* at times.'

'She's a pill,' Felicia said boldly.

The receptionist laughed again.

'So she hasn't been in here today?' Striker clarified.

'No. She shouldn't be in until one o'clock. And you can pretty much set your watch by it. Mrs Ostermann is always extremely punctual and orderly with everything she does. Even the group sessions. God forbid one of them comes in even a minute late. She kicks them out and sends them home.'

Felicia asked, 'Which group is that?'

'Oh, all the groups. But especially the SILC classes – are you familiar with the programme?'

'Yes, we are,' Striker said. 'Does she confer with Dr Ostermann before sending his patients home? These are, after all, his sessions, right?'

'Yes, they are. But Mrs Ostermann does fill in.'

Striker found this interesting. 'Fill in? A *nurse* holds the session in place of a qualified psychiatrist?'

For a moment, the receptionist's face tightened, as if she was worried she had said too much. 'Maybe I shouldn't—'

'Hey, it's okay,' Striker told her. 'I'm not going to press Mrs Ostermann on anything. You got my word on that. I just find it surprising.'

'It's not without its merit,' the woman replied. 'Mrs Ostermann does have extra training.'

'What kind of extra training?' Felicia asked.

'I don't really know, for sure. But she took much of her training in Europe, and she's not one to talk about it. Not one to talk about anything, really. Especially not with staff.'

'Where in Europe?' Striker pressed.

'The Czech Republic.'

He nodded. 'How would you know that when she never talks about it?'

'Dr Ostermann did once. A long time ago. Over a year maybe.'

Striker rested his arm on the front counter and tried to look casual. 'Really? And you remember it.'

The woman's face took on a distant look. 'It's kind of hard to forget. Dr Ostermann was talking to Dr Richter about what courses were considered *transferable* from overseas. During the conversation, he mentioned that Mrs Ostermann had grown up in the Czech Republic and had had problems transferring her university credits.'

'Which university?'

'Charles, I think. I'm not sure exactly where it is.'

'It's in Prague,' Striker said. 'Charles Bridge.'

'And what next?' Felicia asked.

The woman's cheeks reddened further. 'Next? Oh, Mrs Ostermann got angry. *Very* angry. I'd never seen her so . . . enraged – she is a very private person, you know.'

Striker nodded at this.

Private, he thought. And full of secrets.

He took out a business card and wrote down his cell number on the back. When he handed it to the receptionist, he made sure they had eye contact. 'If Lexa or her children return here, I need you to leave the building right away. Do you understand me, Pam?'

The woman looked confused. 'Leave the building?'

'Immediately,' he stressed. 'Make an excuse. Leave to check on one of the patients. And then, the first chance you have, I want you to leave the building and call my cell. Right away. Do you understand?'

The woman nodded slowly.

'And if Dr Ostermann comes in?'

Striker smiled wryly.

'Then I don't think my number's gonna help.'

Eighty-Three

After fully debriefing the receptionist on what had happened with Dr Ostermann's suicide and the subsequent disappearance of his family, Striker and Felicia asked to see Lexa's office.

The receptionist, still looking rattled, nodded daftly. She opened her desk drawer and pulled out a key. 'She locks it,' she said, and led them down the hall. When they rounded the east corner, they came across one room with a dark red door. 'This is Mrs Ostermann's office. She wanted it on the east side of the facility; all the other doctors are on the west.'

'I didn't realize the facility was so big,' Felicia said.

'It's actually not,' the receptionist said. 'It's just a strange layout.' She unlocked the door for them. Before moving out of the way, she fixed Striker with a hard stare. 'Please . . . if you're going to take anything, let me know. I should at least keep a record of things.'

'Of course, Pam,' Striker said. 'Have you ever been in there before?'

She shook her head. 'No one has. Like I said before, Mrs Ostermann is a very private person. She doesn't even allow the other doctors inside. It is always under lock and key, and to be honest, I think she would fire me on the spot if she ever saw me in there – no matter the reason.'

Striker nodded. He said goodbye to Pam, then went inside

the office with Felicia and closed the door behind them. As he turned around, he scanned the room.

It was very drab, and surprisingly, very sparse. Just a black walnut wood desk, a burgundy leather chair, and a computer terminal. No plants or flowers decorated the shelves. No pictures or diplomas adorned the walls. There weren't even any photographs of her family.

Felicia saw the oddness of it too. 'Talk about taking minimalism to the extreme.'

Striker walked over to the desk and opened both drawers. Not much was inside them, except for basic office supplies and a short row of file folders. Striker went through them all, carefully reading each one. All of them contained numerous patient files, but none of the names stood out to him. He took down the names so they could run them through the system later.

Then he looked at the computer. The screen was black, but when he moved the mouse the screensaver vanished. No password. No logon. Just right to the desktop. Striker started browsing through the system. He found nothing, not even one file.

'A new computer,' he said.

'Or a fresh install,' Felicia added.

He looked around for an external backup drive, but found none. He then scanned the office shelves. They were filled with medical and psychological textbooks. They all looked brand new. Like they had never been touched.

He opened one – *The Diagnostics and Statistics Manual* – and felt the inflexible give of the book's spine. None of the pages had been marked up, and no hidden papers were tucked inside the book.

He went through all the books, flipping the pages of each one and finding nothing inside. When done, Striker put the last book back, and paused. At the end of the shelf sat a lone file folder. Red in colour. He picked it up. On the tab were the words: *Medical Billing Codes.* He opened it up, saw the list of codes, and showed it to Felicia:

```
10-14141ML-MG900412,
09-29292TIG-SR730128,
```

and more. The list was several pages long.

'Strange,' he noted. 'If these are Medical Service Plan codes, why not just print them out from the government website? Why go to all the bother of writing them down yourself?'

Felicia looked them over. 'And what do they mean, for that matter? Look at them, they're all in a different format.'

Striker was confused. 'I don't follow you.'

'Most computer programs use similar codes,' she explained. 'Look at PRIME, for example. Everything there is separated by four-digit codes: 2117 is a Suspicious Circumstance. 2118 is a Suspicious Person. 2119 is a Suspicious Vehicle. They are all listed in a pattern. But not these numbers. They're all over the map – as if they're from more than one system.'

Striker looked back at the numbers, and saw she was right. They took the file folder with them, left the office, and stopped at the receptionist's desk on the way out. Pam was still sitting there, looking lost and out of place.

Striker approached her. 'Do you have a book on Medical Service Plan codes?'

Pam blinked as if coming out of a dream. 'Medical Service Plan? Well, no. No, we don't. We would never have use of it.'

'Why not? How do you bill?'

'Because everything here is private. All the medical goes through Riverglen.'

Striker frowned at that; they would have to look the codes up later. He started to leave, then stopped.

'Are you familiar with MSP codes?' he asked.

The receptionist nodded. 'At the other clinic, I do all the billing – and they're completely covered by medical.'

Striker open the folder. He showed the list to Pam. 'Are these Medical Service Plan codes?' he asked.

The receptionist looked at the list for less than a few seconds. 'Not that I recognize.'

Striker closed the file.

'Thanks,' he said. 'I didn't think so.'

Eighty-Four

Striker and Felicia pulled out of the Mapleview parking lot and headed north on Boundary Road. He drove right to the lane behind the Esso gas station on Hastings Street. It housed an On the Run coffee shop, and was a common place where Patrol grabbed coffee after their morning briefings.

'More caffeine?' Felicia asked.

Striker nodded. 'I need one. It helps me think.'

They exited the vehicle, grabbed a couple of coffees, and returned to the lane. They stood outside the car, drinking in the frosty air because Striker liked it that way. The cold always invigorated him.

'Everything we know so far about Lexa Ostermann has been a lie,' he said. 'From the way she presented herself as the frightened victim at her home, to the role she's been playing at the clinic.'

Felicia sipped her coffee. 'Hey, give the psycho credit. She was good at it. She definitely made it look like Ostermann was the one in control of their household, and it was the exact opposite.' She shook her head. 'My God, when I think of her lashing that poor man and him screaming out, "Red. Red! *Red!*" it turns my stomach.'

'Personally, I would have picked *stop* for a safety word. Creates less confusion.'

Felicia laughed, and Striker continued.

'The point is we thought we knew the woman, and she had the wool pulled over our eyes. It makes me wonder what else we don't know about her that we think we do. The vital stuff.'

'Like her name,' Felicia said.

'Exactly. Name, date of birth, place of birth – all those details.'

Felicia took out her phone. 'I got a contact in Victoria,' she said. 'I'll look into her maiden names.'

Striker was glad to hear it. Victoria was the central location for the Vital Statistics Agency, the place where legal name changes and marriage records were kept for all of British Columbia.

'Check the marriage records, too,' he suggested.

She gave him one of her *I'm not an idiot* stares and waited for the call to be answered.

Striker let her be. Dealing with any form of the Canadian government, be it Stats Canada, Canada Revenue, or the Vital Statistics Agency, was always an exercise in frustration. Furthermore, he needed Felicia to do it, because he didn't have any contacts there. To make use of his time while he waited, he called Central Dispatch once more to see if there had been any hits on the Ostermann family.

Sue gave him her trademark response. 'Have I called you?'

'No.'

'Then there's your answer.'

Sue Rhaemer was more on top of things than a cherry on a sundae, and she had never let him down once. He could tell by her tone she was irritated he was even questioning her.

'Thanks, Sue,' he said. 'I'm just desperate here, is all.'

'You owe me a Coke.'

'Over ice,' he said.

He hung up the phone and looked at Felicia. She was still

dealing with her contact at the Vital Statistics Agency, and the look on her face was one of tentative hope. When she began writing information down in her notebook, Striker felt a glimmer of optimism. She hung up and smiled at him.

'Well?' he asked.

'Anytime you need info, you just come to momma, darling.'

Striker laughed. 'I've heard that before. Come on, Feleesh.'

'Fine, fine. But get this: Lexa married Dr Ostermann exactly ten years ago this month.'

'*Ten* years ago?' Striker asked. He thought it over. 'That would mean that Gabriel was only eight when they got married, and Dalia was five. So the kids were either born out of wedlock, or—'

'They're not siblings,' Felicia finished. 'At least not by blood. I verified it through Vital Stats. Gabriel was born a lone child to Wilma and Erich Ostermann eighteen years ago. Wilma died of cancer six years later, and barely two years after that, Erich remarried to Lexa.'

'What was Lexa's maiden name at the time?'

'Smith.'

Striker found that unsurprising. After Lee, Smith was the most common surname in all of North America – definitely the most common among Caucasians. It made searching information on her more of a hassle, and he doubted the validity of the name anyway.

'Is the name legit?' he asked.

Felicia shook her head. 'Phoney as a three-dollar bill. If you go farther back into the name records, she was originally named Jarvis from a previous marriage that lasted only three years – but that marriage took place fifteen years ago.'

'Which would match Dalia's age.'

Felicia nodded. 'Exactly. Lexa has had a list of names over the years. And it doesn't stop there. She had requested a previous name change even before that – when she first came to Canada by way of Toronto. Her immigrant name was Novak.'

'Novak?' Striker said. He thought of the name for a brief moment, then brought out his iPhone. 'I don't know a whole lot of Czech names, but I do recognize Novak.' He punched the name into the Google search engine, then nodded when he saw the result. 'Big surprise. Smith is the most popular name in Canada, Novak is the most common name in the Czech Republic. Where did she emigrate from?'

'Berlin,' Felicia said.

'Yet the receptionist back at Mapleview said Lexa was from Prague.'

'And Lexa was none-too-happy about her knowing.'

Striker Googled Charles University, and got the number. He looked at his watch and saw it was slowly approaching noon in Vancouver. It would be around 8 p.m. there.

He called up the Information and Advisory section of Charles University and was relieved to find a person who was fluent in English. Less than ten minutes later, he got off the phone and gave Felicia a hard stare.

'She went there all right, under the name Novak – and for *eight* years.'

'Why so long? Did she change her programme?'

Striker offered a grave stare. 'She didn't go there for a nursing degree, she's a friggin' doctor. She minored in *psychology.*'

Felicia's face took on a stunned look, but then she nodded. 'It actually makes sense, when you put it all together. Lexa gets her medical degree over there, and comes to Canada.'

'But not all her courses are transferable,' Striker pointed out.

'So she finds a man who's also a forensic psychiatrist.'

'Erich Ostermann. Who just happens to own his own clinic.'

'Where she'll have access to all the patients she wants.'

'Not patients,' Striker said. '*Victims.*'

Felicia thought this over for a long moment, then shook her head. 'There's one small problem here. Why not just take the extra courses required to make her degree recognized over here? I mean, think of it, she put in eight years towards it. Why down-grade to nursing after all that?'

'I can think of two reasons,' Striker said. 'One, it's easier to hide in the background when the police come knocking – every-one thinks of the doctor, not the nurse.'

'And two?'

'Because she couldn't. Lexa Novak was already on the run.'

Eighty-Five

It was a blur, really. A muddled white haze that slowly pushed away the darkness. And William was there, calling for him to *Get up, Gabriel! Get up! You must get up!* And then William was shaking him. Shaking him fiercely. Shaking him so hard his entire body shook like a child's rag doll.

'Get up, Gabriel.'

And the clouds slowly thinned.

'Get up!'

Slowly lifted.

'GABRIEL!'

And he could see blue sky once more.

The Adder lifted his head off the cold, hard earth and it felt like it weighed a million pounds. As he awoke, so did the pain – a cold sharp stabbing sensation. Like a trillion needles poking the skin all over his body, from his head to his feet.

But his legs, they were the worst.

Sharp, *biting* pain, and yet they were also numb. Strangely, achingly numb.

It made no sense.

With all the strength he could muster, the Adder sat up and looked at his legs. They were half submerged in the icy waters of the lake, and they were whiter than the ice.

'Get up, Gabriel!' he heard from behind him.

Whispers.

Desperate panicked whispers.

And he knew that it was Dalia. Somewhere behind him. Up above. Her bedroom window perhaps.

He was too weak to turn around and look.

'Gabriel, you must get inside!'

Without thought, without real intention, the Adder tried to bend his knees. Tried to remove his legs from the icy cold waters of the lake. But his muscles refused to obey the commands of his mind. They were like dead chunks of flesh attached to his body. Useless pieces of meat.

He rolled over, on to his belly, and felt the cold sharpness of the rocks against his skin. To his left, less than an arm's reach away, were his clothes. But he could not reach for them. His mind was slowly clearing now. Ever so slowly. And his rationale was coming back in blips.

The cabin . . .

The cabin was the only chance for survival.

And so inch by inch, arm pull by arm pull, the Adder dragged his body from the lake. Dragged himself up the gravelly beach. Across the frozen lawn. Even up the slippery wood of the porch steps. The back door was still wide open, and he wondered why.

A test from the Doctor? A goal?

Or one of her many taunts?

In the end, it did not matter. He pulled himself inside, his useless legs dragging behind him. When he reached the kitchen, he saw the Doctor.

She was seated at the table, a steaming cup in one hand, her newspaper in the other. She sipped her drink, placed the cup carefully back on the saucer, and then looked down to face him. 'Welcome home, Gabriel,' she said. 'I trust you have learned yet another lesson today.'

He said nothing back. He could not. And after a moment, the Doctor stood and walked away. Out of the front door of the cabin.

As he lay there, waking, returning to life, the heat from the furnace vents blasted on his torso and legs. His skin went from that strange numbness to a cold piercing fire. He ground his teeth and wanted to scream. Wanted to wail with every ounce of strength his lungs had left.

But the Adder did not.

Instead, he lay there, his mind number than his body, and he thought of the only thing left in this world that brought him any true pleasure. The final doorway. The moment of release. The only exit from this world.

The Beautiful Escape.

It was coming once more, and this time for Jacob Striker. The thought almost made the Adder smile.

It was going to be a truly wonderful moment.

Eighty-Six

Striker wanted to run Lexa Ostermann and all her aliases through Interpol – the International Criminal Police Organization. Interpol's primary purpose was to facilitate cooperation between police departments from almost two hundred countries. Essentially, it was a spider's web of information. Starting there was their best bet.

They headed back for Homicide.

When they got there, Striker was surprised to find the office busy, and upon speaking to fellow detective Jana Aiken, learned that there'd been another gang shooting on the Granville Strip.

Nothing interesting.

He found his way to his cubicle and sat down. The computer was still running, but locked, so he logged on and quickly checked his email. No message from Larisa. No voicemail either. Frustrated, he initiated Versadex and loaded the Query page for Interpol.

As far as Striker knew, Lexa had no criminal record, not that it mattered. The database listed everything from wanted criminals to missing children to stolen property. Striker was hoping Lexa would be there, in some form or another; how, he didn't much care. All he wanted was a lead.

Instead of starting with Ostermann, Striker typed in the oldest name they knew of:

Lexa Novak.

For a date of birth, he typed in an age range of thirty-five to forty-eight.

The query came back within thirty seconds to a positive hit, low score, meaning that the details provided matched perfectly but the details provided were few and vague. There were over thirty hits.

Striker sorted through them all until he found one that matched:

Lexa Novak. Forty-six years of age.
167 cm. 59 kgs. Caucasian.
Hair: blonde. Eyes: blue. Build: medium.
Place of birth: Mesto Roztoky, České Republiky.

Striker looked up the name of the town and saw that it was not far from Prague. He looked for any tattoo or scar descriptions, but found none. He scrolled down the page and came to a Remarks section.

What he saw made him smile.

Policie České Republiky
Person of Interest. Identity Fraud.
Contact Detective Lundtiz. 974 852 319.

'*České?*' Felicia asked.

Striker nodded. 'Police of the Czech Republic,' he explained. 'We got a legitimate possible.'

He picked up the landline and dialled. The number took a long time to connect, but then it started to ring. The man who answered spoke in limited English, but managed to convey to Striker that Detective Lundtiz was now *Inspector* Lundtiz, working in the Unit for Combating Corruption and Financial Crime.

He patched Striker through.

After another set of rings, Striker's call was answered by a receptionist and, after again explaining who he was and why he was calling, he was transferred to the main line.

As Striker waited for the inspector, Felicia got the call from one of the cops she knew in Burnaby South. The privatized file from Gabriel's childhood was ready. She gave Striker the thumbs up, then left to pick it up from the Burnaby North detachment.

Striker waved goodbye and waited on hold.

After a long pause, the phone was picked up. 'Good evening, Detective Striker, this is Inspector Lundtiz.'

Striker was surprised to hear that the inspector spoke with good English and had almost no accent. 'Good evening, Inspector. Thanks for taking my call. I'm enquiring about—'

'Lexa Kaleena Novak,' Lundtiz replied. 'Yes, I know her quite well. *Intimately* well, I would say. I spent many months following this woman before she disappeared on me. That was many years ago. Almost twenty, I would think. My God . . .'

'Well, she's been found in Vancouver, Canada,' Striker said.

'Has she killed again?'

The words shocked Striker. 'Has she killed there?'

'Undoubtedly. Proving that, however, was another matter.'

Striker said nothing for a moment, then took out his notebook and a pen. 'What exactly do you know about this woman?'

'A great deal.'

'I've got the time.'

The inspector cleared his throat and began speaking. 'I have the file right in front of me, though I went over it so many times, I practically know it all by memory. Lexa Novak was born in the city of Prague. I'm sure you've heard of it, Charles Bridge and all.'

'I'm aware of it.'

'She grew up one of three sisters. Katerna was eldest, followed by Nava, and then Lexa. The family was upper class. Very well known. Her father, Dagan, was a well-respected man in these parts – a doctor with his hand in politics.'

'Sounds powerful,' Striker noted.

'He was. I remember him. And with Lena for a wife, every man around the town envied him. Lena was beautiful, Lena was the perfect wife and mother, and Lena brought with her a family fortune.'

'*Elite* upper class,' Striker said.

'Entirely. And from an outsider's perspective, they were living the dream. But home life was very different. Dagan Novak was a *sadist*. He took great pleasure in dominating his family, abusing them in all ways – psychologically, physically, even sexually, once the girls reached a certain age. Life in the Novak family was an existence of helplessness and torture. I am ashamed to say the police of this time failed the family utterly.'

'They knew?'

'It was reported. But because of Dagan's social and political connections, the matter was – how do you say it? – *conveniently overlooked.*'

Striker frowned. It was a situation he had seen before as well. 'What happened to the rest of the family?'

'Lena, the mother, supposedly left the family and relocated to Paris, where she had other family connections. Yet when I tried to locate her, the search quickly reached a dead end. I have no doubt that Dagan murdered her.'

'And the other girls?'

'The story is quite sad, I'm afraid. Even beyond the abuse.'

Striker shook his head. 'I don't follow.'

'The eldest of the sisters, Katerna, had to be hospitalized when she was but sixteen years of age. For severe schizophrenia. Three years after that, Nava was also afflicted with the illness.'

'A genetic link.' Striker thought this over. Given the history, it was unsurprising that Lexa had turned to a career of psychiatry. 'Lexa must have lived in constant fear of acquiring this illness.'

'The illness haunted her, tortured her . . . And I think it was the turning point of her freedom. The so-called fuse that set her off. It was not long after the middle child was hospitalized that her father took ill. His symptoms came on slowly, gradually, his skin paling, his body weight diminishing, and then his hair began falling out.'

'Arsenic?'

'In his tea, we believe.'

'And yet you never charged her?'

'We couldn't. The family had a cook. They had a maid. Even a live-in nurse for when the children came home for visits, which of course became exceedingly rare as the illness progressed. In short, Lexa was surrounded by other suspects. There was no way to link her to the poisoning. And to be honest, at the time, I wasn't entirely sure she was involved. I had placed more of my focus on the nurse, still feeling Lexa to be a victim of her father's evil-doings.'

To hear that Dagan Novak got his own justice didn't particularly bother Striker. 'So she got away with one.'

'Yes, she did. Then, when Lexa was nineteen, she met a man named Victor Devorak. He was a young man, a good-looking man, from an estimable background. Within one year of being married to Lexa, he also developed a strange unknown illness and eventually passed away. Lexa moved on, and within two more years she had met and married another young man, also from a rich family. His name was Kavill Svaboda. He lasted longer than her previous husband – almost three full years. But then, four months after Lexa obtained her medical degree, he passed away from unknown causes.'

Striker said nothing as he thought things through. Most everyone around this woman had died, and her two sisters had ended up sick in mental hospitals. The diagnosis was schizophrenia, but he now wondered if Lexa had also played a role in that. He didn't know enough about the illness to speculate.

'So two husbands in just over, say, six years. And they died in a similar manner to her father. Did you bring her in for questioning?' Striker asked.

'Of course I did. After the death of both husbands. The woman was a star. Charming and open. Confident. Secure.'

'Like most psychopaths. Were there any more deaths after that?'

The inspector let out a tired sound. 'I wouldn't know. She disappeared. Just upped and left the country. And no matter how I tried to track her down, I could never find her. One of my contacts had traced her as far as Brussels, but it was an unconfirmed sighting. And after that, the trail went cold. Plus the woman in Brussels had been many months pregnant.'

'Lexa does have children.'

The inspector made a sad sound. 'That is a truly horrible thing.'

'How long ago was that sighting?'

'I'm not sure any more.' Twenty years? The inspector made an uncomfortable sound. 'It's odd . . . when my receptionist told me she had the police from Canada on the phone, Lexa was the first person I thought of.'

'Any advice you can give with this woman?'

'Only this, Detective. *Catch* her. Never let her escape. For there is one thing I learned above all else with Lexa Novak. She will never stop killing. She simply enjoys it too much.'

Eighty-Seven

With the conversation with the Czech police inspector finished, Striker hung up the phone and sat back in his chair. He thought of the Ostermann family.

Dr Erich Ostermann had been evasive and secretive from minute one, and now that they had discovered the man's sexual perversions, that those actions all made sense. As a whole, the world may have become more accepting of people's sexual preferences, but there was little doubt that the professionals and politicians Ostermann hung out with would be less than understanding should his sadomasochistic goings-on ever come to light.

As for Dalia and Gabriel, they had been oddballs from the start. Lexa was the one who had surprised Striker the most. When he had first met her, she had come across as the beautiful, trapped wife of a powerful and dangerous man. Striker had found himself wanting to help her, intrigued by her charms. He now found it frustrating to see how easily she had played him.

And he looked forward to capturing her.

He was deep in thought on this matter when his cell phone went off with a text message. He picked up the cell and looked at the screen. What he saw made his heart clinch. There was a message. From Larisa.

From: Logan, Larisa
Subject: Lost

The message was brief, to the point, and the underlying sense of panic was unmistakable:

I'm not going back to the hospital. Not ever. But I'm afraid, Jacob. I think someone's been watching me. This morning. A woman with dark eyes. She felt very . . . *off*. Everywhere I turned, she was there. And I'm scared. Part of me just wants to end it all. I don't know what I should do . . . I want to trust you, but . . .

The message ended there, and it tugged at Striker's heartstrings. Here was the woman who had been there for him during his darkest hours, and when hers had come, he had fallen way short of doing anything remotely helpful. He looked at the message details. It had been sent only two minutes ago.

Quickly, he typed back:

Larisa, wait! Where are you?

He waited for a long moment, but received no response. Bad thoughts flickered through his mind as he thought over her description.

A woman. With dark eyes.

Striker got on the phone with Bell, his service provider. He gave them his badge number and position, his phone number, and told them to trace the text sender. The technician was resistant at first, and Striker lost his temper.

'This is a matter of life and death,' he explained. 'I know your company policy – I've done this a hundred times. Now trace the goddam call and tell me where it's coming from. Or if anything happens to this woman, I'll be sure to hold you criminally responsible. Not the goddam company, but *you*.'

The clerk made an uncomfortable sound, then asked him to hold. Seconds later, he came back on the line. 'The text is coming from the Whistler Blackcomb area,' he said. 'Any closer than that, I can't give you.'

'Can't, or won't?'

'*Can't*. It doesn't show up as anything more specific than that.'

Striker cursed. He hung up the phone without saying goodbye and went over his options. Whistler Blackcomb was a two-mountain ski resort a hundred kilometres from the downtown core, which translated into roughly a two-hour drive.

An hour fifteen, if he needed it to be.

By population, the resort was the largest in North America. Normal population ranged from a steady flow of ten to fifteen thousand, but with the post-Christmas ski season set to begin, the two main resorts were overflowing with triple that number. Not to mention the numerous villages that clustered in pods around the outer perimeter. Looking for someone there would be like finding the proverbial needle in the haystack.

He cursed out loud. Thoughts of alerting the other police jurisdictions flickered through his mind, but he wiped them away when he recalled the last fiasco with Bernard Hamilton of Car 87 at the coffee shop in Metrotown. If Larisa felt he had tried to trick her again, she would run. And that was something he just couldn't risk.

There was no other option.

He dialled Felicia. She picked up on the first ring.

'Lonely Man's Hotline.'

Normally the comment would have brought a smile to his lips. Not today. 'Where are you?' he said.

'Heading back from Burnaby,' she said. 'Should be less than five minutes. I got the report on Gabriel.'

'Good. You can read it over and explain the whole story to me when we're on our road trip.'

'Road trip? To where?'

'Whistler Mountain,' Striker said. 'We're going after Larisa.'

Eighty-Eight

How long it took for the feeling to return to his legs, the Adder had no clue. Time, as always, was unimportant to him. At first, there was only numbness below his waist, and then slowly, constantly, the feeling came. The pain grew. And with it came mobility. By the time he heard the front door open and close once more – the sign that the Doctor had again returned – he was finally able to stand.

Only then did he realize he was still completely naked. All his clothes were outside by the lake.

He moved from the den and the roaring gas fire back into the kitchen, where the Doctor was making herself a second cup of green tea. She kept her eyes straight ahead and did not so much as glance at him when he entered.

'You're going after the girl,' she said.

'The girl?'

'Larisa Logan.'

The words made him pause. 'She does not matter.'

The Doctor's reply was terse. 'Do not think, Gabriel. *Listen*. And follow orders.'

He said nothing, he just nodded slowly, and the Doctor continued.

'Larisa Logan is the only person that can connect us to the deaths.'

'But the police already know.'

'Proof and knowing are different matters.' The Doctor laughed out loud. 'Besides, they have to find us first, Gabriel. It's time for a new look for this family. A new identity that can never be traced – which is why I took the other DVDs. *Your* DVDs. They are more evidence connecting us.'

A strange sickness hit his stomach. 'My DVDs—'

'They are *destroyed*, Gabriel. And you will make no more of them. Do you understand me? You will make no more.'

'I will make no more,' he said softly.

'Good. Then we are understood. Now go get your clothes and get some rest and leave me be for a while. I have much to go over, much to plan. You have caused me quite a bit of work.' She took her cup and walked into the den.

The Adder watched her go. When she had disappeared from view, he opened the sliding glass door. Outside, the sky was greying over, darkening.

It made the lake look like charcoal.

He turned his eyes away from it and walked down the porch steps. When he reached the edge of the lake ice, he grabbed his clothes. On his way back to the cabin, he knelt by the steps, retrieved his disc – his beloved Disc 1 – and tucked it in between his folded pants and shirt.

Then he returned inside the cabin. He made his way up the stairs to the second floor. At the top, Dalia was waiting for him. Her eyes were wide and hollow, and wet with tears, as if ready to cry. She tried to speak to him, but nothing came out, and she covered her mouth with her hand.

The Adder did not respond. He brushed gently past her, into her room, and picked up her laptop.

Dalia took in a deep breath. '*Gabriel, no,*' she whispered.

But he did not listen.

He took the laptop with him and headed for his room. Once inside, he shut the door and made his way into the closet. He closed the doors behind him, powered on the computer and logged on.

Then he slid in the disc.

Eighty-Nine

As Striker made his way out through the front doors of the annexe, his cell phone went off. He looked down at the screen, saw the name *Sue Rhaemer*, and felt a jolt of hope. It was Central Dispatch. Maybe they had a hit on one of the Ostermanns. He answered the call and stuck the phone to his ear. 'Sue,' he said. 'What you got?'

She laughed softly. 'Calm down, Big Fella, nothing about the Ostermanns, so you can get rid of your hard-on.'

Striker felt his renewed optimism disintegrate. 'Then what's the occasion?' he asked, not bothering to hide the disappointment in his voice.

'The occasion is Bernard Hamilton,' Sue said.

That made Striker take notice. 'Bernard? Now what has the idiot done?'

Sue chuckled at that. 'Nothing too crazy, really. But it's strange. He keeps calling me up and asking me questions – about you.'

'About me?'

'And the case you're on. This one with Larisa Logan.'

Striker felt his fingers ball up. 'You didn't tell him anything, did you?'

'No, I told him to buzz off in my usual polite way. But he did pique my interest. So I got a little creative up here and ran his

GPS history. A weird thing came back – Bernard's position is the exact same as yours, and it has been all day long.'

Striker thought that over. 'Are you sure?'

'Hundred per cent. And it was the same yesterday. Wherever you put yourself out, he does, too. It's almost like he's been following you – or at least following your unit status, seeing where you went, then re-attending.'

'The devious little—'

Striker cut himself off. He couldn't believe his ears. The prick had no shame, and his motive was obvious. Bernard was planning on following their leads, then sneaking in and making the grab on Larisa right from under their noses. Not only was it a shitty thing to do to one of your fellow officers, but it was putting the woman at greater risk.

He had had enough.

'There's something wrong with that guy,' Sue said.

'Darlin', you don't know the half of it.'

'Bernard's not supposed to be using us to check up on you. Want me to do something about it? Speak to one of my superiors down here?'

'I'll deal with it myself,' Striker said. 'Though I might need your assistance, if you feel like helping me put the screws on him.'

'Shipwreck, you've come to the right girl.'

Striker smiled. 'I'll call back.'

He hung up the phone, and walked out on to Cordova Street. Felicia was already on the sidewalk, waiting for him with two cups of coffee in her hands. She handed him one, then took a quick look at his hard expression and lost her smile.

'What's wrong?' she asked. He told her everything he'd just learned about Bernard Hamilton, and she let out a worried sound. 'He's gonna screw up everything.'

Striker just shook his head and smiled at her.

'Here's what I need you to do.'

Fifteen minutes later, Striker parked on the corner of Burrard and Pender and waited for Felicia to get out. She hopped out of the car, closed the door, and stood ten feet away on the sidewalk, in a nook to get away from the wind. Once she was ready and gave him the thumbs up, Striker grabbed the radio mike. He depressed the plunger and spoke.

'Detective Striker to Radio,' he said.

Sue Rhaemer answered. 'Go for Radio.'

'Did you get that address I asked for?'

'The one for Logan?' she replied. 'Yes, I sent it to your screen.'

'Thanks,' Striker said. 'Can you get my partner to switch to the Chat channel?'

Sue Rhaemer raised Felicia over the air, and Felicia responded.

'Switching to Chat,' she said.

Striker ramped the radio up to the next level, and waited to hear Felicia come across the air. 'Felicia on Chat,' she said. He waited a few more seconds, to be sure that Bernard would be eavesdropping on the conversation. Then he depressed the plunger.

'Hey, Feleesh, where are you?' he asked.

'Fifth floor. Why?'

'Get down here. I know where Larisa is hiding out.'

'Awesome, where?'

'She's up in Shaughnessy. 5142 Osler Street. Apparently her aunt lives there and has been letting her hide out for the last two days. I've got confirmation she's there right now. We'll be pushing our way in. The chief wants this done ASAP and kept under wrap.'

'I'm coming down now,' Felicia said. 'Pick me up.'

'Will do,' Striker said. 'Leaving Chat.'

He ramped the radio channel from Chat back to Dispatch. Then he called the Central Dispatcher. Sue Rhaemer answered on the first ring. She was already laughing.

'Did it work?' he asked her.

'I'm checking his GPS now,' she said. 'And . . . Bernard is heading *due south*.'

Her reply made Striker smile. It was perfect.

He thanked Sue for her help, then said goodbye. Felicia returned to the car just as he hung up. She crashed down in her seat, giggling, and closed the door behind her.

'So?' she asked. 'You think he was listening?'

'Oh, he was listening. You can count on it.'

Striker put the car into Drive and headed west. They'd gone less than a block before Felicia spoke again. '5142,' she said thoughtfully. 'The Shaughnessy area? What's that Osler Street address for?'

Striker just grinned and kept driving.

'Trust me,' he said. 'You don't want to know.'

Ninety

'Whistler,' Felicia said again.

Striker nodded. 'Larisa's text was pinged there.'

He drove down Hastings Street towards the Stanley Park Causeway and, from there, the Lions Gate Bridge. Once into North Van, it was just one long winding Trans-Canada Highway stretch to the Whistler Blackcomb ski resort.

'Whistler or Blackcomb?' Felicia asked.

'I don't know yet, one of the villages.'

Felicia looked at him like he was crazy. 'You know how many people are up there right now, Jacob. The ski season's on, for God's sake. There'll be more than—'

'I know, Feleesh, I know. But she's up there. Without a doubt. What if something happens and we're all the way down here with no way to get to her? I can't think of any other choice we have at this point.'

'I can. It's called the Feds. They have units all over that area.'

Striker cast her a hot stare. 'Absolutely not. If Larisa thinks we've sent another cop after her, it's all over. I won't let that happen. We do this one on our own.'

Felicia said nothing for a moment, then shook her head. 'It's not our jurisdiction, Jacob. You have to get permission from Car 10.'

'You know as well as I do what Laroche will say.'

'We have to tell him, Jacob. He's the Road Boss.'

Striker felt his knuckles tighten on the wheel. 'Not this time, Feleesh.'

'I really think—'

He pulled over to the side of the road and slammed the steering column in Park. When he turned to face her, his adrenalin was starting. 'I'm not doing anything that's going to jeopardize my chance of getting Larisa back. You're right. Calling Car 10 is the protocol, but you know what? I'm not doing it. Because I know what Laroche's response will be. He'll get all the different jurisdictions involved, we'll have another boondoggle like we had at Metrotown, and the next thing you know Larisa will be gone forever. Well, forget that. I *owe* her this. And I'm more than willing to risk my career doing it. You can get out right now and I'll completely understand. But know this: *I am going.*'

He reached over and opened the door for her.

Felicia just looked back at him with a surprised look in her eyes. Then he saw the anger. For a moment, he thought she might actually leave. But then she grabbed the door and slammed it shut. 'We're not going to get there any faster if you leave the car in Park.'

Striker said nothing. He just got the car back on the road and drove down the highway.

Destination: Whistler Blackcomb ski resort.

They were just entering the district of West Vancouver when the conversation about Larisa Logan ended and Felicia finally got down to business with the Gabriel Ostermann file. She grabbed the thin folder and opened it up. Striker glanced over and saw a police report as well as an addendum from the Ministry of Children and Families.

'The file looks thin,' he noted.

'Well, in this case, less is more,' Felicia said. 'You ready for this?'

Striker nodded. 'Go.'

And she read through the report.

'This all took place ten years ago, just after Lexa and Dr Ostermann got married.'

'Gabriel must have been only eight years old,' Striker pointed out.

Felicia nodded. 'Which is why the Ministry of Children and Families was involved and also why it was privatized.' She turned through the pages. 'The file itself was a 911 call that was later changed to a Sudden Death call. As it turns out, the Ostermanns were away on vacation at a place called Lost Lake. Gabriel and his younger brother, William, were out playing in the snow.'

'William?' Striker asked.

Felicia nodded. 'Apparently Lexa had *two* children she brought into the marriage – Dalia, and William . . . Anyway, Gabriel threw a Frisbee to his brother and William missed it. The toy went over his head and landed on the lake.'

'Which was frozen at the time?'

Felicia nodded. 'Yeah, exactly. So the Frisbee lands on the ice. The kids had been warned by their parents not to go near the lake because winter was ending and the ice was too thin. Well, the kids never listened. Gabriel was the oldest and heaviest, so he stayed ashore. William was the youngest and the lightest, so he went out to get it.'

'And the ice broke,' Striker said.

'Yeah. The kid went right through. Worst thing is there was a chance to save him. Apparently, the boy managed to grab on to the edge of the ice and hang on for quite some time. He kept calling for someone to help him, kept calling out for his brother. But Gabriel just froze.'

'Wow, completely?'

'Damn near catatonic,' she replied. 'It was apparently all caught on video by one of the neighbour's surveillance systems. Gabriel couldn't bear to watch. So he turned away from the boy. Fell down in the snow. Covered up his ears with his hands.'

Striker pictured the moment in his mind. 'Jesus.'

'When help finally came, it was too late. William was dead. Sunk somewhere beneath the ice. And Gabriel was damn near catatonic.' She leafed through the pages of the report, shaking her head with sadness. 'The ministry was involved quite a bit after that. They've made many notes about Erich Ostermann's detached fathering skills and even more about Lexa's treatment of the boy. How she blamed him for William's death.'

Striker thought about this and nodded. 'Lexa was pregnant in Brussels,' he said. 'Maybe William was her only biological son. And Dalia was born from her marriage to Gerald Jarvis. Before she married Erich Ostermann.'

'What's your point?' Felicia asked.

'That they're a blended family.'

'They're a freak show is what they are,' Felicia said.

Striker nodded. 'With Lexa as a mother, how could they be anything but?' He thought of what it must have been like to be an eight-year-old child growing up under her evil care – an eight-year-old that she blamed for her only son's death. What life must have been like for Gabriel Ostermann was unthinkable. 'It makes me think that Gabriel is less mentally ill with any known psychological diagnosis and more . . . programmed into what he has become.'

'Lexa made him,' Felicia said. 'There's no doubt. The one question is, did his father know?'

'Dr Ostermann?' Striker scowled. 'How could he not? You saw how he treated the boy – like a subject, not a son. The man was wilfully blind to it all. Had to be with all of them living there. Pride and power, just like with Lexa – till he got caught.'

Striker looked down at the file. He saw no attached envelopes.

'Where is the video?' he asked.

'That's the strange thing,' Felicia said. 'The neighbour swore they had one, but when the police went to collect it, the tape was gone. It just vanished, and was never found again.'

Striker frowned at that.

'Nothing vanishes,' he said.

The tape was still out there somewhere.

Ninety-One

An hour later, Striker looked in his rear-view mirror and saw Brandywine Falls behind them. The waterfall was hard to see in the five o'clock dimness. The entire canyon around them was a charcoal-grey colour, so deep it was all he could do to make out the treeline.

'We're getting close,' he said.

Felicia just nodded. 'And then what? We wait around for another call that might not even come? Or another email message she won't respond to?'

That irritated Striker. '*No*, we start hitting the pavement. You know, good old-fashioned, hard-nosed police work. We'll start with Whistler and make our way into Blackcomb. Show her picture around. See what we get.'

Felicia remained unconvinced. 'We don't know if she's even in one of the villages any more. She could be in one of the smaller towns around the perimeter. Or even headed back to Vancouver.'

'She's *here*,' Striker said. 'And if you can come up with a better way of locating her, then let me know. I'm all ears.'

They drove on through the swerving bends and rising hills in silence, Striker thinking of what lay ahead and any possible routes their investigation could take, and Felicia going over the computer files for the millionth time. When the traffic thickened and Striker saw a sign that signalled Whistler Golf and Country Club ahead, he spoke.

'We're almost there.'

Felicia looked up from the computer screen. 'My eyes are going buggy from the screen and I feel carsick from all this reading. I need a coffee before we start. And some food. We haven't eaten a thing since this morning; aren't you hungry?'

Before Striker could respond, his cell went off. He snatched it up, looked at the screen and saw a number he didn't recognize. He pulled over to the side of the road, into one of the runaway lanes, and answered.

'Detective Striker.'

'Shipwreck,' came the reply, the voice deep and gruff. It took Striker but a second to recognize it as his old friend Tom Collins, previously from Financial Crime.

'Hey, Tommy, what's up?'

'Those names you gave me to run through our insurance databases,' he said. 'You jerking my chain here, or what?'

Striker thought of the list he'd given Collins. Every name and date of birth had been one of the people listed in Lexa Ostermann's folders.

'I don't follow,' he said.

Collins explained: 'I thought these were all supposed to be victims of identity theft.'

'They are. Why? What's the problem?'

'The problem is they're all *dead*. Every single one of them.'

Striker said nothing for a moment. 'There were over fifty people on that list. How many of them did you—'

'Every single one of them.'

'Jesus.' Striker gave Felicia a glance and saw the curiosity in her eyes. He ignored it for the moment and asked Tom, 'How? What was the manner of death?'

'All sorts, really. Accidents. Unexplained natural causes. A lot of suicides.'

Striker thought this over. 'And what kind of policies did they have?'

'That's where it gets interesting. They had good life insurance policies. *All* of them. Over half of the claims have already been paid out. I've done the math here. Accumulatively, we're talking twenty-four million dollars from fourteen different insurance providers. And like I said, nearly half the claims haven't been finalized.'

Striker let this information sink in. Twenty-four million. The number was staggering.

'I thought life insurance didn't cover suicide?' he said.

'That's a common misconception,' Collins replied. 'Life insurance doesn't cover suicide in the first two years, the reason being that most people who are truly suicidal aren't in a mindset to wait two years before doing themselves in. But if someone already had a policy, and two years later they killed themselves, yeah, it's usually completely covered.'

Striker sat there with the phone stuck to his ear and watched the tail lights of the cars passing by them along the highway. Little rectangles of red slowly disappearing into the night. As he watched them, he thought everything over.

Stolen identities. All the name-change forms. And twenty-four million dollars in life insurance money.

'You still there?' Collins asked.

'Can you give me the policy numbers and the names of the insurance companies?' Striker asked.

'No problem.' Collins began reading them out.

Striker wrote them down in his notebook, one by one. When they reached the fourteenth name, he stopped writing and looked up. Something occurred to him. He told Collins to hold on for a second, then turned to Felicia.

'Where's the folder we got from Mapleview?'

'Which folder?'

'The one from Lexa's office. With the medical billing codes.'

Felicia reached into the back seat and grabbed the red folder. When she opened it up, Striker saw the first page – the one with the long codes – and he made the connection.

He pointed to one of the lines.

10–14141ML–MG900412.

'Look at that,' he said. 'The first seven digits match Mandy Gill's life insurance policy number.'

Felicia looked at this and nodded. 'You're right. And the rest?'

Striker looked at the next two letters. 'ML – Manual Life, the insurance provider.'

'Shit, you're right,' she said. 'And look at the second half of the code – MG900412. MG . . . that would be Mandilla Gill. Followed by her date of birth. April twelfth, 1990.' She looked down the page. 'Jesus, she has them all listed right here. It's *ten* pages long.'

Striker nodded. He got back on the phone and told Collins he would have to get back to him. When he turned to face Felicia, he saw that she was sitting there with a troubled look on her face.

'What?' he asked.

She spoke, almost hesitantly. 'It looks like Lexa and Dalia and Gabriel have been stealing people's identities, taking out life insurance policies, and then, after systematically bankrupting the victims, murdering them for the insurance claims, but making it look like accidents and tragedies and suicides.'

Striker nodded. 'Complicated and devious, but yes.'

'I have a problem with that. With the theory . . . it doesn't make sense.'

'In what way?'

'*Why?* Why would they do this? By marriage, Lexa is part

owner of the EvenHealth programme. It has to generate hundreds of thousands of dollars per year. And she gets a percentage on every SILC class any other clinic runs. They have a Beamer and a Land Rover. A mansion in Point Grey.'

'And your point is?'

'She doesn't have to do this. She doesn't need the money. She's *loaded*.'

Striker looked back at her and shook his had. 'You're missing the point. It's not about money, Feleesh. It never was.'

'Then what *is* it about?'

'Domination, manipulation, control. Lexa is the one running this thing, and she has been for years. She *owned* Ostermann. And she's the reason why the kids are as screwed up as they are. She doesn't do this for the money. Or for security. Or for anything materialistic. She does it for the thrill of the hunt. She does it because she's a psychopath. A serial killer. And she lives for one thing and one thing only – the *game*.'

Ninety-Two

The Adder sat in the darkness of the closet with the laptop in his lap. Disc 1 ended, and he was filled with the heavenly bliss, that *peace* he felt every time he watched the video.

Disc 1.

William's Beautiful Escape.

Two hours ago, out by the lake, he had thought it was his turn for the Beautiful Escape. When the Doctor had injected him and he'd felt his body melt into the ice below, the darkness had been warm and overpowering. Heavy magnetic waves had pulled him towards places unknown.

But now he was here again. Back in this world.

Back in the cold.

The thought did not stir his emotions. Not much ever did.

But the Doctor had. Earlier in the day. With one injection, she had broken all boundaries between them. Wiped away the invisible lines. In essence, she had betrayed him.

The whole thing was bemusing to him.

The Adder had no idea how many victims the Doctor had killed in what she called her 'business'. And he didn't really care. He knew the truth. This entire process was not a business, but a *game* to her – one of dominance and power and sadistic need. With every fresh death, she seemed to climb one more rung on that ladder in her mind.

But the joke was on her, because the Adder knew one thing about the game that the Doctor did not – there was no end to that ladder. It just went on for ever and ever and ever. Which left them with this demonic game they played. Just Gabriel and Mother; just the Adder and the Doctor.

In a never-ending game of Snakes & Ladders.

The thought made the Adder feel bad emotions again, so he leaned forward and hit Play, and once again William's Beautiful Escape played out on the LED screen. The converted video was old and poor in quality. There was only static for sound. But that did not diminish it at all.

The Adder watched the young boy fall through the ice, and he saw himself there too – also just a boy – shaking, trembling, crying hysterically, then crumbling to the ground with his hands over his ears. Unable to look. Unable to face what was happening.

Unable to run for help.

Back then, this moment had been his own personal Hell on Earth; but over time – over several hundred viewings of the feed – the Adder had come to see the truth behind the moment. The reality. The only real importance.

Death; it was the only reason for living.

And William had been released from the chains of this cold world. He had been set free from this Hell. Utterly, totally free.

The Adder watched the screen with his eyes turning wet as the emergency workers came rushing in and pulled his little brother from the lake. His body was soaked, his skin as white as any angel. Inside his blood and meat were frozen, but his soul was soaring, soaring, *soaring* far away from here.

'You're free,' the Adder whispered. 'Fly away, little bird. Fly away.'

The film ended, and suddenly there was a blinding brightness.

The Adder raised his hands. Looked up at the closet door. And knew what had happened before his eyes even adapted.

The Doctor had found him.

Ninety-Three

From the runaway lane where Striker and Felicia were parked, the drive to the Whistler Blackcomb ski village was less than twenty minutes. Before pulling back on to the Sea-to-Sky Highway, Striker thought of Lexa and Larisa. What were the odds they would both be here in the village?

Not likely. And yet here they were.

A woman with dark eyes. That was what Larisa had texted.

The more he thought about it, the more he feared that finding Larisa might be as simple as finding Lexa. For they were both after Larisa. In a race – one Striker didn't want to enter.

Lexa was an expert in finding her victims.

And that worried him.

Striker scanned through the notes he'd made on the files. They clearly showed that Lexa's victims fell into one of two categories. They were either the marginalized people in society – the sex-trade workers, the mentally ill, the poor, the secluded and alone.

Or they were the extremely well-to-do – victims who had good jobs. Victims who had money. And extremely good credit. Victims who had been carefully selected, because they had no family. No friends. People whose entire life was work. People who no one would bother to worry about if they went missing or passed away from an unexpected tragedy.

Striker took the box from the back seat and passed it to Felicia. 'I've been through these already,' she said.

'Not like this,' he said. 'Go through the files one more time, but this time look for victims who had *status*.'

'Status? Why?'

'Because with status comes money. When you get the top ten or fifteen income earners, run their name through the property registries and see if any of them owned property up in Whistler or Blackcomb.'

Felicia's eyes took on an excited look. 'One of them was another doctor,' she noted. 'And one was a lawyer, I think.' She opened the box and started pulling files.

Striker drove back on to the highway and continued north towards the village. Ten minutes later, Felicia had compiled a list of the twelve most well-off victims. She got on the phone with her contact at the land registrar's office, and began making notes. By the time Striker drove around the last curve of road and saw the bright halo lights of the ski resort, Felicia had already finished narrowing down their targets.

'We got three,' she said. 'Four, if you count the lawyer who owned a cabin back in Furry Creek.'

Furry Creek. Striker was frustrated to hear that; they'd passed Furry Creek Golf Course over thirty minutes ago. To backtrack now would waste more time. 'What about the other three?' he asked.

'All up here,' she said.

'A guy named Robinson – he was a stockbroker – owned a cabin right up on the mountain. In Whistler Creekside, on Nordic Avenue. The next guy, a man named Bellevue – he had old family money – lived on Panorama Trail. Last person's name is Sutton. He lived just off the main drag.'

Felicia pulled out her iPhone and opened Google Maps.

'These cars should have satellite navigation built into them,' she griped.

'Welcome to city funding,' Striker replied. 'Just start querying.'

'Which one first?'

'Whichever is closest,' Striker said. 'And hurry up. We've finally arrived.'

Ninety-Four

'I *knew* it!'

As the Doctor stood above the Adder, looking down on him, the mask she wore crumbled once again, revealing the monster that lay behind it. Without thinking, the Adder closed the laptop and hit the Eject button.

'The moment I saw the other DVDs, I knew you had more,' the Doctor spat. '*Give it to me.*'

The Adder felt his heart hammer inside his chest.

'No,' he said.

The laptop's DVD player ejected out the disc. The Adder gently took it from the DVD tray and tried to place it back in the case; before he could, the Doctor reached forward and snatched it from his hands.

'I'm *destroying* this thing once and for all!'

'No,' he said.

And now there was a tightness spreading throughout his chest. Into his lungs. Into his heart. A strange empty feeling ballooning inside him.

'NO!'

But the Doctor refused to listen.

She stormed out of the room with his precious DVD in her hand. It was his one and only copy, with the original lost – his last connection to William – and this time the Adder did what he had never done before.

This time, the Adder *acted*.

Ninety-Five

The search for the first of the three properties ended as quickly as it began. The first place, a private cabin previously owned by David Sutton, had been bulldozed to make way for a new set of condominiums that were already being sold as timeshares.

From there, they drove across the small village to the address for a man named Reginald Robinson. They'd barely set up on the place when a grey Audi Q7 pulled into the driveway, and a family piled out.

Striker spent less than a minute watching them unload their snowboarding gear before realizing this was another dead end. He approached the father, showed the man his badge and credentials, and explained that they were looking for Reginald Robinson.

The man's response was direct. 'He doesn't live here. Hell, we just bought the place last summer.'

'Do you mind me asking from who?' Striker asked.

'A doctor from the City.'

'Dr Ostermann?'

The man nodded, and his face took on a nervous look. 'Yes, I believe that was his name. Is everything all right? Should I be concerned?'

'You're fine,' Striker said. 'Thank you for your time.'

They left Robinson's lot and drove to the last place on their list. As they made their way there, Striker felt a sense of futility wash over him. The last address they had was slightly farther out, on the east side of the village. If it was negative, they had nothing. It would be canvass time.

Not five minutes later, the road turned from asphalt to gravel, and they came to a T in the road. The right lane turned back towards the highway; the one to the left turned from gravel to hard-packed dirt, and ran straight.

Striker looked down that way. With the night fully cloaked and a fog brooding through the trees, all he could see was a mass of blackness, with the odd porch light piercing the haze. He parked the car on a small outcrop of gravel on the side of the road, then took out his flashlight and shone it all around the road, looking for a street sign. He could find none.

'Google Maps says this is it,' Felicia said. 'Panorama Trail.'

He nodded. 'It's desolate.'

'If we drive in, anyone there will see us coming a mile off.'

Striker agreed. Walking in was the best choice.

They got out and started up the trail.

The man who lived here before his death was Luc Bellevue. No transfer of property form had ever been filed, so by all accounts the place should have been used by his remaining family.

Striker and Felicia followed the bend of the road.

On the left side, a small lake appeared that was backed by tall thick trees that looked completely black in the night-time shadow. The air above the lake was dark and seemed clouded in mist. Everything was very, very quiet.

They marched on. A hundred metres later, around the long curve of lake, a cabin came into view. It was small. Quaint. Made of logs. It sat on the north side of the lake and backed right down to the shoreline.

When they reached the front of the cabin, most of the windows were dark and had the drapes pulled tightly across. Striker spotted movement in one of them. It was fast and fleeting, but it was there.

Someone was home.

Ninety-Six

The Adder found the Doctor downstairs in the study.

'Please,' he said. '*PLEASE!*'

It was the tenth time he had begged her. He knew of nothing else to say.

She walked past him into the kitchen, a smile stretching her lips and her ice blue eyes holding him in their grip. It was as if she was enjoying this moment, *relishing* it. And the Adder knew that she was. Cruelty had always been one of her strongest traits.

'I need it,' he said.

The Doctor made no immediate response. She just stared at him for a long moment, and the smile slowly fell from her lips. Her eyes darkened. Her jaw turned tight. 'You *disgust* me,' she finally said. '*You* should have been the one who died that day, not my precious William. *He* would have learned. *He* would have listened. *He* would never have caused the damage that you have caused us.'

She held the disk delicately between her long fingers. When her eyes met the Adder's – when the faintest hint of a smirk formed at the corners of her cruel mouth – he understood full well her intention.

'No, please! *NO!*'

But his cry meant nothing.

The Doctor tightened her grip and snapped the disc in two.

And the Adder let loose a howl that filled the room. He lashed out and grabbed the Doctor by the wrist, and bent it backwards. She let out a cry, half of surprise and half of pain. She tried to pull away from him. When he did not let her, she raised her free hand and smacked him across the face – a hard, full-forced *SLAP!*

He did not so much as flinch.

'I wish you were never born,' she spat. 'I wish your whore of a mother had drowned you at birth – then my William would still be alive!'

'William is dead,' the Adder said. 'He has been for a very long time.'

Her eyes narrowed. 'You have never been anything but a wretched, pathetic failure, Gabriel. And a poor excuse for a son.'

The words were meant to hurt, but they had no effect on him. The Adder took them all in, thought them over . . . and then he nodded strangely.

'But I'm not your son, am I?' he said.

'What?'

'I am my *father's* son. And you are no longer his wife. You are not my mother. Not any more.'

'How *dare* you!' She slapped him across the face again, across the same stinging red mark that already marred his skin, and broke away from him. When he offered her no real reaction, but only smiled, she reared from him.

'You stay back,' she ordered.

'You're not my mother.' He stepped towards her.

'I said, stay back! I *order* you to stay back. You will listen to me. I am your doctor, Gabriel! Your *DOCTOR!*'

The Adder reached out and wrapped his long fingers around Lexa's slender throat.

'The game is over, Doctor,' he said. '*You lose.*'

Ninety-Seven

Striker stepped off the dirt road on to one of the trails that snaked through the heavily forested area and paralleled the lake. Moving slowly and through shadow, he hoped to be hidden. When he and Felicia moved forward, making their way on to the private lot, they heard arguing inside the cabin.

He stiffened at the sound. He turned and looked at Felicia.

'Male and female?' he asked.

'It *sounds* like it, but I can't tell for sure.' Felicia crept up to the window and peered inside. 'I can't see anything. Let's just go in and get them.'

Striker motioned her back. 'Not yet.'

'Why not?'

'Because we don't know who's in there yet. If Gabriel or Dalia or Lexa are in there, or if they come up the road and spot us, they'll run. They'll get away. And they'll never stop killing. We need *containment*.'

Felicia agreed. 'Then call in the Feds. The Whistler Police has units ten minutes away from here. Get them here and we can cordon off the whole house.'

Striker thought this over. 'If Lexa or Gabriel or Dalia see them, they'll take off and be gone again, and this time maybe for good.'

'They can use plainclothes cops.'

Striker frowned. The talk had gone full circle, back to square one. A decision had to be made. He took out his phone, being careful to block the light of the screen with his body, and called 911. All he got was a dropped signal. He put the phone away.

'No reception,' he said.

The decision had been made for them.

He pointed to the southwest corner of the cabin. 'Cover that. Scream if you need me and I'll come running.'

Felicia just tightened her grip on her SIG and slowly made her way through the trees, around to the other side of the house. She'd barely been gone a minute when Striker detected a lone figure walking up the road: average height, long black hair, slender build.

Dalia.

Striker watched her as she walked up the road towards the cabin, then crossed the yard. Even in the darkness, he could see that her face was tight and lost. Something was wrong; he could feel it.

Ninety-Eight

The Adder stood outside on the frozen grass, his hot breath fogging up the cold night. Small bits of broken ice covered the toes of his runners, and the bottom of his pants legs were wet. In front of him, her upper body submerged face down in the freezing water of the lake, was the Doctor.

He looked down at her body and felt nothing. Because it was nothing.

Just a bad roll of the dice.

Behind him, the soft *swish* of a sliding door could be heard, and then there were footsteps on the deck. He didn't bother to turn around. It was Dalia, he knew. Coming back again after running away – as she had done so many times before. Escape and return. Escape and return. Escape and return.

It was her life.

'Gabriel?' she asked.

Her steps came closer, and suddenly there was a gasp.

'GABRIEL! Oh no! Oh no! Oh no! Oh no! What have you done, Gabriel? *What have you DONE!*'

She screamed and then screamed some more. He said nothing to her. He did not so much as look in her direction. And seconds later, he heard her run off. Somewhere around the house. In that moment, he had lost her. She was gone. And he would never see her again.

Go after her.

It was a soft thought in his head, a whisper from the angels.

But he did not. He could not. For there were other plans now. And they were all that mattered. Running after Dalia would be changing the goal of the game – and that was the one thing that could never be changed. He had no choice in the matter; the rules were long written.

It was sad. On some deeper level, he knew this.

But what did that matter? He now wondered . . . had there ever been a choice? Perhaps it was always meant to be this way. Fated. Perhaps tonight's game would even lead to his own death.

The thought was enthralling. If Death did come, he was prepared for it. He accepted it. He was *happy* for it. At last, his own time. His own Beautiful Escape. And he smiled because either way he would win this game – in the biggest release of his life when he freed Jacob Striker from this world, or in his own release from this torment. Either way, he was ready. Ready for the final throw of the dice. And why not? Nothing could last forever.

All games eventually came to an end.

Ninety-Nine

It happened fast. One moment, Striker was trying to move to a better position in order to see what all the screaming was about; the next moment, he saw Dalia racing around the house. She plunged through the trees away from him.

A second later, Felicia went racing after the girl.

'Stop!' Felicia called. 'Vancouver Police, Dalia! STOP!'

In one brief moment, both women were swallowed by the darkness.

Striker started after them.

He got only a few feet before coming to a hard stop. There was no doubt that whoever was inside the cabin – Gabriel, Lexa or both of them – now knew of the police presence. If Striker went racing after Dalia, then Lexa and Gabriel would be free to escape. Maybe this time forever.

He was torn.

Felicia needed him. But if he allowed Lexa and Gabriel to escape, there was no telling how many more victims they would kill. Maybe not here, but in another town. Another province. Another country. Everywhere Lexa went, she left a trail of death in her wake. And over the years, she'd programmed Gabriel into being the Adder. All in all, it made one thing clear.

'They have to be stopped.'

At any cost.

Striker turned back towards the cabin. It looked smaller now. Secluded and empty. Almost all the inside lights were off, and from this new location, Striker could hear the *chug-chug-chug* of the generator running out back.

Where Dalia had run from.

Striker readied his pistol, then made his way around the lot towards the back of the cabin. He reached the corner of the house, raised his pistol and peered around the edge. Everything there was quiet and the lake was eerily still. Fog floated across the water and through the trees like a living beast, so thick that Striker could not see across the lake. Out there, across the thin ice, there was only a rolling mass of cold murky blackness.

But no Lexa.

And no Gabriel.

Striker rounded the corner and made his way towards the cabin. The sliding glass door was wide open and the kitchen light was on. He walked up the slippery wooden steps of the porch, came flush with the entrance, and looked around the area.

No one was there to be seen.

He stepped forward into the kitchen and listened to the sound of his shoes against the hard tiles of the floor. Slowly, cautiously, he made his way through the first floor, and then the second.

The place was empty.

They were gone.

Frustrated, he made his way back outside. He stood on the porch and shone his flashlight around the lake. At first he saw nothing.

Then he discovered the body.

It was a few feet out from the edge, where the ice thinned and turned to freezing lake water. As he closed in on it, he saw that it was lying face down. He crouched low, reached out with one hand, and grabbed hold of the arm. When he flipped it over, a sense of desperation filled him.

It was Lexa.

The Adder had killed her. He was spiralling out of control.

And he was gone.

One Hundred

The voices were back, the laughter and giggles echoing in his head. But this time, the Adder managed to control them. He had lost his most precious of all precious videos and he did not have the headphones he needed for his iPhone, so he could not even listen to the white noise.

It did not matter.

A new sense of control filled his body. Electric. Empowering. Like ice water in his veins. Ever since breaching the line – ever since killing the Doctor – a sense of invulnerability had filled him. He was unstoppable.

Completely, utterly, one hundred per cent *unstoppable*.

And he nearly laughed out loud as he realized that.

He moved slowly through the wooded grove. Speed was not necessary. What mattered here was silence. Stealth. Besides, there was little point in running through the forest blind. Broken ankles were bad for the killing business.

As he walked steadfastly, thoughts of Jacob Striker filled his head. The big detective had looked so determined back at the cabin, so intense and powerful. The Adder had watched him from the shadows, impressed.

It had been foolish to do so – he should have been gaining as much ground between them as he could. But something about the detective intrigued the Adder. The man had a magnetic presence.

Like a tar pit sucking him down.

He headed straight north and, when he found the proper trail, increased his speed towards Green Lake. That was where Striker would eventually find him. It was a certainty. Because the Adder knew something important that no one else had known – not Detective Striker or Detective Santos or even the omnipotent Doctor herself. He knew where Larisa Logan had been hiding.

And he was determined to get there before Striker.

One Hundred and One

'Felicia!' Striker called out.

It was the tenth time he'd screamed her name, but to no avail, and now he was beginning to panic. He made his way back to the main road. Once there, he tried her cell again. The signal was weak, but the call went through, and it was picked up on the second ring.

'Jacob?' she asked.

'Jesus, you scared the shit outta me. Where the hell are you?'

'I'm back in the village. She ran here. But I've lost her.'

He was angry now. 'I didn't know if you were dead or lying in the forest somewhere. I've been looking everywhere for you!'

'I'm sorry,' she said. 'Are you okay?'

'I'm fine.'

'And Gabriel?' She asked the question almost tentatively.

'Gone. He killed Lexa.'

Felicia made a shocked sound. 'My God.'

'He's spinning out of control, Feleesh. Gone right off the deep end. And he knows we're here after him. No point in hiding that any more. Call the Feds. We need more units. We got to catch this guy before he escapes. I'll meet you back in the village. By the flag pole in the centre square.'

'Okay. I'll call the Feds right now.'

'And, Feleesh. Be careful on this one. We've lost sight of them, but that doesn't mean they've run off.'

'I can take care of myself, Jacob. Just get here.'

The line went dead and Striker started hiking back towards the cruiser. He'd gone less than ten feet when his phone vibrated again. He snatched it up, expecting to see Felicia's name on the screen, but instead he saw that he had another text message. The send time was only a minute ago. He opened it up, saw Larisa's name, and read the text:

Jacob, R U there?

He immediately typed back.

I'm here. Where are you?

After a moment, she responded:

I have proof, Jacob. A video. The doctors at Mapleview are killing people for money.

You need to come in.

They'll send me back to Riverglen. To the doctor.

I won't let them. I'll be with you.

He received no response, so he typed back:

Larisa? U there?

You can't stop them. And I can't take this any more.

Let me help you!

Striker waited for a long moment, so long he thought Larisa had ended the conversation. But finally a text came back:

> I'm so tired, Jacob. I'll leave you the video I have of Sarah. No. 5 Old Mill Road. I hope it helps you stop them. Thanks for being my friend.

Striker got a bad feeling from her text. He recalled her PRIME files, remembered her emotional instability. He typed back:

> Don't do anything foolish, okay? I'm coming right now!

No response.

> Larisa?

Nothing again.

Striker sprinted back down the trail to the cruiser. Once there, he punched the address into Google Maps and located it. He started the engine. Hit the gas. And left a trail of dirt and gravel in his wake.

Old Mill Road was only minutes away.

One Hundred and Two

Striker drove so fast he almost lost control of the cruiser on the icy gravel. When he reached Old Mill Road, he floored it. The road was narrow and old, unpaved. Tall rows of cedars and Douglas firs bordered the road, blocking out any of the weak moonlight that managed to struggle through the heavy blanket of fog.

The road was a strip of blackness.

He spotted a house at the end. Even in the pale glow of the cruiser's headlights, the place looked ramshackle. Old. And dark. All the lights were off and the front door was wide open.

Striker wasted no time. He jumped out of the cruiser, taking out his flashlight and pistol at the same time.

He reached the front door, used the frame for cover, and flashed his light inside. Everything was dark and still and empty. He hit the light switch, but nothing happened. And he realized there were no sounds coming from the generator.

'Larisa?' he called out. 'Larisa, it's Jacob – are you here?'

When he received no response, he made the decision. There was no more time for delay. Flashlight illuminating the way, gun aimed ahead, finger alongside the trigger, Striker stepped into the darkness.

He moved quickly, not allowing himself to slow for even a

second. He made his way out of the small foyer, through the living room, kitchen, den and then the bedroom.

But there was no sign of her.

He took the stairs into the basement more slowly, keeping his body tight to the wall. When he reached the bottom and his shoes touched the hard concrete of the cellar floor, he scanned the area around him and spotted a long narrow hallway. There was a doorway to the right and one straight ahead at the far end of the hall.

The doorway on the right was open; the one at the end was closed.

Striker moved forward to the first doorway. He stopped and aimed his flashlight into the room, illuminating all four corners.

And that was when he found her.

Slumped in a chair at the far end of the room was the woman he had been searching for these last three days.

'*Larisa!*' he said.

He moved forward through the darkness. Came to within ten feet of her. And stopped hard. Her head was turned down and her eyes were half open. Dangling from her right hand was an empty pill case, and at her feet was a DVD case with the name *Sarah Rose* on it. Striker gently placed two fingers against her neck and felt for a pulse. She was warm, but he could feel no beating of her heart.

'Please, Larisa,' he said. 'Please.'

He was running out of time.

One Hundred and Three

Desperation flooded him. Striker took out his cell to call 911; it rang on him before he could even dial. He stuck it to his ear.

'Striker,' he said.

'Where are you?' Felicia asked.

'Number five Old Mill Road,' he said. 'No time for talk. I got Larisa here. She's overdosed on pills. Call 911 for an ambulance and get your ass up here now.'

He hung up without waiting for a response, then grabbed Larisa and placed her on the floor, so he could begin CPR. Keep her heart going till the medics got here.

His phone vibrated again. He looked down and read the words:

    I have proof, Jacob. I'm scared.
    I have proof, Jacob. I'm scared.
    I have proof, Jacob. I'm scared.
    ;o)

He stood back up, momentarily confused. 'What the hell?'

And his phone went off with another text:

Congratulations, Hero, you found her – or have I found you?

Snake eyes!

SNAKE EYES!

SNAKE EYES!

One Hundred and Four

Striker tore his eyes away from the text, knowing for certain the Adder was here. He placed his back to the wall, moved slowly to the corner of the room, and kept scanning with his flashlight and gun. With the exception of him and Larisa, the room was empty. Dark. Quiet.

There was only one way in, and only one way out.

For a moment, he considered staying put. Keeping all his attention on the doorway and waiting for back-up. Then he heard a door slam out front. Thoughts of being trapped in another inferno flashed through his mind, as did the notion of Gabriel Ostermann escaping once more.

He got moving.

Gun aimed ahead of him, flashlight illuminating the way, Striker made his way back across the room and turned towards the front foyer. The door leading out front was just a stairway away.

It was closed.

Striker took a step towards it, then heard a shuffling sound behind him. He stopped and slowly turned around. He looked back down the hallway. On the right side was the doorway into the room where Larisa's body lay on the floor. At the far end was the only other room the basement owned. The door there had been closed when he'd first come down the stairs.

Now it was open.

He moved to one side of the hall, out of the main line of fire, and took aim on the open doorway. He called out:

'Vancouver Police, Gabriel. I know you're here and I've got every reason to believe you're armed and dangerous. Come out with your hands where I can see them and you won't get hurt.'

No response.

Striker listened for a moment, heard nothing else. He slowly left his position of cover and made his way down the hall. When he came to within ten feet of the open doorway, he shone his flashlight inside the room.

From the cover of the door frame, the weak beam of his flashlight caught a vague shape. Someone was hiding in a small nook of the wall. In the closet. He took aim on the figure and called out once more:

'I see you, Gabriel. Don't move!'

But the figure only turned slightly and shuffled out of view; as it moved, Striker caught a brief glimpse of the man's face. There was no doubt about it.

It was Gabriel.

The Adder.

'I said, don't move, Gabriel!' Striker ordered again.

When the Adder disappeared from Striker's line of fire, Striker seized the moment before it was lost. He moved forward, ready to fire. It wasn't until he had stepped right into the room that he realized his mistake. What he was staring at wasn't a closet; it was the wall. And as he looked at the wall, he saw a poster on it – but the writing was all *backwards*.

Then he realized. It was not a wall but a full-length mirror.

The Adder was *behind* him.

He spun to the right just as he felt an arm wrap around his neck from behind. There was a sharp pinprick and, almost immediately, a numbing sensation ran from his neck throughout the rest of his body, snaking out like long pulsating tendrils.

Striker shoved back, but it was too late. He felt his body melting on him. His legs gave out. And he went down firing.

He hit the floor hard. Felt the air explode from his lungs. And watched the darkness sweeping into his sight from all corners of his periphery. He thought of his daughter, Courtney, and then of Felicia and Larisa, whose life depended on him escaping this moment.

But the last image Striker saw, as he was sucked down by the heavy blackness, was that of Gabriel. The Adder was staring back at him, his pale twisted expression the only visible beacon for him in a dark and cold vacuum.

One Hundred and Five

First came the sound.

There was a faint, wailing noise in the background, like the soft banshee cries of some strange beast coming to take him away. The wail grew louder and louder until it was right on top of him – an overbearing echo in his ears. Until Striker realized the source of the call:

Sirens.

Striker tried to open his eyes, and then he realized they were already open. The strange supple warmth slowly washed away from him and was replaced by a stark coldness. The darkness slowly ebbed away, and Striker looked up to see three people on top of him.

Two men dressed in white . . .

Paramedics.

And one between them. A face that made him smile and relax and brought back all the warmth that had been stolen from his body.

'Feleesh,' he said. His voice sounded weak and very far away.

'Just relax, Jacob,' she said. 'They're giving you some drugs. You need to stay still.'

He tried to get up; she pushed him back down.

'You need to *relax.*'

'Larisa . . .'

'They got her, too, Jacob. She's breathing and en route to Whistler hospital.'

He let go. Felt his body melt into the floor. And he lazily looked left.

Lying on his back was Gabriel Ostermann. Two other paramedics, both women, were hovering over the Adder, examining his chest and stomach area. In the centre of the two was a large meaty hole. Striker saw this glistening redness and the vague recollection of past gunfire returned to his ears.

His bullets had found their target.

Centre mass.

The simple action of looking at the Adder drained him, and Striker let his head fall back to the floor. He looked up, straight ahead at Felicia, who was hovering like an earthbound angel. Behind her, one of the female paramedics let out a surprised sound.

'Jesus, this guy's still alive,' she said.

And Striker realized they were talking about Gabriel Ostermann.

'He keeps whispering,' one of the women said to her partner. 'I can't make it out. What the hell's he saying? *I'm the Villain?*'

Striker understood the word, and he breathed heavily as he spoke.

'He said *William* . . . he said, *I'm coming, William.*'

And then the medications pulled him under and he did not wake for a long time.